EMMA SMART

EMMA SMART

JONATHAN TREITEL

BLOOMSBURY

First published 1992

Copyright © 1992 by Jonathan Treitel

The moral right of the author has been asserted.

Bloomsbury Publishing Ltd, 2 Soho Square, London W1V 5DE

A CIP catalogue record for this book
is available from the British Library.

ISBN 0 7475 1114 4

Typeset by Hewer Text Composition Services, Edinburgh
Printed in Great Britain by Clays Ltd, St Ives plc

ACKNOWLEDGEMENTS

I should like to acknowledge the assistance of the Katherine Blundell Award, administered by the Society of Authors.

TO MY PARENTS

§ I

The Snowman's Tale

'Why have you got such big teeth, Grandma?'
And the wolf replied . . .

1

The first thing I saw after passing through customs at JFK was a bulky suede coat with a neck above it, and, in the place where a head would normally be, a square of brown cardboard felt-tipped with:

WELCOME TO THE
REAL NEW YORK
Professor Emma Smart

I had a fit of embarrassment, so I waved my right hand in a very small fanning motion and whispered an inaudible *yoo-hoo*. The bearer of the greeting must have heard me, all the same, because he lowered his cardboard and staggered towards me, booming, 'Long time no see, Emma! You're looking great!' He widened his arms in a pre-hug but I blocked him with my collapsible suitcase which fortunately didn't. So instead he lifted his big unshaven chin and pouted, angling for a kiss. 'Oh,' I said, 'it's you.'

It was my old friend, Frank. ('Friend' is not the exact word – but let it pass.) We'd known each other at Cambridge (the real Cambridge, I mean – not the imitation version erected in Massachusetts), where I was a senior research fellow in the department of pure mathematics and he was hanging about the place with the aid of a temporary lectureship in something arty. Not the person I would have chosen to meet me, but I didn't really know anyone else in New York.

'Sure is.' He grinned. 'Who do you expect?'

I noticed Frank was putting on his American accent. He's one of those cosmopolitan multi-ethnic types who speak a dozen languages badly. He once admitted to me in a rare moment of honesty (I was about to say 'frankness', but I prefer my puns more subtle) that he found it useful to be American in Britain and British in America. 'The

3

foreigner can get away with breaking the rules,' he said. But it must be queer not having a definite nationality . . . As for myself – one is English, of course.

'By the way,' I said, following the above train of thought. 'I was held up for half an hour at immigration. The officials can scarcely speak English and have apparently never heard of an academic exchange visa. And then . . . I told the customs man, "I have nothing to declare except my – " "Aw, lady, give me a break. I hear that gag a million times." ". . . except the contents of this suitcase."'

Frank laughed – but not as much as my anecdote deserved. 'Yeah,' he said. 'They're notorious at Idlewild.'

'At doing *what*?'

'Idlewild. It's the old name for this airport. Sounds snazzier than JFK, huh? Anyhow, Kennedy was a classic Cold Warrior, so I'm anti his whole, y'know, the memorial razzmatazz operation thing.'

'Indeed? You're supposed to be a literary critic, not a poet. One can't alter history for the sake of euphony. Besides, I distinctly remember you telling me that moral considerations should play no part in the interpretation of society.'

'That's not exactly my point of view. What I said was – '

'Yes it is. I have a remarkably accurate memory, and – '

'Okay, Emma. You're right – as always.'

Sarcasm is both wonderful and oppressive. The very idea that a sentence can mean the opposite of what it states! What a liberation from logic! What an amazing joke! But it's also scary. I remember when I was an infant Daddy used to say, to make me work harder at my calculus, 'Oh, Emmy doesn't need to swot. She knows everything already.' And I'd become angry and red-faced the way children do: then I'd stay up all night practising Lebesgue integration. But now I wonder if possibly Daddy meant every word. There is the finest of lines between sarcasm and a declaration of love . . . In all the months I had been planning to come to New York I had imagined it as a hotbed of sarcasm – the city is an artificial creation, after all, constructed from the delusions and nightmares of successive generations of immigrants, a hot-air balloon inflated by the gusts of their own rhetoric; perhaps just because it's so implausible (if it didn't exist, no one would invent it) it's home to the most brilliant, creative mathematicians in the world, whose imagination soars limitlessly. And now I came to think of Idlewild as the epitome of New York. The airport seemed to be inhabited by a race of white-liars: a shaggy beggar was demanding 69

4

cents 'for a cup of coffee'; a blank-faced pious girl was asking passers-by 'to fill in a personality questionnaire'; a machine was enticing air passengers to buy 'life insurance' by credit card . . . The ceiling was high and bright. Mysterious cool air currents were blowing from nowhere. Voices were chanting over the PA system: *Would Mister Impossibly Unpronounceable please pick up the white courtesy telephone* . . .

I have an extremely clear mind usually, so on the rare occasions when my imagination gets the upper hand I tend to shake off the mood by becoming bossy. I tapped my forefinger imperiously on Frank's sign. 'You have committed an error. Strictly speaking, contrary to the allegation here, I am not a professor. My official ranking is – '

'Yeah, well. Sure. But you're really an associate prof. . . . a don . . . I mean, the American equivalent of . . . I mean, as it were . . .' He wobbled the cardboard as a visual analogue of his muddled thoughts. 'You don't have to be bashful, Emma.'

I couldn't help giggling. 'No one has ever called me *that* before. Shy, yes. Bashful, no.'

Which is true. Often when introduced to strangers at receptions in the senior common room or during coffee breaks at international conferences I become dreadfully nervous and twitter away twenty to the dozen at the top of my voice. Or else I stammer: I open my mouth and nothing emerges – and suddenly lots of words gush out, and I daren't pause for fear I won't be able to start again. But I never lack confidence in my own abilities. Of course I was much more timid ten years ago when I came up to Cambridge: one was this tiny 11-year-old undergraduate with long blonde hair and blue eyes, elfin, looking like an illustration to the Brothers Grimm. I remember my first day at college. All on my own, I got out of the taxi and walked through the great arched gateway towards the porter's lodge. Suddenly I was surrounded by a pack of newsmen: reporters were barking, photographers were poking their lenses at me and letting off flashes. The best I could manage was to follow Mummy's advice on dealing with strangers. I shook them all by the hand and mumbled, 'How do you do? My name is Miss Smart. I am pleased to make your acquaintance.'

A crowd was surging towards us: a man trundling a huge box on tiny strap-on-able wheels; a woman leaning backwards to balance a tall case on her hips and breast, her arms around its back, swaying, as if she were dancing with it cheek to cheek; a mother shepherding several children accompanied by lots of tiny colourful bags; a couple about my age, each with a colossal rucksack riding high on the back . . . None of them looked at us as they elbowed past: their faces were tilted up, searching for waiting friends and family, or the car-hire stand, or the bank or the tourist information place.

'Let's get,' I said to Frank, 'out.'

He shrugged. He waved his free hand vaguely over the handle of my suitcase, but – feeling lazy or reckoning this offer might violate his non-sexist principles – converted the gesture into a squeeze of my elbow. I handed him my case anyway. We made our way towards the exit.

We had got as far as a row of orange plastic chairs near an air-conditioning vent when I said, 'Just a moment.' Frank wiped the seats with a newspaper featuring a photograph of some smiling moustached Pole and meanwhile made some irritatingly knowledgeable comment on the political situation in Eastern Europe. We sat down. He hitched up his trouser legs to avoid crumple; he unbuttoned his suede coat revealing an expanse of beige fisherman's jersey; he smirked unnecessarily. (Frank is far too aware of his own swarthy handsomeness. At Cambridge his nickname was sleazy-Frank – all in one word, like Puss-in-boots.) I set the cardboard sign across both our laps as a makeshift table. Then I dipped my hand into my carrier bag and fished out a couple of plastic glasses (snitched from the plane) and a bottle of duty-free Moët et Chandon 1986.

'You can't!' said Frank.

'Well, I don't usually. One aspires to be a Perrier-with-a-twist-of-lemon lady. But seeing as it's a special occasion . . . You haven't forgotten what today *is*, have you?'

'I mean, you can't. It's illegal in the States, drinking in public. We usually put the booze inside a paper bag.'

I gave him an are-you-joking frown and he returned a no-I-really-mean-it nod.

A dishevelled man happened to be passing, pushing a shopping trolley loaded with assorted scraps of paper, plastic, string. I took from my purse a 50-pence coin – heavy, silvery, heptagonal: already it struck me as exotically European – and proffered it to the tramp. He bit it suspiciously. By way of exchange I took one of his brown-paper bags: it cloaked my champagne.

People often suppose brilliant theorists are no good at practical things, but actually I'm quite dextrous. My thumbnails made short work of the foil on the bottle top. I deftly untwisted the wire cage. Frank – who gets jittery about the slightest illegality, despite his brave tales of high jinks on his tours through totalitarian countries – juddered his fingers across his elegant coiffure, especially the *distingué* grey bits. He gazed down greedily as I rubbed the cork between both palms, easing it off. It shot up with a bang. A security guard awoke, pointed his gun at us, and fell asleep. The lovely fizzy stuff flowed into the glasses (I poured neatly: not a drop was spilt), which we raised.

'Cheers!' I said.

The air-conditioning vent was humming to itself. The disembodied amplified voices kept crackling. *Would Missis Implausible please go to inaudible* . . . In front of us we could see the huddled masses yearning to be free flowing from immigration into New York through one-way glass doors. On the far side, a baggage carousel was bringing unclaimed cases round repeatedly, and a gang of freeloading small children too: we couldn't hear them but we saw their mouths widening and narrowing in what might have been screams of joy. Every so often the automatic doors behind us opened to the outside world: we felt a blast of crisp polluted air on the back of the neck.

'And cheers to you too,' said Frank.

We sipped.

'Happy birthday,' I said.

Frank's eyebrows went up. 'But it's not my . . . I'm a Pisces on the Aries cusp and you're a . . . Oh, *of course*. Happy Twenty-first, Emma. At last you're a real grown-up woman.'

'Not quite, perhaps. But I honestly think I'm on my way.'

I liked the happenstance of my birthday falling on the date of my entry into the New World: my mind is neat like that. An optimistic coincidence. To be sure, I had chosen to fly in on this date: 2 September 1989 – I believe one creates one's own luck.

I had another glassful, and Frank had three. He dripped a little champagne on the sign: my name became hazy. For some reason we both found this funny. Frank chuckled. I tittered in that high-pitched way which Daddy often tells me I really must grow out of. 'Naughty Emmy,' I told myself, smacking my own wrist. This was even more hilarious: I laughed until I ran out of breath. Frank did his asymmetric smile. I suppose one must have been a trifle tipsy.

We gave the tramp the remainder of the Moët et Chandon. He chewed, gargled, and spat it in the style of an expert *dégustateur*. He also gratefully accepted the sheet of cardboard, adding it to his stash.

'Well, come on, Frank,' I said, jumping up. 'Where's the taxi rank? Show me this Real New York you're so keen on.'

7

Frank didn't answer. He stood up. He put his hands on my shoulders and leaned towards me. His suede coat flapped on either side of me. His eyes were half closed. I noticed how long his lashes were and the roughness of his skin. His lips were slightly parted.

'N-n-n-n-no,' I said. 'Not that again.'

2

Three days later, by arrangement, Frank dropped in on my apartment. He poked his head through the door. The agreed plan was that he would pick me up and take me on a tour around the city. He wiped his huge red–black running shoes on the WELCOME mat. He swayed from the hips in his little–lost–boy pose. Then he gave a smile and said, 'You're looking very . . . settled already.'

'Mmm,' I said noncommitally.

'Mmm,' he said appreciatively.

'Yes. One's accommodation is rather agreeable. Do come in.'

He strutted over the fitted carpet, lifting each foot high and lowering it with precision, like an elephant at the circus.

I shut the door behind him, fastening the array of complex latches and bolts which is *de rigueur* in this city.

He lifted his arms as if to give me a quick hug – then thrust his hands back in the pockets of his tan leather jacket and looked down at his feet. Frank knows perfectly well that his 'shyness' is attractive – all those averted gazes and head shakes and heavy pauses – and he knows I know he knows I know he knows (iterate *ad infinitum*). That he is genuinely rather shy is neither here nor there.

I determined to resist his charm. It seemed proper to establish a decent, non–intimate relationship at the outset. 'How do you do?' I said, shaking his hand.

I had him hang up his jacket and scarf on a hook on the corridor wall. 'Before we go out, I'll give you a guided tour of my place, whether you want to or not. It's only fair.'

First: the sitting room/study. Three walls were lined with high pinewood bookcases packed with upright hardbacks. The fourth wall was windowed and venetian blinded; extending across its entire length was a shiny pinewood desk on which an anglepoise lamp was poised at an angle like a heron on a lake. The ceiling and floor were done in contrasting shades of off-cream: a tranquil effect. Assorted chairs were all over the place. Then I led him into the kitchenette: a Mondrian-esque arrangement of tessellating oblong units and workspaces; the microwave oven stared blankly. Next the bathroom; I drew his attention to the flooring of shaggy carpet tiles – an anti-puritan moral: cosiness before practicality! Finally I permitted him a brief peek into the bedroom.

'Super,' he said.

'Indeed? You'll be calling it "groovy" next.'

'Right on! Dig it, man.'

Frank was being sensitive about his age, as usual – he was 35 – and, by implication, the fact that he still hadn't got tenure. After his Cambridge lectureship was over, he'd worked for an independent film company for a while, contributing his chiselled profile to arts programmes on Channel 4. Then he'd managed to wangle an assistant professorship at Nixon University, a liberal arts college at the northern tip of Manhattan. Good money, he claimed (when he'd got the job he'd sent me an aerogramme with dollar signs scrawled all around the border), but no prestige or security.

'It's great. It's big, Emma, for the Village.'

(One dislikes the custom of referring to Greenwich Village as 'the Village', because (1) it's not remotely village-like, and (2) it's certainly not *the* one – but I decided to let the illogic pass.)

'Yes, it *is* rather nice.' (Mummy always told me to accept compliments gracefully.) 'The bedroom is soporific. The sitting room has lots of places to sit. The bathroom is equipped with an infra-red ceiling light which I'm sure has some dreadfully useful function . . . But it's not mine: I'm just borrowing it.'

I directed him back to the sitting room.

'Oh, do sit down. Stop peering at the fittings. If you're about to recite an elaborate semiotic analysis of the stains on the walls and the dimmer switches for the spotlights, one really doesn't want to hear it.'

I sat upright on the black vinyl sofa and tucked my legs underneath. Strategically I gestured at a low-slung steel-framed canvas chair located on the opposite side of the room. He dropped into it, spreading his jean-clad legs wide.

'So, what you been doing with yourself, Em? Done the tourist thing already? Oohing at the Statue of Liberty and aahing at the Empire

State Building? I guess visitors to the Big Apple go places that people who live here all year round never find time to see.'

I noted the falsity of tone in his use of the journalistic idiom: 'Big Apple'. Also the implicit assumption that he was a permanent New Yorker – he'd only been living here for one and five-twelfths years.

'Actually, Francis,' I said in my snootiest voice, 'I've been far too busy.'

Which was the truth. I'd had to buy things for the apartment: a jug kettle, a toaster, two light bulbs, an alarm clock, a bottle of blue scented lavatory cleaner . . . And I'd gone up to the Institute for Advanced Studies, the place that was supposed to be hosting me during my sabbatical year in the States, to sort out my office and find out what was what. I'd had a long chat with the admin./secretarial staff (from my Cambridge experience I know that's where all the important decisions are made) – i.e. Fanny and Bridget – about how to use the photocopying machine and the coffee machine and sign up for computer time, and how to get in/out after eight when they lock the front door, and what to do if one is mugged on the subway, and women's talk about what a pretty bangle I or she or she was wearing and watch out for groping Professor Honthorst. I'd even found time to phone Potts at NYU and Ostrovsky at Columbia about their latest work on the Smart–Potts–Ostrovsky conjecture: one flattered oneself that one's own research was in advance of theirs. And I'd glimpsed fragments of New York through the windows of taxis: it didn't look so different from the centre of Cambridge or London – blown autumn leaves and men in business suits.

'So you haven't done anything, Emma?'

'No – that is, yes! Certainly not. I mean . . .' I snorted. 'What I have accomplished is . . . a great deal.'

'Sure is,' he said. 'It's a bargain. Who from?'

'What?'

'Who are you borrowing the apartment from?'

'IBM only knows. I got it through the inter-university exchange scheme. They told me my flat in Cambridge is lent to a lepidopterist on sabbatical from Osaka. His residence is being used by somebody or another who's visiting Osaka . . . And so on round and round – a set of unidirectional one-to-one relations composited in an intricate network. A mainframe computer in Illinois keeps track of it all.'

'Uh huh.'

'In fact,' I said, warming to my topic, 'it's a paradigm of – '

'Yeah, yeah,' he said negatively. He and I had had this discussion far too many times before.

The point is: I specialise in a sub-branch of a kind of mathematics called differential geometry. I learnt about it at the age of 12, in the same month as one's first period. It came as a revelation – the maths, that is (well, the other thing, too). Differential geometry states that one can analyse a complex system in two ways: in terms of *either* very small 'differential' changes *or* the overall shape: the 'geometry'. For example, imagine standing on a flat field in England. One can see the horizon all around, and so one can deduce that the surface of the earth is curved. Or conversely: if one knows the earth is spherical, one can deduce that the field must have a horizon. In summary: the local determines the global and the global determines the local. So one starts off by knowing a bit about the local and the global, and one soon discovers one knows more than one thought one did! Frank – who claims to be something called a 'post-modernist' – doesn't disagree with me about the facts, but he draws a different moral. He says: everything influences everything else, and so nothing really exists in its own right, so nobody can really know anything. I point out that it's only trendy arty academics who don't know anything, and we mathematicians know a great deal, thank you very much . . .

We had had this argument often enough in the past, so were able to imply it by means of a few heavy sighs each.

Then Frank said, 'What's the guy's name who lives here? Maybe I know him.'

'I just told you. I haven't the faintest.'

'Surely he left you a note, or his name on the mailbox, or something?'

I shook my head.

Frank succeeded in rising from his chair. 'I'll solve the mystery!' he hissed in a stagey voice which gave me a fit of the giggles. He stomped around jerking his head from side to side – presumably imitating some genre of fictional detective. (In a manner of speaking, detection is his job: he's often mentioned that the post-modernist literary critic is a kind of private eye, gathering clues and drawing ingenious deductions . . . Actually I think he just enjoys playing Sherlock.) He began rummaging through a bookcase, searching for an owner's name written on a fly leaf. He climbed on the desk to reach books on the top shelves. 'Here's an inscription!' He opened a book, twisted it round, and screwed up his eyes. 'It says . . . "With best wishes from the author." Huh. I could've written something more revealing myself.'

'Of course you could. You're a critic. Revealing the author's intention is what you're supposed to do.'

'Author shmauthor!' He put on his professor-knows-best voice. 'The authorial presence has been deconstructed. All that remains is the polysemous text itself, and the process of its interpretation – '

'In plain English, the author has been dethroned, and the critic – namely, you – is king.'

'Paradigmatically speaking – '

'So you're saying you're more important than the creative writer?'

'It's not a question of importance. It's bound up with the ontological status of a text. Like, it's the gourmet – not the sturgeon – who decides caviare is delicious.'

'B-b-b-but,' I stammered, trying to give myself time to come up with a convincing rebuttal.

Meanwhile Frank was looking frightfully silly, extending his arms in oratorical gestures while prancing about on the table top. He did have an unfair advantage in this argument though, since he was towering above me, delivering his pronouncements like Moses on Sinai. He kept coming out with pretentious name-dropping and a pushy first-person plural such as: 'Let us remind ourselves of the fundamental distinction made by Saussure . . .'

'Yes, yes,' I interrupted. 'But you can't get away from the fact that fiction writers are creative, and mathematicians are creative as well, but critics are just analytical.'

Overlapping with my last sentence, Frank had been saying, ' . . . to come back to the distinction that Barthes has taught us, the process of textual analysis is reducible to two elements: the *signification* and the *signifiation*, the former being, as it were, the "meaning" which manifests itself in the sensorium of the reader, and the latter being the process whereby the very text struggles to give itself meaning. The role of the "author" is empty.'

He was evidently quoting some lecture notes or article: all the same I was interested. 'You mean, it's like maths divides into pure maths, which has all the ideas, and applied maths, which uses those ideas; and there's no need to worry too much about who discovered any particular bit, since that doesn't affect the truth.'

'Uh . . . See, "truth" is not at issue – '

'Well, truth may not matter much to you lit. critters, but we mathematicians do try to keep on the right side of it . . .' I tapped him on the ankle. 'And talking of truth, I can tell you a fact about the Mystery Man – the chap who owns this flat. He's a linguist.'

'How the hell can you know that?'

'Look at the book covers, dum-dum.'

'Ah, sure.'

The volumes mostly had giveaway titles, such as: *Swahili Anaphora,* or *Proceedings of the XXVIIth San Diego Conference on Meaning,* or *Irregular Lexeme Formation in Certain Hungarian–Slav Pidgins,* or *Seventeen Problems with Indirect Speech.* I also noted a selection of paperback thrillers and detective stories, including such classics as *Who Killed Roger Ackroyd?* and *Poirot's Last Case.*

'We're not beaten yet!' he said, jumping down. 'Look. You take the kitchen and I'll check out the bathroom.'

So I examined what was left behind on the kitchenette shelves. A half empty bag of rice and one of sugar. A roll of sticky, translucent Saran Wrap. No revelation there. I called out, 'Judging by his cookery books, he's a vegetarian. Also he bakes his own bread' – noting a bit of dough encrusted between the pages of the *Tassajara Bread Book.* Meanwhile I could hear Frank slamming open the bathroom cabinet. He was yelling, 'The guy's got dandruff and dry skin.'

We met again back in the sitting room, panting with the thrill of the chase.

'Didn't you get any mail addressed to him?' Frank asked.

'No.'

'Didn't he leave you any message?'

'Well, yes, but – '

'Where?'

I pulled open a drawer and showed him the stack of useful information I'd found waiting for me in the apartment: maps and guides to the city, leaflets on where to walk your dog, what to do about noise pollution and AIDS; even a pad of ruled paper inscribed in fading spidery handwriting with notes on where best to buy peanut butter and coffee, opening times for museums, parks, playgrounds, the number to phone for frozen pipes or rape or public-transport information in Spanish . . . but no signature.

'Hmm,' said Frank. 'Well, I reckon he's got us beat.'

'Or *she*?' I murmured.

'Guess it rings a change on the cliché of the absentminded professor. This guy is absentbodied.'

'I hereby name him/her – Professor Absent!'

Frank nodded thoughtfully. '"Professor Absent."' He visually represented the " " scare-marks by wagging the first and second fingers of both hands on either side of his head, as if mimicking a bunny rabbit's long twitchy ears.

'Now, we've got to be logical,' he said. 'What do we know about Prof. Absent? He's rich – because he owns a fine apartment in the Village. His interior decorator goes for nouveau sixties-style lighting and furniture. So the Prof.'s in his, I guess, late fifties. Likes *haute cuisine*, and skin care, and making lists.'

'And he's academically quite successful,' I said, 'given that he's presumably a visiting professor somewhere else. And he's not too rich, or else he wouldn't bother letting his place out.'

'Intellectually speaking, as it were . . .' Frank chewed his upper lip, deep in thought.

'One doesn't know his precise field,' I said.

'Uh. He's into the linguistic turn, I guess, the attack on preconceived notions of literature and society . . .'

'You can't know that!'

'And he wears Gucci shoes, Savile Row suits, and . . .' Frank waved his thumb triumphantly.

'You're making him up! Cheat! Cheat!'

' . . . *and* bow ties!'

'No, no, he doesn't! He's a typical boring American academic type. He has a horrible brown polyester suit and – '

'He won't be seen dead in brown polyester! He gets his Harris tweed special from Scotland, and a little tailor man in Hong Kong – '

'He's my invention! I thought of him first!'

'Okay, Em, okay.' Frank patted the air ten centimetres above my head.

'He's mine! He's all mine!'

'Easy, *eee-zeee*. It's a collaborative effort.'

'Oh, all right . . . But I *did* think of him first. Or possibly *her*.'

Frank was busy bellowing, 'To Professor Absent!'

'To Professor Absent!'

So we both raised and drained an imaginary tankard. Frank did a rather elaborate mime about banging the bottom of the thing and sucking out the last drops. He had me tee-heeing till I choked; then I coughed.

Meanwhile he was spouting a long-winded joke about how Professor

15

Absent is the presiding god of New York, absent and ineffable, well-intentioned and not much use. (Frank, you see, had some sort of religious upbringing which is why he makes such a fuss about being atheist. As for me – well, one is Church of England *faute de mieux*, not that one takes it seriously – Mummy used to arrange the ornamental cabbages at Harvest Festival . . . things like that.)

He sank back into the canvas chair. With some difficulty, he contorted his left leg and hooked it over the side, the better to display his crotch. He dangled and swung an elephantine shoe.

It should be made clear that I am not, in fact, notably physiologically attractive. Granted, Daddy's nordic colouring has passed down to me in the genes – and whenever one reads about a 'blonde' in the papers it always turns out in paragraph two that she is the mistress of a pop-singer, or her half-clothed body has been dragged out of a canal – but I have also inherited Mummy's square face and goggle eyes. I'm averagely plain. I used to 'make the best of my features' by doing my hair long and wavy and parted asymmetrically – but since one attracts so much attention anyway as a crack mathematician there seemed little point in seeking more: a year ago I chopped my hair shortish and took to wearing plain, practical, not unattractive, neat clothes. Really, one is the kind of blonde who only seems beautiful to dark-skinned foreigners: one was always being followed round Cambridge by Senegalese language students, or Persian tourists would offer one a peanut . . . In fact I had only ever had one 'boyfriend': Frank – and that didn't last long: we both soon agreed it would be more 'mature' to have a less intimate relationship. (Well, I'm *supposed* to be immature: that's what a 'child prodigy' is all about; but if a man hasn't grown up by the time he gets into his 30s, ah, one begins to wonder.)

'Now come on,' I said teasingly. 'Do it.'

'Do what?'

I put my knees firmly together, folded my arms across my chest, then flashed at him my demurest smile. I whispered, 'Do what you came here for.'

'What's that?'

'What you're intending to do.'

'Oh yeah?'

'What I want you to do.'

'Really?'

'What you promised.'

'Yeah?'

'Uh. Okay.'

'Now.'

Frank set about rising from his deep chair. He tried rolling backwards over one of its sides like a high-jumper doing a fosbury flop, but it was too steep. Then he had a go at sitting upright-ish and somersaulting forwards, but there wasn't enough leverage in his knees. Then he worked out the solution. He tucked his knees up to his chin, looking like a dwarf, or a child on an adult-size sofa, and swung backwards, forwards – once, twice, thrice – building up momentum, and sprang out sprawling on the fitted carpet.

He picked himself up. He put on his leather jacket and wound his sleek white silk scarf around his neck.

'Emma, you lucky woman, you. You are about to be shown the Real New York by a real New Yorker.'

I made for the front door – but he barged past me. He set about opening it: he fiddled for a while with the multiple locks, chains, latches, and security bolts.

3

A word about upbringing. It's impossible to get to know a city without walking its streets; or to comprehend a mathematical proof unless one works one's way through the definitions and lemmas which go to make it; or a people without grasping its history: just so, to understand a human being, one must have at least a nodding acquaintance with that person's biography.

In my case, it all goes back to Daddy.

Daddy was born in 1925 in the master bedroom of our house on the farm. The house is called The New House, which means – as always in England – that it's very old. (Jacobean, actually.) And one is supposed to call the grounds the 'farm' – not the 'estate' – because one doesn't want to sound vulgar and *nouveau riche*. Not that Daddy had a silver spoon in his mouth – well, not exactly: it was tarnished, at least – because as a second son (Uncle Harry was already a vigorous 7-year-old) he wasn't expected to make very much of his life.

What a cherub he was! Look at him in those early photographs, posed in a sailor suit or on a chestnut gelding. His hair was luxuriant gold; his face was wide-mouthed and big-eyed (chinlessness isn't considered a defect in children); his expression had that combination of vacancy and breathlessness which is considered as attractive in infants as in sex symbols. From the age of 5 – when he sneaked a glance into Uncle Harry's schoolbook containing Euclid's proof of the Pythagorean theorem – he knew he wanted to become a mathematician. Nobody went to the trouble of discouraging him. Eccentricity is quite commonplace, almost banal, in a family such as ours. Of course it's more the done thing for a younger son to become a lawyer, a parson, a something in the City . . . but dons too are socially quite acceptable.

And then came the war. Daddy was called up. Our family has

traditionally gone into the navy (the 'senior service', one calls it, if one is in an old-fashioned mood) rather than the army – so Daddy found himself at sea. He had a reasonably pleasant time of it (he says): zigzagging across the Atlantic, operating the radio communications system, vomiting into the ocean, gazing at magnificent sunsets, growing a trim beard, reading monographs on tensor calculus.

After the war it was many months until he was demobbed: perhaps because he was so good at his job, or blame it on bureaucracy. But at last he went up to Cambridge to read mathematics. One obtained a first-class degree, of course. He embarked on a Ph.D., specialising in the foundations of hydrodynamics. Back then this field was thought of as unexciting, almost dry (to make a reasonable pun); of course, a decade or two later, when it was realised it could be incorporated into a general analysis of Chaos Theory, it became awfully trendy – but that was too late for Daddy.

Well, no doubt Daddy would have become a don. Not a genius, no, but a perfectly competent mathematician doing his bit for human knowledge. One can imagine him as he might have been: a bumbling bachelor, a fixture in the college, passing the port to the left and the sherry to the right, offering earnest advice and undrinkable homemade elderberry wine to the undergraduates, acquiring a jovial nickname such as 'Smudger' or 'Gog' . . . But then Uncle Harry died.

No one knows the whole story, and honestly it doesn't matter. A shooting accident, apparently. Uncle Harry in the barn. Uncle Harry snapping open a shotgun. Uncle Harry fiddling with a rod and an oily rag, to clean the damn thing. Uncle Harry clicking the gun shut. Uncle Harry peering down the barrel, checking he'd done a decent job, while his fingers danced casually over the trigger . . . There was an almighty to-do. And poor Daddy was given no choice. Daddy was now the eldest son, the head of the family: master of the estate, the tenants, the honour of the Smarts. He had to resign his fellowship. He was whisked back to take command of The New House.

Make no bones about it: Daddy was stuck with his inheritance. There was no question of selling off the farm or letting a hired manager run it. Indeed for generations we've been disposing of our acreage, bit by bit (it's only a medium-sized estate now, with wheat and cabbages and sheep), and buying stocks and shares, but one can't get rid of the whole lot because that's one of the things. Land. A family like ours *must* own land: we're supposed to be 'rooted' in it, as if one were a turnip or something. Otherwise we'd just be parasites living off unearned income, like those people who work in the City whom one doesn't invite to dinner.

Yes, one's attitude is rather negative. No, one can't work up any enthusiasm for the upper classes (or 'upper middle classes' as one euphemistically and confusingly describes them nowadays: only the Queen and the Duke of Edinburgh admit to being upper – and one is not sure about the Duke). Yes, one has to concede that one's country and caste are something of a backwater. No, one is not too regretful. Yes, indeed one did do important things in one's time, such as writing Tennyson and governing India – but if one hadn't, somebody else would have, and probably better.

. . . Now, Uncle Harry had been engaged to an incredibly suitable young lady from a neighbouring county: a big-boned, oblong-jawed, agricultural type who seemed to like nothing better than grooming the horses, pruning the privet, and mucking out the sheep. Who came with a fine dowry. Who was actually fond of Uncle Harry. Whose accent was proper. Whose family was the right sort . . . Who was now at a loose end, weeping, despairing . . . So it seemed the decent thing for Daddy to propose to her.

Mummy and Daddy rub along all right. They don't talk to each other much, except for essential communications such as, 'It looks like thunder,' and, 'Pass the salt.' They move along separate, non-intersecting worldlines in and around the bright, chill estate. The New House is located near the summit of a hill, for strategic rather than climatic reasons: a wind blows through the gaps in the warped window frames. Often it drizzles: moisture seeps into the box room, the drawing-room, the spare bedroom . . . Usually Mummy is outdoors, trudging about in her Wellington boots, murmuring that she must just unblock a silage clamp, or whistling for the sheepdog. She is happiest attending to her beloved rose garden. 'I can't think where I misplaced my secs,' she might remark, with reference to her secateurs; then: 'Ah! there they are at the back of the sewing box. What would one do without one's secs?' Once upon a time she and Daddy must have been aware of – indeed, cultivated – this droll pun; now, thanks to continual devotion to the English virtue of suppressed emotion, they are unaware of any joke . . . And in due course Mummy strides indoors: she steps into her worn slippers; she puts on her grey-mauve housecoat; she arranges snipped blooms in tall glass vases: those sensual masses of Crimson Joy, Peace, American Beauty, hybrid tea . . . Daddy glances at them and goes, 'Hmm.' As for

Daddy . . . ah, what does Daddy do now that his children have left home?

My brother Edmund, the eldest child, looks rather like Daddy, and shares his shyness if not his intelligence. Edmund survives on his income from the trust fund. We see him for a month or so every few years, when he hitches in from Heathrow; in between visits, he says, he is traipsing around India in an apricot-coloured robe. Obviously he won't be the inheritor of the Smart tradition: by now my parents are resigned to that.

And I am the second child. While I was still in my nappies Daddy was teaching me two–plus–two. I learnt my times tables before I was old enough to go to kindergarten. Geometry at the age of 4. Algebra at 6. Calculus at 8. Daddy was determined I would become a mathematician. And so I have.

Now, one can't escape from the past just because one understands it. (That's the mistake Freudians and Marxists make, as I have often pointed out to Frank – when he alleges 'there's a lot to be said for' both.) Of course I do appreciate that my whole life as a mathematician is just the substantiation of Daddy's dream – but it's real none the less. Sometimes I muse about not being mathematical: what kind of existence might one have had instead? Perhaps one might have grown into a properly conventional young lady, fluttering around dances in a long frilly dress, aspiring to marry a gentleman with the right antecedents, an ample bank account, an estate in the country . . . But I think such an ideal is unrealistic outside the novels of Jane Austen: a well brought up modern girl *has* to break out one way or another. Some become punks or Methodists, lesbians or hairdressers (or indeed all four simultaneously) . . . why not a mathematician? Besides, if one weren't a mathematician, one would be nothing. I mean that literally: if one were to meet someone precisely like oneself but unmathematical (as I do in my nightmares), one simply wouldn't recognise that person.

No: one is made by one's past – biography and history – whether one likes it or not.

4

We set out into New York.

Frank metaphorically took me by the arm (he made a move towards doing it literally, but I side-skipped prophylactically) and gave a running commentary on the street-life outside my apartment. That 'guy' over there, he said, pointing, was sporting the very latest fashion in lapels. That building with the funny Disneylandesque towers was a library: built in eighteen-somethingty-something. That lady dragging bags was of the kind known as a 'bag lady'. That café at the corner – where blank faces behind glass were staring out at us or dutifully eating high sandwiches filled with a dry red meat – was a very well-known café about which he could tell an interesting anecdote if he chose . . .

'How terribly clever of you to have invented this nice big city all on your own!'

'Very witty,' he said, meaning the opposite. He continued with his travelogue voice-over. 'I live over there, in the East Village, of course.'

'Of course.'

'We are now approaching the junction of Greenwich and Charles . . .'

'You call it Charles *tout court*! Well I never! One assumes you have been personally introduced.' No sooner did this clever-clever remark escape my lips than I felt embarrassed. One does tend to be snappy and dazzlingly waggish, as a means of asserting one's identity – especially given that one is actually smaller and always younger than everybody else – and because cleverness, after all, is what one is good at. Now I wanted to admit I was sorry – but that would have been even more embarrassing.

While I was thinking these apologetic thoughts Frank had led me out on to a broad boulevard. We were strolling down it in the midst of a flowing crowd. The season was a peculiar combination of late

22

summer and early winter: bright sun, crisp air. Some folk were marching along in bermuda shorts and gaudy T-shirts; others were wrapped up in quilted layers, earmuffs, woollen hats, sullen expressions.

By way of making it up to him, I said, 'You're like Virgil guiding Dante through Paradise.'

This wasn't a very effective compliment. Being a literary fellow, he likes to get in first with that kind of simile. He grunted. 'Or through the *Inferno*.' I let him have the last word.

Then I noticed several blue metal containers, about the size of a minimalist sheep, parked at intervals beside the road. These were embossed with the mysterious letters USMAIL. I explained at some length that these were the shrines of the shadowy Usmaili sect, bent on subverting the world as we know it. Frank laughed – but not as much as he might have done.

I looked around me and tried to see the city as a projection of Frank's psyche: stylish, knowledgeable, thoroughly hiding its neurosis. I noted a playground guarded by a wire fence behind which adults were endlessly aiming basketballs; a knick-knack store where a vortex of shoppers was being made to buy things no one could possibly want: pornographic baseball caps, mock-sushi earrings, second-hand shoes . . . Newspaper headlines reported demonstrations in Bratislava and Cracow – places one had thought featured only in history books or fairy tales . . . Everything seemed both shocking and oddly reminiscent – much as Columbus must have regarded the New World.

Frank interrupted my thoughts by announcing, 'And this is Sixth Avenue.'

To cheer him up, I put on my ooh-silly-little-me voice. 'Then why does it say "Avenue of the Americas" on the street signs?'

A patronising smirk. 'That's its *name*. But what it *is*, is Sixth.'

'Oh, I see. Like Buck House in London. Referred to as Buckingham Palace only by members of the middle class and foreigners.'

Which made me realise why this district looked so familiar. It was just like an idealised England! Cambridge, say. The same masses of American tourists. The same honking Japanese cars. The same genre of street beggars, wistfully playing the harmonica or vending sweet incense. The same scatter of shiny litter: twisted foil, greasy paper, orange peel . . . The same cathedral-light: a slow slosh of glimmer and shadow. A yellow M signalled a fast-food joint – just like the dear old McDonald's down the road from Trinity College!

I glanced at my companion. Frank, handsome and striding, was in his element. With his generically foreign looks and nervy smarminess, he fitted in among all these visitors from New Jersey or Puerto Rico, Teheran or Brooklyn. His clothes too, showy but not individualised, seemed designed to pass unnoticed. And then I happened on a vision in the mirrored window of a florist's: behold (framed romantically by bunched carnations, roses, maidenhair ferns) a young woman in green corduroy trousers, a striped shirt (borrowed from Daddy), a tufty boyish hairdo . . . myself! I too seemed to be an indefinable but recognisable type. I was exhilarated: at last I had found a city where I wouldn't stand out! Of course I knew I would always be different from other people really – but at least it wouldn't show!

I tried to explain this to Frank. I gesticulated excitedly at the reflected image of the two of us, looking like a normal couple (not that I wanted to *be* a couple with him – but . . .).

He said, 'Yeah,' a few times. He spat at a prickly-pear cactus growing in a pot of dry sand. 'It hurts me to see it so dry.'

'But don't you see? One looks just like a real person!'

'Nah, not here . . .' Then he mumbled something I couldn't quite catch.

'I don't altogether follow. Kindly explain the meaning of "thnick".'

'D'know. What is it?'

'Just now, you were referring to – '

'Emma. I give up. What's the answer?'

'But you yourself said – '

'Em. I never heard the word in my life.'

'But you – '

'So *you* tell *me*.'

'Now look here, Francis. I distinctly heard you say that the Real New York is only to be found in a "thnick" neighbourhood . . .'

As I spoke – suddenly, simultaneously in both our minds! – my quoted syllables (while we were stepping from the pavement down a flight of grey stairs) resolved into what he had actually said; we gave each other our special look.

New York, like any system, may be analysed in two ways: locally and globally. The local structure is grid-like: at any point one has the choice of walking backwards or forwards, right or left. The natives define location in terms of: 'Go two blocks down and it's half a block on your left.' Every point is accessible from every other nearby point –

if one doesn't mind jaywalking. But the global structure is based on the subway system. Now, I have travelled by underground railway about several cities. The geometry of the London tube is an oval crossed out with many wiggly lines. The Paris Métro is a complex of tentacles pinned at one central point. The superbly designed Moscow system (which I had the pleasure of trying out during the Some Approaches Towards A Resolution Of The Smart-Potts-Ostrovsky Conjecture conference there last year) is a minimalist arrangement of two concentric wheels with connecting spokes. But the New York subway is a fast-flowing river. Imagine you're a fly, fallen into the metaphorical stream somewhere around Coney Island. The flux of the subway system will carry you up Brooklyn, swerve through Manhattan, flush you northward into the furthest reaches of the Bronx. Should you want to struggle perpendicular to the flow, that's just too bad: the system isn't designed for your benefit. Well, I've simplified everything for the sake of clarity (which is what applied mathematics is all about); in fact there are subtle vortices and cross-flow currents: the ingenious fly can paddle around the river using these. Also many isolated creeks persist: the only escape route from them is to rise to the surface, walk a block or two across the city, and (if one wishes) buy another subway token, and switch to a different line . . . Ah! the analysis of intraconnected systems is my obsession: my specialisation: what I'm awfully good at and will one day make me renowned.

Dark winds and gusty smells. An insinuating rumble. Air pockets carrying trapped voices. A shifting gloom. The world had transformed itself (Alice down the rabbit hole!) into a deliciously eerie Gothic horror setting. We were in the subway station. We bought tokens from a glassed-in figure with an implausible nose; dropped them in a turnstile. A crouching, pouting boy (resembling one of those gargoyles over the gate of my Cambridge college) pressed his mouth on the slot and sucked out my token. Frank cuffed him aside. I grinned at the ingenious lad, and inserted another token. Passed through. What a quaint, old-fashioned technology. This place could be the vault where they keep the city's history. Ceiling girders were encrusted with a century of dust and cobwebs. Dim figures surged by: leaping over the turnstile like ghosts in a hurry, or like runners in the hundred metres hurdles – not a modern race, though, but one taken from a pre-war Olympics, as viewed on a flickering monochrome newsreel – or older still: the line-up of warriors on the Elgin marbles . . .

We descended another precipitate flight of stairs, deeper into the underworld.

A colossal shudder. A clank. A moment of stillness – like that tense pause with the mouth in the 'cheese' position while the photographer takes a group portrait – and the doors of the train had opened and shut – and we were inside.

Remembering the interior of one of those subway trains is like trying to recall a dream. It was primitive: unsoft chairs, slippery vertical steel rods. Posters berated/comforted haemorrhoid sufferers and trainee typists. It was hot and it was cold. There was a low white noise. We were standing and clinging. Darkness slid past. At intervals the doors opened and faces tumbled in, like goldfish swept along with the gush of water from a shattered glass bowl. I was quite content down there since I knew this was only the prelude to my adventures in the city: the smoky-dark frame around the gorgeous painting. I avoided eye contact with anyone and brooded on differential geometry.

We emerged into a narrow place. The sun was behind a cloud; I shivered. The image of the subway – long dingy rumbling thoughts – persisted, jarring and darkening my perception of the alley. Frank was loping ahead. He pointed at a cross street and waved back at me. 'Look! Little Italy!'

A brisk transformation scene. Suddenly golden sunshine is dripping on piazzas and palazzos; a tower is leaning; a tenor is belting out a bittersweet love song; gondolas are gliding across grape vines and olive groves and plates of saucy pasta . . . No, in fact we were in a nondescript corner of the city. Women were carrying heavy bags. Men were idling in doorways. A drug store. A bar. A grand mini superette plastered with EVERYTHING SLASHED! and LAST DAYS!! and GOING OUT OF BUSINESS!!! (one admired the subtle deceit in that one).

'They're speaking *English*,' I said. '*This* isn't up to scratch.'

'With an Italian intonation, if you listen carefully.'

'Well. Yes. But . . . I want a thnick!'

'There, there,' he said, rubbing my chin the way one does with nervous fillies or sobbing babies. 'There, there,' he said – but this time signifying directionality.

He was standing in front of 'La Bella Hibernia', a shop decorated in the national colours: green, white, orangey-red. A bell tinkled as we entered. An aroma of cheese and olives and spilt Guinness. Tin boxes of panettone. Cellophane packages of crunchy things with sesame seeds. Scale models of soda bread in authentic plastic. A choice of gleamy bottles of herbal vinegars and whiskeys. Long red salamis dangled from the ceiling. This month's special offer was potato-flavoured rigatoni, also tea towels printed with popes. A female assistant was trying to interest a black man in a mug bearing the message: KISS ME. I'M IRISH–ITALIAN.

She said to Frank, 'One moment, sir.'

'I'm just looking,' he said in a Britishesque accent.

'Oh yeah?'

'Actually, yes. Rather!'

'Oh.'

The black man left the shop holding the mug in both hands as if it were something precious.

I said to the assistant, '*B–b–buon giorno.*'

'Me no speakee Spanishee.'

Frank mollified her by buying some special, exceptionally Irish-Italian sausages. He took them away in a gaudy plastic bag.

'Oh. How interesting,' I said in a polite voice as we returned to the subway.

'You ain't seen nothing yet.'

Half an hour later we were in a Russian neighbourhood in Brooklyn. No Red Armies marched. No blizzards erased onion-shaped domes. No bears danced a crouching dance. No hammers and sickles threw vodka glasses over their shoulders. Frank did however find a shop which sold – *inter alia* – a special kind of native sausage. He bought half a pound and put it in his carrier bag.

We advanced across Brooklyn and Queens by subway and bus, visiting Serbian, Korean, Iranian, Norwegian and Jamaican neighbourhoods, not necessarily in that order. Each was subtly – but only subtly – differentiated, like Cabbage Patch dolls. And each had a shop offering a unique sausage. Frank's bag was getting quite full. He held it with both hands.

'Presumably you like sausages,' I said.

'No, not really.'

Dusk was approaching. My mind felt the way one's stomach does when one has eaten disparate foods – satisfied, craving, excited, disappointed, confused, optimistic. We were seeking a bus stop:

27

everyone we asked said it was one block further on – like the end of the rainbow. I still had confidence that Frank would eventually lead me to the really real New York: he's awfully 'good with' places – in the sense that some other people are good with children or geraniums or dogs. A gang of dogs was trailing us: miscellaneous mongrels with lopsided ears, punkish bald patches, comic limps, musical coughs. Every so often Frank would toss the curs one of his sausages; that would delay them for a minute while they tussled with each other for the meaty scraps; then they would lollop after us again with their tongues out.

'I think they're trying to be friendly,' he said when we finally caught the bus, and he threw out the bag containing the last sausage. A young man picked it up and strolled off munching.

'If this is the real New York,' I said, 'show me the unreal.'

Now it was dark. We were in some obscure backwater of the city – yet another ethnic neighbourhood, this one inhabited by emigrants from some Central European country – I couldn't remember which sort. A wind was flapping, pushing clouds between the street-lamps and the moon. A slight mist softened the lamps and the car-lights and the glowing shop windows. A yellow bus went past with children's faces pressed against the windows. A skateboard painted in luminous colours slid down the road with nobody on. The streets were starting to empty of adults and young children, and fill with lounging teenagers.

Then the mist turned to rain – the youths fled. Gusts lifted the rain in great curves, and slapped it down on gleamy tarmac. The storm shaped itself in great swishing blades. A noise of hiss and smash, as if some enormous thing were being destroyed in the distance. The rain became heavier and darker; thunder rolled, echoing from side to side. Frank stood on tiptoe, raised his arms in the air, and imitated the thunder: '*Drrr drrr!*' His version was louder and more authentic-sounding than the original. I tittered with joy and fright. We were soaked and happy, thrilled and fearful. One was alone.

And suddenly we saw, standing up four-square in the middle of the downpour, a solid, well-lit, multi-storey building. 'That's it!' said Frank. He grabbed my arm and we ran towards it.

28

5

The glass door opened. A doorpost groaned. A floorboard creaked. A voice yelled, 'You are bringing the cold in with you!' The door slammed shut.

Think of an explorer who has just climbed over a mountain pass and, pausing at last on the rim of the valley, leans forward, gazing down at a whole new land. What comes into being is at first no more than a sense of misty space – which resolves into a panorama of multicoloured polygons – then a set of nameable things, finally individual details – sights and sounds and smells – take on clarity. The explorer advances cautiously, bravely, optimistically into the future . . . We were inside the building (having scampered up three flights of a spiral iron fire-escape), out of the wet. We found ourselves on a shallow podium connected by way of a few steps to a large, low-ceilinged area. One made out a scatter of tables and chairs of various designs and uncertain ages – some of oak, plastic, or that textured wood known as distressed pine – dotted here and there amid elderly Persian rugs; and a few very comfy looking armchairs were grouped in front of what seemed to be a gas fire. Soon it was evident this territory was inhabited: real people, assorted and fading, camouflaged or contrasting with the furniture, became visible as they shifted a leg, an arm, an eyebrow. Some were chatting in clusters, others were eating, drinking, playing cards or chess; still others swayed gently like sleepy sheep, doing nothing very much except making mm-hm noises of agreement from time to time; solitary figures were reading newspapers or books, or paring their nails, or repeatedly clicking a cigarette-lighter. The scene was rendered shadowy and dramatic by the illumination (overhead bulbs were secreted within reddish fringed lampshades, behind us pebble-glass windows were gleaming

29

intermittently), so emotions (happiness, wonder, puzzlement, disappointment . . .) were manifested in terms of blatant wrinkles drifting from forehead to forehead. Now, at the furthest reach of this room, extra objects sprang into reality: a luminous green EXIT sign; a steaming espresso machine; a bar with bottles of bourbon and beer and a barmaid; shiny stacks of plates and glasses on a counter; a door through which a red-haired man in a tweed suit who somehow looked familiar was passing. An aroma of smoke, stew, old wood, wet coats. The beat of the rain against the front door and windows; the hiss of the gas fire; the bubbling of the espresso machine; a murmur of conversation *not in English*. Ah, an uncompromising foreignness – yet the time-worn random quality of the place was nothing if not English-ish. How strange to come across such an uncontemporary, unhurried, unabashedly un-American zone in New York – but its very oddity could be seen as a sign of New York-ness, arguably. No one paid us any especial attention.

We were separated from the body of the room by a low railing; on it was a plaque engraved with a notice in fancy Gothicky lettering; I didn't recognise the language. Frank translated: it just stated this is a social, political, dining and cultural club (which seems to cover all the possibilities, surely?) and that it is reserved for members only but visitors are welcome (ditto).

We sat down at a table in a corner. I felt at home here instantly, whereas Frank . . . Frank, actually, tends to frequent the kind of dive which is featured in glossy magazines (his favourite is that dreadfully trendy joint, The Red Cabbage Café): he hides his insecurity behind the mask of 'style'. Certainly no one could call this place stylish – or rather it was, but in a fashion quite its own, bearing no obvious relationship to anything anywhere else. To start with – as became glaringly obvious now that we were down amongst them – most of the inhabitants were not young. In fact, old. Not to say ancient. Well, older than Frank and me, anyway. Some were positively archaic. Now, I'm quite used to that, since practically everybody I meet is venerable compared to myself; one is frequently being poked in the tummy and asked, 'Oo's a liddle girly-wirly?' (to exaggerate – but not very much). Frank, on the other hand, is wary of old folk. He is scared of growing up (he doesn't want to conclude like his detestable parents: deracinated, philistine, unloved, over 50 . . .); hence he hangs out with teenage pop stars and junior members of the minor aristocracy; he has been known to gallivant around Cambridge with Swedish au pairs or juvenile ice-skating champions, for want of better – under the delusion this will keep him eternally young. (One of one's own motives for befriending him in the first place, indeed, was to save him from himself: if he *must* be obsessed with youth, one argues, at least let him make the acquaintance of brilliant youth.) Not his type at all, these oldsters. They had kitted themselves out in the kind of clothes one is apt to discover in the dusty cabin chest under the four-poster in the housemaids' quarters: tweed knickerbockers; a check motoring cap; a long brown leather coat with round buttons; a plumed hat; a fur muff, slightly got at by moths; tan kid gloves; a detachable collar with a faux-ivory stud; a Fair Isle sweater, on the small side; a fat gold pocket watch; correspondent shoes; spats; a three-piece double breasted suit in darkest black . . . They seemed to have thrown together their outfits in the spirit of oh-what-a-lark, like children at a fancy-dress party pulling items out of the dressing-up box. They were so unfashionable as to be almost fashionable. If, at some remote point in the future, one were to become ordinary and unbrilliant and irresponsible and old, one might dress like that.

'Do you know anyone here?' I asked Frank. Actually he always knows someone anywhere: that's rather the point of him.

'Hrr, hmm. See that guy over there?' he said, gesturing with his chin.

'No.'

'The old guy.'

'Which?'

'*That* guy.' He was referring to the red-haired man I'd noticed before. 'The guy in the fancy-shmancy suit and the no necktie and the piggy face and the . . . the dyed, I guess, hair. Well, he's none other than a Michelob for me no make that a Heineken and a what you want, Em?'

'Er. May I have a cup of tea please? With just a dash of milk. No sugar.'

I looked up – and the waitress was already striding back towards the bar.

'Yes?' I asked. 'Who *is* he?'

But I was addressing the long, shapely, layered hair on Frank's nape. He had turned round in his chair, and was already deep in conversation with some fellow in a silvery grey suit and a trim white beard who looked like a middle-aged, dapper version of King Lear.

31

The man nodded politely at me and gave me a once-over with his eyes, the way men do. 'Hello. I am the well-known critic, thinker and bon viveur, H. H. Gritz.' Simultaneously Frank was murmuring, 'H.H. needs no introduction, of course.'

The two of them ignored me, and set about having one of those long, tangled conversations in which each tries to work out where and when he has met the other before: it turned out to be at a publication party for some anthology of domestic and imported verse. Then they commenced impressing each other. Frank was saying, in his best Cambridge accent and intonation, 'Epiphenomenally speaking, to put it mildly . . .' Meanwhile H.H. was declaring, 'Speaking as an intellectual . . .'

Other inhabitants were doing things they obviously always did, with the air of actors in a long run – that combination of boredom, ease and subtle innovation. A bald man was talking about sex and money and the marvels of a certain fellow, who turned out to be himself, to a white-haired man who was asleep. A chorus of nodding folk was propped against the bar. A silent, pale barmaid was pouring out drinks. A man in brown was disagreeing with a man in black.

The scene struck me as the kind of scene that is shown in films. (Which is odd, because I hardly ever watch films. As a dedicated mathematician, one has to deny oneself various time-consuming simple pleasures.) Imagine a flickering screen filled with dim characters wearing hats indoors, and smoking, and grunting in Americish . . . The club seemed both alien and universal, both taking place on a backlot decades ago and Coming Soon To A Theatre Near You.

The waitress returned with the drinks. Her appearance was most peculiar yet attractive: one wondered why no one had ever thought of looking like that before. She was somewhere between the ages of 50 and 500. Her round tanned face was covered with intersecting shallow wrinkles, subdividing her skin into a tessellation of quadrilaterals – rather like the quilted satin material which is sometimes used for bedspreads or dressing-gowns. She was plumpish and smiling. She wore buttercup yellow harem trousers and a frayed grey woollen cardigan covered with a long sky blue apron.

She flapped a red check tablecloth and spread it on the distressed pine table-top. 'Your tea-ea-ea . . .' she said, making the vowel very musical.

'Thank you.' I had a sip. Ordering tea in foreign parts is a risky business, but, to my surprise, 'Jolly nice, really.'

'Hiya!' she sang, as if heralding an important announcement. 'I'm Barbra.'

'Oh, are you really?'

'Many people call me Barbara – but that is *wrong*.'

'Yes. I suppose it would be, rather.'

'For short, see, it was either Bar or Bra – and I ask myself, which I am prouder of, my boozing or my boobs . . .' She pressed her hands on her ample breasts. (One wishes one's own were more evident; but then one can't have everything.) '. . . So my friends call me Bra.'

'Not at all. Don't mention it. Emma Smart, actually.'

She pointed at her apron. 'You think I'm a nobody waitress, yes? But' – dramatic pause – 'I wait tables to keep the wolf from the door, only.' She glanced at the door. She raised her hands and opened her eyes and mouth in mock-shock.

I giggled at her act. And she giggled too. And I giggled some more – but now with her rather than at her.

'Emma, I will tell you a secret. I'm really a very important translator.'

I liked her blatant boasting. How un-English! Wouldn't it be fun if one could cut all the polite guff and understatement and actually-one's-by-way-of-being-something-of-a, and instead come straight out with: Hallo, I'm a brilliant mathematician?

'Hallo, I'm a brilliant mathematician.'

'Hah! We are two brilliants.'

She chucked my cheek but I didn't mind. She sat down opposite me.

'What do you translate, er, Barbra?'

'What do I not translate? I translate all the famous writers of my people.' She began pointing at faces around the room and associating them with their actually quite modest literary and cultural achievements. 'There is —— who was awarded a Rockefeller fellowship in nineteen sixty-two; I translated his research proposal. This is —— , a selection of his poems appeared in a nineteen seventy-seven edition of *Partisan Review* – translated by me . . .' And so she went on, outlining potted biographies of X, Y and Z. I didn't catch the names.

I was feeling rather ignorant: a pretty rare and undignified phenomenon. So I tapped Frank on the shoulder, and whispered, 'What country do these people come from?'

He mumbled back, 'It's twenty after six.'

Which is just typical of him! He's simply incapable of responding to

33

a straight question with a logical answer. Now I brought to mind why I had broken up with him two years before . . . But one wasn't about to engage in a demeaning contretemps – besides, Frank was busy smarming up to this H.H. fellow. One has to admit that Frank does this kind of thing very professionally: he puts on a British accent, and alternates gruff agreement with academic dubiousness: 'You're absolutely right . . . as it were . . .' So the flatteree gets the impression Frank is both sensible and independently minded. Also, Frank arranges himself stiffly with his sit-me-down well back on the seat, blinks seriously, and smiles asymmetrically. One might suppose the H.H. Gritzes of this world would be rather bored of being buttered up to – but not so: it becomes addictive, presumably. As for oneself, when people declare one is an amazing prodigy etcetera, even though it's true, one still gets all squirmy.

'. . . and —— over there, he has a collection of essays forthcoming from the University of Nebraska Press, some translated by me. And —— is working on a major dramatic monologue, the real thing . . .'

The man in the red hair was seated by himself at a table on the far side, dipping a spoon into a ruddy soup and crumbling a roll between his elegant fingers. His shirt was open – a touch of affectation, arguably – his neck showed his age. He swerved his tongue around his protruding lips, licking off soup. There was something about him which made him look kingly – perhaps it was that nobody spoke to or looked at him; indeed, everyone seemed to have turned away to avoid his gaze.

I nudged Frank's back. 'Who?'

Frank followed my gaze. 'L. Z. Allgrobsch, of course . . . Yes, H.H., you certainly have a point there . . . so to speak . . .'

Of course. In the flesh, Allgrobsch was rather shorter and plumper than he appears in the photographs on his book jackets. One was rather impressed. I had read several of his stories, as they came out in the *New Yorker*; in fact I had bought his latest collection, *Greater than Infinity and other stories*, on account of its title; the hardback was still sitting on the shelf in my rooms at Cambridge: one had been meaning to get round to it for ages.

What is wonderful about Allgrobsch's stories (as the Nobel Prize committee spokesperson said) is the way they begin as a lighthearted fairy-tale and end as tragedy. How he achieves that effect is a mystery, since there is no obvious darkening of the tone. The reader is strolling along, and gradually the way angles down and becomes

34

slippery and leads to a crevasse . . . Take for example the title story of his latest collection but two, 'The Bubble Blowing Party'. It is set – like all his fictions – in the land of his birth, before the war. It describes how three young women – all crossed in love – decide to cheer themselves up by blowing soap bubbles. They playfully vie to blow the most beautiful bubble. The story consists of a detailed account of this contest. Although it is never explicitly stated, the reader somehow becomes aware that they are going to continue blowing bubbles until they die, and indeed the whole town is doomed. Yes, one concedes this plot sounds ridiculous in summary; nevertheless . . . Or there is his tale about the two men who ate meatball upon meatball until they exploded. (Surely that can't be correct: one must be misremembering. Well, anyway, one recalls the tragic, shocking tone.) Or the one about the man buried in snow (he burns or freezes or is shot – one can't recollect). And everyone knows his 'The Ice Skater': a simple, lyrical piece about a young girl who goes skating along a river in the old country; she travels further and further into the frozen land; we see the snowy farms on either bank, and the townscapes; we understand that the river is a curse and she is condemned to skate on it eternally.

'Do you know Allgrobsch personally?' I asked Frank.

'Yeah, well, I guess we have . . . uh . . . on various occasions.'

'Oh, that's a pity,' I said.

I asked Barbra. 'Allgrobsch, er . . .'

'Yes.'

'Have you translated him?'

She replied stiffly, 'I have translated many eminent writers of our language . . . '

'Yes. But – '

'. . . such as —— and —— '

One still couldn't remember what language or country Allgrobsch wrote in or came from. Jolly frustrating, that. 'Frank. Where from?'

'. . . and ninthly . . .' H.H. was saying.

Frank was muttering, 'Oh definitely, H.H., there's a lot to be, ah, from that, one might regard, perspective . . .'

I jolted him in the small of his back with my elbow. He hissed at me out of the corner of his mouth. 'It's their club.'

Silly Frank! I imagined a country named Club, inhabited by Clubbies who spoke Clubbish. I got a fit of the giggles. I tried gulping some of my drink to suppress it, but the upshot was I spluttered milky tea all over the tablecloth. Barbra must have found this funny, because the wrinkles in her face started deepening and rippling. She accidentally brushed some spilt tea on to me, so I brushed a bit back at her, so she retaliated in kind, so we were both pointing and dipping our fingers in the tea and flicking it at each other while I was trying to explain about the Clubbies and she was trying to tell me something about Allgrobsch but we were both hee-heeing too much to talk clearly.

A number of people had now moved over to our corner of the room, attracted by the laughter or the intellectual conversation or the new faces. The table was small so plates of food were balanced on laps and glasses were held in hands. The newcomers arranged themselves in a loose semi-ellipse.

I discovered Barbra and I had stopped giggling. After laughter one always feels melancholy for a while. I listened quite attentively while various smiling and nodding faces introduced themselves. Frank greeted them all personally. I nodded and said my how-d'you-dos.

'Is there much interest in your literature nowadays?' I enquired politely of no one in particular.

'Oh, yes,' said a tall man in black.

'Well, no,' said a short man in brown.

Barbra said, 'Why, only last month we had this conference, it was real big, at the State University of – '

H.H. interrupted. 'We have become Comp. Lit.' He smiled wryly.

I asked, 'Do the young speak your language much?' Frank kicked my shin under the table.

'Oh, the young,' said the man in black.

'The young, oh,' said the man in brown.

'The weather is wet,' said H.H.

Everyone glanced away, shrugged, peered into their coffee.

'And of course,' I continued in my best clear voice, rather hoping he would overhear, 'there is one world-famous writer in your language, whom I'm sure you all admire – L. Z. Allgrobsch.'

A heavy silence. The espresso machine was whistling faintly. A table-leg sighed. The rain outside battered the front wall; the wind soughed and rattled the translucent door.

'Ah,' said Barbra.

'He doesn't write in our language any more,' said the tall man.

'He's written directly in English since nineteen fifty-nine,' said the short man.

36

At the far side of the room, Allgrobsch was rising, lifting his arms as if about to say something dramatic. The spoon dropped from his hand and clattered in the empty soup bowl.

Somebody near me thumped on the pine table. 'Cursed be the English language,' a voice shouted, 'which has stolen L. Z. Allgrobsch from us. May it vanish from the surface of the earth!'

6

Extract from the preface to
The Bubble Blowing Party and other stories

. . . How I hated my childhood! The weather was always bad; the food always nasty; the land of my birth unwelcoming. Politics irritated me; my family irritated me; everybody in the town irritated me. The adults were all scared and boring: each did whatever they were supposed to be doing, day in and day out. They lived without hope.

(But now I am old myself, and I forgive them. I realize their hopelessness was truly justified.)

So I retreated into bookishness. The great science-fiction classics had been translated into our language: I read Jules Verne and H. G. Wells and Sir Arthur Conan Doyle. I dreamed of becoming Captain Nemo sailing beneath the oceans; or voyaging round the world in eighty days; or discovering ancient monsters along with Professor Challenger; or waging war against Martians . . . Or, failing that, I decided that one day I would become old, and famous, and a writer of stories set in imaginary lands.

And now I am old, and famous, and a writer of stories set in the town of my birth in the 1930s. For everything I grew up with has become fantasy. My childhood is as far away as Betelgeuse . . .

© L. Z. Allgrobsch 1984

38

7

Everybody turned round. Allgrobsch was rising slowly, his arms were extended, his hands were sliding like a windscreen wiper, his mouth was opening . . . And suddenly Frank had vaulted over the distressed pine table; his trailing foot was kicking aside the red check tablecloth; he ran towards Allgrobsch. And Barbra's fists were pushed against her cheeks, squeezing them inward. And the pallid woman at the bar had fainted. And a score of faces and voices were distorting and falling apart . . . Now Allgrobsch was dropping. First his legs lost rigidity; then his torso swayed jerkily like a scrap of dried leaf caught in a gust; his head swung forward and banged into the empty soup bowl. Just then Frank managed to grab his shoulders and haul him upright, but Allgrobsch's body was as limp as a dummy's and there were red soup marks all over his face.

Hushed shouting and noisy whispering. Shoe soles thudding in all directions over the frayed Persian carpet and soles loud on the wooden floor. Crying voices. Moaning voices. Practical voices with sensible suggestions. The non-melody of a touch-tone telephone being dialled. 'Hello? Hello? Emergency. Hello?'

And the door swung open, letting in great boulders of cold wind and spray and street clamour.

Frank spreading Allgrobsch on the table. Frank thrusting a crumpled up tablecloth under Allgrobsch's head as a pillow. Frank half climbing, half leaning over Allgrobsch . . . Deliberately and powerfully, Frank pressed his fists up against Allgrobsch's lungs, forcing the old air out; then he pressed his mouth over *his* mouth, and blew new air in.

The door was flapping on its hinges, banging irregularly against the frame, dispatching gouts of chilliness. H.H. was shaking. A bald man was quivering. A white-haired man was waking up. The man in black and the man in brown were leaning on each other for support. Barbra was emitting a high, chortling scream. The barmaid was mouthing *where am I?*

A roar and growl of vehicles drawing up outside. Flashing, rotating red/blue/white lights. Sobbing sirens.

'I'm sorry,' Frank said, 'there's nothing more I can do,' as he lowered the body gently on to the table. Its face was wiped blank of emotion and its mouth was hanging open.

8

Two Coals and a Beet

How do people acquire their nicknames? In some cases it is obvious. In my home town in the old country, for example, Dav 'the barber' was in fact a barber. Govya 'the beautiful' had an exquisite figure and face. Gam 'the pious' was generally agreed to be pious — in so far as anybody could tell, since he worked long hours selling fish at his stall in the market, or else mumbling to himself. But his wife, Fehma, was never referred to by anybody as Fehma 'the part-time seamstress' (which she was) or Fehma 'with the twisted nose' (which was also true) or even Fehma 'Gam's wife' — no, she was known as Fehma 'the artistic'. Nobody knew the reason at the time — and we're certainly not going to find out now, now that the town has long been destroyed and its charred ruins lie beneath a canning factory, a minor road and a patch of mud. One theory is that she once sketched a panorma of the town, as seen from the river, on the back of an invoice for two dozen perch. Or some tell the story of how — a decade before I was born — she praised a little girl (Govya, maybe) for looking like 'a real Botticelli' — and she was teased about her pretentiousness ever after. But I favor the hypothesis that Fehma got her nickname because she was completely, utterly, non-artistic.

It is one hour before dawn. Fehma the artistic learns that her husband is to be taken away soon. How she comes by this knowledge is a mystery: the gossip network is silent in the small hours; but somehow rumors do manage to insinuate into the most unlikely places — just as gusts penetrating through invisible gaps between tarred rafters are responsible for what is sometimes noticed on winter mornings, on awakening and glancing into a corner of the bedroom — a small pyramid of snow.

And why Gam? He is an insignificant fellow, quiet, unimportant, who does little except pray and cope with his stock of fish. Ah, there is no cause for such an event. Some things have no explanation worth seeking.

41

Fehma sets a dim candle on the bedside stool. She hustles her husband off the straw mattress. She pushes him upright. She slides his feet into leather boots. She presses his nightcap firmly on his head. An amiable and loving man, he consents unquestioningly. As always on getting up, he takes his clay pipe from its place on the pine dresser, waves it a few times, and taps out the dottle on the floor. Carefully, slowly, affectionately, he stuffs the bowl with a pinch of his favorite mixture, tamps it down; grips the stem in his teeth; leans forward to light the pipe at the candle flame; the tobacco glows; he sucks in rich smoke. He holds it with both hands, moving his fingers along the stem like a flautist.

Meanwhile his wife is searching for a hiding place. Should she conceal him in the attic, under her pile of satin panels and lace trimmings? But no, the material is certain to be rummaged through. Or what about the chest in the basement: maybe he could lie at the bottom of a delivery of frozen flatfish? But surely that would be an obvious place to be investigated. She eliminates in turn, for assorted excellent reasons, the broom closet, the boot box, and the space behind the stove. Finally she takes her husband by the hand and leads him down the stairs and through the front parlor. 'Come outside.'

Outside it is bitterly cold. The cone of light from the doorway illuminates individual snowflakes, each spiraling downward in a different, quirky way. Thick snow covers the land. There is that eerie luminescence which snow always seems to give off, even when there is no moon to be reflected. She stations her husband beneath the eaves, beside the front door, and orders him to stay put. She tightens her lips as if she were humming – and maybe she is, accompanying the wind's tunelessness. She takes his pipe from his hand: he surrenders it reluctantly. She holds it, quite still, like a conductor about to begin Beethoven. Then she drapes her husband with a smelly blue canvas – the one he fastens over the cart to keep the weather off his fish. She tugs and adjusts it, constructing compromises between its linearity and the irregular shape of a human body, until she is satisfied. She ties it loosely with lengths of string and black velvet ribbon. She inspects his wrapped face, simplified and blurred. Her sharp sewing scissors snip a little hole over his mouth. A puff of his breath emerges and steams in the chill air. With one firm tap – like launching a toy boat on to a pond – she pushes the stem of his pipe back through the gap; he bites on it; soon aromatic smoke is wafting into the night. Snowflakes melt and sizzle where they hit the bowl. 'Ah . . . My Gam.'

She crouches at his feet. She angles her head down and shuts her eyes like a worshipper offering obeisance to an expressionless idol, or like a classical statue illustrating one of the servile virtues. Her gloved hands scoop snow, and plaster it on his boots. But this process is too time-consuming. So she staggers to her feet. She fetches a shovel from the cart. She pushes it deep into a drift, then whacks great white masses all over his legs and hips. 'I know you feel cold now, but soon the snow will warm you. They say Eskimos who live in igloos the whole year round are as cozy as millionaires.' She sees nubbed ripples swim to and fro across the blue material: she deduces his hidden elbows and knuckles are on the move . . . so his arms must have broken loose: she pushes them back into their pristine arrangement. She heaves snow on his torso. Soon he is buried up to the neck. She pats and slaps the coating into a rough oblong shape.

Dawn is breaking. A pink gleam. The snowfall eases. She heaps snow on his head. All that can be seen of him is overlaid with snow: not a man but the idea of a man. An occasional crumb of snow slides down the figure's skull, shoulder, hip – like an avalanche glimpsed on a distant mountain. She turns his pipe upside-down – the way a key is twisted in a lock – the contents of the bowl drop on to the ground, glow a moment, and die away. 'You can breathe through the pipe?'

She slips back into the kitchen. She returns with three lumpy objects. She is balancing them awkwardly like a juggler about to perform. She slams them on to the snow-head.

Two coals become his eyes: they are rather closer together and less symmetrically disposed than in real life, giving him a shabby, dishonest air. A round cooked beet – one of the few root vegetables she has left this winter – freezes into place just below his actual mouth. Its roundness suggests a pout of desire or dissatisfaction. The dangling pipe is propped above that. A purplish red juice leaks diagonally across the broad snow-neck.

She kisses the beet.

The enemy arrives. Two soldiers, one fat and one tall, bang through the house: prying in the boot box, inspecting the broom closet, peering behind the stove, rumpling the mats, kicking the doors, upturning the bed, breaking the mirror, toppling the wardrobe, knocking over the candle on to the straw mattress, snatching bits of lace from the attic store to give their women or wives or the pawnbroker, cracking the stair balusters and prodding their bayonets into the basement flatfish store. 'Where is he?' 'I don't know, sir.' 'I said: where is he?' 'Sir, I don't – ' 'I said: where – '

The soldiers stomp to and fro outside, making deep footprints in the drift which – the snow is so loose and wind-driven – soon erase themselves. The tall one passes his time spitting. The fat one eyes Fehma the artistic *lecherously, but she is old and cold and her nose is crooked. The tall soldier notices the dark patch of ash on the ground. He jokes, 'Look! The snowman is smoking!' The fat soldier chuckles. He flicks the bowl the right way up: a few snowflakes settle in the bowl and begin to clog it. The tall soldier says, 'I don't like snowmen.' The fat soldier says, 'I hate snowmen!' The tall soldier swings round, aiming his gun at the snowman's chest; he clicks the safety catch; his finger tightens on the trigger. Instantly his bare neck is splashed with a rounded mass of snow. He staggers back, laughing with shock. He grabs a fistful of snow from the ground and hurls it at the fat soldier, who, outraged, chucks more snow back. The two soldiers, guffawing nonstop, engage in a snow fight. They score hits alternately on a chest, elbow, calf, face. They stuff snow down each other's pants. Fehma the artistic retreats under the eaves.*

I am watching all this from the highest window in my parents' house. I am a little child and nobody tells me anything. I understand what I understand. I see the shadow of a woman. I see a pair of playful young men in uniform, gleefully tossing snowballs at each other. I see the grandest, most beautiful snowman in my life.

A sheet of white paper is resting on the sill in front of me. I have a box of colored pencils which I love: I was given it only recently and then I realized I had desired it for years. I was planning to draw the view – but now I change my mind. I will write a story: the first I have ever attempted. I grip a pencil in my fist. Slowly I set down the following in big, rainbow-colored letters.

MY LIFE, BY A SNOWMAN

I AM A SNOWMAN. I FELL FROM THE SKY. I LAY ON THE GROUND. SOMEBODY PICKED ME UP. NOW I AM A SNOWMAN. SOON I WON'T BE A SNOWMAN.

§ II

Best of All Possible Worlds

. . . but the birds had eaten all the crumbs!
The children were lost in the dark wood.

9

Suddenly it had become winter.

'Have you heard anything new about him?'

'Him?'

'Honestly, Francis. You can be dreadfully obtuse at times.'

'Ah, *him*. Well . . . uh . . . did you see the article in the paper, the . . . eh . . . Times?'

'Really? I didn't know it was sold here.'

'The *New York* Times.'

'Yes, well of course one gets *that* here. Show it to me, please.'

It was three days after Allgrobsch's stroke. We were taking a stroll around Washington Square (conveniently located midway between our accommodations). The idea was that we would build up a thirst and an appetite; then work them off in some nearby café. We were moving quite rapidly to ward off the cold but not so fast as to slither. A heavy frost had coated everything – grass, tarmac, paving, a rolling discarded orange – giving a delusion of snow. Snow was indeed predicted (according to the weathermen): there was no reason why it shouldn't fall any moment.

Frank was very sleepy that morning – he kept rubbing his eyes with his fists in a rather babyish way. He pulled a crumpled bit of newsprint from his suede coat pocket and pressed it flat against his conveniently large palm. He browsed down a narrow column. 'Hmm,' he said, and made some comment on the migration of East Germans to the West via Hungary.

'What's that got to do with anything?' I said.

'It's a cataclysmic turning point, a watershed, a *coupure*. Historians of the future will envy us.'

'Never mind *them*. What about *him*?'

He turned the scrap of paper over.

L. Z. Allgrobsch, the well-known fictional story writer, is under observation in St Kevin's Hospital, Brooklyn, following a stroke Tuesday. According to a hospital spokesman, Mr Allgrobsch is in critical condition.

'What does that mean,' I asked Frank, "in critical condition"?'

'Aw, I write it on students' essays, sometimes. They give me what is supposed to be an independently researched term paper on a . . . I d'know . . . some kind of lit.crit., and I see it's all copied from the *Encyclopaedia Britannica* or my lecture notes or . . . So I write, in my special red ink, "Your grade is in critical condition." Then they come see me and I tell them if they want a passing grade they'll have to . . . It means: bad, lousy . . . there's nothing good in their work, zero, zilch, nada . . .'

'Gosh.'

'When the papers say: "He is in satisfactory condition," that means it's fifty-fifty; and if he'll probably live, his condition is "fair". But "critical" is . . . They don't hold out much hope.'

'Oh dear. Poor old Allgrobsch.'

He crushed the newspaper into a ball and flicked it into the distance. 'He's gone critical already.'

Frank seemed in good humour, inappropriately. He was swinging his arms in big strokes as he strode on the paving around the emptied fountain in the middle of the square. I had to run a few steps to catch up with him. Then we were forced to jump on to the grass to dodge a gang of revellers careering all over the place on rollerskates or skateboards or some similar mobile fad.

I felt it only fair to tell him, 'You know, you were awfully *good*. When Allgrobsch had his stroke, everybody else went into a state of blind panic. But you just went right ahead and did the oral resuscitation, and . . . well, one was surprised how reliable you were in a crisis. You're really a much better person than you give yourself credit for.'

'Yeah. I know.'

I blushed. 'What I meant was . . .'

'Sure. Sure.'

It's true, though if one were in a crisis one wouldn't want to be accompanied by a genuinely 'good' person who'd carefully weigh the pros and cons; no, one would opt for a morally wonky but bold fellow like Frank. Well, 'bold' only in the sense that, having decided to do something, he does it willy-nilly. Of course, he contemplates his strategy in advance, and often chooses retreat or cowardice. In fact I've never known anyone so subtly aware of how his actions will be perceived and reacted to by others; for example, his coat was buttoned incorrectly, and there were dubious white and brown stains on the sleeve, and he'd scuffed his shoes – those Italian ones with the ridiculous laces . . . Clearly he was deliberately aiming at the careless intellectual/lovable little jackanapes image. And how come he always has precisely twenty-four hours worth of stubble on his chin? That must take a great deal of planning.

Frank stopped, turned round, and said, 'Y'know, Em. you are a pixie.' I was wearing my green anorak with the hood up.

I wasn't sure if this was supposed to be a compliment. I said, 'You're looking pretty messy yourself.'

He leered at himself, and quoted Shakespeare or whoever, '"A sweet disorder in the dress/Kindles in me a wantonness . . ."'

I thought it safer to change the subject. 'I didn't even know there *was* a St Kevin.'

'You bet. He was Irish, of course, a follower of St Patrick. A pagan king asked him to renounce his faith and marry the king's beautiful daughter. But St Kevin said no. So he was roasted on the spit and his flesh was served to the dogs.'

'Yee-ugh. Trust you to know a fact like that.'

'Yeah, well. I made the story up. But I guess it's true, anyhow. Or another story just as nasty.' He was smirking amiably.

Perhaps what was putting him in such a good mood wasn't the Allgrobsch affair at all but some unrelated joy. (Which is often the way. Or conversely: one might be having a chat with someone who is plainly desperate to sneak away – and it turns out not to be anything one said or did: it's just that one's interlocutor has to catch a train or go to the loo . . .) That morning, when I went over to the East Village to meet him, he was just coming out of his apartment building as I arrived. He was accompanied by a brace of gaudy young women. He was in the middle and had an arm around each of their necks. He was facing forward and they were looking back, in the attitude of the Three Graces. At first I hazarded that he had broken a leg or at least sprained an ankle, and they were kindly supporting him; then I realised he was hugging them simultaneously. He did the introductions. 'Hi, Em! Hey, ladies, this is the genius mathematician I was telling you all about. And

Em, meet my' – switching mid-sentence into a British accent – 'jolly good old chums, Mare and Lalage. They work at' – back into an exaggeratedly American accent – 'the Red Cabbage Café, that hip dive where all we wonderful folks hang out.'

Mare – the one with the dyed gold hair and the fake leopard-skin stole – tilted her head round coquettishly, waved her hand, and lisped, 'Ooh, you're just like I imagined you.'

Lalage – all I saw of her was a Dracula cloak and a black satin turban – boomed at Frank, 'Who the batshit is she?'

He kissed them each, gave their bottoms a simultaneous goodbye slap . . . and the pair of nymphets jogged off down the street.

He informed me, 'They just moved into the apartment above mine.'

'That must be very convenient for them,' I said. 'I'm sure they're honoured.'

Now, the four of us meeting like this was a complete coincidence, not in any way plotted or thought out beforehand by Frank with a view to stirring up jealousy – I don't think.

Frank and I couldn't stroll any further along the path because a police car was parked there, blocking the way, like a cow on a country lane. So we turned and walked back, towards the great archway on Fifth Avenue.

We passed a black boy who hissed, '*Smoke!?*'

I murmured, 'Awfully sorry, but we don't have any to spare.'

Frank and the boy looked at me oddly.

We kept on encountering different boys going '*Smoke*' interspersed among the pigeons and the tramps and the hot-dogs and the Dutch tourists in hippy gear and the ambling policemen.

I remarked to Frank sniffily, 'Cigarettes are in high demand, here.' One doesn't smoke oneself, and Frank (who used to have bunches of cigarillos or Gauloises dangling from his lower lip) had become a born-again non-smoker: the kind of man who, when somebody else lights up, pulls open the window to let masses of chill air in, leans out, inhales ostentatiously, and says, 'Ahh! I feel fit.'

He explained that the boys weren't proposing to take but to sell, and it wasn't (a quick moue of disgust) tobacco they had on offer anyway.

One doesn't like having one's naïvety exposed, so I said grumpily, 'Why can't people *say* what they *mean*? I hate all this deceit and power play and . . . and machination and bitchery and . . . and manipulating other people to make them do things they'd probably do anyway if only one asked them politely . . . It's simply dreadful!'

50

He stopped still and looked into my eyes. 'No you don't, Emma. You love it, really.'

I said, as sarcastically as I could, 'I bet you say that to all the girls.' I looked down at the hard ground – which I kicked, stubbing my toe.

'Look,' he said. 'Everything is a plot.'

'I didn't know you were so keen on theology?'

'Well, sure, *that* everything too – the trees and the cars and the' – he waved a hand broadly – 'and the clouds in the sky. But I meant' – in a dramatic hush – 'suppose Allgrobsch's death was murder?!'

'He's not dead yet.'

'Yeah, okay. His "imminent demise", then. You read whodunnits. So tell me. *Who done it?*'

Soon after we had first met, I had admitted to him – in a moment of brute honesty – that I flip through detectives stories for relaxation. In fact I have worked my way through almost the entire *oeuvre* of Agatha Christie; I'm less fond of her country-house settings because they are too naturalistic, but some of her mysteries in exotic parts are jolly ingenious. I usually skip the middle third of the book to make the task of unravelling the puzzle more testing.

'Don't be silly. Allgrobsch just had a stroke. Lots of perfectly ordinary people do. For instance, I remember, my mother's great-aunt Dorothy . . .'

'Yeah. But just suppose. It has to be somebody in the club, right? That's one of the rules. Could the murderer be, say, that waitress you were chatting to?'

'Certainly not! Barbra is much too nice a person.'

'Okay. Good. We're eliminating suspects one by one. How about . . . that guy with the bald thing and the line in dirty patter?'

'No. Too obvious a suspect. Couldn't be the one. What do you say to the barmaid?'

'Who? Oh, her. No, she didn't say anything. And the murderer always makes some innocent-seeming comment in Chapter One. That's how it is.'

'H.H. Gritz, then?'

'Ye-e-es. He's a reviewer for the *Voice* – and they're notoriously bloodthirsty. We can't exclude him . . . Or maybe Professor Absent sneaked down the chimney?'

'Look, Frank. This is ludicrous. And it's in bad taste. A man is dying in St Kevin's . . .'

Frank began a grin which turned into a yawn and back into a grin.

51

'Aw, Emma. It's not a *man*. It's an *author*. And we post-modernist literary critics have proved that authors don't exist.'

'Well, yes, it is rather odd the way one always assumes they've passed away years ago. Do you remember how the Classics don, old Podger, anyway he invited his special guest to the Founder's Day organ concert in the college chapel, and it turned out to be none other than that awfully famous, what'shisname, you know, the one who – '

'That's not exactly what I had in mind.'

We started walking slowly towards the arch. Frank said quietly, 'I'm going to find out the truth about Allgrobsch.' I was about to mention there is such a phenomenon as carrying a joke too far, but there was a seriousness in his voice. His eyes looked old, and it wasn't just from lack of sleep. 'I'm going to write Allgrobsch's authorised biography.'

'But you can't.'

'Why not?'

'Well, for one thing . . . You don't know enough about him.'

'I'll do research.'

'And how can he authorise you? He's in critical condition.'

'Aw, I went to his publisher, and H.H., who's his literary executor. The deal's sewn up.'

'Already?'

He nodded.

'How can he have an executor? He's still alive.'

'Yeah?'

'I mean, he is expected to get right as rain, eventually, isn't he?'

'I checked with the hospital. He's in a coma, and he'll never come out.'

'Oh dear. That's . . . simply awful.'

'Nah, no sweat. Makes it easier to write the biog., all in all, when the subject can't contradict the author. And no hang-ups over libel . . . So I explained to the publisher I'm a distinguished professor of comparative literature, and I know Allgrobsch's work in the original, and I'm his old pal: we used to hang out together at the club, where I also met many of his compatriots and colleagues . . . H.H. supported me . . . I'm the ideal biographer.'

'That's a fib! *And* it's . . .' I searched for a polite expression of my disapproval.

'Why the hell? I'm doing Allgrobsch a favour, free publicity and all. And he's doing me one: I'll win fame and tenure from this book, hopefully.'

'One would be like a vulture feeding on a corpse.'

'Nuh-*huh*. Allgrobsch was an autobiographical fictionalist, right? He's already nibbled away all his own flesh. I'm just sucking the marrow from the bones . . . Look, you're the one who has the big thing about logic, and about trying to be *good*. I want to be a good guy, too, y'know, in my own funky way. What harm does this do anyone? I'm immortalising him! If we go one block to the right, there's an ethnic little place that does an okay cappuccino and an amazing spumoni. I'll show you a transcript of my interview with H.H. – I've got a great source right there.' He handed me some clipped sheets of word-processed paper. 'Boy, I need caffeine.'

I sniffed heavily but could think of no answer – or rather none that was wholly fair and honest and relevant.

I thought about how much I disliked Frank – indeed I had always done so. The trouble with him, fundamentally (one is aware it isn't fashionable to say this), is that *he is no gentleman*. A gentleman wouldn't have seized the opportunity of somebody else's near-fatality to advance his own career; or if he would, he would at least have pulled a long face and muttered something about how mortified he was to find himself in this position. Call it 'hypocrisy' – but hypocrisy is at least a nod in the direction of virtue. Frank's jollity was simply *infra dig*. Now, one doesn't claim to be perfect oneself: one admits one is sometimes arrogant, bossy, childish – but one certainly knows how to comport oneself in the face of tragedy . . . On the other hand, of course, his ungentlemanliness was part of his attraction. A wholly good man could not be lovable: a woman needs somebody who is prepared, if necessary, to be wicked on behalf of them both – so that she herself may remain unblemished, innocent, eternally pure.

On several occasions I had tried to tell Frank about my ambivalent feelings for him – relating them to my childhood in The New House, with Daddy and Mummy and the sheep and cabbages . . . He would go, 'Hh hm,' and change the subject. He just didn't seem to care. 'The cult of the individual is dead,' he'd say, or, 'We have deconstructed personal identity,' or, 'The ego is irrelevant in the twentieth century.' I'd try to counter him on his own ground, pointing out that Freud (and Frank, in certain moods, claims to be a Freudian) thought that all our mental hiccups can be traced back to our upbringing, didn't he? Frank would reply, 'Maybe Freud thought he was analysing individuual psychology, but really he was into epistemology.' Well, I was a bit miffed at his attitude. Naturally I concede that my own placid childhood was boring compared to his – jetting around the world in cosmopolitan luxury – but all the same he might have taken a decent interest . . .

And now he was proposing to obsess himself with the details of another man's life. Well, I could put a name to the emotion that was afflicting me – jealousy. But women are *supposed* to be jealous, aren't we? I should feel proud to have acquired this feeling, rather grown up. So, on mature reflection, I had every reason to be content.

We passed under the archway. Yet another infuriating boy tried to sell us a forbidden substance.

I stamped my foot heavily on the tarmac, hurting my stubbed toe. I waved both arms and screamed, 'Shoo! Scat! Go away! How many times do I have to repeat it? One – doesn't – want – any!'

I had a lump in my throat and my cheeks were burning. I ran towards the uptown subway station. In the distance I could hear Frank's voice calling, 'Hey! Em. The café's over here,' and many little shifting voices around me hissing '*Smoke*' . . . And I imagined palls of soft grey smoke rolling in from the horizons: little flames were crackling and sprouting underneath.

10

Interview with H.H. Gritz (edited extract), New York,
5 September 1989

– Yes.
– Ah, yes.
– Yes.
– Dreadful, yes. Of course the physicians insist he can't see anyone now, not even his oldest and closest friends. Otherwise . . .
– A *complete* surprise. He'd always seemed fit and healthy, though of course at our age . . . I remember, back in 1962 as I recall, no, '63, we both came down with a touch of the influenza that was going around then, Spanish flu, it was called, or possibly Portuguese . . .
– A *very* great writer. I've always said as much. In fact I've stated my views in print frequently. It's no secret, I think, that I as much as anyone helped establish his reputation. And when the Nobel Prize committee phoned me to ask my opinion . . . Well, who knows if my recommendation might not have tipped the balance?
– Well, it's hard to say. There are so many facets of his work . . .
– Just so.
– Yes, indeed.
– Not exactly political, no . . . though of course the *oeuvre* of a great writer of our time necessarily has its political resonance.
– The burning passion. I would have to single that out, should you press me. The sheer intensity of his vision. The profundity of his insights. The honesty and dedication with which he pursued the – for him – sacred task of preserving our homeland in the form of literature, as a fly might be carried down to eternity within a – how shall I put it? – droplet of amber . . . Of course, *de mortuis nil nisi bunkum*, as the saying goes. Not that he's dead yet, strictly speaking . . .
– Ah, yes, old friendships are the best. They have a tolerance, a broad-spiritedness, an *elasticitas* indeed, which cannot be found in the passing acquaintanceship favoured by a younger generation. Not that our friendship was so very antique. We didn't meet until after the war. The

fall of '46, if my memory serves me. We were both residing in London then – as were many of our compatriots: such as . . .

– Lyon's restaurant near Swiss Cottage, to be precise. It was much patronised by the intelligentsia. We used to reconnoitre there often – we appreciated its quick service – the waitresses there were known as 'nippies' – and my! they were nippy indeed . . .

– Ah, there was a something about him. Call it an aura, if you like, a charisma, a *signum* . . . I spotted his potential at once.

– You see, I already had a certain reputation in critical and cultural circles, whereas L.Z. was something of an unknown. He's a few years my junior, of course. He had published some poems in lesser periodicals – nothing outstanding. But I was struck by – call it genius, if you like.

– Well, I can't put my finger on it, exactly. It was his intelligence, of course, and his determination. And he knew he wanted to be a great writer, from the start. You only had to talk to him for a few minutes to understand that. Of course some people regarded him as a *poseur*, but I recognised the genuineness of his ambition, the generosity of his egoism . . .

– It's difficult to be specific . . . For example – and I know this sounds ridiculous – he used to construct jokes, puns, based on your name – on everybody's name. A trivial feat, to be sure, but the focused ingenuity with which he pursued this simple task – well I knew that here was a mighty talent *in posse*.

– No, I don't recall what pun he made on my name.

– Naturally I was in a position to advance his career. And I believe I did so. It's one of the greatest satisfactions, after all, for someone of my pre-eminence, to assist budding figures . . .

– Ah, veritably. The root of all evil, to be sure. But it has its uses. I had the good fortune to have a good fortune . . . er, I trust you're not proposing to print this interview verbatim . . . Suitably edited, of course, as an appendix to your biography. And naturally I have final text approval . . . No, yes, yes. I have a reputation to maintain as a verbally adept man of letters, a *littérateur* . . . Do you know what my old friend Vladimir remarked on a similar occasion? 'I speak as a cretin but I write as a genius' – I would hardly be so extreme myself, but . . . As Tom wrote, 'Words slip, slide . . . ah, perish, sometimes break under the burden . . .' Now, what were we talking about?

– Since I had inherited substantial assets from my parents, I considered it my duty to use my wealth to ease the lot of those poorer than myself, especially artists, writers and so on. I lent L.Z. a significant sum.

– No, I can't put a number on it. You'll have to see my accountant about that . . . Of course, he paid it all back in later years, when he had become famous and rich.

– No, I merely provided seed capital, as it were. I believe creative artists should not be pampered. A little poverty helps toughen them up . . . Like vines, really. All the best vintages grow on poor soil. For example, a little vineyard I happen to know in the Minervois region . . .

– So glad you agree.

– No, I was not his major financial support in the early years. I ceased aiding him soon after he arrived in New York. You'll have to get in touch with my accountant . . .

– Far from it. No, no, it was simply that he obtained another, more significant source of finance, hence my own pittance would hardly be . . .

– I'm glad you asked me that question.

– If I could get back to that point later . . .

– I'd rather you didn't press me on that one.

– We had a few differences in the course of time, an occasional disagreement. Who doesn't? It's no secret, I presume, we didn't always see eye to eye over some of his transitional work . . .

– That would be in the early sixties, yes, when he switched to writing in English. I felt that the sacrifice involved in abandoning the polyphonic *richesse* and *gravitas* of his mother tongue was scarcely compensated for by the brevity and allusiveness of . . . But in the long run, who knows?

– Ah, we can set no rules for genius.

– No, I can't accept that.

– Definitely not.

– There is no doubt whatsoever in my mind that I have always behaved towards poor L.Z. with the utmost consideration and tolerance, especially in view of . . . And I will continue to do so, so long as he may live.

– What? I might remind you, young fellow, that you are dependent on my continued support in your endeavours . . .

– Apology accepted.

– Ah, yes.

– Yes.

– Yes.

– A horrible, frightening business.

11

I entered my office. I switched on the fluorescent light and stared into its flat brightness. It shone down on the whiteboard which stretched right across one wall creating a sheet of uniform dazzle, like a snowscape or the window of a furnace – a *tabula rasa* . . . My thoughts moved – as they always do, as they always must – on to the subject of mathematics.

People get so scared when one says one is a mathematician. I've learnt to recognise that averting of the gaze, that flustering of the hands, that mumble of, 'Gosh! You must be very brainy,' or, 'I was never much good at sums,' or, 'Weather turning rainy, eh?' What the dickens do they suppose a mathematician *is*? One doesn't eat special mathematical food or sleep on a mathematical bed; one doesn't have mathematical emotions or a mathematical body; a mathematician is just somebody who does mathematics. That's all. One is no different from ordinary people – apart from being smarter and having a temperament which makes it possible to spend one's waking hours in a small room scribbling symbols on sheets of scrap paper, working towards some all-inclusive theory, and one's nights dreaming about it.

And why bother? 'I'm sure it's not boring, sometimes,' people remark, or, 'What do you want to be when you grow up, young lady?' or, 'What are you hiding from?' (to quote Frank, once, on a certain awful afternoon in Cambridge). But one is not hiding from anything and one won't grow out of it and it's never boring. Mathematics is the most important thing there is. It's the most *real*. Any other ideas washing about the place – in physics, economics, philosophy – are just impure versions of mathematical truths.

And so it can serve as a consolation. Ordinary people, racked by guilt and insomnia, have no recourse other than to hit the bottle or count sheep jumping over a stile. But as a mathematician one can fix one's mind on something bigger than oneself . . . One is never alone.

Oh yes, one has tried an assortment of other escapisms, with varied success. By all means relax with luscious art (Gauguin, Mucha, Botticelli) and fantastic literature (Dickens, Tennyson, Agatha Christie, Allgrobsch) and fragrant music (ah! Debussy . . . I detest the kind of music which *pretends* to be mathematics – that Bach which Frank is always playing on his stereo). Naturally one feels an affinity with other creative minds – but one also looks down on them, since, as a mathematician, one has something important to be creative *about* . . . Also one has been drunk six times. And in love, possibly, once.

. . . So if one encounters some distraction – a tiff with an ex-boyfriend; a famous writer getting a stroke within spitting distance – one gets straight on the subway and goes up to the Institute for Advanced Studies on the Upper West Side, and enters a rather pleasant second-floor office with soundproofed walls and a big desk and a double-glazed view of a blown plane tree losing its last leaves, and turns on the light, and seats oneself on the comfortable swivel chair, and swivels, and thinks.

The afterimage of the fluorescent fixture – a rough white oblong – remained on my retina, blanking out a portion of my view as I rotated: now the door handle became invisible – now a selection from the bookshelf – now a paragraph in an open *Proc. Am. Maths Soc.* – now a sparrow perched on the tree outside . . . I closed my eyes to think more clearly but the afterimage lingered: a hovering, slowly fading, luminous slot.

What I was trying to think about on that particular late September morning was my attempted proof of a special case of the Smart–Potts–Ostrovsky conjecture. Potts and Ostrovsky in person were coming round to see me at eleven, so I had one hour to sort out my ideas. 'Be calm,' I said to myself, 'and be clear.'

. . . But Frank's chuckle kept resounding in my memory, accompanied by the recurrent crash of Allgrobsch's head hitting the soup bowl . . . The needle was stuck in the groove.

So I went to the administration office, did my hallos to the personnel, Fanny and Bridget; poured a cup of coffee into a polystyrene cup, gulped it, searing my throat; swallowed iced water from the iced-water machine . . .

'Is she okay?' asked Fanny or Bridget. 'Is she sick?' asked Bridget or Fanny.

'I think she's looking pale.' 'I think she's having a hard time.'

'No, there's really no need . . .' I was saying.

But they were holding out the First Aid kit like a waiter urging a selection from the cheese board – aspirins, bandages, antiseptic ointment, a tin of chicken soup, the morning-after pill, bandaids . . .

They were each resting a cool hand on my forehead and looking at each other sympathetically.

'I think she's too hot.' 'I think she's not feeling too good.'

I looked from one to the other, comparing their complexions and the shapes of their eyelids . . . They were in steady profile like figures in Egyptian tomb paintings. I felt incapable of communicating with them right then.

'No. I'm quite all right, Branny . . . Honestly, Fidget. I'll be f-f-f-f . . .'

I fled from the administration area. Scampered along the corridor; past the photocopier room – which, as always, was emitting its flashes of light and its stamping sounds as if inhabited by a junior thunder god – returned to my office and (although it's considered rude in America to shut one's office door) shut my door; and at last (a good mathematician must *always* be a good mathematician) began scribbling neat, orderly ideas on a pad of yellow paper.

The afterimage had reduced to a translucent fuzzy patch.

My specialisation is a branch of differential geometry called 'scope theory'. It's not easy to describe it to a layman – but one must, I suppose . . .

I remember trying to explain my work to Frank the first time I met him. It was in the senior common room of my college when I was a mere junior research fellow, a whole two and two-thirds years ago. Frank had been invited to dinner on high table by Sydenham-Blom (a fruity ancient biochemist), who was on the committee of some organisation awarding a grant Frank was angling for. Anyway, old S.-B. toddled off after dinner. And Frank – presumably on the grounds that I was the only unattached female – sidled up to me holding out a cigarillo.

'Rather not,' I said. I backed away as far as the marble griffin by the fireplace. 'One doesn't know if you're offering that thing or asking for a light – but either way: no thank you.'

'I'm Frank.'

'Oh.'

'They call me sleazy-Frank.'

'One had heard.' I certainly had. He was notorious. According to rumour, he was in the habit of standing in front of the condom machine in junior common rooms across Cambridge, asking plaintively of anyone in skirts, 'Can you lend me fifty pee?'

He tucked the cigarillo back in his top pocket; it poked out. He was wearing a cream baggy suit with buoyant lapels (in a style out of date even then) and a thin scarlet tie which had worked itself round his neck, resembling a fresh fatal wound.

'And you're the famous Emma Smart, huh? Pleased to know you, Emma.'

He held out his right hand. No response on my part. Thirty seconds later he pincered his right hand between his left finger and thumb, flipped the palm over to admire his knuckles, turned it back again, peered at it, remarked, 'My love line is very long. Tell me all about your work.'

'I'm a scope theorist. It's really not possible to explain it to a layman . . . If you'll excuse me . . .'

Frank was exactly the kind of fellow one dislikes: lecherous, apparently self-confident, pushy, crude, deliberately handsome, unbrilliant. And he was a smoker, to boot. (My theory is that the tobacco habit carries the implication: 'I'm desperately suicidal and only you can save me' – and one falls for it, every time.) One had fantasised about falling in love, of course: but one's ideal had consisted of the mind of a genius mathematician incarnated in some unimaginably perfect body. Anyway, not *him*.

I tried to push past him without doing so literally. But he held his ground. 'Excuse me. One really must move away from the fireplace, or one's tights will char.' He still didn't budge.

He was looking down at his crotch. His face was so sad – the mouth loose, the jaw drooped, the eyes thin – like a naughty schoolboy who had been punished but doesn't understand why. Of course I knew that his pose was – well, not exactly artificial: but he certainly was aware of its effect. All the same, I didn't want to hurt him.

I manoeuvred around him to get away from the heat, pushing right up against his torso, perforce. His unshaven jaw scratched my forehead. I gripped the tip of his red tie, pulled it clockwise round his neck through one hundred and eighty degrees, and stuffed it back where it belonged. I said, 'Oh. Might as well tell you about scope theory, I suppose. It can't do any harm.'

Consider a family tree diagram: a structure of relationships. Now

61

imagine scribbling over it, in a different-coloured ink, lines connecting everybody with noses of the same shape, for example, or joining all grandfathers with grandchildren . . . various kinds of similarity relations. And then imagine constructing a new diagram showing the interlinking of all these similarity relations – 'simrels', for short . . .

Frank inserted a pretentious addendum at this point. 'Where does "scope" come in? Anything to do with the Greek *skopein* meaning "to see"?'

'No,' I said firmly. 'Actually it's a rather poor anglicisation of a term invented by the Russian mathematician Yuri Ostrovsky. May I continue?'

I tried to explain that the two kinds of diagram – the family tree and the simrel diagram – are mutually 'translatable' using a 'scope' – and it turns out that the scope is a fundamental object which comes in various categories.

He asked, 'So you're interested in family trees, huh?'

'Of course not! One is not a genealogist! One doesn't do applied maths. I'm *pure*.'

'So the scope is a kind of dictionary, for moving between the two ways of seeing the thing?'

I was surprised he understood even that much. 'Well, yes. Metaphorically speaking, anyway. Strictly speaking, it's just a formal mathematical entity. It's geometrical.'

'You mean, like a triangle or a circle . . . ?'

'Well, actually it's more of an infinitely discontinous n-dimensional geometric object . . . But you're on the right track.'

The same kind of mathematics (as I went on to show) can be used to understand, for example, a complex decision process. Think of a network of situations connected by decision-lines. Again, one can calculate the simrel diagram and the scope.

Frank was yawning at this stage. So I skipped most of the argument, and said, 'Anyway, the breakthrough came back in nineteen eighty-four when Ostrovsky showed the maths of scope theory is formally similar to that of differential geometry . . . You know what *that* is, don't you?'

He shook his head.

'Ohhh. You don't know anything! Diff. geom. is all about relating the local and the global in a differential system – and scope theory too is about the local and the global – and I *said* you wouldn't understand it, and I don't know *why* you made me tell you all this, I simply *don't know*.'

I was giddy and breathless. Frank was grinning. Various dons were turning round to stare at me and clear their throats. One felt a complete ninny, a silly girl. I wanted to jump in the fireplace, vaporise, and vanish up the chimney.

Ostrovsky came in first: a recent Russian *émigré* in a crumpled sports jacket, displaying a tanned baldish head fringed with grey hair which gave him a monkish air. He wasn't as old as he looked – but he was nearly 40, which is *old* by the standards of pure mathematicians, about the age most of us retire and fade into physicists or vice-chancellors.

'Hello, Emma,' he said. 'You're looking lovely.'

'Hallo, Yuri,' I said. 'Yes, the weather has turned rather chilly.'

He grunted. He picked up the special wiper for use on the whiteboard, fiddled with it, and clicked its handle against his teeth.

Next came Chuck Potts, a shaggy little fellow in faded jeans and a baseball cap. He was only 24, and was evidently a former child prodigy (we can always recognise each other). He had all the symptoms: a tense expression shifting unstably like a *perpetuum mobile*; an aggressive shyness; a young-old body, like a dwarf's. He was trailing a smaller version of himself.

'Hey, Emma. Meet my grad. student, Jed. I'm bringing him along for the fun.'

Jed looked as if he had just been weaned – gosh, they get younger every day.

Potts whispered in Jed's ear, 'See? She's just like I said, hey?' Jed sniggered.

'Hello, Chuck and Jed,' said Ostrovsky.

'How do you do,' I said. 'And how do you do.'

We turned to face the whiteboard. Its smoothness and sheen and cleansability seemed to exemplify the spirit of pure mathematics. (Of course in the old days one used a blackboard; the only people who still do are the cosmology gang – because there's a brand name of chalk called Cosmic Antidust; and because they feel the urge to retain contact with something physical: the scrape of rock against rock.) Ostrovsky – as the oldest person and the obvious genius – naturally took charge. He fidgeted with the boardmarkers: blue, red, green, plus a yellow one – a jokey extra – whose ink is almost invisible. He's one of those mathematicians who deliberately cultivate disorder for the sake of creativity – the kind, indeed, which is misinterpreted in the popular mind as 'the genius with his head in the air'. He made semi-legible marks using all four pens on different parts of the whiteboard; he murmured his ideas; he drew arrows and circles connecting his jottings; he wiped out equations with his cuffs or his palms, and wrote over them.

Jed piped up, 'Oy, Yuri. You missed out a Z in that equation over there.'

Of course he pronounced the Z in the American manner, *zee*, which sounds like a winter wind, like the letter in the middle of blizzard – much ruder and more final than the British *zed*.

Ostrovsky grunted, wrote a big blue Z over the entire whiteboard, and went on scribbling and murmuring. Soon he had sketched out a vague, intuitive approach to re-representing the Smart–Potts–Ostrovsky conjecture in a different formalism.

One ought to explain the SPO conjecture, I suppose. It was discovered simultaneously by Potts and myself, and we recycled some of Ostrovsky's old ideas – so he got his name included too. I was awarded my doctorate on the strength of two pages worth of work on it. Meanwhile, over in New York, Potts was reaching more or less the same conclusion by means of a three-hundred-page formal proof. In fact I did explain it to Frank when he called round at my room in college three days after I'd first met him. He was very apologetic, and wearing designer jeans and a buff satin jacket with a hole in the elbow, and carrying a big bunch of parsley.

I couldn't very well turn him away.

'That's very. Yes, *very*,' I said. 'Shall I put it in a vase?'

'Well . . . I. . . . I was passing through the market, and I felt like . . . nibbling a little . . . ah . . . I guess you'd call it parsley.'

'Quite.'

He sat down in my chintz armchair and tucked the vegetable between his knees.

'I was hoping . . . ah, Dr Smart . . . Emma . . . you'll tell me more about your work.'

He bent his head and bit off some herb. He chewed it slowly like a grazing sheep; the green stuff poked from his mouth. 'D'you fancy a sprig?'

'Well, in order to understand the SPO, it's necessary to get a handle on Ostrovsky's Best Of All Possible Worlds theorem. And in order to understand the BOAPW, consider a network of possible situations connected by simrels. The BOAPW states just that it is possible to

64

define a notion of "bestness" such that there exists a best possible situation. (This is not as obvious as one might think, since the network might be broken or infinite or both.) It turns out the proof depends on various subtle properties of the scope. (Strictly speaking, the BOAPW is only true for "most" networks – where "most" can be precisely defined in context.)'

Frank was already lost. He shrugged and made a silly smile. He gazed down into his parsley.

'Look,' I said, 'suppose you're choosing a restaurant to have your lunch at. How might you select the "best" one?'

"Well . . . I guess I could . . . always go for the cheapest.'

'Exactly! In the case of restaurants there exists a possible definition of "bestness" – namely, price – which makes it possible to find a BOAPW. But that's not obvious for other things.'

'But . . . hey, hang on. The cheapest restaurant isn't always the best.'

'Of course it's not the *best*! But it is the "best" – if one defines it that way. One could pick another definition of "bestness" such that the most expensive was the "best". In that case, the "best" might well be the worst. Understand?'

'I *think* so.'

'The Smart–Potts–Ostrovsky conjecture just states that there exists a strategy for finding the best alternative; in fact, "most reasonable" strategies will do.'

Frank chewed a sprig pensively. 'You mean, like . . . it's okay if I check out the prices at the different restaurants in any order?'

'Exactly. That illustrates the SPO conjecture.'

'Uh huh. So basically, what you're, ah, saying, is you're an optimist?'

'No! One is not a philosopher! I'm a pure mathematician. I've described certain formal properties of intrarelated networks. That's all. I've indicated that there are strategies to reach a "best" situation – but I'm not claiming this "bestness" is actually *good*.'

'Yeah, but your ideas – '

'They're not *my* ideas. They're *true*. I'm just the one who happened to discover them – along with Potts and Ostrovsky.'

'Sure, but why did you do *this* maths? This is all to do with your personal, ah, psychological and societal make-up. Right?'

'Wrong! Well, no . . . yes. Or rather, you're right – but it's irrelevant. Look, an apple fell on Newton's head so he discovered gravity. But gravity isn't true *because* of the falling apple!'

65

At this point I realised I was shouting. 'I'm sorry,' I said.

'No. *I'm* sorry.'

'No, no. I really shouldn't have – '

'It's all my fault.'

'No. I – '

'But I'm the one to blame.'

'Of course not.'

'Please do accept my sincerest apologies.'

Frank opened his mouth, then closed it. He shrugged. 'Okay.'

'What?'

'I accept your apologies. You win.'

'But . . .'

'Yeah?'

'Nothing.'

One was most aggrieved. Frank had deliberately, callously exploited the British convention on apologising. As a quasi-Englishman he knew the rules but didn't feel bound to play by them. What's more, there was no polite way to point out his rudeness to him. One sulked a little.

Eventually Frank said gently, 'Yeah? You were telling me about your, ah, the SPO . . .'

'Well. Yes. Quite. Thing is, there's a lot of work still to be done on it. Defining "most" and "reasonable" is very tricky. In fact nobody's yet discovered a precise definition. That's why it's called the SPO *conjecture* – it's not even a hypothesis yet – let alone a theorem.'

'So you don't yet know what you're trying to prove?'

'But that's what maths is all about! Ordinary people have quite the wrong idea: they think one has a straightforward but knotty problem to which one devises a solution. It's not remotely like that. Rather, one begins with a vague, ill-defined intuition. One then tries different ways of making it more specific: the trick is to ask *the right question* – not trivial or impossible or meaningless – then, getting the answer is often a piece of cake.'

'Uh huh. And when you finally get the answer, it'll be an answer to a question you specially made up to make it easy to get an answer to, right? Isn't that kind of . . . cheating?'

I felt angry. Then I saw Frank was grinning at me. I had to giggle. 'We're not cheats! We can't be! Everything we find out is true. It's *real.*'

Ostrovsky was trying to advance nearer to a bit of reality. He sketched out a proof that, for any given scope, a strategy that is 'not reasonable' is 'quite distant' from any other 'non-reasonable' strategy – which would imply that 'most' other strategies would be 'reasonable' (he hoped).

'I'm afraid you'll think me awfully British,' I said pugnaciously. 'But let's be clear about what's what.' Then I pointed out at length certain lacunae in Ostrovsky's approach. I wrote up my argument in my neat small handwriting in blue on one corner of the whiteboard. I proved, to one's own satisfaction at least, that 'quite distant' is fundamentally ill-defined.

'In fact, let's do it *my* way.' (One is perfectly self-confident – not to say arrogant – when discussing mathematics.) I outlined my proposal to show the BOAPW is true for infinite simrel networks too. A rather daringly abstract idea.

Then it was the turn of Potts and Co. The two Americans exhibited a great sheaf of fan-folded computer paper. They had applied a limited (to my mind, ridiculously limited) but clear version of the SPO to solving a problem in numerical decision theory. They showed off the print-out.

'It's not very *fundamental*,' I said.

'No, ma'am,' said Jed, 'but it *works*.'

So the meeting broke up. We were all in good humour, each convinced one's own approach to the SPO was better than anybody else's. Ostrovsky felt he was bolder than the rest of us. 'In six months I will have proved the Ostrovsky–Smart–Potts conjecture!' he said immodestly. His hands and chin were crisscrossed with blue and red ink marks in a garish stars-and-stripes effect. Potts said, 'You wanna bet? I'll cash out the Potts–Smart–Ostrovsky conjecture while you're still playing with your lemmas!' Then he and Jed slapped their raised hands together in a kind of vigorous pat-a-cake. I murmured that my own ideas might lead to a powerful new proof technique of the Smart–Potts–Ostrovsky conjecture.

After they left I stayed in my room, swivelling on the chair with my eyes shut.

He nibbled the parsley down to its base.

'You're a genius, Emma!' he said, tossing the stems up in the air.

'Yes, one knows.'

'Will you . . . Will you come to dinner at my college on Friday?' He thrust his hands into the pockets of his satin jacket, nervous-seeming.

I could think of no polite way of refusing. One could hardly tell the man one couldn't stand him, given that one had just frittered away no less than (I glanced at my watch) one hour and twenty minutes in chatter with him. I decided it might be safer to meet him on my own territory.

I suggested, 'Why don't you come to the Founder's Day Organ Concert in the college chapel here instead?'

A little to my surprise, in view of his reputation, he made no attempt to grip my thigh or compliment me on my supposed beauty. Instead he ran out into the court, shouting to the whole college, the old brick buildings, the cobblestones, and the sky, 'Yippee! I got a date with Dr Emma Smart!'

I worked all afternoon in my office at the Institute.

And in the evening I went out into the cold and dark. I came downtown.

I dropped in on the twenty-four-hour bookstore round the corner from my apartment, and shopped for Allgrobsch's *The Bubble Blowing Party and other stories*. I took it home.

I climbed under the sheets. I rotated the dimmer switch. I turned on my Panasonic: Debussy's *La Cathédrale Engloutie*. I looked up at the walls of my small bedroom, leaning protectively over me. I checked my own emotions, and was pleasantly surprised to note one wasn't at all depressed. One felt rather proud of one's inner resources: one could aspire to the reality of mathematics or the fantasy of literature, just as one fancied. I decided to treat myself to an Allgrobsch before going to sleep. How comfy to communicate with a man only by means of his publications: if only all human contacts were so straightforward! Which story would I choose? (One loves that moment of choice, teetering between possibilities: such as passing through the college gates for the first time, or arriving at an airport, or running up three flights of a fire-escape to enter a thnick club . . .) Enough of fact: let's try fiction for a change.

12

So Cold That

'Once upon a time, a duck lived on that pond in front of the fishmonger's, which is connected via a muddy brook to the river Vlas which flows past our town, which leads on, by way of numerous canals and waterways, to the great rivers of Central Europe, and so to the Atlantic, the Mediterranean, and the Black Sea.'

'Yes I know,' says the little boy.

'And it was bitterly cold,' the father continues. 'So cold that breath froze in the air. So cold that the wolves, dodging through the forest, had to wear mufflers, mittens, and big woolly hats.'

'Yes I know,' says the little boy.

'And the pond began to freeze.'

'What was the name of the duck?'

'The duck could only make one sound — so all the other animals decided that should be his name. His name was Kwa.'

'Kwa, kwa,' says the boy.

'And it was so cold that . . .'

'Yes I know.'

'. . . the pond completely froze over. So the poor duck had to escape. Where would he go? He thought about hiding in the barn, behind the stacks of hay. But there's no water in the barn: and ducks need water. Then he thought about jumping down the well. There's plenty of water down the well. But there's nothing to eat: he'd get very hungry. So where would he go? Poor duck!'

'Poor Kwa!'

'Finally he set off along the brook. Of course it was frozen too: he had to struggle over the slippery surface on his flat webbed feet. He saw, sealed under ice, little golden fishes with their mouths open. He saw a red leaf that looked as if it was falling into the depths but wasn't. He felt very sorry for himself, so he said — '

69

'Kwa, kwa!'

'He arrived on the river Vlas. It was almost covered with ice, but there were cracks between the blocks, and a few holes which fishermen had made. He dipped his beak into the cold water, ate and drank. He waddled away downstream, for he knew these gaps in the ice would soon disappear. Wasn't Kwa a brave duck?'

'Yes I know.'

'At last he got to the thicker part of the river, where it goes past the steel mill and the bakery. He saw hot steam rising from chimneys. He smelled the good smell of bread. The waste heat from the steam mill had melted the river near the bank. He swam and fished there. Kwa was a lucky duck!'

'Kwa, kwa!'

'But the puddles froze over at night. He saw flocks of geese and swans flying overhead, and he wished he could fly like them, but he couldn't.'

'Why not?'

'Because he couldn't.'

'Why not?'

'Because . . . So brave Kwa went marching down the river, merrily waving his wings and singing – '

'Kwa, kwa, kwa!'

'And in no time at all, in two shakes of a lamb's tail, before you can say – '

'Kwa, kwa, kwa!'

' – he had reached the great city of Blomblomblom, which is a very great city indeed, though not so great as other cities such as Warsaw or New York or London or Budapest, and which has a lot of buses and streetcars and trains going to and fro along the . . . What sound do trains make?'

'Kwa, kwa!'

'. . . Going to and fro over the bridges and beside the waterfront. So Kwa said to himself, "I reckon this is a fine city. I'll stay here awhile . . ." Are you asleep yet?'

'Kwa, kwa!'

'But the weather got even worse . . .'

'Yes I know!'

'He had to go again. It was a beautiful sunset. Red and orange and yellow and green – '

' – and blue and indigo and violet.'

'He skipped off down the river, singing and whooping, twirling his wings, happy as a – '

'Hippopopopopotamus?'

'. . . *And the geese said to him, "Honk, honk! We're geese and we're flying south because it's winter. What's your name, little duck?"'*

'*How does he sleep?*'

'*"My name is Kwa –"*'

'*How?*'

'*He had a woolly blanket.*'

'*How does he stop his blanket getting wet?*'

'*He had a rubber sheet. He had two, actually, one to go underneath and one on top. Kwa was a very clever duck! As clever as you!*'

'*What's his name?*'

'*I told you. His name is –*'

'*Yes I know!*'

'*Only ducks and human beings can say their own names. And wolves too. What do wolves say?*'

'*Kwa, kwa!*'

'*. . . And the railroad trains shouted back to him, "Hello! I'm a railroad train! Chuff chuff!" And he shouted –*'

'*I'm hungry.*'

'*Yes, Kwa got very hungry. But he knew if he just kept going another few hours, or maybe days more, he was sure to get to some place where –*'

'*I'm thirsty.*'

'*But Kwa wasn't afraid! He hopped over the ice, singing and . . . and singing, saying to himself, "I'm a brave duck. Kwa, kwa, kwa!" And . . .*'

'*It's dark.*'

'*Yes I know. But –*'

'*It's dark. I'm scared.*'

'*Kwa, kwa, kwa! No, Kwa wasn't scared! Not our brave Kwa! He knew he only . . . Waving his wings, he . . . Kwa . . . Kwa . . .*'

The father rests his head on his son's lap. And, although he knows it won't help, the little boy strokes the old man's eyes, his cheeks and his beard.

© L.Z. Allgrobsch 1963

13

During that winter, New York shrank to the size of a small room. I felt that if I stretched my arms I could touch its boundaries. My apartment, which had seemed so spacious, suddenly became cluttered with my belongings – books, an IBM clone, a tin-opener, a thousand miscellaneous objects which suddenly revealed themselves as essential . . . and the genial, omnipresent ghost of Professor Absent (his toenail clipping arrived under the bedroom rug; his blue jigsaw piece – a fragment of sky? – was holed up behind the refrigerator). The apartment was overheated, stuffy, and smelled of me. As I tucked myself up in bed, or huddled in front of the computer monitor, I felt like some tiny woodland animal – hedgehog or squirrel – in cosy hibernation. And I felt proprietorial towards a section of my apartment building too: the lobby, the stairs, Raoul the janitor, the lift, and certain corridors . . . I got on nodding terms with my neighbours in the apartment opposite: Mona the literary agent who would be visible late at night or early in the morning, staggering in/ out half-hidden behind a stack of manuscripts in leaky envelopes and manilla folders (I used to find stray numbered sheets of typescript – fractions of a steamy romance or a gardening manual – on the landing, which I'd stuff back under her door) along with her teenage son Arnie, who was odd. I felt they belonged to me, a little, too. And when I stepped ouside I was still in my territory: the cars, the roads, the polluted air were all mine. Everything seemed so miniature in New York, so toy-like, compared to the grand perspective and high sky of my English childhood. Here the horizon stopped at the far side of the road; the skyscrapers were as cute and simple as houses sketched by an infant; the sky (just because of the height of the buildings) was a ceiling of low cloud. My demesne incorporated a portion of the Village (yes, somehow that expression slipped past my

72

lips: the place turned out to be rather villagey after all); suddenly I was often being stopped by tourists seeking directions, and I found myself naming the streets (Greenwich, Charles, 12th and Christopher . . .) in much the same tone that Mummy uses when stating which field the flock is grazing in. And beyond that, I owned bits of Manhattan: my office at the Institute, of course; and my plane tree seen through its window when the venetian blind is tugged just so; and my sparrow that perches on the plane tree . . . Also my grocer's, my delicatessen, my launderette, my Chinese restaurant, my subway station; my zigzag of roads connecting these places, which I marched through bravely, warm in my lime green anorak with the hood up, despite the banked snow and the screaming wind.

And – spiralling still further out – I possessed the club, where I used to go whenever I had some free time, to chat with Barbra and the rest of the clubbies, or just to sit quietly in the corner, listening to a murmur of conversation in pleasantly incomprehensible clubbish and accented American. There was a seat in a corner there that was mine; a table was mine; and a creak in the floorboards and a shadow and a favourite tea (Earl Grey) were all mine. What I loved about it was . . . what I am trying to get at, really, is that I was regarded there as peculiar, young, different – but not *because* I was a prodigy. One can get so bored of all that.

Nor was there any distraction from Frank, thank goodness. On the strength of a generous advance from his publisher plus a bribe from his university, he was busy researching Allgrobsch's life in the New York Public Library, the Library of Congress, the libraries down and up at Princeton and Yale; and even flying off to England – even Canada – even Argentina – to see old acquaintances of Allgrobsch, or to unearth fragments of correspondence and juvenilia. (Frank can be quite diligent, when he sets his mind to it. After all, he didn't reach his present academic position *entirely* by virtue of charm and sleaze.) I used to receive jokey (at least one assumes they were intended to be jokey) postcards from him: Big Ben and the Royal Family from London; a plain black card entitled 'Toronto by Night'; a 'Somebody Went To Buenos Aires And All I Got Was This Lousy Postcard' postcard. He even sent me transcripts of interviews with various old acquaintances of Allgrobsch, which I put aside to read when I had a spare moment.

What's more, by December I had succeeded in establishing certain mathematical results. I bought a picture postcard featuring a smiling toothless George Washington (the touch of kitsch, I thought, would appeal to Frank's sense of irony) and wrote on the reverse:

Dear Frank
   I have proved the Best Of All Worlds Hypothesis is meaningful even for infinitely large networks! Weather continues cold. Hope all's well.

Yours, Emma

Then I realised I had no idea where to address it. So I stuffed it behind the radiator in the bathroom. I imagined that one day, long after I'll have gone, Professor Absent, crawling on his knees to retrieve his dropped bifocals, would stumble across this card, and ponder its message. That way I would achieve a . . . Well, not immortality, but at least a prolongation of my existence in New York.

I had become quite fond of dear old Absent. I had decided that he (he was definitely a *he* now) was elderly but nice. He had false teeth and wore spectacles, and his hair was thinning; but there was a twinkle in his eye and he was happy to cuddle me – in the chastest, most avuncular manner, of course. I would browse through the drawer in the sitting room cabinet where he had stowed his helpful notes about bus routes or museum opening hours, written in a loopy hand on yellowing notepaper, read them (though I had no especial intention of taking a bus to a museum) and bless his considerateness. How unlike Frank!

In fact Prof. Absent bore a marked resemblance to a companion of my childhood, a certain Otto. There were three of us chums, actually, living together in The New House – as faithful as the Three Musketeers or the members of the Trinity – namely: myself, Otto Man (a dusty brown creature with a broken spring at one end) and Shay Zlong (elegant, mauve, rosette-patterned). We used to play together in the dappled corner of the drawing room. Otto and Shay would lie down beside either wall; I'd run between them, sometimes favouring Otto's male, and sometimes Shay's female, comfort. They used to embrace and tickle me, and in return I taught them differential calculus. On occasion (I confess) I played them off against one another: I'd whisper to each that I preferred the other; that way they'd both vie to hug me as hard as they could . . . And meanwhile Daddy would be aloft in his study, reading an article on hydrodynamics; and through the leaded window I'd see Mummy in her Wellingtons trudging through the rose garden, deadheading a Dorothy Perkins with her secateurs.

But now I was 21, too old for such childishness, surely? One was an (almost) grown-up young woman, perfectly capable of standing on one's own two feet. One was a splendid mathematician, busy making important discoveries in the foundations of scope theory. Everything was hunkydory. So why should one be upset just because Frank was more interested in the life story of an almost dead man than in oneself? Why indeed?

'Am I right to care about him?' I asked.

'Me, I care about nobody,' said Barbra, shaking her bosom, which was covered, along with most of the rest of her, in a glorious oil-slickesque lurex flying suit, 'except you, Emma' – chucking my cheek – 'and my good friend, because he is so rich and handsome' – pointing at some bald man seated on one side of her, browsing in a newspaper in some foreign language, shaking his head – 'and my other good friend, because we all know he is a saint' – he was the white-haired fellow on the other side, snoozing peacefully in an armchair – 'and all my many lovely people in the club, and the President of the United States, and the First Lady, and the Emperor of China, and most everybody in the world, I guess.'

'I see,' I said. 'Have you heard from him lately?'

'Oh sure! Your friend comes in the club always. He asks everybody more and more questions about Elzee – '

'What?'

'Elzee. Elzee Allgrobsch . . .'

'Oh. Yes.'

'And we tell him Elzee is a great guy and a fine writer and a tribute to his community.'

'He's back in New York, then?'

'Where else?'

'Ah. It's funny he hasn't got in touch with me yet . . . isn't it?'

'Well . . . in his condition . . .' She tapped me sympathetically on my anorak sleeve.

'What? Is anything the matter? You would tell me if anything's the matter with him?'

She shrugged. 'He's alive.'

'Yes, but . . .'

'The physician says he could pass away any day . . .'

75

'What!'

'He's in a coma for ten weeks, and – '

'Oh. *Him*.'

'They say he won't live till the New Year.'

'That's all right, then. I was awfully scared for one dreadful moment.'

It was teatime. The meal commenced. Barbra was off duty for half an hour (her apron hung at the ready over the back of her chair) and was making the most of it. She had a bowl of some dark stew; she pushed her spoon deep into the stuff, then brought the spoon well inside her own mouth before sucking vigorously. Her face wrinkled up with gustatory pleasure. Personally, one doesn't care for the ethnic food (except for some of the puddings, and possibly a soup or two): it's more oily and strongly flavoured than one is used to. I was drinking a nice cup of tea, made with a Twining's Earl Grey bag, and nibbling something called an English muffin – which wasn't remotely like anything I'd had in England, but tasted really not bad, all the same.

We were in 'my' corner of the club: the shadowy part at the back. Behind us was a wall hung with framed monochrome photographs from their country: pictures of moustached men leaning on pitchforks; or a grinning crone in a black bonnet; or a frozen waterfall; or the first steam train in a certain district; or a panorama looking down from some high spot on to black roofs, a hillside and a narrow winding river. Although, in my current position, I couldn't actually see those pictures, I knew them by heart. They moved me terribly – much more so than the portraits of one's own tiresome ancestors hung up alongside the Great Staircase in The New House . . .

And somehow they all reminded me of Frank: one doesn't fully understand why. Perhaps it was the impression of generic foreignness, and that air they all had of somehow being terribly important, which – although one consciously knew it to be misleading – one couldn't shake off. Also, when one thinks of the world before one's birth, one is struck by an unslakable nostalgia. Which perhaps accounts for the appeal of an Older Man – not love but curiosity: one is desperate to know what he Knows . . . Or possibly it was simply that everything in the world reminded me of Frank.

I tried to explain these ideas to Barbra, in general terms, without mentioning Frank by name. She smiled and said unconvincingly, 'I know just how you feel.'

'I really *mean* it.'

'Sure. Everybody is nostalgic for the past, the time we were young. You're nostalgic about a guy you saw a few weeks ago. When you get to our age – like my buddies and me – we're nostalgic about . . . uh . . . decades and centuries back . . . George Washington crossing the Delaware.'

We were surrounded by males – I mean, we had been all along, but now it sprang to my attention. A man in black was playing backgammon with a man in brown. A bald man leaning behind Barbra's back was telling a string of unfunny dirty jokes ('Lawyers *do it* in their briefs. Realtors *do it* for real . . .') to a dozing, white-haired man. Two men were passing through a door marked Men's Room.

I remarked, 'I always think "men's room" sounds funny . . .'

'Men! Who needs them?'

'I mean, one might suppose the entire male population was permanently cosseted in that one room!'

'Ah, men! What would we do without them?'

'Of course, as a mathematician, one spends a lot of one's time in largely masculine company . . . In fact, everywhere one has ever been is predominantly male: Cambridge, the academic world, the streets of the Village, this club indeed . . . Statistically, fifty-two per cent of the New York population is supposed to be female, yet one wonders where they all go? Do they inhabit some special Amazonian district? Or arguably it's all a question of perspective, and from the point of view of someone else, who moves in rather different circles, the city suffers from a dearth of men . . .'

'Men! I don't see any men here?'

'One wonders what their function is . . . They don't understand us, in fact, or themselves – '

'So what's new? When I was young, when I was your age, all the men were . . . and now . . . yet!'

'No, what I mean is: ignorance and dullness can be very attractive, don't you think? Why else do so many women find themselves hitched up with such dreadful mates? It's the lack of subtlety, of perceptive acuity, that comforts and relaxes us. We don't have to be on our guard with them – or rather we do, but in a different way from when we're with other women . . .'

While I'd been yammering away Barbra had snapped into what was supposed to be (I think) an 'on-guard' mime: her right hand was fixed in a salute (or possibly a screening of the eyes against an imaginary sun); her eyeballs jerked left and right. Then she gestured at the men's

77

room with a glance. She made a dismissive pout. We had a little giggle. What we were laughing about can't be stated verbally: her facial expression somehow implied a rather risqué mockery of male pretensions.

The world had become an agreeable grisaille. The ceiling was shadowed with grey. The woollen number worn by the barmaid who was taking away Barbra's empty bowl was charcoal grey. I was sipping the last drops of Earl Grey. The pebble-glass windows and door, as dusk approached, were smeared with grey. I felt as one does when one is in a plane flying through clouds, and everything becomes inconsequential.

Barbra released my hand with a little pinch. She peered at her own freckled knuckles. She said in what was for her a quiet voice, 'I know men like the back of my hand. I was married to them.'

'You've been married?' I said redundantly, keeping up my end of the conversation.

'Have I been married! A thousand times! A million! I had three separate marriages . . .'

'Gosh. What were they like?'

'Ah, a bunch of lowlifes . . . Wonderful superstars . . . No, they were like me and you, except they're different on account of they're not the same, you understand?'

'I think so.'

'The first, he was young. And I was young. And you don't marry good when you're inexperienced. And the second, I wasn't happy then, I was depressed. And he's depressed. So the marriage is depressed. And the third time, I'm old and he was old and why do you want to marry old people?'

'I'm sure I don't know.'

She shrugged.

I asked, 'Do you keep in touch?'

'Uh-oh. You know what they say, the first million husbands is the hardest.'

'Any children?'

'Yes, a few hundred. Six. Four boys and two girls.'

'What are their names? Where do they live? Do you have their pictures on you?'

'It's not so easy, Emma. They're all grown up, now. They have their own lives . . . California, Maryland, Hawaii, Teaneck . . .' She was shaking her head and looking older than usual.

78

I wanted to say something comforting, on the lines of: If I were your daughter, I'd always want to be near you . . . but . . . So instead I tried to imply my sympathy by talking about something altogether different (the way people do in Chekhov plays or Allgrobsch stories).

'My! this muffin is scrumptious. I can't think why anybody should dislike it.'

She smiled wryly. 'Maybe it's not so good a muffin as you think.'

'Oh, I'm sure it is.'

'Who knows?'

'Try it.'

I offered her the last quarter of a buttered muffin. She ate it slowly; crumbs collected in a wrinkle at the corner of her mouth.

'You're a good friend, Emma. Not British at all.'

'Er, thank you?'

'You know, your name sounds English . . .'

'Well, it is.'

'. . . so maybe I should call you Em, but . . .'

(Frank has been known to drawl 'Em' on occasion, making it sound like a slangy, hip acronym.)

'. . . or maybe "Ma" . . . but you're not really . . .'

'Emma is fine,' I said. 'One is quite used to it by now.'

'It's a headache, like the thing I was saying before.'

'You mean, about your relationship with your children?'

'Nuh, I mean . . . *Men*, yes? I know them like you know . . . What do you know?'

'Differential geometry?'

'Yeah, like that. I translate them, even. It's an intimate relationship. His mind gets inside my mind. I forget I am me and I think I am him.'

'Really?'

'No-o . . . I like to kid myself I'm a partner in the creative process. *But* . . . Translating is a female role, a nurturing. It's like a kindergarten teacher, or a nurse, a wife, a model, a flight attendant . . . We're like the girl who shows you where the emergency exits are hiding, and what you do if the air runs out of oxygen, and do you prefer chicken or beef? Somebody else does the flying.'

I chose my words with care, honesty and reassurance. 'Many people would say that the translator's role is that of midwife, and that you play a vital part in propagating the culture and literature of your people.'

'Yeah, but when you get to my age, you ask yourself: so what if you're playing a vital part? Who cares?'

'Oh, we all ask ourselves that.'

Barbra gazed into my eyes, no doubt wishing she were young, energetic and amazingly brilliant. I stared at the dusk-pink window and wished I had her maturity, her experience, and the courage to wear a glossy multi-coloured top.

We looked around at the clubbies. I noted H. H. Gritz's absence, and asked her about him.

'Uh, him. H.H. is always too busy to come see his old friends.'

'According to an interview Frank did with him – Frank showed me a bit of the transcript – Gritz says he gave Allgrobsch a lot of support . . .'

'H.H. says a lot of things.'

'. . . especially of a financial nature,' I added, prying rather too blatantly, I confess.

'Well, Elzee had his ways of getting money.'

'Oh? How?'

'He had his ways.'

'According to H.H. – '

'Now, Emma, you're not going to hear anything bad about poor Elzee from me. And I'm not saying H.H. is lying or he's not, but everybody remembers different. When you get old, you twist the truth' – pointing down her own throat – 'even me!'

She tittered. She dropped a spoon on the Persian rug and picked it up again. She squeezed my hand. The barmaid refilled my tea cup with hot water and gave Barbra her favourite Budweiser with blackcurrant cordial. Barbra looked round and changed the subject. She said, with the air of quoting some proverbial saying, 'Old folks are funny folks.'

She pointed out to me various oddities concerning the physical appearance and habits of the clubbies. X was snoring through his left nostril. Y was tugging his right earlobe. Z had a mild case of dandruff. These details – touching or irritating, depending on the observer's mood – were, she asserted, typical of the persons concerned; they'd been having them for the last half-century. 'The critics say Elzee's so original when he makes all his characters have a nickname about what they always do – or maybe they say his characters aren't rounded – but I tell you, look at any real people.' She addressed the bald man seated to her left. 'Are you rounded?'

'Not me,' he said.

'Are you?' she asked the white-haired man on her right.

He didn't reply.

'And what about you?' she asked the man in black.

'No way.'

She jabbed her thumb at her cleavage. 'I guess I'm kinda rounded myself.'

She chuckled. I joined in out of politeness, though it's not the kind of joke one would have made oneself.

An idea formed itself. Why shouldn't I try to beat Frank at his own game? Perhaps I could find out some juicy titbit about Allgrobsch. It seemed best to proceed indirectly: to work the conversation round to Allgrobsch's biography without letting on that I was interested in it.

I said, 'I-I-I-I-'

'Well?'

'One is awfully sorry. One suffers from an occasional stammer – or possibly I mean stutter; stammer/stutter is one of those pairs, like negro/black or disabled/handicapped, one of which is supposed to be "good" and the other not, only one can never recall which.' At this point I realised that irrelevant words were pouring from my lips, the way they do when a stammered blockage is broken. 'I'm sorry. What I was meaning to say is . . .'

'Yes?'

It was no use. I would never be able to persuade my tongue to be duplicitous. I can no more tell a whopper than George Washington. It seemed simplest to be open.

'What was Allgrobsch *really* like? I mean, *is* really like? I mean, I know you've told Frank everything you know – but perhaps there are a few little matters . . .'

'Elzee is a great writer and a fine upstanding human being . . .'

Judging by her tone, an unsaid 'but' was dangling at the sentence's end.

The bald man tapped me on the knee. 'Elzee is a warm-hearted, generous man . . .'

Again, an unspoken 'but'.

'He knew long words like you wouldn't believe . . .' said the man in brown, swallowing another final 'but'.

'*But* . . .' I said.

'Ah, *but* . . .' said Barbra.

'*But* . . .' said the man in black.

The white-haired man murmured in his sleep, '*But* . . .'

'I asked him to lend me a copy of *Somewhere, Rain*,' said a petulant voice. 'His own book, yet. And you know what he says? He says, buy a copy in the bookstore like everybody else.'

'I bought him drinks at the bar, and he never bought me one in his life,' said a slurred voice.

'Once I had a big sneeze,' said a nasal voice, 'and Allgrobsch had a fresh Kleenex in his pocket and he wouldn't give it me. He said he was saving it up.'

Barbra leaned close to me. 'I know what you're thinking,' she said in a strong whisper. 'You and your Britishness, you say kind things about everybody. But Elzee was a no-good person. Period. You know his story about the duck?'

'Oh, yes. As a matter of fact – '

'Sure. Well, let me tell you – '

'The story was rather moving.'

'Moving! I'll tell you about moving. He plagiarised it. In sixty-three, I remember it like it's tomorrow. I'm telling my little son, my Oswald, a story I make up about a duck that goes quack quack, and Elzee is listening . . . and he makes a few changes and sells it to the *New Yorker* for one thousand dollars!'

'But writers are *supposed* to use materials at hand, little scraps of folk tales and eavesdroppings and *objets trouvés*. It's part of their job.'

'Sure, but – '

At this juncture Barbra – having been tapped on the shoulder by the barmaid – put on her sky blue apron, loaded saucers and bowls and tea cups and cutlery on to a tray, and carried them off to the kitchen.

I thought of what I had been told about Allgrobsch. Why did the clubbies have such an animus towards him, especially considering he was on his death bed? It seemed jolly unfair. Jealousy, was it? Or possibly they disliked the idea of an outsider becoming interested in 'their' great writer? Well, naturally it would be most improper to incorporate that kind of negative attitude in a literary biography: I certainly wasn't going to pass on their gripes to Frank.

To be honest, on first reading I hadn't cared all that much for Allgrobsch's stories. One has to admit, of course, his technical mastery, and his cleverness, and his evocation of doom and evil, and his compassion, and that malarky. But, well . . . if one were a writer (which of course one wouldn't be, since one doesn't have the right kind of imagination, and one has something better to do with one's life anyway) one would write a very different kind of fiction. It would be a roughly contemporary novel, with lots of dialogue and gossip about real believable characters just a bit larger than life. Whereas Allgrobsch's stories contain (no doubt deliberately) flat characters who don't accomplish very much; and the setting is evoked rather than described; and the stories are so short that just as you're getting interested in the plot, it stops.

Nevertheless – in the teeth of all the anti-Allgrobsch-ism at the club – I began to identify with him. The worst that could be said of him, apparently, is that he was dedicated to his art and perhaps a trifle eccentric. Like myself, he was creative, undeniably brilliant, rather cut off from the surrounding populace. Like myself, he put his all into the service of his talent. No doubt he was somewhat conceited, insensitive, impatient with fools, stroppy, immature – but these are minor defects.

A sudden insight struck me. Consider the attitude of the clubbies towards Allgrobsch (I recalled my first visit to the club): the way they'd sat half angled towards him, the way they'd glanced at him surreptitiously; now note their admiration and their envy, their bitchery about him, their petty objections (*vide* H.H. Gritz); the simple fact that they can't help talking about him. What was this reminiscent of? Evidently, everyone in the club was, in a way, in love with Allgrobsch . . . And now he was comatose in an intensive-care unit, with catheters and wires joining him to a life-support machine: he was inanimate as a sofa . . .

I determined to find out as much as I could about his life.

14

Interview with O.U. Pertman (edited extract), Geneva,
16 December 1989

– Come in, come in. You are Frank, yes? Delighted to be of assistance, Frank. You must forgive my English, I have not used her for many years.

– So, sit.

– Ah, no . . . please, no . . . How you say?

– Tape-recorder, yes. Please switch out . . . Ach, that is very better.

– Ah, *non, nein* . . . We speak English only. Is good language, yes?

– My dear friend, Allgrobsch, my old friend – Yes, I hear. It is sad. He is eating his soup and suddenly poof!

– Poof!

– You are literature man, Frank? I am not knowing literature. I read but I am not knowing. I am businessman. I think he is good writer, yes?

– First I meet him, 1946, London. Restaurant's Lyon in Swiss Cottage, quick nippies, yes! We speak about old country. He has much memories.

– He has memories of people. Perhaps he tells false stories, perhaps true stories. He has story of duck goes *Ka, ka!* He has story of shoemaker. He has story of meatballs . . .

– He makes me laugh! His stories very funny, yes? Very . . .

– Yes, Frank.

– No, Frank.

– No, not 1946.

– I give him not money.

– Because I am poor! But then I make money in 1951 and 1952 and 1953 and . . .

– I give him money, yes, Frank. I give him plenty money. 1959. I go to Geneva. He go to New York with my money . . .

– Because he is my good friend. Because he is my good writer. Because he need money . . .

– I have not wife, I have not child, I give money to good writer . . .

– Ah, you ask many good questions, Frank. You are good asker, yes? You are famous writer, also, Frank? I am honoured to hear and say with you.

84

– Ah, there is much years ago . . .

– My memory is old, Frank. You want coffee? You want little cream cake?

– About the new history, Frank, you hear, I listen on the BBC World Service, the politic revolution from Bohemia. She is good? She is bad? What you think . . . ?

15

I nibbled a fishy thing in sweet and sour sauce, and sipped from my glass of Californian chablis. I replied, 'One more spontaneous upsurge in Eastern Europe is neither here nor there. It's not as if one were acquainted with those sort of people, personally . . . Allgrobsch. You were about to tell me everything you know about him.'

'Yeah. Well . . . Allgrobsch was something of a recluse. Not like a real Howard Hughes, an oddball, or anything, but he doesn't tell the media about himself and his life, y'know?'

'Yes, one does know.' When I first went up to Cambridge, various glossies and Sundays wanted to do photofeatures on me, snaps of one clutching a rag doll in one hand and an introductory Galois theory textbook in the other, with snide captions such as 'LITTLE EMMA WOWS THE PROFS' or 'SHE'S ONLY ELEVEN BUT SHE KNOWS HOW', and of course Daddy told them to buzz off and quite right too – not that it stopped them aiming their zoom lenses at me when one was on one's way to breakfast, but . . . 'Yes, I do understand just how Allgrobsch feels.'

'So, there's nothing on him in *Who's Who* and the standard references. But I picked up some, as the Bard says' – Frank simpered, in so far as one can simper while simultaneously talking and eating prawn crackers – 'so to speak, unconsidered trifles. My exhaustive research project is underway. Like for example, I've been going through his manuscripts, his financial records . . . Did you know he claimed a thirty-five dollar tax-deductible expenditure on typewriter ribbons in nineteen sixty-three but zero in sixty-four? These details tell the professional historian something.'

'No doubt.'

'And I've been doing oral interviews. I sent you the transcripts . . .'

'Yes. I had time to glance through some. Pertman's in particular. It was really rather – '

'. . . and these are the facts. He was born in May nineteen twenty-five, in the town of – '

'What did he look like?'

'Like any other baby, I guess . . .'

'One builds up a picture in one's mind eye. I imagined him as an eccentric tubby chappy with a big moustache, rather like Hercule Poirot, actually . . .'

'. . . with pink skin and a hairless head and a damp bottom.'

'What?'

'What?'

'For goodness sake, Frank, what are you on about?'

'I'm telling you about baby Allgrobsch, right? Like you asked.'

'Can't you listen? We were discussing Pertman.'

'Aw, *him*. Yeah. He's a little neat guy in a dark suit.'

'Can't say much for his command of English.'

'Uh-huh. I tried him out in other languages: Swiss-German, Flemish, Slovak . . . He's equally bad in them all.'

'How did you get in touch with him in the first place?'

Frank blinked. He picked up a slippery off-white thing with his chopsticks, playing for time. 'Yeah, I went through Allgrobsch's old address book, from his London days. Phoned around. Networked from acquaintance to acquaintance. That's how it goes.'

'A little . . . underhand, isn't it?'

Frank shrugged. 'Well, Pertman's not so important. He's lying, I guess. Or maybe not. Anyhow, there's no record in his accounts he gave any money to Allgrobsch. I checked.'

'Why would he mislead you?'

'Y'know. Allgrobsch is famous. This guy, knew him in the early years, wants to look good in the biography.'

'How eccentric. To keep up appearances in real life is one thing, to desire to do so on the pages of a book is quite another.'

'Yeah, but it's a very important book.'

'And what's the truth? Was he Allgrobsch's patron?'

'Who knows? We don't believe in omniscient narrators any more. My biography is going to be written from a, hah, explicilty anti-intellectual-imperialism point of view, stressing the inherent limitations of examining the past, by virtue of its, y'know, self-reflexive dynamic.'

'To translate that into plain English, you're going to parade your own ignorance.'

He smiled.

'Speak for yourself,' I said.

'Uh, yeah . . . Like I was saying, Allgrobsch was born in nineteen twenty-five. His father was a successful phonograph importer. His mother was a mother. They lived in a small town, but when Allgrobsch was a youth the family emigrated to Poland. They stayed in Warsaw one year. Then they were in Lithuania briefly. Then Paris. They arrived in London in nineteen thirty-nine – '

'Wait a minute!' I said. 'Do you know the exact dates of those moves?'

'No. Like I told you just now . . . Europe in those days . . .'

'What I'm trying to establish is: did he in fact spend his childhood in a small town in his homeland – as described in his fiction?'

'Well, he writes about it, doesn't he?'

'Go on.'

'Now, he stayed in London during the war. He published some early poems in émigré newsletters and journals . . . Came to New York in nineteen fifty-three and – something about the city, I guess – he was stimulated to produce fiction. His early stories are available now, yeah, in translation, check out his collections, *The Skater* and *The Barber's Song*, but back then he was untranslated, a nobody. A little later he was maybe financially supported by – ah, Pertman – he kept Allgrobsch's head above water while he pulled his socks up – you know?'

'In a manner of speaking, yes.'

'And on second December nineteen fifty-nine – the date's pencilled on the original manuscript – he wrote his first story in English. We all know the rest of the biography,' he declaimed, waving his arm in some grandiose oratorical gesture, addressing in his imagination a cheering audience of learned professors and buxom floosies giving him a standing ovation and a come-hither wink respectively – and puzzling a populous Chinese family having a birthday celebration around the adjacent table.

'No,' I interrupted, 'we *don't* all know the rest of the biography. You tell me.'

'He became famous and successful, and not poor not rich, and lived happily ever after.'

'Until he had a stroke.'

At this point, the waiter – a grim, small figure, with that queerly donnish scowl that is served up only at the better restaurants, and remarkably good timing – approached. 'Are you ready to order, sir?'

I nudged the 'free' hors d'oeuvres and stroked the stem of my wine glass. Frank tapped the vast, unwieldy, gilt-embossed cerise velveteen menu jacket with his horn-rimmed reading spectacles (he uses them when he wants an air of grown-upness). We were both nervous, the way people are when they meet each other after a break: Frank had just returned from his travels and I was back from a brief visit to my family. The time of year, too, was uncertain of itself: it was during that indecisive week after Christmas, when it's neither last year nor the next.

The waiter repeated his request.

Frank pointed out to me, knowingly, that the Chinese name for this restaurant was the Osmanthus Bush Prosperity Tea House as opposed to the English name: The Happy Yum Yum.

'Oh, I didn't know you could read Chinese,' I said, rising to the bait.

'Uh, just a few hundred characters . . . What do you fancy?'

'I'll have whatever you're having,' I said, 'provided it's not too foreign.'

Frank ran his finger down the list of appetisers, tapping intently at points of interest. He was unhurried, presumably following the keep-the-waiter-waiting-that's-what-he's-there-for principle (as favoured by the *nouveau riche*). He waved his spectacles. He rapped the menu and ordered something, chattering away in fluent lingo. (The only Chinese I know is *I love you* – taught to me at Cambridge by an over-optimistic geology postdoc. from Hong Kong.) Meanwhile the waiter displayed patience. Frank (who insists on charming anybody within earshot, even a middle-aged waiter in New York's Chinatown) launched into what was, judging by Frank's crooked smiles and eyebrow-raising, a frightfully amusing anecdote.

A pause. The waiter said, 'No Mandarin, sir. Only speak Cantonese.'

So I took charge of the menu, and commanded, 'Two twenty-threes, two seventeens, two ninety-sixes with an eighty-four, two hundred and fifteens for dessert, and may we have another bottle of forty-three, please? Thank you.'

The waiter vanished into wherever waiters vanish.

I chattered fairly randomly to plug the silence. 'Did I ever tell you about my Great-Uncle Sydney who was rather pious and odd, and taught himself classical Aramaic so that he would be able to argue with St Peter at the pearly gates?'

I wanted to ask Frank point-blank about his biography of Allgrobsch but I had cold feet. (Also literally: wodges of snow were melting off my boots, dampening the scarlet carpet.) I decided to work the conversation round to this topic by means of the following stratagem.

'I remember, when I was three and I went to London for the first time – Aunt Matilda took me to the zoo – I had an extremely enormous ice-cream with a glacé cherry on top, and then we went to Madame Tussaud's where of course I didn't realise they were supposed to be dummies, I thought they were real people standing very still, and then we had high tea at Fortnum's and then – this is what I remember best of all – we walked back home through Chinatown. The funny smells, and a kind of gold dragon . . . So I asked Auntie, and she told me what's what, so for years afterwards I was under the impression all Londoners were Chinese: indeed, I thought China was a part of London.'

'Uh huh.'

'So . . . well, one wonders . . . many children have a completely wrongheaded view of the world . . . Did Allgrobsch recycle his life in his stories?'

'Sure,' said Frank. 'That's what writers do.'

'Oh, one does hope not. I'd rather think Allgrobsch made the whole caboodle up from scratch. Much more fun.'

'Yeah, well,' he said, warming to the topic, 'the relationship between the subject's own life and his fiction is fundamentally symmetrical and intertextual. And this is, as it were, reduplicated in the way my biography relates to both his life and his fiction.'

'Is it?'

'A, so to speak, dialectical *mis en abîme*.'

'Of course.' (Pretentiousness doesn't cow me: one has survived enough Cambridge senior common room chit-chat.) 'But story writers make everything up, don't they? That's the whole point of the thing. If they'd wanted to tell the truth, they'd have become mathematicians or scientists instead.'

'Ah, but your so-called "truth" . . .' he said.

'My *what*?'

'. . . is the interface between observation and imagination. So Allgrobsch's fictions are as "true" as an account of what we see around us in this restaurant . . . the gold-painted ceiling, the Chinese family slurping soup at the next table, the waiter bringing us our order . . . Ah, thank you. Put the tofu right here.'

90

'Tommyrot!' I said, using one of Daddy's expressions. 'One mustn't go around blurring reality like that. Let's face it: some things are true – such as two plus two makes four – and other things aren't – music, for instance, or fiction. The dictator of what's that country that's always in the news lately got overthrown for failing to make that very distinction.'

Frank dipped a crunchy thing in a gooey thing, and ate it.

'Look over there,' I said, 'at what is actually a largeframed looking glass – if one believes the laws of optics. But if one trusts Lewis Carroll instead, it's a door into another world. So, go on then, I dare you, walk straight through!'

'He inspected his glass of chablis, and sipped a little. '*Romania*,' he murmured.

'In fact,' I continued, 'writing a biography of a story writer is a pretty rum thing in the first place. I mean, everything that's interesting and important about him takes place inside his head . . . So I suppose you *have* to believe his stories are all based on his life – otherwise there wouldn't be much for you to write about.'

Frank shunted half the stir-fry on to a plate for me, and half for him. He spooned some brown sauce on top of the portions.

Meanwhile he said, 'Ah, no, Emma. You're getting hold of the wrong end of the . . . the . . .'

'The stick?' I suggested. (One gets so bored of his slow drawl: what is he *doing* in the pauses between his words: does his brain go into suspended animation?)

' . . . of the multi-faceted process. I'm not trying to construct a "true" life story of the guy. I'm a professor of comparative literature, not a reporter for *People* magazine. I don't iron his life out into a fake linearity, no. My plan is to write the book on a kind of post-modernist framework, using in-depth analyses of four of his fictions as, ah, thematic vortices, and arranging the biographical elements around those. See, I'm engaged in an ongoing demythologisation, deper-sonalisation, deconstruction . . .'

'Poppycock!' (Another of Daddy's handy words.) I was getting jolly upset and red-faced: I wasn't at all sure I could handle the winter greens in black-bean sauce in my condition. 'Allgrobsch's life is fact and his fiction is fiction, and that's that!'

'Sure. And I'm analysing, from a neo-post-marxist perspective, both the economics and the "economics" of the interrelated financial and "literary" processes of production . . .' He stared into my eyes and bit

91

his lower lip. 'Don't look at me like that, Emma. All I want is to win some success as a literary scholar, and get tenure. Is that too much to ask?'

A pause. I said, 'Mmm,' dubiously, converting it halfway through into an appreciation of the food.

There followed a blurt of general conversation. He made some remark concerning the election to choose the New York mayor, which had clogged the front page of the local newspapers for months; the contest was between two Americans with identical splendid intentions and smiles: one was black and the other wasn't. I mentioned that in India (according to a geologist from Bombay who was invited once to our high table) the political parties all have symbols – a cow, say, or a flower – so the illiterate voters know what's what; and in New York they take this principle one step further by having rival candidates with different skin pigmentation, do they? It took Frank several seconds to realise I was joking. He assured me this distinction wasn't compulsory. Then I told him my maths was going all right (he nodded) and that I was pleased to see him (another nod). I added that he was looking tanned, and he said I was looking okay.

I said, 'Oh, Frank, this isn't at all how I'd imagined it.'

'Hmm?'

'Well, we're meeting again, and having a nice lunch, and I'd expected we'd have a cosy chatter, and, er . . . And instead all we do is quarrel about Allgrobsch! Honestly, it happens to me all the time: one wants to talk about one thing and one finds oneself gabbling away about something altogether different. I wish I could manage my conversations in a proper grown-up way.'

'Ah, some of us golden oldies have problems with that, too.' He did his lopsided grin, and toothpicked out a bit of stir-fried spinach that had caught between his incisors. 'So let's start again, huh?' His voice quavered down and up. 'Hello, I'm Frank. Hello I'm Emma. How are things? How do you do? Sure, okay. Very well, thank you. How was your Christmas? How was *your* Christmas?'

I couldn't help chortling bang in the middle of my Peking duck . . . Which is how come Frank and I managed to remain on speaking terms during that winter: we annoyed each other, but we also gave each other the giggles. Yes, one knows it's not a 'mature relationship' – but nobody can be mature *all* the time.

'Oh, Christmas,' I said, 'you know. All one's antediluvian relations . . . I spent it with my family, in The New House . . . Everybody saying how pretty I used to be when I was seven . . . and how they remembered me doing something horribly cute in my nappies . . . No snow, only drizzle. And Aunt Matilda and Uncle Charles, Great-Aunt Peggy, Cousin Imogen with her triplets . . . all patting me on my head and telling me how tall I'd grown . . . As if one were a prize marrow or something. And Aunt Mary actually alleged I spoke with a *soupçon* of an American accent. She imitated my voice, in her just-teasing way, "Mathemadics," she droned, and "Ree-search".'

Frank laughed – briefly but genuinely.

'And how was yours?' I asked.

'Busy busy.'

'But I'm glad to be back.'

'Me too.'

An intimate moment. We eyed each other while sucking the orange slices. He took something from one of his inner pockets and laid it on the table. It was about the size of a cigarette packet. It looked like a slab of crumbly cement.

'It's for you,' he said.

'Oh. It's . . . just what I've always wanted.'

'I visited some contacts of mine in Eastern Europe just before Christmas. In Bratislava, they're having a ball – and boy, you should see them in Budapest . . .' He told a slightly droll anecdote about how some Hungarians in Transylvania had mistaken him for a Romanian and vice-versa. Then he tapped his gift. 'This is a souvenir I picked up with my own hands in Berlin. It's a piece of the Wall.'

I appreciated the gesture. By Frank's standards, it was unusually thoughtful. I wrapped it in a paper napkin for safekeeping.

A member of the Chinese family at the adjacent table blew out twenty-one candles on a gateau.

He poured me another glass of wine.

'Ooh, one really mustn't,' I said, as I took an ample swig, 'I get quite tiddly. I know you and your kind' – wagging a chopstick at him – 'you're the type Mummy warned me against: a swarthy chappy with intentions. Not properly brought up: and that's a fact. You get innocent maidens under your spell across the supper table. You offer them a harmless-seeming cube of tofu, and then – foof!'

'Foof,' he repeated solemnly.

'We won't ever bicker seriously, now will we?'

'No way, Em.'

'We won't get jealous of each other because you're so handsome and

I'm so brilliant, the way Barbra does with Allgrobsch and it's all to do with that silly little duck story . . .'

'Duck story?'

I clapped my hand over my mouth. 'Oops! Silly me. I hadn't meant to tell you about that. It was supposed to be a secret.'

'Aw, we don't need any secrets.' He patted my nearer set of knuckles. 'Anyhow, Barbra told me the same. She's bitter.'

'All the clubbies are like that.'

'They are?'

'I wish I were better at keeping mum. Mummy used to chant over my cradle: *Honesty is the best policy*. One can't get away from a thing like that.'

'The guys at the club told me the same as they told you. At first they're shy with strangers, they keep their eyes close to their chests, but then they spill the beans. I don't believe them. They're just envious. And they hate him because he writes in English, and because now he's dying, taking himself away from them finally.'

'We won't ever hate each other, will we? We won't keep secrets from each other?'

'Certainly not.'

Frank picked up my right hand, removed the two chopsticks gripped therein and laid them on the chopstick rest, placed the tips of my fingertips in the vicinity of his lips, and kissed them lightly . . . Thereafter, in the following weeks, it became customary for him to kiss my hand on parting. I know this sounds like a terribly old-fashioned courtship – and perhaps it was. I took the Wall home with me.

Frank summoned the waiter and waved a fancy credit card embossed with a hologram depicting the solar system. The thought of offering to pay half the bill crossed my mind – but it's very difficult to resist Frank's will if he really wants to do something.

16

The Man Who Liked Winter

Nobody promises to do anything. We're not saying we'll definitely go skating on the frozen river; but we're not saying we won't. We're not committing ourselves to give Glar the beggar a gratis potato on Friday; we just work potatoes and Fridays into the general conversation and leave it at that. There's no question of parents arranging to marry off their children; but sometimes the father of a girl meets the father of a boy, and the discussion happens to drift on to the topic of delightful hypothetical grandchildren. In our town it's thought folly to make resolutions at New Year; instead the terrors and mistakes of the previous year are lamented. For any declaration of intentions is bad luck and absurd – since who knows what will come to pass?

Of course every rule has its exception. We have just one inveterate, incorrigible promiser in our town – Memed the millionaire.

Memed truly was a millionaire – on paper, at least – for a few brief weeks some years ago, when the stock exchange soared like a toy kite on a windy day, before it swooped the way kites do. Watch his arms burrow inside the stuffing of his hen-feather mattress: his gloved hands emerge. 'These are my shares,' he says, displaying a stash of elaborately and subtly printed certificates. 'Worthless, the lot of them.' He embraces the papers; he tosses them in the air and catches them. He indicates a document printed in curvaceous lettering, illustrated with a three-color engraving of a steam train: 'Here are my railroads.' Next, a representation of a large brick building; letters and numbers in a squarish no-nonsense font form paragraphs beneath: 'And these are my textile mills.' Finally, a depiction of a hole in the ground: 'My gold mine.'

At this point his wife, Nara the philosophical, joins in the conversation. 'He was poor when I married him,' she tell us, 'and now he is poor again. What have I lost?' (Actually Memed is not poor. He has some savings under the creaking floorboard and a fine pair of candlesticks. But it is not our custom to boast of present successes: we describe only ones which have long since vanished.) He replies, 'You have lost the dowry your father gave me.' She says, 'Yes, yes!' Then they both slap the mattress hard: little pale feathers rise in the air, making everybody sneeze.

Memed is optimistic. 'I was rich once, so why not twice?' He has invested in various schemes over the years. He opened a business importing American jigsaw puzzles – but they were so difficult, what with their quantities of random blurred detail, that almost no one could solve them, and he had to refund the purchase price to dissatisfied customers. Then he went into advertising. He hired men to roam the streets wearing a pair of boards, fore and aft, painted with alliterative mottos (composed by Nara) in favour of lovely laundries, superlative sausages, and dramatic dry goods stores. But his employees could not be trusted to march to and fro all day long; they would sidle off for a quick beer, and be found several hours later dozing in an alley, impairing the reputation of the promoted product; meanwhile little boys would scrawl disruptive graffiti on the rear board, such as 'I AM A LIAR' or 'KICK ME'.

Now, though, Memed has come up with a surefire idea. Let him tell it in his own words. He sits back in the high-winged armchair while his wife warms his slippers on the hearth. He says, 'I propose to sell time.' He smiles, coughs, hawks phlegm on the fire and waits for it to sizzle. 'It's winter now and the land is frozen. Folk don't venture out unless they're desperate for work or to see a friend, or they have nowhere to stay. But in a few months it'll be spring – then summer, and we'll all go mushrooming in the woods and boating on the river. And we'll get so hot, so sweaty, we'll want . . . What will we want, Nara?' She pats the slippers on to his feet, adjusts his socks, and chimes in dutifully, 'We'll want to cool down.' 'Yes!' he says. 'We'll desire coldness more than anything. We'll look back to those wonderful mid-winter days when huge drifts of snow blocked the roads and coldness was ours for the taking . . . But, panting in August . . . what can we do?'

Memed looks round at us: we don't know the answer.

He continues, 'I'll tell you what! We can buy a piece of the past, or future. Off we go to the ice factory, where winter is manufactured by an expensive Czech machine which keeps breaking down, and we purchase a big block of smearily transparent frozen water. We take it home. We crack it with special hammers. We put fragments in our long drinks: our cherry juices, our vodka-on-the-rockses, our Manhattans . . .'

He smacks his hands together. 'But is this satisfactory? Of course not! The ice factory is unreliable. Its product is overpriced. We pay through the nose for what isn't, let's be honest, the genuine article. What we want is winter – not some artificial substitute.'

He leans forward. His head wags against one wing of the armchair, then the other. He whispers loudly. 'Soon, very soon, I'll dig a big hole in the ground. I'll let it fill up with snow, naturally. I'll cover everything with a thick blanket of straw, and over the straw I'll lay canvas. In six months' time I'll pull back the canvas, exposing the straw. Off with the straw, revealing the smooth sheen of perfect ice. Which I'll sell. What costs nothing will bring me my fortune! The change of the seasons will make me a millionaire again!'

Nara smiles and throws another stick on the fire.

Memed sets about putting his plan into action. He digs the pit. He shoves in snow. He heats the snow with a charcoal fire so it melts, then refreezes into solid ice. He heaps straw on it. He stretches a giant sheet of dirt-green canvas across his valuable asset: it looks like a small plot for growing cabbages or turnips. Then more snow drifts over: it becomes entirely invisible. Little birds hop across, leaving their marks; and look! there is the spoor of a single wandering fox . . .

And what will be the outcome (we ask)? Will Memed really be able to undercut the ice factory? Has he taken overhead costs into account? Will he actually make a profit? Will he make plenty? Will he make a million? Will Nara be able to retrieve the candlesticks from the pawn shop, set them on the mantelpiece, fix pure white paraffin candles in them, light the wicks and illuminate the whole room? Will summer come soon?

Memed answers many times, 'Yes.' He is seated cross-legged on top of his private glacier, cosy in his woollens, narrating a story which is true, maybe. 'Once upon a time,' he says, 'an explorer from our very own town journeyed south. He traveled by horse and automobile and rail and foot. He came to the happy lands of perpetual spring where folk smile all day long, drink wine and eat olives. Then he climbed inside a big ship. He crossed the blue sea. At last he arrived in a country where the sun is king. And what did he see? He saw sand. Sand. Nothing but sand. Only sand, stretching away boundlessly. And a few wandering men. And just a little water, brackish and warm, from the occasional well. So the explorer told the desert dwellers about a wonderful substance, as hard as rock, as transparent as glass, as cold as night . . .'

Nara joins her husband on the ice. She loosens his collar and rolls up his sleeves. She wipes the sweat from his brow.

17

MY NEW YEAR RESOLUTIONS
by Emma Smart

(1) I will grow older.
(2) I will work hard at my maths.
(3) I will be nice to other people, especially those less fortunate than oneself.
(4) I will become more mature.

The trick in devising a list of resolutions is to combine surefire ones (such as 1 and 2 – one is bound to age and do lots of mathematics) with worthy intentions (3 and 4). Every January 1st I make the same resolutions, so all I have to do is dribble a little whiteout over last year's date, then type in this year's. I tape my list on top of my computer's external disc drive: it can't be overlooked, that way.

What kind of year did it turn out to be? Early January was very cold with masses of snow (and bloody riots in obscure bits of Central Asia no one has ever heard of – but one can't get upset over everything) so I had a splendid excuse for staying at home or in my office and developing an extension of the SPO to infinite simrel networks. Then, later in the month, there was a freakish warm spell: rain drilled holes in the drifts; the city turned to slush; one couldn't step outside without getting dirty water in one's thermal socks . . . which was yet another reason for holing oneself up with books, learned journals, a notepad and a computer. And then the thermometer dropped below zero again: slippery ice everywhere – cars sliding and hooting all over the city; fragmented windscreens and cracked-off wing mirrors littering the tarmac as if the sky had shattered; policemen slithering; bag ladies falling back on their bags; the mugger lying down with the mugged . . .

98

a third justification for huddling in one's study. Perhaps the pre-eminence of the north-eastern United States in present-day mathematics (I wondered idly) has something to do with the climate? But no: to a true mathematician, any season, any meteorological condition, any news report of a superpower getting tough or tender, anything at all . . . is an overwhelming argument for doing mathematics.

A knock on my door: odd, that. One had very few visitors anyway (just occasionally Ostrovsky or Potts, or Fanny and Bridget from the Institute; for one doesn't encourage that sort of thing: one's home is not a *boîte*) and they always had to cope with the entryphone system (a buzz would be heard inside one's apartment: one would thumb a control on the wall; a crackly voice would plead; then, on pressing a different button, the grille at the apartment building entrance would unlock, letting the visitor in). But who on earth could it be? I pressed my eye over the peephole – the fisheye lens therein always had the effect of making anybody outside look rather fishy, with a long nose and rounded cheeks. My visitor did in fact have a permanently submarine appearance, what with his lank beige seaweedy hair, his washed-out eyes, his endlessly drifting hands.

'Hallo, Arnie,' I said, having unlatched, unbolted and pulled open the door; and shut, bolted and latched it behind him. 'Do come in. Now what can I do for you?'

Arnie – like teenage boys in general – was mopish, having recently caught acne and existentialism (or whatever). I'd only ever encountered him before in the capacity of errand boy for his mother, my neighbour Mona the freelance literary agent – she'd send him over to my place to borrow a bottle of erasing fluid or anti-dandruff shampoo (one might have thought she'd be more organised in view of her job: but not so). And she was so busy nannying her authors (on the few occasions I'd spoken to her she'd always been in mid-crisis: an author to be lunched, an author to be sobered; an author to be visited in the psychiatric ward, an author to be sued for libel for claiming the President of the United States was a practising Satanist, an author's funeral to be attended . . .), it was no wonder she couldn't take proper care of her son. And he had no father, apparently.

Arnie wandered in and slumped on my sofa.

'Yes?' I said. 'And what does your, er, mom, want now?'

'Nothing.'

'Er, excuse me?'

He scratched bits of his head, and said forcefully, 'I'm not here for her. Mona doesn't know I'm seeing you. I want to talk to you alone, Emma.'

'Oh, yes. Certainly!'

I was baffled. Surely the boy had something better to do than take up my valuable time while I was trying to generalise the SPO conjecture?

Anyway, how does one entertain American boys? I seemed to recall something about feeding them milk and biscuits. 'I think I know just what you want.'

I opened a packet of Pepperidge Farm and arranged the snacks on a floral pattern plate (courtesy of Professor Absent); I poured a carton of homogenised medium fat into a glass. 'Here's your milk and, er, chocolate chip cookies.'

He ate and drank my offering greedily (not to say messily), so presumably one was doing the right thing.

'How is your . . . ?' I said. 'How is Mona?'

'Uh, you know . . .'

'Oh, really?'

'Yeah.'

'I see?'

'Sure.'

'Well, er . . . my, it's getting rather late,' I said.

He licked his thumb, pressed it on assorted crumbs which had gathered in the folds of his jeans, and put the thumb back in his mouth baby-wise.

I decided to try a mild insult to drive him out. 'I must say, you're quite a big lad now.'

'I'm a junior.'

'Yes? Well, I never. Junior high school already.'

'I'm a junior in senior high school.' The American nomenclature is pointlessly ambiguous: why can't they just call themselves Lower Sixth Formers like normal people? 'I'm graduating next year. I'm applying to MIT and Caltech. I want to be a theoretical quantum cosmologist.'

'I see . . .'

'And you're a mathematician, right?'

I hazarded a guess as to where this dialogue was leading. 'Yes, but I'm a *pure* mathematician. I really don't have much to do with physicists or the administrative staff or the admission tutors – or whatever you call that lot here – or anybody at all who can give you an unfair advantage in getting accepted by your first-choice college. So frankly – '

'No, uh . . . I want to talk with you about physics. I have some ideas, see . . .'

He took a crumpled sheet of paper from his jeans pocket and showed it to me. He jabbed at equations with the blunt end of a propelling pencil. It turned out that he had scribbled a few interesting notions – of the type that many clever undergraduates come up with: an amusing derivation of the Einstein $E = mc2$ relation starting from the Laplace formula for soundwaves in an ether, an estimate of the size of the universe given the assumption that overall potential energy changes balance those in kinetic energy . . . All quite ingenious but simplistic (there was no sign he had understood General Relativity).

For his age, it was quite commendable. I tried to combine non-cloying praise with non-scathing criticism. I referred him to a *Scientific American* article on the Dirac Large Number Hypothesis. 'You'll find some relevant stuff there.'

'Mona doesn't understand me,' he said.

'No, well – '

'She won't quit nagging me to play tennis, go swim, see a movie . . .'

'No doubt she's entitled to her opinions.'

'I mean, she's okay, I guess. But she doesn't know shit about science.'

'Ah, I'm afraid you'll come to realise that the vast majority of the human population – '

'She's my *mother*.'

A brief silence ensued.

I seized the opportunity to do a spot of missionary work. 'By the way, Arnie, you seem a bright lad. Are you *sure* you want to be a physicist? There's a lot of fundamental work to be done in pure mathematics . . .'

'I'm sure.' He smiled wanly.

'Pity.'

'Yeah, I guess I'll . . .' He got up awkwardly and sidled towards the door.

'Well, goodbye, Arnie,' I said.

He chewed his lower lip.

I went through the business with the multiple locks.

Just as he was walking out, he glanced over his shoulder at me and muttered, 'Christ! I wish I had a mother like you.'

Not until I had shut and bolted the door firmly did one let one's laughter ring out. Emma Smart as a mother-substitute! What a notion! What a scream! My, one was chuffed.

I went back into the study and leaned over my computer. I read the list of resolutions out loud to myself, and mentally ticked them off. All four accomplished in the course of a single afternoon!

18

Resolutions – on further reflection – are stranger than they seem: one first hypothesises a world in which one will have accomplished something, and secondly one attemps to ease this real world into the shape of the imagined one.

And who better at doing that than mathematicians?

Conferences are my cup of tea. I'm at my best there, strolling around, greeting and being greeted by figures I had previously known only by reputation or phone or fax, or at other conferences – swapping ideas and complimenting one another. And the best part of any conference is the beginning, meeting the new faces, peering down at names written semi-legibly on 'HELLO I'M —— ' labels: I relish the tang of expectation.

Columbia was rather a good setting for the 'What's New In Scope Theory 1990?' bash. The place used to be known as King's College, New York (and still would be, but for the nefarious activities of a small group of disloyal elements – as I pointed out, lightheartedly needless to say, to assorted United Staters): the spaciousness and variegatedness of its main court are reminiscent of those of some of the newer fangled Cambridge colleges. A chill day, of course, with fresh snow on the ground: but a scatter of sunshine had jemmied through the clouds: some wistful undergraduates were sprawling on the steps in full ski costume, facing the rising sun.

Meanwhile we mathematicians were scurrying past them, pushing through the swing doors into the lobby of one of the buildings, picking up glazed doughnuts from a buffet table. I chatted to Habib from Rochester, Chang and di Piero from Northeastern. Flixheim from Cornell – Ostrovsky was one of the organisers: he was nervous and happy, clucking around like a mother hen. Potts and Jed were absent:

103

they'd recently managed to kid some official at the Office of Naval Research that their kind of stuff was just the ticket to defeat the forces of anti-Americanism, so gaining them oodles of oof; that Monday they were down in Washington hoping to win the jackpot from the Department of Defense too. (I'd spoken to Potts on the phone. He'd argued that since his work has no possible military application, all he was doing was diverting cash from nuclear missiles into his own pocket: to hear him talk, you'd think he and Jed were the Robin Hood and Friar Tuck of the modern world.) Also I was managing to avoid bumping into a compatriot of mine, Blogham-Smith, on sabbatical at SUNY; he (in between explaining his work on differential geometry) was strutting around with a disposable cup of darjeeling balanced on one shoulder, squawking at it, 'Pretty poly! Pretty poly styrene!' This pun – admittedly not very droll in the first place – was made less humorous by the fact that Americans refer to the substance as styrofoam. He had a bad case of dandruff, to boot. Fortunately one was able to avoid addressing him in good conscience, since he is an Oxford man.

It occurred to me that an ordinary person passing through here might regard the conferees as eccentric or boring or absentminded. After all, these are the popular stereotypes; the world is envious of mathematicians and so supposes they are defective in some way. Nonsense, of course one would find a similar variety of personality-types at a conference of accountants or plumbers.

And then came the talks. Chang's was good; I asked a question which set him thinking. Flixheim's was poorer, I didn't manage to get a word in edgeways during the question period. But I more than made up for that at Blogham-Smith's where I offered no fewer than three helpful suggestions.

And in the afternoon (after a quick chicken sandwich, a nice cup of tea, and a brisk stroll) it was my turn.

I stood on the stage, with my mouth hovering over the microphone and my hands sliding transparencies into the projector. All had been prepared with care. I sketched out the Best Of All Possible Worlds Hypothesis, for the benefit of any ignoramuses or graduate students in the audience. I then demonstrated my stylishly inductive proof that the BOAPW was also definable and valid for infinite networks. I stated my next subgoal: to prove that most strategies will lead to the BOAPW in an infinite network (i.e. a partial proof of the SPO). And, fairly triumphantly, I got most of the way towards that proof: I succeeded in proving that an infinity of strategies succeed and an infinity fail . . . so all I had to do was show that the first infinity is infinitely bigger than the second infinity.

(I had tremendous difficulty trying to explain this simple concept to Frank – until I hit on the following illustration: 'How many points are there in a line? Infinity, of course. How may points are there in a square? Likewise infinity. Which infinity is bigger? The latter, surely. How can one prove this? By showing the line fits inside the square. [Actually this example is invalid, for reasons I couldn't be bothered to explain to him. Never mind. What he doesn't know won't harm him.])

There followed a session of questions from the floor. Habib raised an objecton which I quashed. Ostrovsky offered a rather useful comment on a possible technique for counting the infinities to prove my result. Of course, one was grateful for his assistance (as I said). But also disconcerted: if I adopted his ideas, I'd have to call my result the Smart–Ostrovsky theorem, instead of the Smart theorem, and that wouldn't do at all.

After my talk was over, I remained behind in the lecture hall, tidying my transparencies away very slowly. I like the feel of transpariencies, their cool fish-like wriggle, and their appearance too: the way the multicoloured symbols in my handwriting stand out on oblongs of gleamy nothingness . . . Meanwhile, intermittently, I gazed up at the images projected on the screen – a magnification of my own thoughts, as if one's head had become see-through and one's mind were public. I rumpled and shifted the transparencies: a shimmering Venetian effect. And then I tided them all away; collated them in a file. The projector remained on a while, displaying pure light.

What is my contribution to mathematics? It's not a question one asks oneself too often: it's best not to be too introspective on these matters; the centipede who tried to puzzle out its own motion couldn't walk. Shall I ever be a truly great mathematician, one of those few giants who transfigure human understanding? I have a white-hot analytical mind – so do we all. And I'm unusually imaginative and hard-thinking, of course. But do I have that devastating creativity, that devil-may-care explosive intellect? Ostrovsky has it, perhaps. Possibly even Blogham-Smith – unpleasant though this is to contemplate. But Emma Smart . . . What about her? Is she too conservative, too much of the perpetual Daddy's girl? Or can she unstopper the bottle and liberate her genius? One wondered. I recalled the Thanksgiving Parade which is held in New York each November; inflated cartoon figures glide above the streets. I hadn't seen the actual parade myself, since I'd been too busy working that day, but on the night before, I'd accompanied Fanny and Bridget to the place by the Natural History Museum where the floats are assembled and the figures are pumped up. Klieg lights blazed; a convoy of trucks was parked; mechanics injected lighter-than-air gas into Mickey Mouse's elbow and Popeye's buttock – the mythical characters swelled a little, and poked a limb at the stars . . . But for safety's sake they were not permitted to rise from the ground: nets covered them, holding them down.

And why be a mathematician anyway? The short answer is that mathematics matters. Granted. Take scope theory, in particular. 'One is seeking to know if things usually turn out for the best.' Not a misleading explanation – provided one adds the caveat that 'best' doesn't necessarily have anything to do with goodness in the normal sense. Or one could propose the justification: 'One is finding ways of relating the global and the local.' Correct too – and certainly this is an important topic (that's what politics is all about) – but it would miss the point. My mathematics – all mathematics, at bottom – is pure. It has nothing to do with applications ultimately, and morality doesn't come into it. One clothes one's thoughts in the language of applied mathematics and ethics (all those terms, such as 'reasonable strategy' and 'best'!) not out of picturesqueness or funkiness, but because one's imagination takes shape that way – even though one's goal is superhumanly abstract and amoral. One must tell the truth – not because it's good or handy – but because it's true.

19

'The trouble with Allgrobsch . . .' a voice was suggesting.

'Allgrobsch's big mistake . . .' a voice was arguing.

'Where Allgrobsch gets it wrong . . .' a voice was insisting.

All around me the clubbies were picking holes in Allgrobsch's fictions, pointing out supposed errors of fact.

'This is quite unlike what one does in England,' I informed Barbra. 'There, it is the custom to gloss over the defects of the dead or dying – in public, at least. One draws attention to the virtues of the late lamented.'

'It's bad enough he writes in English – and now he's not writing in anything,' said Barbra. 'I guess we feel he's deserting us a second time.'

'Oh, how is he?' I asked politely. 'Has anyone visited him in hospital?'

Barbra commented, irrelevantly, 'I love the way you British say "in hospital" instead of "in *the* hospital". Like "in school" or "in jail". Like you think it's a state of life.'

'Yes,' I said. 'It is. And *you* call it the "horse-piddle". What kind of state is he in?'

'He's much better,' said a deep voice.

'He's much worse,' said a high voice.

'He's exactly the same,' said a quavering voice.

'I must say,' I remarked, 'the ambience here has become more . . . spirited than on previous occasions.'

'It's gotten a little noisy. Spring's in the air!' Her hands shot up and fluttered in what was presumably a free interpretation of burgeoning blossom or lolloping lambs or something.

'Surely not.' I pointed to the welts of my shoes and the hem of my khaki corduroy trousers: snow was visible.

'Well, we're optimists. You have to be when you're old.'

Actually, I'd come all the way out here for a change of scene, while I was mulling over the developments in scope theory, working out the simplest and most efficient way to categorise the scopes for an infinite simrel diagram. I was seated in my favourite corner, beneath the old photographs. 'One had hoped for a little peace and quiet.'

'You should be so lucky.'

Barbra sprang up and attended to somebody waving his or her hand. She was supposed to be waitressing throughout; she could only chat to me in intermittent spurts.

Also, mention of Allgrobsch reminded me of Frank, and one didn't really want to dwell on all that. After our last encounter I'd been distracted from my research for a whole day – and of course mathematics must come first.

A voice was insinuating, 'Note how he claims in his boating story that the river Vlas turns left after it leaves the town, but everybody knows it turns right!'

A voice was objecting, 'In the story about the blacksmith, Allgrobsch gives him a blister on his thumb, but of course they always get it on the pinkie.'

A voice was commenting, 'The hero of "The Counterfeiter" tries to remove an ink stain with vinegar, when gasoline is much more effective.'

'Honestly,' I said to Barbra as she scurried past carrying a trayload of dirty plates, 'what a pettifogging attitude! Surely one appreciates that fiction is not supposed to be historically accurate.'

'Emma, I'm surprised at you. How would you feel if someone wrote a story about – about a mathematician in Cambridge, England, and he made a mistake about – '

'To be sure, a failure in verisimilitude might lead one – '

'See! You wouldn't like it.' She swung round and perched on the edge of the table, balancing the tray against her sky blue apron. Her head was backdropped against a framed monochrome photograph of a hilly landscape, like a face on television.

'So we're not happy either when Elzee gets things wrong. Mind you, I'm not saying he *does* make mistakes, but we have to check it out.'

'But fiction exists for the sake of nourishing the imagination, not as a substitute for journalism or history. It's the channel whereby the author communicates his fantasies to us, often it's the only route along which these thoughts *can* be transmitted . . .'

108

A pause while both of us thought the same thought: an image of an unconscious figure on a hospital bed.

I continued, 'After all, no one objects to *Alice in Wonderland* on the grounds that white rabbits don't in fact wear large pocket watches and speak fluent if somewhat dated English!'

'Sure. But all Allgrobsch's stories are set in a real place and time. So the details have to be correct. Okay, let's pretend . . . Here is a novel set in London, England.' She held an imaginary volume in both hands (a rather tricky activity, involving balancing the tray between her breasts and wrists). 'It's written by an American who never went to England, yes? And it's full of errors. The beefeaters eat dim sum; the Prime Minister says, "It's a whole new ballgame," for example . . .'

'Actually the beefeaters don't really eat beef: the name is a corruption of . . . And Americanisms are catching on, due to the influence of Hollywood, especially among the middle classes. But, yes, I do appreciate your point.'

'And it's worse when it's *too* correct. Too much local colour. Like, the characters are always speaking Cockney and wearing bowler hats, and meeting each other in front of Big Ben and drinking tea.'

'Granted,' I said, lowering my cup of Earl Grey delicately on to the saucer, 'some glaring howler might disturb the equanimity of the reader. But that scarcely justifies this perverse *search* for trivial deviations from exactitude, with all the misplaced enthusiasm of the Spanish Inquisition rooting out subtle varieties of heterodoxy!'

'Uh-uh.' She shut her imaginary book. 'The big mistakes nobody minds, because of course they're intended. The Alice books, for example, like you said. But it's the small wrong things, the tiny flaws, they destroy your belief completely.'

'One's imagination should be quite robust enough to stand up to such an assault. Only someone with an inherently suspicious character – '

'See. Suppose you go home, and you see somebody has smashed all the windows in your street. So what do you think? You're upset, yes, you're angry, you curse and you swear at the young hooligans . . . But this is all. Now, suppose every window – they're not broken, but instead all the corners are now rounded instead of square like they were in the morning. So . . . A thing like this can make you crazy.'

'One can scarcely compare – '

'And it's the same with fiction. I know. I translated plenty. On page eighty-six the man in the blue suit puts tobacco in his pipe and on page eighty-eight he stubs out his cigar on his tan pants. You don't know

109

what to think. You throw the novel in the fire.' Her hands made a hurling motion.

A whine: 'The truth about the old days . . .'

A bray: 'If only he'd asked me . . .'

A roar: 'I could've told him the facts . . .'

'But surely a mere solecism,' I said, 'one itsy-bitsy fact more or less – '

'There's a morality in facts, Emma. Think how you feel when somebody chops down a tree that was standing there since you were a child. It was an ugly tree. You never liked it. But now . . . It's the same when you read a story set in your home town and the writer puts a street in the wrong place, or has a car turning right on a No Right Turn intersection . . . It happens when I'm translating, often. Like a certain writer – I'm not saying the name – the story is about an old man who takes the train from Baltimore to New York. So he gets off the train at Grand Central . . .'

She stopped talking suddenly.

'Yes?' I said. 'Go on.'

'You understand? The train from Baltimore doesn't come in at Grand Central. It goes to Penn Station. So how should I translate it? It was a big headache. Is it better to have a true translation and a false fact or a false translation and a true fact?'

'Why not contact the writer and ask his advice?'

'He passed away already.'

'In that case, change it, of coure. One might as well not antagonise one's living readers.'

'Sure, Emma. But there's a problem. The old man comes out the station, he walks down Forty-second Street. Now Penn Station is on Thirty-fourth, so . . .'

'Well, make an appropriate alteration. Have the character run uptown first – '

'He's an old man, with chronic arthritis.'

'He can take a taxi – '

'He's poor.'

'Oh, well then, revise it so he walks down Thirty-fourth Street instead.'

'But he walks toward the United Nations building, which is on Forty-second, and – '

'Oh, forget it. Just translate another story instead.'

'So now you understand the problem, Emma?'

'Er, what did you do in the end?'

'What?'

'The story. Did you change the stations?'

'Uh . . . Who remembers? It was a long time ago.'

Questioning voices faded away.

I thought about Barbra's anecdote. 'Actually, you know, your account proves my point. There are so many tiddly little facts about, it's impossible to tidy them all up, so why bother?'

'Shame on you, Emma. There are so many little equations about, so why get them right, yes?'

I blushed. My mind was not operating with its usual superfineness. Naturally one was right and she was wrong, because mathematics is all about discovering the truth whereas fiction is about making things up – but it would hardly be tactful to emphasise that. 'Erase my last argument, please.'

'At least we should try to be accurate. Thus we honour the world.'

'Well, we mathematicians do things rather differently. When one writes an article for a learned journal, one arranges it in the form of a proof – an argument, if you prefer – from premises via lemmas to conclusions. Of course one's written proof bears precious little relation to what actually went on in one's head. One leaves out all the intuition, and scratching together of odd ideas, and all that brouhaha. It's the *idea* that counts, not the history of its discovery.'

I was reminded of a mathematicians' in-joke. Whenever the great mathematician David Hilbert was giving a lecture and he couldn't carry out one vital step of the proof, what he'd do instead was say, 'Obviously,' and jump ahead to the next step. Everyone always assumed that, since he was so clever, the missing link had been obvious for him!

I grinned at this recollection. Barbra grinned back. I tittered. She tittered sympathetically. I burst into uproarious giggles. Which set her off. She was rocking on the distressed pine table-top, rumpling the red checked cloth, shaking her tray till all the stacked plates and cups rattled.

'What's the joke?' she panted.

'*Obviously*!' I yelled. And giggled some more.

'*Obviously*,' bellowed a deep slow voice. A hand was gripping my shoulder. I glanced round. '*Obviously* it's absurd. *Obviously* it's ludicrous.'

Frank's face loomed. It was handsome (of course) and ghoulish under the overhead light; razor nicks decorated the chin.

111

His sternness had darkened the mood. I realised I wasn't laughing any more. Barbra's chortles had died away into silence.

'How do you do?' I said.

'I had one hell of a task getting hold of you,' he said, spitting the words. 'You weren't answering your phone. Your office didn't know where to locate you. Finally I went round to your place. The peculiar boy in the apartment opposite knew where you were, somehow.'

'Ah, yes,' I said. 'He *is* peculiar, isn't he? It's a long story . . .'

I was in the club to avoid Arnie's attentions as much as for any other reason. He'd been pestering me for weeks with questions about quantum mechanics and special relativity; knocking on my door at very queer hours.

'Come with me,' said Frank.

'Perhaps you'd care for a coffee?' I said, maintaining the social decencies.

Of course he was perfectly entitled to visit the club should he so wish, but why was he seeking me here, and addressing me so peremptorily? One had supposed one had an understanding, a gentleman's agreement, that our relationship was easygoing, informal, and one would not inflict any serious personal problem on the other. What on earth was the fellow up to?

'Come outside, Em. Now.'

'Or an English muffin, possibly? They're a lot tastier than one thinks.'

I smiled nervously at the space where Barbra had been. She had gone to return the plates to the kitchen.

Frank squeezed my nape, and tugged upwards as if to lift me onehanded.

I rose and followed him through the translucent door, and down the winding fire-escape.

A grey afternoon. Snowdrifts by the walls and in the gutters. An old roomy Buick was parked at the kerb; a brace of young women – evidently the type Frank specialises in – were leaning against the car.

'Hi, guys!' said Frank, waving at them. 'This is Emma. And Em, meet a couple of my' – switching into a pompous British military accent – 'dear old comrades from the Red Cabb' – jumping temporarily into French? Spanish? ' – *age* ooh la la olé Café, Doris and Midge.'

Doris, the black one in the lilac wedding dress, pressed her hands over her mouth and nose and sniggered. Midge, the giantess with the ivory neckrings, looked at her feet.

'F-f-francis,' I said. 'Now, look here. Have you really come all the way out here just to interrupt my actually most interesting and informative conversation with Barbra and several other clubbies merely to introduce me to two of your . . . two persons?'

'No.'

'Well, then?'

Frank looked from Doris to Midge to me, in the attitude adopted by Paris deciding which goddess to give his golden apple to. (One always identified with Athene oneself, who sprang full-grown from her Daddy's head – the brainy one who did not get the apple, nor did she want it, thank you very little.)

'See, Em, I just made the most amazing discovery, and I want you to be the first to know about it.'

He opened the car door, in what might arguably be interpreted as self-mocking male chauvinst style, and ushered me in. He shut the door behind me. He walked round and sat himself down in the driving seat.

'We won't be disturbed here.'

I looked about nervily. Doris was peering in the wing mirror to adjust her false eyelashes. Midge was clicking her luminous orange fingernails against the windscreen. It was quite late already, so some vehicles had already switched on their headlights; glares slid past us.

'Y'know,' said Frank, 'all those guys at the club, all saying Allgrobsch was mistaken, they've got it wrong.'

'You were listening to them?'

'Sure. I was in there a while. Longer than you . . . Thing is: I checked the exact dates. His family emigrated to Warsaw when he was only a kid of three. He can't be remembering anything from his childhood: he made it all up, surely.'

'That's exactly what I told you.'

'Did you? Ah.'

'Yes. The last time we discussed this matter, you said quite the opposite.'

'Not so . . . The core of the biography is, as it were, the process of depersonalisation under the pressure of external factors, the progressive fictionalisation/defictionalisation deconstruction situation.'

'Last time you said he was directly adapting his autobiography into fiction.'

113

'Yeah, well, that just goes to show, like Saussure said, the fundamental wobble of the signified . . .'

'In other words, you're alleging that fictionalised fact and fictionalised imagination are the same?'

'Yeah . . .'

'Then, if it makes no difference whether any fact actually occurred in his life, why bother writing his biography? Why not just do a critical study of his fiction?'

'Em!' He banged the horn angrily. 'I've come all the way out here specially to do you a favour, right? So shut your mouth and let me get a word in.'

I bit my thumbnail apologetically.

Midge's bottom, covered in some stripy deckchair material, was thumping rhythmically against the window on my side. Doris was concentrating on her lip gloss.

'Thing is, Em, I just found a document, in private archives in Florida.' He sucked in his breath. 'It's a greetings card, from Allgrobsch to his former publisher, a Ms – ah, mustn't say the name in case of libel – now retired, dated twenty-eighth February nineteen sixty. Reproduction of Holman Hunt's *The Scapegoat*, which maybe had some private significance and maybe didn't. Handwritten message: "Best of Luck with the New Book from myself and my wife. Signed: L.Z. Allgrobsch."'

He handed me the card. Also a pink folder containing a stapled transcript of the interview with her.

'*Wife?*'

Frank nodded. He tapped the padded driving wheel.

'You're sure you didn't misread it? It defintely was from his wife, not his poodle or his . . . ? Oops, sorry.' I do tend to get silly at moments of tension.

Frank stared hard at me.

'Gosh!'

'It explains a lot. Like for instance his Kite story of March nineteen sixty can be interpreted as a parable of the hidden wife. And of course the *coupure* of fifty-nine, when he switched to English . . . His use of the first person plural in his stories of that period is definitely significant.'

'How queer.'

'I guess there's something sneaky going on, Em. How come nobody mentions the wife? We're going to find out more about her.'

'*We?*'

'I can't question the guys in the club directly. You know what they're like. They clam up.'

'Indeed. Do I gather from your conversation that you want me to act as your – '

'Yup.'

'Your – '

'Yeah.'

'I don't think that's very nice.'

'C'mon, Em. Just for me.'

'In that case, certainly not.'

Bang in front of the car, Doris and Midge were playing each other at paper-stone-scissors: I could see at my eye level their right hands – one black and beringed, the other white and bony – forming and re-forming themselves into elegant temporary shapes.

'Think about it, Emma . . . See, you got no choice. Now I told you about his wife, you're going to go back in that club and you're going to keep thinking about her, and you're going to bring the subject up casually in conversation whether you want to or not, and you're going to get some response, and you're going to tell me what you hear because you're too well brought up to keep a secret, so you're going to be my stalking horse whether you want to or not.'

20

Interview with [NAME DELETED] (edited extract) Miami Beach, 4 February 1990

– Sit down, young man.

– The same to you, too.

– So you're the Frank, huh?

– So you came all this way to interview li'l ol' me. Have a macadamia cookie: I brought it with my own hands from the Seven Eleven.

– Oh.

– You already looked through my old papers? Found anything?

– Uh huh.

– And have a shot of this. You need something to get you through the long hot afternoon.

– Don't mind if *I* do?

– Who's your publisher?

– Uh huh. They're paying your expenses?

– How much is your advance?

– Okay, sure, I can respect that. You have to be confidential sometimes, not give away secrets. Confucius he say: let sleeping dogs lie . . . Now what do you want to interview me about?

– Allgrobsch, hhh. Let me tell you something about that man. You think, because he's famous and he won the Nobel and all that, we made a million on him? We did not. I published him – I was personally responsible for selecting him, dealing with him, the grief – from 1961 through 1972 – all the way through *In the Town of Sadness and other stories* . . . And suddenly he becomes famous. And what does he do? He signs a contract with some bigshot company for ten times what we're paying him. Judas! Them, they're not a publishing house! They're a conglomerate with interests in piggeries and ball-bearing factories. So tell me, how can we compete?

– No, I don't remember anything you can use. Well, I didn't know him personally, you understand. We never met: maybe three times in eleven years. He's not like some authors, you know, always phoning, always knocking on your door, always question question . . . I am telling *you*. Like

116

there was one Doctor Pogelwitz, an astronauts' diet-book, okay – so what kind of publicity does any reasonable human being expect? – and he actually phones me on my personal number . . .

– Another shot?

– Don't mind if *I* do?

– Am I glad I took early retirement!

– We had a little correspondence, sure.

– No, I didn't keep it.

– Sure I edited him, not editing, really . . . just, like, in the early collections, *Somewhere, Rain* and so on, he was using British spellings – 'colour' and 'honour', you know? – and we were taking them out, so he puts them in again, so we take them out again . . . Crazy! But then, after *Twins*, he used American spellings and it was okay.

– No, he wasn't picky. Confucius he say: you scratch mine and I scratch yours.

– No.

– No, we don't believe in showing the author the proofs. Confucius he say: what they don't know won't harm you.

– Another shot, don't mind if *I* do?

– If you give an inch, they take a mile: that's what Confucius he say.

– Like there was one self-help author, I'm not mentioning any names, Arthur 'Unbutton Your Psyche' Smith, so he insists on spelling 'seize' the wrong way: 'Eye before ee except after cee,' he is chanting at me over the phone. And you are asking me why I got the hell out the business? *That's* why I got the hell out . . .

– Did *who* have a *what*?

– Oh.

– How should I know? Wives, girlfriends, boyfriends . . . They're worse than the authors themselves. I mean, anybody who marries an author has to be crazy. No, I never heard . . .

– Well, if you tell me he wrote it on a card to me, then I guess he did. I'm busy. I don't have time to read correspondence from authors.

– Okay, sure. You're the expert.

– Uh huh.

– Money, hhh. Always a problem.

– Not so big a problem with Allgrobsch . . . Until he deserted us, the rat . . .

– Well, see, we gave him our usual contract: zero royalty on the first ten thousand, rising to two point five per cent up to twenty thousand, then three per cent above that . . . and we keep the foreign rights and the movie rights and everything, of course . . .

117

– Uh huh.

– Sure.

– What do you think we are? A charity? A benevolent fund for indigent scribblers? And we offered him a three hundred dollar advance on *Skater* – that's worth a lot more in 1972 dollars than you think.

– Look, he didn't need the money.

– He was too.

– Yup.

– Sure.

– Sure I'm sure! He was a darned sight nearer a zillionaire than I'll ever be. All the time I dealt with him.

– What you mean, how do I know?

– I dealt with the IRS, right? A pain in the you-know-what. I knew his income tax situation.

– Of course I haven't kept any records.

– What am I? A computer?

– I don't know.

– I said, I don't know.

– Confucius he say: I don't know.

– It's your book: you write it.

– Gee, we seem to have finished the bottle . . . And nothing for you to nibble neither . . . Look, you give me twenty, no fifteen, okay ten bucks and I'll go down the Seven Eleven and buy some more cookies . . . please, young man? . . . Some yummy munchies . . .

21

Figure of Eight

We are flying kites on the hill above the town. We have made the kites ourselves, gluing sheets of newspaper on to wooden splints. If the rain or the snow or the hail falls, the paper will dissolve, and that will be that. We are children, of course – since only children are ignorant enough to think that sending a little thing into the sky counts as an achievement – except for two of us who are lovers, since lovers also aspire to folly.

The names of the lovers are Nalev the blue and Dirnda the old man's daughter. Nalev is named 'the blue' because once, when he was a baby, he spilled a bottle of blue ink on his head. The color faded years ago but the name has stuck. And Dirnda is known as 'the old man's daughter' because she is.

Today is a good day for flying kites. The wind is strong. It blows from one direction only: we know where we stand with it. If we face it and open our mouths, its cold force inflates our lungs. If we turn our back on it, it blows us along the same way it is going itself.

Today is the first day of the flying season. Before, it was too cold to run about for pleasure in the open: and then it was too rainy; and then too calm. But now everything is perfect. True, the ground is mulchy, it clings to our soles, and little ominous clouds potter about the sky – but we are too young or too much in love to worry about things beyond our control.

Pretend a man is hovering in the sky, at kite height, peering down at us. What would he see? He would see humans running across the hilltop in strange loops and figures of eight; if he traced the complete route of any individual, it would resemble the kind of shape scrawled by infants with pens in their fists . . . He would not regard us as wise.

Now interpret the action from our point of view. We are furling and unfurling the kite-string; in response to the invisible high gusts tugging at our kite, we have to dash about. Or so we suppose. The storyteller (who is living many years later, in an age when all those kite-fliers are scattered around the world, and are old and dying or dead) would like to draw a moral at this point: whatever seems randomly crazy is, if properly interpreted, sensible. But wouldn't it be just as effective and much less exhausting to squat in one place, on a tree stump or a rock, and manipulate the kite from there?

The kites are the shape known as 'kite-shaped'. They always are and they always have been. Nobody knows why.

What we see when we gaze around us are running people, and a few trees, and rocks and grass, and sky . . . The wind drums on our eyeballs, blurring everything. Everything is slashed by the diagonal lines of the kite-strings. And below us are the chimneys of the town; some of them puff codes of black smoke. And below that is farmland. And right at the bottom is the river, as thin and curvy as a kite-tail.

Can we read the black and white of the newsprint on the kites? No, it has merged to gray.

The children and the lovers are talking breathlessly about must-see places: Paris and Timbuctoo, New York and the moon. If only we could travel there . . . Or Everest, too. Yes, Everest! It is the highest place of all – everybody knows that – so if we stood on the summit of Everest we would see the whole world below us, and we could fly our kit with impunity since there would be nothing higher that the string could snag on.

The little gray clouds swirl, and the children too, and their sweet nagging voices . . . An older child tells a younger child: 'Every cloud is the shape of a country. Look. Every country has its cloud. There you can see Poland. And there is the United States. There is New Zealand. There, Peru . . .'

The wind stops. The kites begin to fall.

One kite in particular – a broad one bearing a headline in heavy lettering – drifts dangerously near a branch of an elm . . . But suddenly the breeze picks up and the kite is lifted.

A cloud is jostled. Part of it narrows. Part of it broadens. A section of it is pinched off.

That kite rises even higher – higher than a kite is supposed to go – further than the length of its string. So we can deduce that its string snagged and snapped on the long, finger-shaped bough of the elm. Everybody watched the kite soar . . . nearer to the clouds. Eventually it is so lofty it becomes invisible.

Watch the children from on high: see them with their mouths wide open and their eyes narrow . . . Then you can no longer see them at all.

And what about the lovers? The storyteller wanted to commemorate

120

them. He went to the trouble of stating their names and a little tender fact about each. But now the story is almost ended and still they have achieved nothing.

The storyteller (he is a little boy, now, back in that windscape) shuts his eyes and makes a wish. What it was must never be told, or else it will not come true.

22

It's not as if it were *his* wife. Nevertheless, Frank had set off again around the globe, searching for clues as to her whereabouts. He'd send me picture postcards inscribed with melodramatic messages – foolish and risible – devised with his characteristic touch of the Lord Peter Wimseys.

From Boston: *Chilhood acquaintance of Allgrobsch denies any knowledge of her!*

From London: *Her initial on a Dutch pawn ticket! She begins with W!*

From Amsterdam: *Allgrobsch's Dutch publisher remembers her. She was wearing a black dress, he thinks!*

From Sydney: *Have found her laundry bill! 3 blouses, 1 skirt & 5 socks! Yes 5!*

From Hackensack: *Carved on a park maple: LZ loves WW. Could this be significant?*

And my answering-machine tape became coated with shy rambling messages overlaid with long-distance hiss. (He never managed to telephone when I was in.) 'Ah, hallo, Emma, this is . . . Oh I just spoke over the bleep, I think. Well, again, it's me, Frank, here . . . Just want to say . . . [*incoherent mumble*].'

It seemed that I was standing in the centre of the world, in this New York, while he whirled around me, buoyed by his own centrifugal force.

His absence was very nearly as disturbing as his presence.

Which reminds me of what might – by a fair stretch of the imagination – be termed our first 'date'. It was during Lent Term of 1987, at the Founder's Day Organ Concert in the college chapel. The evening had – the way most meetings do – a symmetrical shape. It began with a slow percolation of black-gowned dons (Frank and oneself somewhere in the middle) in through the low chancel door (the great entrance to the nave having been sealed, on the bursar's insistence, to reduce heating bills) while the organ grumbled and trilled its welcome. We inched our way forwards, past the undergraduates who were sticking wads of used chewing-gum on the underside of pews, passing notes, playing strip poker, writing last-minute essays, chatting to their stockbroker by means of a portable telephone, lending earplugs, and so forth. Frank avoided my gaze; he kept wince-smiling at any undergraduate who might reasonably be expected to have a crush on him and hailing any don whose face he thought he recognised. We reached our allotted places at the front.

Frank still didn't talk to me. Nor did he seize the opportunity to massage my kneecap or recite scraps of Catullus at me – as I'd been afraid he might. Instead he passed the time smarming up to various eminences, telling them how much he'd always admired their work in his own humble way . . .

This discourse was interrupted by the usual mumble from the Master (he's an ex-mathematician – used to be a top-notch algebraist until his brain crumbled) about how glad one was to see so many blah blah on this notable blah. Then the organ roared. Our organ scholar at the time (long-haired fellow in a torn black leather jacket – Tim something – Old Etonian, of course; whenever one dropped into the chapel between services he was always belting out 'heavy metal') was dutifully extruding the melancholy repetitive stuff with faint variations which is called for on such occasions. (In one's opinion, admiration for this kind of music is simply a sublimated desire for mathematics: no wonder its supporters are invariably arty types who have missed out on a proper education.) Frank closed his eyes, fixed an expression of profound yet not unquestioning appreciation on his face, and quite possibly enjoyed the first half of the programme.

At last the interval! This is always the high point of any concert – when boyfriends get girlfriends tipsy, undergraduates adjust their Walkmans, academic wives swap recipes for watercress soup, and ambitious types make useful contacts. I turned to make some polite remark to Frank to the effect that the music was no doubt jolly likeable if one liked that sort of thing – but he was busy replying, 'Yes, certainly,' to the Master.

To his credit, he's quite open about it (as he explained to me some weeks subsequently). 'We call it networking,' he said. I asked him if such obvious flattery was actually effective. He said, 'Ah, sure. They

dislike me at first because they reckon I'm a pushy, greasy half-caste
. . . but they change their minds. See, if you're old and dried up, you
can't help wanting to be admired by a youthful, sexy guy.'

More gloom and boom on the organ. More chatter from the Master.
More generalised disruption from the undergraduates – busy swapping
matchboxes or giving one another tattoos, or whatever they do.

Everybody exited. Dons were dispersing towards organic chemistry
labs and pub snuggeries. Now if ever was surely the time for Frank to
make his move.

'That was very . . . er,' I said noncommittally.

'Uh, it was . . . yeah,' he replied. He marched off fast over the lawn
to grab old Podger (an eminent if gaga classicist)'s equally senile chum
in animated conversation.

I was bewildered. I pulled my gown about myself. I couldn't make
head or tail of Frank's behaviour. Was he a Napoleon of seduction,
deliberately playing hard to get? Had he had no interest in me in the
first place, and had merely been using my invitation to the concert as
an opportunity to get in with more powerful dons? Was he – hard
though this might be to grant – in some respect genuinely shy? I gazed
across the court at his back, inexpressively gowned, almost
camouflaged amidst the dim shrubbery.

I returned to my rooms and slogged away at my mathematics (to be
precise: a tricky contour integration on the complex XYZ-plane).

Which was what I was doing (among much else) in the weeks while
Frank was away. I was classifying the scopes on an infinite simrel
network (using some of Ostrovsky's suggestions, actually). I was
beginning to see light. It looked as if I'd be able to establish that the
infinite number of strategies which achieve a 'best' situation are
infinitely more common than the infinite number which don't. Just a
few little lemmas to go . . .

In the evenings, when I was too tired to work, I used to wander
around the flat searching for signs of dear old Professor Absent. A
black hair revealed itself behind the stove. A yellow button turned up
under the mattress. Often the shower fluctuated from its steady state,
permitting itself flashes of extreme heat – that must have annoyed him,
I thought. On top of the bedroom wardrobe I stumbled on his
Scrabble set: it was still set up with words from his last game, such as
ZOON and JISM; somebody had established QUIXOTIC across two
triple-word scores. I put the game back, undisturbed. Junk letters

arrived in my mailbox, emblazoned with 'IMPORTANT' and 'URGENT' and 'PERSONAL' and 'YOU MAY HAVE ALREADY WON $50,000'. They were addressed to 'The Occupier', which seemed rather a cruel way of putting it.

And when I was too tired even to search for Absent, I'd turn off the lights and lie back on the living-room sofa. I'd test my wakefulness: for example by trying to solve Rubik's cube in my head – and realise that I couldn't just then. I'd wonder: is my brain when sleepy rather like normal people's when wide awake? Do they really go through life in a state of premanent drowse? Would that explain why they apparently act illogically, and tell pointless anecdotes, and repeat themselves, and speak so slowly, and go *Uh*, and can't make up their mind what on earth they really want?

I'd lie on my left side and pretend I was cuddled up with Otto Man. Then I'd roll over on to my right and have some girls' talk with Shay Zlong. I'd wriggle on my front, and rock from side to side, chatting or laughing with the two of them. And when I'd had enough of all that, and was sated and exhausted, I'd stretch out on my back, eyes open, and (while dramatic imaginary organ music moaned in the background) stare up at Professor Absent.

Hello, Absent would say, as he pushed his bifocals further down his nose and stuffed a little baccy in his pipe. *And how's my favourite Emma today?*

Oh, jolly good actually, I'd reply.

Still missing our boyfriend, are we? he'd continue.

Boyfriend, I'd reply with a start. *Oh, one certainly wouldn't call him that. Merely an acquaintance . . .*

Absent would casually puff a smoke ring.

Well, I'd concede. *One doesn't deny a certain attachment . . . but really that's ridiculous. After all, it's not as if either of us had made a definite commitment . . .*

Aha, he'd interject. *So all those liaisons at Cambridge –*

What liaisons? I'd interrupt. *To start with, it all happened years ago. And for another, we never did more than –*

Than what? A little dottle would fall on his shoes. His bifocals would slip off his nose.

Such prurient prying is really quite infra dig. I'd retort sharply. *And in any case . . .*

Yes? He'd catch the spectacles, and cradle them gently in both palms.

125

. . . And in any case, I'm a v-v-v . . .

He'd smile sympathatically but patronisingly.

Oh, honestly! You must have heard of us, at least. We're always cropping up in the Brothers Grimm. 'Once upon a time, long long ago, in a land far far away, in a splendid palace, dwelt a beautiful, wise, lonely virgin . . .'

126

23

Which reminds me . . . At the age of 6, having just read a certain novel by Jane Austen (in fact, the one named after oneself), I asked Mummy, in that insufferable way children do, 'What is love?'

'What, dear?' she said. She gave a rose tree a stern shake. 'Look, Emmy. There are definite aphid on my Reine d'Hollande. I shall have to give the whole thing a jolly good spray.'

'Love, Mummy. What is it?'

'Ah, yes, Emmy. Well, there's no need for one to worry about a silly little thing like that.'

'Why, Mummy?'

She clicked her secateurs for some seconds. 'Do you remember that time you went to stay with Aunt Matilda at the seaside?'

'Of course, Mummy. It was only four years, seven months, two weeks and one day ago.'

'You were homesick.'

'Yes, I was. I cried and I cried.'

'Well, dear. Love is rather like that.'

She peered into the crimson interior of a Dorothy Perkins and made *tch tch* noises.

Mummy,' I said. 'Have you ever been in love?'

She pursed her lips. 'Actually one has, yes.'

I was rather surprised – given that she and Daddy weren't exactly Romeo and Juliet.

'Oh, when he was young . . . was Daddy really handsome?'

'Oh, no, dear. Not with Daddy. Not exactly . . .'

Of course one was exaggerating, the way children do. I had only been mildly unhappy during my fortnight at Aunt Matilda's. In fact, I am fortunate never to have suffered the extremities of homesickness. One is resilient. To be sure, while residing in America one missed England . . . Cambridge . . . The New House . . . etcetera. But let's face it, there is nothing all that wonderful over there. One's gentle longing for a decent crumpet and a nice cold field with English sheep can hardly compare with the clubbies' attitude towards their lost homeland: their desperate, aching, ever unrequited desire.

I looked out across the room. First I peered down at the busily lunching clubbies – then I viewed the furthest limit: the hissing espresso machine; the barmaid reaching for a beer bottle; the green EXIT sign; the sepia oblongs which I knew to be framed old photographs; the doors to the lavatories, the kitchen, and the corridors leading to parts of the club where I had never ventured . . .

It was a certain noon in mid-February; St Valentine's Day, to be precise. That very morning I'd discovered in my mailbox a card depicting a procession of ants bearing red hearts with the motto. '*Here's kissses and hugs/ From your Love Bugs/ You know I'm ever true/ 'Cos I'm biting only you!!!*' Unsigned, of course. I noticed that the envelope was addressed by means of a word-processed stick-on label. Rather cheap, that. Well, no doubt Frank had a great many cards to dispatch. Also a single red rose turned up outside my apartment. Which was hardly Frank's style. No doubt it was intended for Professor Absent?

. . . and then I looked down at happy or sullen faces, wondering who had received what that day, or who hadn't. I was visiting the club because . . .

. . . why? Of course there was no question of my doing what Frank wanted: one simply wouldn't dream of asking casual questions about Allgrobsch's alleged wife, or even nudging the conversation in that general direction – not that that would be difficult to accomplish if one so wished: one could lead on to it from a chit-chat about Allgrobsch, or about Frank, or about wives, or women, or men . . .

. . . so there could be no reasonable objection to my being here, then, provided one didn't mention the above topics, and deliberately made a point of avoiding them, and indeed resolutely quashed them should they happen to turn up . . .

. . . which would of course be impossible . . .

. . . but I was here anyway. Perhaps the clubbies' homesickness had infected me a little: I too felt a desire to retreat within this building – this museumed fragment of a defunct Europe – although it could hardly have had less in common with my own background.

Only a few months ago the regulars here had seemed to me mere types, elderly eccentrics in queer clothes and accents and nostalgias (all except Barbra, who was far too vital ever to seem generic, and H.H., who was comprehensible because his behaviour fitted into a familiar academic context). It's shocking how difficult one finds it to think of strangers as other than simple cut-out figures – blame this on one's country and class. One was brought up to think there were only a few score families in the county one could invite to dinner, even at a pinch; as for the rest . . . well, the Chinese were busy looking after China, the middle classes were running banks, dental surgeries and things like that, and so on. Naturally there were a few exceptions to prove the rule: Mummy was really quite matey with Mrs Branston, an accountant's wife with a green thumb from the village; Daddy kept up with an Irishman he'd known in the navy . . . But now, at last, the clubbies were coming to life. Oh, it wasn't a sudden resurrection – not at all like that Stanley Spencer which the vicar at home has (in reproduction) on his drawing-room wall, where all the folk jump out of their graves and start hooting, 'Long time no see,' to their old chums. It was awfully gradual. For example, there was one fellow who always wore a black suit: I now had nicknamed him (in the private language one uses for chatting with oneself) 'Mr Black'; I knew his real name, his age (58), that he was a widower, drank bourbon, collected baseball cards, wrote lyric poetry, and had almost visited England in 1956 but had decided at the last minute, in view of the political situation, to take a Caribbean cruise instead. Similarly I was acquainted with Mr Black's buddy, Mr Brown (retired from the plumbing supply industry, sucks Lifesaver mints, amateur historian) and the white-haired occasional journalist whom I thought of as Mr Dozy – because he was; and Mr Richman (bald, tells dirty jokes, proud of his fake Rolex watch); and so forth. To be sure, they weren't a hundred per cent known to me yet, but I was on my way . . .

I greeted them by name as I walked through the room towards my usual table. They greeted me in their various manners – 'Hiya, Emma!' 'Howdie, Em!' 'Good afternoon.' 'What's up, Professor?' a slap on the back; a pinch on the arm . . .

I took my seat. Various familiar faces turned towards me and made comments on the weather, or politics, or how good I was allegedly looking, or cracked jokes. I replied to them *en masse* with a polite noncommittal smile.

Mummy always says that one should converse alternately with the person on one's right and the person on one's left. That's not the way it was working here. Dozens of dialogues were taking place, swirling around me and across me: I was at the midpoint of a vortex of speech. I tried to participate: nodding, pursing my lips, muttering at intervals, 'Oh quite . . . Yes . . . Simply shocking, isn't it? . . . Do you think so? . . . Yes, one does, rather . . .' Then I realised with a start that the conversations had drifted out of English: everybody except oneself was arguing earnestly in Clubbish. Of course, I could understand odd words here and there – such as 'coma,' and 'capitalism' and 'diagnosis' and 'Gorbachev' and 'St Kevin's' – like recognising scraps of melody in a musical conceit, or reading a mathematical monograph in Japanese. One felt rather out of it.

Barbra waved to me; in due course she came across with my regular Earl Grey, plus other assorted items, which might have been a bottle of brown sauce for Mr Brown, and a shaker of black pepper for Mr Black – or, there again, probably not.

She ruffled my hair, but I didn't really mind. Then she wiped her hands on her apron. (One wishes she had performed those acts the other way round.) She joined in the conversation, protesting forcefully about something.

A minute or two later, the conversation had somehow muddled back towards semi-English. (Don't they *know* what language they're speaking? How very peculiar.) Now I could understand whole half-sentences.

Mr Black: 'We'll all be sorry when – '
Mr Dozy: 'What a shame if – '
Mr Richman: ' – even if he's not Mister Nice Guy.'
Mr Brown: ' – could happen to me or – '
Barbra: ' – we'll miss the – '

Meanwhile a stray thought crossed my mind: all, or almost all, of the clubbies had, at some point in their lives, been in love. Grown-ups do, don't they? And what of Emma Smart? To be sure, one liked Daddy, and Mummy too, and one had had a crush on one's vicar at home and one's first-year tutor at Cambridge with the hairstyle, and I was still involved in my thing with Frank – a flirtation, surely, nothing more. But 'love' – that emotion people have in novels – something that could hurt worse than homesickness, that could wrench one's soul apart and disrupt one's career as a mathematician – would I ever experience it?

A voice was inserting itself into the general conversation. 'Oh, but surely at least one person loved him.' The voice was girlish and was speaking English and had an English accent and was (I recognised suddenly) mine.

Everybody looked at me. Faces angled towards me, then away. Questions were asked in hushed tones.

Barbra patted my hand. She whispered to me, 'Can you help carry the dirty dishes back to the kitchen?'

I nodded.

She lifted a trayload of soupy bowls and coffee-stained cups – an arrangement of approximate geometries and off-greys, like an urban street scene. I bore a single white porcelain salt cellar, holding it in both hands.

'Now you listen, Em,' she whispered when we were out of earshot of the others. 'What did you hear?'

'About what?'

'You know.'

'Ah, yes.' I could think of no polite way to white-lie. 'You mean, about Allgrobsch's w-w-w-w . . .'

'Yes, I do mean about his w-w-w-w.'

'Well, certainly,' I said, rather huffed. 'I do understand. One doesn't discuss certain matters. I would be the last person to pry, to attempt to discover further details of – '

'No.'

We were in the kitchen by then – that white space beyond the main room, through the exit doors, filled with the roar of rushing water and the rumble of machinery, bright synthetic light, steam and food smells. Barbra set her tray down on a steel workspace beside the dishwasher.

She smiled grimly at me; her eyes buried themselves under their lids. 'See, Emma. You're a mathematician, yes. So what you put on paper is everything you know. This is your job – '

'That's not exactly – ' I began.

'Me, I'm a translator, and let me tell you the whole big secret of translating is knowing what to leave out. Some things you just can't say. You don't let them out of the bag. You can't ask a person to lay herself bare.'

'No. Quite . . . I can see.' I twirled the salt cellar in my hands. I backed against the side of the dishwasher. 'D'you mean, his wife actually lives near here, in New York? She has visited this very club . . . sometimes . . . often?'

'What is this, Emma? An interrogation?'

I blushed. 'No, actually, if you'd rather one didn't discuss these – '

She tugged the salt cellar from my hands and crouched to insert it into the dishwasher. She arranged other plates and saucers and bowls alongside it in the rack. I took the salt cellar back. 'It's clean. It just needs refilling.' Meanwhile she murmured, 'This is confidential, yes? You won't go tell your Mister Big Inquisitive?'

'What?'

'Your Mister He-Man I'm-So-Clever Pooh Mature?'

'Oh *him*. No, no. Wouldn't dream of passing anything on.'

She shut the dishwasher door.

I fiddled with things aimlessly.

She said, 'Allgrobsch's ex is in the club.'

I looked diagonally down on Barbra's mass of grey-black hair – 'You mean, she's pregnant!? Oh, the *club*. What, she's here now? Where? Surely not?' as I dropped the salt cellar; which shattered into a thousand remarkably small irregular polygons.

She pressed a control and pulled a lever.

The dishwasher began banging against my bottom: soon it and oneself were rocking and whirring inwardly.

24

Bird's Eye Maple

In our country the cattle starve every winter until their bodies are a stack of bones so narrow it seems they can swallow themselves; but in the spring when the snow melts we feed them clots of stubble, a greenish waterweed shaped like a bladder, colorless revealed tubers, and buckets full of the pinkish fungi that push up from the roots of house beams, so at least some of the beasts will grow fat again, give us milk and get slaughtered.

Or maybe we misremember. We have become old and we had a saying: 'Old men and smiling policemen are not to be trusted.' But when we were infants we trusted the old. All the young men from our town went to work as pedlars, log-rollers, furriers, iron-workers, tea-tasters, morticians, clock-repairers, night watchmen, pressganged soldiers, bankers, prisoners . . . as far away as Poland or Latvia – and if we hadn't trusted the old, we would have had no one to trust.

How did we know it was spring? (You lean forward and ask that.) We would be huddled together in our one warm room – the children, the women, the few toothless old men together – forming a ring around the embers and the picture books and a tepid turnip pie . . . so what could we learn of the seasonal changes? (Listen . . .) Oh, now we live in a foreign country where nothing is to be heard of an April but the moan of endlessly circling traffic, a chattering television in the next apartment, and the occasional questions of curious visitors – but then we heard the spring. It came as a bang. A single sharp explosion like somebody hammering in a nail close by the forehead. Many tiny crackles afterward. Then some old man would lean forward, pouting his rough lips, and whisper, 'The ice is breaking on the river.' We would be warned solemnly never to state that fact in public – for if a policeman overheard we could be taken away never to be seen again: guilty of metaphor.

We were happy. Soon, we knew, the young men were going to return. They would ride home on the milk cart, their pockets jangling with silver,

133

and they would buy us potatoes, carrots, swedes, bread, salt meat . . . and everybody would join in the big communal feast. We might not be hungry again for almost seven months. And (now that you jog our memory) why, yes, we do remember one feast in particular.

We are aged 5 or 6. We are short enough to wander among the complicated wooden underpinnings — that forest of planks, girders, pegs — beneath the long trestle tables erected on the damp green hillside above the town. The feast will be served here. We have to dine in the open air, for how could any one building be large enough to hold everybody? The tables are arranged along three sides of a square like the stage-set in an old-fashioned theater, on the fourth is cold air, the clustered dark roofs still piebald with snow, the ice-crazed river, the farmlands beyond, and the misty horizon. Yet we are just tall enough, when we tiptoe forward, to peer over the battered pinewood table-top. Govya — that pale young woman: her red hair is so long she could sit on it — is teaching us children our duties. She has spread a broad length of stiff white paper — borrowed from one of her admirers, Vlob the tailor (it's the kind on which he pencils the outlines of coats: he pins it on the thick dark cloth, then sets to work with his shears) — she is instructing us to fold it into halves, quarters, eighths, sixteenths. A dozen children labor at her bidding. We pant: our breath whitens the air. We each have responsibility for one corner of the paper: we feel it bend in the crook of our fingers; we press forward with all our weight and the crease grows beneath our palm. Then she takes a small pair of curved scissors — lent by another of her admirers, Dav the barber — and carves deep into the many-layered paper. She cuts out a semicircle. She blows hard. A curlicue of paper floats free, unfolds itself, stretching like a kite-tail, and flies down the hillside. We run after it but nobody catches anything. We return and we bang eagerly on the echoing table, crying, 'Me, me!' She entrusts the scissors to each of us in turn: we hold our breath as we operate the subtle steel apparatus with two hands; we snick, we lacerate, snipping away ovals and diamonds and oblongs and stars. Fragments of waste paper flutter and vanish. Finally she murmurs, 'Be careful. It is delicate,' while she supervises our act of unfolding. Sides are pulled; creases are smoothed away. We hold the lower edge while she lifts the upper, raising her hands as high as she can; the paper expands into a huge pattern covering her upper body. How our random incisions have led to such a symmetrical design! The breeze swells the paper. Extracts from her body — a triangle of cheek, a segment of nose, a crescent of bright hair and white cloth — are visible through the holes. It is so beautiful that one child (which of us?) cries.

134

*Govya tacks the paper on to the table as a kind of drapery or decoration.
Then she takes out another sheet: the process continues.*

*We smell a rich aroma. Away on our right, near the path leading down
the hill, something tasty is simmering in a row of big black pots. Firewood
burns beneath the pots — crackling brambles and hissing dark branches.
Each family in the town has contributed what it can, according to its
means: the beggar's has donated a potato; the jeweler's has offered a vat of
preserved asparagus. Everything is turning into a wonderful stew. And
bobbing somewhere within the murk are concealed meatballs. Our town is
famous for its meatballs — not that they are particularly delicious, not that
they have any virtue not found in foreign ones, but they are ours. We are
proud of them. They consist mostly of breadcrumbs and assorted root
vegetables, plus whatever scraps of meat can be found: gristle, rind, salted
and cured mutton or beef, a jar of fat. There is this to be said in their
favor: they are cheap and they are filling; for although the inhabitants of
our town may be hungry all year long, on the evening of the feast let none
of us rise until our belly is crammed and we can eat not one crumb more.*

*The pots are in the charge of the young men. They have rolled up their
sleeves; the steam is clouding their white muscular arms and their beards.
They are gripping sticks cracked off old trees, which they push in a spiral
motion within the bubbling food. As they stir, they glance over at us and
especially at Govya. But only briefly. They are hungry, you see, and one
cannot love when one's mind is full of images of nutritious stew and chunky
meatballs. So they return to their work and their philosophical chatter.*

*Vlob the tailor says, 'I guess we do it because it's a tradition. All
traditions should be kept up, I think.'*

Dav the barber says, 'No. It's because we're hungry.'

*Portin the intellectual says, 'Really, it's a kind of primitive
communism.'*

Gam the pious mumbles incomprehensibly.

Vlob says, 'Me, I don't even like meatballs, much.'

Dav says, 'Oh yeah?'

*Portin says, 'Or arguably it's a fertility rite. I've got a big black book at
home listing analogous examples.'*

Gam rubs his stomach.

*Soon the feast has begun. Bowls of hot stew are laid along the tables. Faces
reflected in shiny convex spoons look fatter already. Everybody is seated.
Children are propped on piles of books so they can reach the food easily; we
might wobble atop an atlas, a Hans Christian Andersen, and a volume of*

romantic German poetry in translation. A short prayer has been said. A symphony of slurping and chewing and gulping. Metal chinks against earthenware. The young men keep coming round wheeling cauldrons: more stew, more meatballs: the feeding goes on. And all this while no one speaks or looks at a neighbor.

We have a small stomach and a big mouth so we finish quite soon. We climb down. We hide under the table. We are in an underworld inhabited by shoes – gentle unreliable beasts: usually they are as dozy as cows but sometimes they change forward without warning. The sharp black kind are predictable in their rhythmic furies: but beware the vagaries of the heavy brown things, encrusted with mud. We crawl with caution. The rear of our underworld is a screen of table-legs and human legs; the latter seem thick as tree trunks but are never altogether still. The ceiling is constructed out of planks hacked from old packing cases; we can read the stenciled signs: here was an American tractor; a load of Russian barley; a case of Czech beer. We inspect the soil: bits of dropped food; a pink earthworn appears and disappears. A chill wind hisses. We turn and touch the pierced paper drapery. We press our eye to a gap and gaze at the river: rough white shapes are drifting downstream.

We explore. We scramble across trestles and past ankles. Several legs are unbending, blocking the path. We clamber over or around the obstacles, always finding a way. Scraps of conversation tumble down. A veneer dealer is remarking on the rising demand for bird's eye maple. A pawnbroker is taking a professional interest in a baker's wife's silver pocket watch. Then we encounter a long off-white woollen skirt billowing like a curtain, and, on either side of it, masses of bright auburn hair – we know we are at Govya's feet.

She is saying nothing. But on her left, from the vicinity of the clean lace-ups and the thick gray socks (Vlob's), comes the remark, 'Nice weather, huh?' No response. The brogues on her right (Dav's) shuffle ominously. 'Quite chill for this time of year.' Vlob says, 'I could eat a horse.' Dav says, 'I could eat an elephant.' Silence. A ruddy knuckle becomes palpable through a star-shaped hole in the paper; nearby a red lock sways across a circular hole: Dav is touching Govya's hair! (It might seem unintentional but it isn't.) His fingerwork is so light she probably doesn't even notice. And Vlob's right hand is brushing against her hair too: a hundred gleamy filaments skate across his wrist. Dav: 'I could eat a thousand meatballs.' Vlob: 'I could eat a million.' 'Oh, is that so?' 'Yes.' 'You want to bet?' 'Sure. How much?' 'I bet I can eat more meatballs than you.' 'I said: how much?' 'You're all talk.' 'I said, how . . .' 'Anything.'

'*Anything?*' '*Anything.*' *Their hands reach out and shake each other across Govya's lap.* '*Anything your heart desires.*'

We stare at the clouds and the river. We rub our belly with one hand and pat our head with the other because some grown-up has told us it is impossible.

Several minutes pass. Speechlessness. Dav's toes are twitching urgently within his brogues. Vlob's knees wobble thoughtfully. Then a mumble. Dav: '*I'm up to seven.*' *Vlob:* '*I'm on my ninth, actually.*'

We toddle along the underworld past three pairs of legs. We hear Portin the intellectual explaining the theory of dueling to Gam the pious. '*See, people have got it all wrong. They think the idea is to kill or wound your enemy. But that's crazy. Really it's a kind of trial by ordeal. We want to find out a secret. Whoever wins the contest is the one God favors, so he must be telling the truth. History is written by the victors, they used to say, just because the victors' version is divinely endorsed. Which is why nobody duels any more. Who believes now that God is on the side of the big battalions?*'

'*I'll do eighteen yet,*' *Dav's voice booms down the table.* '*I'm nearing twenty-one,*' *says Vlob's voice.* '*Give me another from the pot.*'

We look round. Dav's legs are slumped forward; his brown shoes are swaying in a mad semaphore. Vlob's hand is snaking under the table, groping around his own waistline, undoing a crucial button; his belly, liberated, expands. We crawl closer. Groans from Dav. Vlob is uttering loud sighs.

And now the sun is setting: there is darkness behind the pierced paper. Gaps appear in the rear wall of the underworld: where have all those legs gone?

'*Twenty –* ' *(Dav).* '*Twenty-two –* ' *(Vlob).*

Dav's legs and bottom are thrashing about, rocking, writhing like an otter teased by vicious boys. His fist grabs a mass of red hair for good luck. Govya screams infinitely faintly. Vlob's right ankle is repeatedly kicking his left. His fist seizes a lock too.

'*Twenty-three.*' '*Twenty-three.*'

We never did find out who won the contest – for at that moment a big pink hand reached down, pincered its fingers, circled in the air a moment, and grabbed our neck. We were hauled away to our bedtime. But who else should turn up at a diner on the Upper West Side of Manhattan in 1952 than Portin the intellectual? He was almost bald by then and dying and eating cheesecake. He remarked that Govya had in fact married a haberdasher from another town, and – this was the last thing anyone had heard – she had had a son who was a student in Paris, another son who became a butcher, a third who went into the family business, and a little daughter with beautiful red hair.

§ III

Greater than Infinity

. . . and she could see nobody. So she lay down on the biggest bed, but it was too hard. Then she tried the smaller bed, but it was too soft. Finally she stretched out on the tiniest bed, and it was just right.

25

A tiny rabbit-squeak emerged from her throat. She pointed at her own cleavage and gasped, 'You don't mean . . .' Her eyes shrank to slits. She swayed forward over the tiled kitchen floor like a runner at the start of a race. A deeper sound pushed through her lips. Her blue apron flapped. Her whole body rippled like a sheet beneath which somebody is sleeping badly. For an instant I thought Barbra was doing an Allgrobsch – but that would be absurd. Apart from any other consideration, it would be a most unlikely coincidence for two people to have strokes in the same place at different times, just while one happened to be on the spot, and coincidences like that don't happen by chance.

Then – for another few seconds – I feared she might be choking. A poster explaining what to do in such cases was taped up beside the dishwasher. (Perhaps its presence focused one's mind on this possibility.) It was illustrated with numbered diagrams of a pair of intertwined androgynes. The first thing is to bang the victim between the shoulder blades. I did this gently to begin with, rapping with my knuckles as if on a door. Then I slapped harder with the flat of my hand. The effect of this action (thanks to the Law of Conservation of Momentum) was to push myself backwards across the floor, which was slippery with shattered salt cellar and traces of liberated salt, so I almost tripped. Barbra rose and spluttered.

The last resort is something called the Heimlich Manoeuvre. One stands behind the victim, hooping her/him with one's arms, then one clasps one's fists together and firmly pushes them up against the diaphragm. Just as I was nerving myself to do this, easing behind her, she coughed and rose and banged my head with her elbows. She struggled free.

'What the – ' she panted.

141

'Are you all right?'

'You – you – '

'I thought something had got stuck in your throat,' I said defensively.

'I was laughing . . .'

'An odd way to do that.'

'. . . at you.'

'Oh,' I added.

'You're as bad as my second husband. Always trying to cop a feel while I was washing the dishes. I divorced him on account of he had incompatibility.'

'One doesn't see anything to be amused at.'

'Hah, Emma.' She chucked my chin. '*I'm* not' – pausing dramatically and/or for breath – 'the' – pronouncing the definite article with a long vowel, as if addressing someone in an old-fashioned second person singular – 'Ex-Wife' – enunciating each syllable. '*I'm* not Elzee's anything! I wouldn't marry him if he gave me all the gold in Fort Knox. Him with his piggy face and his phony accent!'

During this oration I was crouching on the floor to hide my blushes and scoop fragmented salt cellar into a dustpan; I transferred it into a bin.

'But you said . . .' I said. 'So naturally one assumed that . . .'

'Me! Him?'

'Well, who, then? There aren't any other women in the club. Are there?' I changed the subject. 'Isn't laughter strange? It's a bit like sneezing, really. One may or may not want to do it, but once it starts, and one's whole body starts shaking, one just has to wait patiently for it to finish.'

'Ah. Let's go have a drink.'

I constructed a mental list of all the women I'd seen here. Certainly there were no regulars. Mr Black's wife came in occasionally, and some of Mr Richman's girlfriends too. I'd glimpsed other female faces on occasion, always attached to some male. This club (like those on Pall Mall) was fundamentally a masculine preserve. I wondered idly where the women of this community met: perhaps at each other's homes, or in cafés or restaurants or bingo halls or pizza parlours. I had no great wish to associate with them *en masse*: no doubt as a result of my upbringing, it has always seemed to me the natural state of things to be the sole woman amid a horde of men, the one who is glanced at, the focus of attention. Arguably this is unhealthy, and pre-post-feminist, and is symptomatic

142

of a deep-seated insecurity. That's what Frank (who likes to style himself a New Man) has alleged on occasion. Whenever he's just done something especially irritating, he'll point out by way of self-justification that as a mere male he is biologically determined to be unsympathetic, egotistical, lecherous and so on, hence it wasn't really his fault, in fact it's mine for not sticking to wholly female company.

While I was mulling over all this, Barbra had led me to the bar in the main room. We were perched on high aluminium stools. What with her head nodding as she ordered the drinks ('O.J. for my good friend, Emma! Vodkatini for me!') and her gaudy clothing, she resembled one of the more extroverted cagebirds: a parakeet or a cockatoo.

'Well, then,' I said. 'Who?'

'She's in here, now,' said Barbra. And, 'Ah, lovely,' as her drink arrived. She sipped it showily. She pecked at the gratis salted peanuts.

I looked all around the club, at the chatting and dozing figures, at the wisps of tobacco smoke, at the luminous far windows. Everything seemed terribly far away, as if gazing across a moor . . . 'Well, I can't see her. Not unless she's hiding under the table, or dressed up with a false moustache and so forth.'

Some fuss followed. Barbra asked for – and received – extra vodka to stiffen her cocktail. Meanwhile I inspected the scene behind the bar. That monstrous shiny machine which produces such tiny cups of espresso, each the size of an elephant's eye. A pagoda of stacked saucers. The taps roosting over the sink. The array of giant-size liquor bottled racked upside-down for easy access: some of them had their labels inverted too, to make it easier to identify the contents; on others the labels were stuck the normal way: either alternative seemed wrong.

Barbra sorted out her vodka problem and my orange juice turned up at last.

'No, let me pay,' I said, sliding some green notes across the aluminium counter, and receiving change. 'She's definitely not here,' I said. 'I've looked everywhere. I'm beginning to suspect you're making her up and Allgrobsch was really an incorrigible bachelor.'

Barbra flapped her sleeves with amusement or frustration. 'I can see her with my own eyes. In fact, she can hear every word you're saying.'

'Well,' I said, 'well, I like a joke as much as anyone, Barbra, but one must know when to stop.' I banged for emphasis on the counter, which underwent resonant vibration, so having the effect of knocking over my own glass. 'The Invisible Woman does not exist' – spilling juice on the barmaid – 'er. Oops.'

'Hello,' she said, holding out a hand dripping with the sweet coloured fluid, 'I'm Wanda.'

She shook my hand formally. I felt a chill, moist stickiness pass from her palm to mine. Then she wiped us both (making a special effort regarding the fingernails) and the counter too, with a damp cloth, and one felt rather more comfortable.

Neither of us could manage to come up with any further conversation. It would be understandable if she were miffed. And it would hardly have been tactful of me to point out that it was all Barbra's fault really for giving the misleading impression that the Ex-Wife was a normal person.

So Barbra plugged the silence, chattering away, supplying exhaustive permutations of all the lines that Wanda and I might have said had we had more *savoir faire*. 'We were just speaking about you, Wanda, yes, Emma? Wanda is so much looking forward to knowing you, Emma, yes, Wanda? And Emma has heard so much about you, Wanda, Emma, yes? And I'm sure the both of you must have a lot to say to each other, yes, Wanda, Emma; yes, Emma, Wanda; Emma, Wanda, yes?'

Of course at the time I didn't even know her Christian name properly (I got her to spell it out for me later), because it's pronounced in a funny slurred way: something between Wander and Wonder and Fonder and Funder. Just so, in appearance too she was indeterminate: both pretty and plain. She had long, centre-parted black hair with a slight natural wave (if only my hair were like that; I simply can't do anything with mine), and a very white complexion (the kind that's called 'interestingly pale'); green eyes. She was thin. Her bosom was only a little bigger than one's own and not as shapely. She seemed quite tall (an illusion created by her slenderness and her hair) but actually was about my height. She was dressed all in black, for reasons of formality, style, morbidity, period detail, setting off her complexion, or any combination of the above. I estimated her age at somewhere in the mid- to late 30s – which was (doing a quick bout of mental arithmetic) at least a decade younger than she must surely have been.

She set a cardboard sign on the counter stating in English and Clubbish: 'BACK IN FIVE MINUTES'.

In dreams one is always passing through previously overlooked doors in familiar settings, and discovering that a wondrous faery exists just behind the skirting board or a menagerie above the rafters . . . So the three of us walked beneath the luminous green EXIT sign, where I had never journeyed before, between the fire-doors, along a long corridor variegated with oddities – a tropical aquarium, an open door through which I could see two men playing pingpong, a poster in a foreign language – up a flight of concrete stairs, and another similar flight, beyond a chipboard door, and found ourselves in . . .

. . . a cosy little room at the front of the building with a broad picture window. Sunshine was flooding in. A sensation of being on high, as if standing on the battlements of a castle, the bridge of a ship, or an elephant's howdah. Far beneath us, New York rocked gently. It was spring! (It shouldn't have been, this early in the year, but it was!) A precocious flowering cherry was doing just that. Cars shone. Beggars were emerging from their alleys, their heads were merry in colourful woollen hats. Stores were advertising 'SPRING-CLEANING SPECIALS' and 'MASSIVE REDUCTIONS ON WINTER GOODS'. Pairs of children were swinging each other in circles until they both got giddy and fell over.

Which made me dizzy myself. I sat down at one end of a purple settee. Barbra plumped down at the other, so ensuring that Wanda had to fit in between us. All women together! Hmm. Not that one has anything against socialising with one's own sex (I've been out to the Hungarian Pastry Shop several times with Fanny and Bridget; and Häagen-Dasz too: my favourite is choc 'n cherry with a hot fudge topping and crushed nuts), and in many ways it's more relaxing than mixing with men – one doesn't have to worry about being asked if one knows what Freud said about something or about actually getting tweaked – but on the other hand, less so. Men aren't very perceptive: it often seems they register the outline of one's body and nothing else. Whereas women subject each other to a thoroughgoing inspection – as Wanda and I were doing. I was examining the lines on her neck, the electrolysis (?) marks on her upper lip, the patches of beige blemish concealer beneath her eyes; she was presumably doing something equally impertinent to me.

'I'm sorry,' I said. 'I mean, about the . . .'

'That's all right,' she said. 'It happens.'

Her voice was quiet and high, perhaps a little nervous. (Shy people sometimes find my manner threatening – absurd as that may be. I mean: can't they tell I'm shy myself, not very deep down?) I noted that – unlike most of the other clubbies – she had only the faintest accent. And then I reflected on that thought: of course she really had a very strong accent – namely, an American one – but I'd come to not even notice this unless I deliberately focused on it. Queer, this: I realised I was becoming Americanised!

While I'd been thinking about oneself, she'd been asking me something in her soft voice. 'What?' I said.

'No, no,' she murmured. 'It's nothing.'

'Oh, yes,' I said. 'Please. I am happy to answer all your questions.'

'No, really. Never mind. It was . . .'

'Now, go on. Ask me it again. I'm sure it was a frightfully sensible enquiry.'

'I said . . . mm . . . it's nice weather?'

I replied, 'Yes.'

A silence ensued.

'Yes, it is,' I continued. 'Horribly nice weather.'

'The sun . . .' she whispered.

'Yes, the sun. Definitely . . . And the sky, too.'

'The . . . The . . . The clouds.'

A longer silence. It was all rather like a Pinter play. I folded my hands on my lap. I could see Barbra was crossing and uncrossing her legs frantically, eager to interject some brash comment to get the party swinging, yet not wanting to overshadow Wanda.

'Three women were seated in a room just like this one,' I remarked to them both. 'And all three of the women had smuts on their noses, which was very funny! So they all started laughing at each other. Suddenly, one of the women took out her hankie and wiped the smut off her face. How did she know it was there?'

Wanda thought for a while. 'Who were the women?'

'It's just a story . . .'

'Why were they dirty?'

'Ah, well, it was presumably from the locomotive . . . In the original form of this anecdote, you see, it takes place in a train compartment. I just thought it might be nicer to move it here . . . And it's an old story, it certainly goes back before the war, so they probably still had steam trains when it was invented.'

Barbra asked, 'Was there a mirror in the room?'

'Oh no . . . Do you both give up? Well, let me tell you the answer. Call the three women X, Y, Z. So X knows Y and Z are both smutty, and both laughing. X argues as follows: "Suppose for the sake of argument I am not smutty. Then Y is laughing at someone; and Z must be able to deduce that Y must be laughing at her, so Z would wipe off her own smut. But Z has not done so. Ergo – by *reductio ad absurdum* – I am smutty." So she wipes away. QED.'

They were looking at me in a rather concerned manner. Which was odd: that little puzzle-tale had always gone down a treat at Cambridge.

Barbra asked, 'What's the moral of the story?'

'Oh . . . I don't think it has one.'

Silence took over again.

'Do you come here often?' I asked, intending a joke so subtly ironic that even I didn't get it.

'Yes. I work at the bar most days . . . Do you?'

'Do I *what*?'

'Uh . . . nothing.'

I clenched my fists. It was now or never. 'I gather you were . . . married to L.Z. Allgrobsch?'

She smiled – at first nervously and then less so. I could see her face visibly relaxing. Presumably it had been the tension of waiting for me to bring up this topic which had rendered her so tongue-tied. 'Sure.'

'Oh, that's good.'

'Maybe.'

'I suppose you must be feeling rather, well, perturbed, in the light of present circumstances?'

'On account of he's dying, you mean? Well, sometimes I am and sometimes I'm not. See, we split more years ago than I care to remember, so . . . Sure, I know I *ought* to feel sore or sad or angry or guilty, but I went through losing him a bunch of times already. My analyst says – '

'How interesting,' I interrupted. It really was a bit thick, that she should switch from gulping timidity to garrulousness. I'm always rather put out by people (Americans, especially) who reveal their whole life story at first acquaintance. I'm sorry, but one was brought up to consider a decent reticence as a mark of a proper upbringing.

'How did you meet him in the first place?' I asked.

She looked embarrassed again.

'Ah, my father, who was in the white goods supply business . . . And my ex, well . . . It's a long story.'

I imagined Wanda and Allgrobsch as they must have been back in 1959: he resembling his picture on the old book jackets, gazing determinedly and puffing a pipe; and she much as at present, only sprightlier. A handsome couple. Ill-matched as to intelligence, of course. Well, it's obvious from his stories that Allgrobsch had his wits about him, whereas Wanda's conversation wasn't exactly bursing with sparkling insight, and surely one would have to be quite dull to have achieved no greater status than a barmaid by her age. Of course many clever men are attracted to stupid women. Good job, too, on balance: otherwise the entire male population would be flocking around oneself . . . I tried to envision their daily married life.

'I suppose the incessant pipe-smoke must have got you down,' I remarked.

'What?'

Daddy used to be a pipe-smoker, once upon a time, in those mysterious days before I existed. A naval habit. There are old photos of him in his uniform, biting the stem of a cherrywood; he looked rather dashing. But he gave it up not long before I was born. Nevertheless one is always unearthing items of smoking paraphernalia around The New House: an assortment of pipes, tins of Balkan mixture, packets of pipe-cleaners, things for squidging and widgeting tobacco . . . His naval beard still smells of smoke.

And while I'd been thinking about Daddy, Wanda had been talking about her marriage.

' . . . we were only together for so short a time. I was too young, you understand, it was nobody's fault. These things happen . . . You've got to imagine him like he was then: his intelligence, his sensuousness, his creativity . . . We were *so-o* happy together. He wasn't real famous then, but I mean, when a man's a genius you can just see it all over him, can't you?'

'Can one?'

'His genuine *charisma*.'

'So it was . . . romantic love?'

She muttered something in Clubbish to Barbra.

I'm very curious about love. I mean – by way of comparison – that although one is a virgin, one knows all about the physiological side and is perfectly capable of imagining it; after all, it's detailed in countless novels, manuals, paintings, and so on, and evidently it does take place in a million bedrooms every night. But when it comes to love all testimony is flawed: granted, many writers describe it, fictionally and even autobiographically, but perhaps they are following the conventions rather than telling the truth. Indeed, if one were to stumble into love oneself, how would one know that's what it was?

'What?' I said.

'Love makes the world go round.'

148

'Ah,' I said. 'I wish – '

'He was the love of my life and I want the world to know!'

The world was busily existing on the far side of the picture window. I saw shoppers shopping, toddlers toddling, old men hauling themselves along, jogging policemen, shouting bus drivers, panting cyclists on their glittery machines . . . Presumably the world *would* know about Allgrobsch's one great passion quite soon, once Frank had got around to publicising it. Well, why not? Love is private but it's public too; though it's the ultimately personal emotion, it's something we all can aspire to.

26

Frank returned to New York, at last. I checked the messages on my answering machine one evening in early February, and there it was – the familiar drawling mumble. Evidently he'd started talking before the beep, given that all I heard was: '. . . *and that's okay also. So I'll come round to your place then. See you! Ciao!*' Naturally I responded by choosing a time for my return call (eleven on a Saturday night) when I could be sure he'd be out, so my message would go on *his* answering machine: 'Hallo, Frank. Change of plan. Meet you at six on Monday at the club. Bye.'

Why there and then? Why not? On a certain notorious occasion at Cambridge, Frank had explained to me at length the importance of dramatic irony, as favoured by Shakespeare, Frank and other luminaries. Apparently this had justified his squiring some blowsy Girton undergraduate to the selfsame May Ball he had promised to escort me to. It would do him good to have a taste of his own medicine.

'Yoo hoo!' I mouthed, waving across the club room. I felt a touch irresponsible: I was already halfway through a Brooklyn Bijou (a cocktail consisting largely of white plonk and fizzy water, which Wanda specialises in) and was ever so minutely tiddly; besides, I was mounted on the bar stool like an infant on a high chair. Not far behind me, Wanda was busily washing up things and stashing them where they're supposed to go. At the other end of the room, the pebble-glass door was swinging open . . . Enter Frank, strutting over the faded carpet, winding between the tables, bestowing his greetings on anybody he thought deserved the benefit of them. He was sporting expensive jeans and a striped Italian jacket ostentatiously frayed at the lapel: the weary gigolo look. And of course he'd come back with a fresh layering of tan (he's the only human being who can acquire a healthy glow in London in February). He waved back at me. I beckoned to him: he beckoned to me. I pointed at the bar stool adjacent to mine: he pointed at a table in the body of the club room. Our movements were matched, like those of fellow exercisees in an aerobics class. I'd read once (in a women's magazine at the hairdresser's) an article entitled 'HOW TO CATCH YOUR MATE'; the approved technique consists of 'mirroring' his body-language. Doubtless Frank would know all about that kind of thing. Then he gave me that peculiar American gesture which looks like patting a child's head; it means: wait a moment. So I turned to order another slice of orange for my cocktail – and just then he bounced on to the stool beside me, yelling, 'I'll have a gin and French with hey, lovely to see ya my Em, no make that a straight double scotch, did anybody ever tell you you're looking great?'

'How do you do, Frank?'

'Yeah! You are *right*. I *do*.'

'One seems in a high-spirited mood.'

'Wait till you hear! You'll never guess! I'll give you three guesses.'

'Actually, Francis, I myself happen to have just discovered certain information which might be – '

'Huh, Em. Wait for it, wait for it . . . Ama-incredibly-zing! I found the wife! Yessir! I exposed her . . . Sure, you can keep the change . . . Cheers! . . . I'm on her track right now, sniffing her out . . .'

He did his bloodhound imitation, snuffling along the metal counter, pushing his nose almost as far as my fingertips. I giggled a little and withdrew my hand just in time.

'It was no sweat,' he explained. 'A guy in Amsterdam knew a guy in Glasgow knew a guy in Cleveland who . . . Ta da!'

He withdrew a small manilla envelope from an inner pocket, and spread the contents on the counter. Photographs, in black and white.

A wedding, evidently.

He wiped the counter with his sleeve and began distributing the images across its blurrily reflective surface. A close-up of a younger version of Allgrobsch's face. Allgrobsch full-length, in a morning suit. Allgrobsch half-length. Allgrobsch head-and-shoulders. Allgrobsch in profile. Allgrobsch in front of a brick arch, beside a woman in a complete bridal outfit; the veil obscured her features. The same scene from closer up: the bride's face – scared, as they always are – visible through the ruffled translucency. Evidently this was Wanda: she had scarcely changed at all. More images joined these: they overlapped, elided, swirled and swarmed over each other.

Frank ordered another scotch for himself. He asked me if I wanted anything from the bar.

'No, I'm happy,' I answered, nibbling the mint leaf in my drink.

'I'm happy you're happy,' he said, quite possibly basing his philosophy on a bumper sticker.

'Do you know her name?' I asked, pointing at a close-up of Wanda. Wanda herself was taking an interest in the proceedings: she was leaning over the bar, looking down at representations of herself as she had been. By contrast to the photographs – their hazy monochrome – her real face seemed enormously colourful and filled with detail (the fine lines on her forehead; the individuality of each eyelash . . .) Her expression was indecipherable.

'Uh,' Frank replied. 'Not yet, no. But I can hack it! I'll just ask, the y'know, people. Somebody in this club or somewhere is sure to recognise the face.'

'Yes,' I said.

He paid Wanda. He took the toothpick from my drink, held it between his index and middle finger, and mimed smoking it, ultra-debonair. I tittered at this gag more than one would have under less tense circumstances.

'Have you seen this bride around?' I hinted. 'Possibly in this very club?'

He shook his head.

'Surely she wouldn't be,' I added, dropping a big fat clue, 'debarred?'

'Uh-uh.'

'And the face is distinctive, too. The long jet black hair, the pale complexion . . .'

'You can't know that, Emma. Everything's in black and white. For all we can tell, she could have yellow skin and . . . dark green hair.'

'Granted – but unlikely.'

'Besides, everybody looked like that in nineteen fifty-nine. It's the period style, the, y'know, French beatnik look . . . You're too young to remember, Em.'

'So are you.' Frank has this annoying habit of pretending to belong to any generation which takes his passing fancy.

He ignored my comment, of course. Instead he fidgeted with the photos while making some pretentious remark about how the first person plural in Allgrobsch's post-1959 stories could be interpreted as representing the fundamental diploidity of the married state and/

152

or the dialectical instability of the superego, or, there again, possibly not.

Idly, he flicked the corner of one picture: it showed the couple at a slant, more her than him. It was one of those peculiar shots one gets when clicking a camera: his neck was hunched like a tortoise's; her open mouth made her look daft or singing and her left eye was almost shut. One wondered why this memorabilium had been saved.

'She's crying,' he said.

Now that I looked more closely, he was right. A highlit gleam on her left under-eye.

'People do at weddings,' I said – though I couldn't recall a single instance of that occurring at any I'd been invited to; perhaps the phenomenon is more common among foreigners and the lower classes. 'Or so one gathers.'

'A piece of confetti just fell in her eye,' said a very faint voice – Wanda's.

In fact her voice was so quiet that Frank seemed to have interpreted it as the prompting of his own subconscious – for he too said, 'Maybe a piece of confetti just fell in her eye.'

Wanda leaned over the shiny counter: a hazy reflection of her upside-down face swam in the interstices between the scattered photographs. Her long thin fingers rotated that particular picture round to face her.

She repeated, rather more clearly, 'A piece of confetti just fell in her eye.'

'Yeah, a piece of confetti just fell in her eye,' he said.

One had the impression that the two of them were trapped in a time loop – doomed to recite this one phrase *ad infinitum* . . . But then Frank broke the pattern.

'How can you know that?' he said, looking up at her for the first time.

Wanda's fingers were clenched on the edge of the picture. Her head was bowed. A single tear was sliding down her left cheek.

It was one of those moments that seem terribly potent even at the time – like the last paragraph of Allgrobsch's 'The Bubble Blowing Party', when the huge iridescent bubble descends on the eldest sister's nose, or that incident in the market square at Cambridge, of all places, when Frank got down on his knees and swore his undying love for one, and one told him not to be so silly . . . Which jolts back a memory of a more exact parallel: Mummy poring through the old morocco-bound

153

albums in the bookcase behind Shay Zlong in the drawing-room at home, and coming across one of Daddy aged 10, mounted on his black mare Lucifer, and one assumed the moistness in her eyes was a reaction to the pathos inherent in seeing Daddy before she knew him; and then one noticed Uncle Harry holding the reins, there in the shadow of the mare's head . . .

So the revelation scene took place as in some old silent film: wordless, melodramatic, with exaggerated gestures. Frank looked up and down several times, presumably comparing the live with the inanimate Wanda. His mouth opened. She brought him a refill of scotch, and he swallowed the medicinal liquor in one gulp. He pointed at her with his index finger extended. He mouthed a queston. She replied inaudibly. She caressed her own long locks very gently. Suddenly – like a caption trailed across the screen – she said, '*It was true love*.' (She actually said that.)

Frank put the photographs back in his inner pocket, and set his little Sony Cascorder on the counter. He arranged his features in an alert, interested Interviewer's Expression. He pressed the record button.

I'd never seen him actually at work on the biography before, so I was attentive. The procedure is as follows. He begins by reciting, 'Ten nine eight seven six five four three two one let us go then you and I when the evening is spread out against the sky.' He rewinds and plays the message back so he can listen to the sound of his own voice: an activity he rather enjoys. He rewinds again, and leans close to the machine to murmur into it intimately the date, the place, and the name of the interviewee. He smirks a bit, and asks the subject a nice easy question to get her in the mood. 'What is your name?' She looks frightened and mumbles something. He asks further, more searching questions, about where, when and how she first met Allgrobsch, the development of their romance, their marriage, their '. . . ah, marital difficulties', their 'how shall I put it, as it were, divorce', and – what he is most interested in – putative parallelisms between Allgrobsch's life and his fiction. Meanwhile she looks around nervously, answers some questions very quietly and others not at all. Every so often he has to fiddle with his machine, turning up the volume control or sliding the microphone closer to her.

Afterwards, he murmured to me confidentially, 'It's okay. I got the basics in there. You'll see. I'll edit it and show you the transcript.'

By way of celebration, he bought another Brooklyn Bijou for me, and also one for Wanda. For himself he ordered a double Glenfiddich to be served in a large glass, 'to bring out the flavour, the way they do in Scotland': he sipped and chewed the stuff. 'It's got a big nose,' he said appreciatively. He set his whisky on the counter between my and Wanda's cocktails. His tall glass with its inch of brownish fluid seemed (surely intentionally) austerely masculine to the point of self-parody when contrasted with our fizzy drinks decorated with mint and fruit and little paper umbrellas. He took the umbrella from my Bijou and fiddled with it, opening and closing it, and succeeded in breaking it. He stuck it behind his ear then dropped it in the ashtray.

I was feeling faintly tipsy myself, but cleared my mind by sheer willpower.

He kept cradling and thumbing his Cascorder, taking it in and out of his jacket pocket, like a little boy toying with his pet white mouse. He played back a fragment, just checking. There was some problem with the tape-speed control, so it came out sounding peculiar. First a high girlish squeak gabbled very rapidly, '*It was true love.*' Then this was repeated in a deep slow growl, like an ogre's voice, 'IT WAS TRUE LOVE.' But he never managed to get it sounding normal – though, come to think of it, that phrase surely never would.

27

Interview with Wanda Allgrobsch (edited extract), New York,
14 February 1990

– Mm.

– Mm.

– Mm.

– I guess I'll begin at the beginning . . . ?

– We met through Pa . . . My father . . . he lived in Queens before he passed away . . . my father and my ex, they come from the same place in the old country . . .

– Me, I was born in Cincinnati.

– At Pa's funeral, mm.

– I guess it was . . .

– At first sight . . . I'm standing there, by the coffin, in my black, and suddenly – outa left field! kaboom! – I mean, genius is the only word . . . He wasn't handsome in a conventional way, but he always looked after himself, you know. His suits were, kinda European style . . . He kept all his own hair, right till the end.

– Who knows what he saw in me? I mean, I'd know. I haven't got smarts like he has. And I'm not pretty or . . .

– Why, thank you, Frank.

– And . . . But . . .

– Gee, you're embarrassing me.

– El-oh-vee-ee!

– Can you imagine, Frank? After we got married, for almost one year, I was the original Happy Housewife. Every morning I open his Kellogg's, I pour his prune juice, I toast his bagel and fix his egg the way he likes it . . . and I'm saying to myself: 'I am having breakfast with a genius!' Outasight! And at night, it's: 'I am being screwed by the great writer of our time L. Z. Allgrobsch.'

– You want to know what he was like, mm? *Really* like . . . Let me tell you, this guy came in the club one time – a young guy, maybe twenty, and he's walking in a kinda crooked way, glancing over his shoulder all the time, like he's about to rob a bank, and he's carrying a big valise with plenty of papers, and he goes up to Elzee and he says, in a frightened high

156

voice, 'I've been writing these stories and I want you to tell me if I'm any good. Either I'm going to hit the big time or I'm going to jump off Brooklyn Bridge.' And he puts a stack of his stories on the table in front of Elzee. So Elzee reads page one from top to bottom and he doesn't say anything. Not a word. Then he looks at the last page and reads that from top to bottom. Then he looks at the kid – who is shaking by now, ess-cee-ay-ar-ee-dee – and he says, 'Your stories are lousy. You'll never be a writer.' And the kid picks up his stories and walks right out . . . Mm, I *know* what you're thinking, but it's not true. He had a respect for Literature. It was the most important thing to him, and he wasn't going to tell a lie about it, not to make anybody feel good.

– And then we split, mm . . . No, I don't want to . . . talk about . . .

– Mm.

– Uh?

– Mm, you . . . You're talking like there's *reasons* for everything. But it was just – you know – it doesn't mean we didn't . . . It was true love!

– Mm.

– No.

– The *what*?

– Sure, I understand, Frank. You want to write his biography. You don't know him personally, so you want to get through to him, using his stories, and his –

– Like you want me to tell you: he wrote his story abut the monkey in the snow after we saw the monkeys in Bronx Zoo in November, this kind of thing?

– What? What monkey?

– Oh, the *parallels*, sure . . . I d'know.

– I don't know.

– Me, I never read his books.

– I made love to him every night for eighteen months. Why do I need to read his books?

157

28

In Fifth Week of Lent Term in 1987, a month or so after the non-event at the organ concert, I was returning to my rooms, having just polished off a satisfactory scrambled-egg breakfast in Hall. Sunshine. I was walking diagonally across the lawn in the middle of the court, as only dons may (hoi polloi must take the longer route via the perimeter), savouring the aftertaste of coffee and buttered toast, when I was disturbed by a familiar shout in a raucous Cambridgeshire accent. 'Oy! You! Get off that grass!' It was our porter, Sunny Jim, stationed at the gate of his lodge, waving his arms like a human scarecrow. (This is his favourite activity: no doubt it keeps him fit.) The person he was addressing yelled back, 'It's all right! I'm Dr Smart's personal colleague!' Frank; needless to say.

I waited patiently for him to catch me up. This took a while, since he wasn't dressed for a morning stroll: he was wearing a black wetsuit, slashed geometrically to reveal diamonds and crescents of his hairy bare skin, with a matching rubber cape, and flippers.

'I've just come back from a theme party at Magdalene,' he said. 'It went on all night.'

'Aren't you rather hot in that get-up?' I asked. 'Or possibly rather cold?'

'It was a Bring Your Own Fetish party. Somebody stole my whip. I didn't have any choice. I have to see you.'

Naturally one's first thought was that Frank was drunk or high on some designer poison. 'Well, it's been very pleasant chatting with you, Francis, but one really must – '

'I have to talk to you. Alone.' He seemed sober enough.

I considered the possibilities. One certainly didn't wish to continue this conversation in the centre of the lawn. But one couldn't very well send him away: if one attempted to, he would more than likely create

158

an embarrassing scene. Nor would it be a good idea to invite him back to the solitude of one's rooms: it might give him ideas. As for leading him through the college and down to the Backs, well, on such a fine morning, with the sun and the ducks shining and quacking on the river, no no, it would be far too romantic. So I steered him past the porter's lodge (Sunny Jim leered; I responded with a taut smile) and we set out – I marching ahead and he waddling behind – down the winding street towards the centre of Cambridge. There, among the supermarkets and the fast-food stores and the coachloads of tourists, we would be suitably anonymous. And no one would pay any attention to eccentricities of dress or behaviour – it is a university town, after all.

We reached the square where a little market is established: stalls specialise in herbs, fruit, dog biscuits, secondhand books. We passed behind these, separated from them by screens of striped plastic sheeting and dirty translucent polythene. The tarmac, still wet from night-time rain, was glittering like silver. We arrived at a zebra crossing; we accomplished the transition to the far side; I noticed he stepped only on the black stripes, like a chess bishop, obeying some private neurosis. He caught up with me in front of a large puddle – a very public location. We faced each other. A pause took place, during which a blind man passed between us and splashed on through the murky water; as did a pram containing triplets pushed by a (pregnant again) townie mother in high wet, wet-look boots; also one of my students in the Maths Tripos Part III course, to whom I nodded good morning; and the entire Jesus rugby team.

'Do you come here often?' I asked, not entirely ironically. The scene reminded me of one of those pictures of an African watering hole, where all the local fauna – lions, giraffes, big-game hunters in solar topees – gather to drink and get eaten by each other.

'I am,' he said, 'a tragic figure.'

'Yes. I can see that would be rather upsetting.'

'All night long, all the time in the party, while everybody else was enjoying and making merry and having a ball, I was sad. I was downhearted. I was blue. I've been miserable ever since I met you, Emma. You know that, don't you?'

'Oh dear. Was it something I said?'

'I'm pining for you.'

'Ah.'

Of course I still had my long hair in those days, and, in honour of

159

the weather, I had put on a rather attractive candy-striped frock which revealed a quantity of leg; I wished I were wearing something more lecherproof.

'I must have you, Emma! I must possess you here and now!'

Momentarily I thought Frank meant this literally: the prospect would not be altogether unembarrassing. Naturally, one has been propositioned before – usually in even cruder ways – by, for instance and especially, drunkards at academic parties. This despite the fact that one does not have the kind of voluptuous figure which is conventionally supposed to appeal to males. Also there is a certain class of deviant known technically (according to a psychology don who once brought up the topic at High Table) as 'brain freaks'. They are attracted towards persons of superior intelligence, irrespective of any other incompatibility. In my early days at Cambridge, when I was the subject of much media interest, I used to get the queerest letters, parcels, and even phone-calls from these perverts; on one occasion Sunny Jim intercepted the most extraordinary Scotsman, wearing a sporran and little else. So I was not un-used to dealing with such suggestions. The simplest approach is the most effective.

I said, '*No.*'

There was a fortunate break in the proceedings while a group of jolly undergraduates bustled between and around us: they were wearing nothing but draped bedsheets and little laurel head wreaths, and were chattering in Latin. Some of them were actually conversing in that language; others were faking it, rhubarbing, '*Arma virumque cano . . .*' and '*Amo, amas, amat . . .*'

'You yearn for me too,' he said.

A breeze started up. Goose pimples were appearing on a circular patch of his exposed upper knee; I felt an urge to poke my finger through the hole in the wetsuit, and touch. I said, 'Oh no I don't.'

'Oh yes you do.'

'Oh no I . . . No, one doesn't. This is getting ludicrous!'

'Uh, you want me, subconsciously. But maybe you don't realise it.'

Which was unanswerable.

'Emma . . .'

'Now. Let's get moving, shall we? A bit of brisk exercise will do us both a lot of good.' I listened to my own voice: it sounded annoyingly like Mummy addressing her sheepdog.

He threw down his cape on the puddle. 'You may cross on this.'

Well, it *was* made of rubber: probably he'd planned the gesture. I gave him ten out of ten for style, anyway. I plonked my feet on the silly thing. It sank under my weight. I got my toes quite damp. I sprang back on to dry land.

'Now look what you've made me do to my second best brown shoes!' I said.

'What do wet feet matter when you're in love?' he said. And, with a great noise of squelching rubber, he sank down on one knee and held up his clasped palms as if praying to me.

I thought I spotted the Master of my college walking towards us, carrying a Tesco's shopping bag.

'*Get up*,' I hissed. 'You're making us both look ridiculous.'

'Only if you say you love me, Emma.'

'You're making a silly ass of yourself.'

'I don't mind making an ass of myself for your sake.'

'That's stupid!'

The man with the shopping bag was coming closer.

'I know I'm stupid. But say you love me.'

'I . . .'

'C'mon. Repeat after me: I – Love – You . . .'

I gabbled in a low voice, 'Iloveyou.'

. . . and Frank sprang to his feet.

. . . just as the man strode past us – and turned out to be taller than the Master, and to have a darker complexion, and a different nose, and in fact to be utterly unlike the Master in every conceivable way; besides, it's well known that the Master never patronises Tesco's, preferring to get his provisions from Sainsbury's.

Frank was smirking.

'Now, look here, Francis,' I said. 'You know perfectly well you made me say it, so it doesn't count . . . Anyway, why me? You're not called sleazy-Frank for nothing. You're handsome. You're experienced. You're cultured. You're reasonably intelligent, and you can actually be quite considerate, if you put your mind to it. And you've got a reputation, to boot. With all those qualifications, you could have any woman in Cambridge you want, almost. What's more: you do. You've been seen with all sorts of floosies: it's no use denying it. So why do you keep on trying to . . . to be rude to me?'

His expression had turned hangdog again. He murmured, in a tone of utter misery, 'Your college or mine?'

For a moment I almost was tempted. Of course one had imagined that one's first time would be with someone one loved – and Frank was (to put it bluntly) too stupid to be truly lovable. But one did feel a definite twinge of lust for him; and he would surely be skilful, and kind . . . And supposing nobody ever asked me again? One might spend the rest of one's life shrivelling into a sad spinster, like Great-Aunt Rose or Cousin Gertie . . . But on the other hand one woud feel such a fool for giving way before such a blatant seduction technique; surely, when it's right, nobody has to plan it – it just happens, somehow . . . Oh, I wished I didn't have to consider all these pros and cons! If only I weren't so brilliant. If I were dull and normal and unthinking – like all these shopgirls and schoolgirls and a gaggle of giggly French language students wriggling across the square, then I'd be able to sink into Frank's arms, and let him hold me tight, and never let me go.

'No,' I said.

He didn't appear to hear me. He crouched to pick his cape from the mud. He shook it, the way a dog shakes itself. Dirty droplets spattered on my ankles.

'I'm not promising you anything, Emma. I don't say I'll be faithful to you, or . . . the love of a true virgin will cure me, and make me mend my ways . . . You have to give me credit for being honest, don't you? I know you're big on telling the truth . . .'

There was a little in what he said – just a little.

Just then, a group of middle-aged Japanese holidaymakers turned up. The men were clad in the style of golfing Americans, with plaid trousers and open-necked buttondown shirts; the women were wearing expensive Bond Street numbers. They had evidently been shopping locally, for they were carrying a globular cantaloup, a sprig of fresh rosemary, a single dry biscuit, a pre-war Baedeker Guide to England . . . They approached. An older man tapped an Olympus camera and gestured in turn at Frank, at himself, and at his compatriots. Frank (who can get by in languages no one else has even heard of) replied in what sounded like fluent Japanese. A little conversation ensued. Either they misunderstood him or he was desperate to oblige. The shorter women squatted in a row in front of Frank, tittering as they hopped over his flippers; the taller men stood on tiptoe behind him; he was flanked by further women. He was utterly surrounded. The man with the camera handed it to a passing Mexican tourist – then dashed round the back to join the line-up. Everybody smiled. The Mexican stepped back like a wicket keeper at cricket, waiting for the ball. He peered through the image finder.

Everybody said a word sounding suspiciously as if it were going to be 'Cheese' if they ever got round to finishing it: 'Ch . . .' Meanwhile crowds of students and townies and foreigners were drifting through the marketplace. I took the opportunity to disappear somewhere in their midst.

29

I woke up on the morning after the Wanda interview and couldn't get to sleep again. A liquid red light was seeping through the gap in the bedroom curtains. A bird was making a racket. I rolled out of bed; dressed; unlocked my front door; and – without actually having decided – realised I was on the point of going for a brisk walk before breakfast.

I descended to ground level. I took deep breaths of the fresh air: it tasted of Manhattan. The weather was really quite springlike for February. The forecasters had predicted terrible weather on its way – snowstorms and hailstorms – but not yet . . . not yet . . .

At this hour the streets of the Village were pleasantly quiet, as in a real village. I slipped through them in a vaguely westerly direction, pushing my arms forward as if I had somewhere important to get to. Whenever I saw a turning which seemed to have some point of interest, I'd zigzag down it. A black dog with its nose to the ground. A manhole gleaming like a medal. The window of a shut bookshop crammed with a display of identical hardbacks featuring a woman's face with a pin in her cheek. Ten male drunkards clad in strips of black leather were falling against each other; their behaviour and dress were reminiscent of the members of that dining club which used to meet at Trinity Hall. I veered through a right angle and ran along a straight narrow road for the sheer pleasure of feeling my legs moving.

I had the illusion that I was at the still point and images were being flashed on a screen in front of me. A black man in a boiler suit was performing effortfully languid tai chi exercises. An old woman lay supine on an unfolded cardboard box; she'd carefully removed the staples and spread out the sides, converting it into the shape of a flat, asymmetrical cross. One felt all this ought to *mean* something.

Then . . . Blood on the paving stones. A steel tray full of lambs' hooves. Great half-oxen, spattered with clots of blood resembling

164

blackberries, were suspended from hooks. Men with loud voices and stained aprons were rubbing their arms against their sides like grasshoppers; prices were being negotiated.

. . . And I came out on the other side of that. I reached a car park guarded by a tall wire fence. Whitewashed lines on black tarmac indicated the space each vehicle should occupy – big territories for lorries, smaller ones for cars, and tiny ones for compact cars – but none was present so early in the day. Such pathetic absences! I thought of Goldilocks stumbling across beds and chairs and porridges . . .

And finally – like a shaggy dog story's punchline which one thought would never arrive but here it is anyway – absurdly existent – the river itself. The Hudson. Usually nobody in Manhattan thinks of it as an island – but it is, it *is*. I looked out across the water. One small boat was chugging from right to left, like a hand writing Hebrew. A seagull. A great grey flow with New Jersey glued on to its far side.

The air seemed crystal clear – but when I gazed at the horizon, the view was softened with a faint mist. I looked down at the ground by my feet – and the air was transparent again. Up at the distance – the mist reappeared. It was as easy as a conjuring trick. What sort of world is it where even the mist can't be trusted?

A mass of garbage was dumped on the bank: the remnants of a glossy women's magazine; a crumpled burger wrapper; the business section of a newspaper; eggshells; a Girl Scout Calendar for 1989 . . .

That last item caught my attention: it was the One Deliberate Mistake. Everyone knows that boys have Boy Scouts and girls have Girl Guides – at least, that's how it is in England. At Mummy's urging I had once enrolled myself in the Brownies (the junior equivalent of the Girl Guides) but had been thrown out for misbehaviour. I'd taken my partial differential equations textbook to a jamboree, and our leader, Brown Owl (actually Mrs Branston from the village), had said I was cowing the other girls.

I picked up the calendar. It was the size of an *Am. Math. Rev.* offprint; it felt damp. Its pages opened with difficulty. 'BE PREPARED' was printed on the inside front cover: well, *that* seemed authentic, anyway, I flipped through it. Information on public, religious and scouting holidays was inserted at the appropriate date. Diagrams illustrated 'How To Tie A Granny Knot' and 'The Safe Way To Build A Camp Fire'. I reached 2 September – the day I had arrived in the United States – and gazed at the blank space with nostalgia. A cheery song was printed in italics on the final page.

165

Somebody had been using it as a diary. Her name was Linda (or possibly Lirda). I read her scribblings with difficulty since the orthography, spelling and grammar were all poor, and the ink had run a little. In March she had been looking forward to a party. In April she had attended it; she had met a boy she'd described as having 'a great butt'. In May she had gone with him to a cheap hotel near Times Square, but they'd been thrown out for being too young; so they'd found an even more sordid hotel, and it had hurt terribly and she'd bled a lot. In July he had stolen $250 from his parents and they'd run away to seek their fortune like the heroes of fairy-tales. In August she had discovered she was pregnant. A red exclamation mark covered an entire page. In September he'd left her. There are no entries after that . . . and somehow, at some subsequent moment, this diary had been abandoned on a rubbish heap beside the Hudson.

The sheer banality of the story horrified me. I'm used to reading about that kind of thing only through the filter of fiction; if this story had been written by Allgrobsch, say, he would have invested it with a dab of irony, a quirky touch, a moral; he would have made Linda into a tragic heroine or a representative figure – or anyway something more than a poor, silly girl.

I had thought I was 'living in New York'. Indeed, I'd sent picture postcards to various acquaintances in England, telling them what really goes on in this city beneath the surface glitz. I'd presumed my own quotidian routine – shopping at the supermarket and the deli; taking the subway to the Institute; doing my work; occasionally going to cafés with Fanny and Bridget, or visiting the club – while certainly not paradigmatic, was as typical a New York existence as anybody else's. And now I'd discovered that the city was full of Lindas . . . or Lirdas . . . And I don't suppose *they* are 'typical' of anything either.

One feels so ignorant, so young . . .

The immediate problem was what to do with the calendar? One couldn't very well drop it back where one had found it. Nor could one take it home. Really, one shouldn't have read it in the first place – but it was a bit late for that now.

I threw it into the Hudson. A single beam of sunshine broke through the clouds and illumined the mussed calendar floating downstream like a swan.

(The beam of sunshine is a white lie. Everything else is true.)

166

30

Well, one wanted to find out what's what. I thought about getting in touch with Wanda and arranging to chat with her privately, but – what with my work on scope theory, and making arrangements to deliver colloquia in far-flung places (one at Cornell; one at a location called Urbana, Illinois), and the puzzling weather – before I got round even to planning my next visit to the club, I received a call at the Institute.

'Hallo,' I said. 'Smart speaking.'

'It's me.' (A quiet female voice.)

'Who?'

'It's me.'

'Yes. I've gathered that. But which "me" exactly?'

'Emma, I'm – '

'No. *I'm* Emma. Who are you?'

'Wanda . . . I'm Wanda . . . mm, I hope you're not busy?'

In fact I was extremely busy (which accounted for my huffiness): I was bang in the middle of a partial differentiation. But I replied in the conventional manner. 'No, not at all. What is it?'

'You wanna see a movie?'

'Ah . . .' I replied cautiously. In American English (I had come to learn), 'movie' is a code word roughly translatable as 'human interaction'. I didn't want to view a film – not one's cup of tea at all – but I did rather want to get together with her all the same. I had flicked through Frank's transcript of his interview with her, and obviously, reading between the lines, there was a lot she didn't want to tell him but might well reveal to a more sympathetic interlocutor.

'There's a new one just opened,' she said. 'It's about a woman.'

'Well, yes, I can see that might have its points of interest . . .'

'A woman and a man. They meet and they fall in love and then they die.'

167

'Well, perhaps instead we might meet at . . .'

I realised that I didn't really know what ordinary people do when they socialise. This sabbatical was the first time in my life – having been mollycoddled at The New House and in college – that I actually had to look after myself, all on my own. Well, not quite on my own: I had Professor Absent's Helpful Hints, and Frank's suggestions; and of course Fanny and Bridget had steered me round the Institute, and dispensed all sorts of useful advice and gossip over cappuccini or ice-creams at Upper West Side cafés. (To be honest, one was rather proud of oneself for getting on so well with those two: it proved that one could relate to people who weren't of one's own class or nationality, or even intelligence.) But how does one set about 'making friends'? Granted, one doesn't have to be shockingly brilliant to find that problematic – newspapers are filled with Lonely Heart advertisements; vast tracts of New York are devoted to recondite establishments such as 'singles bars' and 'discothèques' which one would never dream of entering. Of course at Cambridge it was all much easier; should one encounter somebody of an adequate intellectual level and pleasing disposition in the course of one's work, or at the cheese counter in the supermarket, one would request, 'Would you like to come to High Table at my college? Lunch on Friday suit you?' And that would be that. The nearest equivalent in New York (and quite possibly elsewhere, for all I know) is the invitation to the cinema. I had had that suggestion made to me by all sorts: Fanny and Bridget and Barbra and Ostrovsky and Frank; even Professor Honthorst; even Arnie . . . A depressing image: two adults set out with the intention of sharing confidences, and end up seated side by side in a large darkened room, not talking, staring in parallel at an illuminated screen.

'Instead,' I suggested, 'why don't we go to . . .' Well, where? A good long walk in Central Park was out of the question, given the weather forecast, as was viewing any district of touristic interest. Inviting her to a café or a restaurant seemed unsuitable: she spends her working life in that ambience. I finally hit on: '. . . the Metropolitan Museum of Art, eh?'

And she agreed.

So there we were, in the process of getting seated at a small table in the cafeteria area within the museum, asking politely whether the other person was *sure* she wouldn't rather have the alternative chair. Eventually she and I settled ourselves. We launched into our cola and milky tea respectively. So far the meeting hadn't gone too splendidly.

We'd met as planned in the foyer. A huge crowd had been milling there, so I'd had to jump in the air several times (earning some queer looks) before sighting her. We'd handed over the entrance fee at the appropriate counter; the price is displayed prominently, but – as she'd revealed, handing over one cent – this sign is just for show, and really one can give anything. (People always do enjoy explaining things to me – perhaps because one looks quite girlish.) To indicate that we'd paid, we'd been given little red metal discs which clipped on to one's clothing – 'buttons', she'd called them, though they didn't button anything. And then we'd seen the most wonderfully gooey Monets (or so I thought; Wanda said, 'When you've seen one waterlily . . .') and lovely Corots with little fuzzy bits.

General conversation to begin with: the way Mummy recommends. It was awkward. She appeared to have no interest at all in visual art (except for modern American stuff, which doesn't count), nor in decent music, nor literature. The only cultural things she cared for were sixties popular music (which was before everybody's time) and modern poetry (tedious 'free' verse: why can't they say what they mean?); she recited something by somebody called Bob Dylan Thomas. Initially one sympathised with Allgrobsch: imagine living with her! (Yes, one does tend to see relationships from the man's point of view: yet another neurotic consequence of one's upbringing – as Frank has often pointed out when I'm trying to be nice to him against his will.)

While she chattered on, I listened – not so much to what she was trying to communicate as to her style of speech. She was shy, of course. Well, who isn't? But her brand of shyness was quite different from Frank's artful lonely-little-boy-ishness, or my own rather bossy stammering; it seemed melancholy, as if it didn't much matter if anyone listened to her anyway. Her speech flowed in and out of silence, rather than contrasting with it in the usual way. And her idiolect was a subtle mixture: at bottom it was a fairly standard American, but this was overlaid with touches of Clubbish intonation and phrasing, and some anglicisms which she might have picked up from Allgrobsch, and touching relics of sixties slang . . . odd that she was still trying to relive her girlhood while I was trying to grow out of mine.

I wondered yet again what Allgrobsch saw in her. Perhaps it was her ignorance he wanted, her innocence, her admiration . . . It can't have been her beauty that he desired, surely; oh, she was pretty enough but (it occurred to me as I inspected her angled face; she passed a hand over it to push back her hair) she was probably more attractive now, as

169

a circa 50-year-old, than she'd ever been in her teens. No wonder they divorced . . . Of course one wasn't jealous of her . . . No, not exactly – or only in a rather abstract way. Besides, one wouldn't really have been contented as Mrs Allgrobsch, but the *idea* of it appeals – he and I, both brilliant, but in completely non-overlapping fields. What a couple!

Meanwhile I distinctly heard Wanda say the word, 'Elzee.'

'What?' I said.

'I went and saw him in the hospital, Tuesday.'

'And . . .'

'And nothing. He's still . . . mm.'

She looked as if she were about to cry. I tried to be sympathetic. 'Well, I'm sure he'll get better soon,' I lied, as one must.

Her eyes were moist. Her mouth was hanging open. Her voice was distorted. 'I luff him.'

'What? . . . Oh, yes.'

'I always – '

'I'm sure. And did he, er, love you?'

She shook her head and gulped hard. 'He's not into that bag. What he wants is – '

'No. I quite understand.' But I wasn't a hundred per cent sure that I did: luff might be rather different from love. I thought it best to analyse this matter intellectually. 'It's an interesting question, really,' I mused out loud, 'and one I often ask myself – as to which one needs more: somebody to love or somebody to be loved by. I suppose, as men do, he felt entitled to admiration; and you, in your capacity as – '

'You don't understand!'

I reached across the table and patted her cola glass sympathetically. It felt cool.

'No, I don't,' I confessed. 'Tell me.'

'It's not my love he wanted, it's my . . . mm . . . I told no one before, but I'll tell you, 'cause you're kind and you can keep secrets, and you're a foreigner . . .'

I was about to object – *But I'm English!* – but fortunately I swallowed the exclamation just in time.

'It was like this.' She gulped a little; swigged her drink; steeled herself for what promised to be a long speech. I pushed my tea round to her side of the table so that she could have a sip of that too, should her mouth become dry in the course of her narration.

'After Pa died – and boy was he rich . . .' She began to talk, not too surprisingly, about money. (Other people are very concerned with that sort of thing. Fortunately one has never had to worry about it oneself. Artemidorus Smart married a silkworm heiress back in the 1720s, since which the Smarts have always had more than a sufficiency.) Her childhood was one of great luxury, she said.

The food service area at the museum is constructed as follows. Imagine a large rectangular sunken sector, roofed with a translucent skylight, in which are tables covered with white cloths, silvery trolleys, bowing waiters, and all that a high-paying diner might reasonably expect. This is rimmed by a higher level zone with wobbly tables around which the cafeteria customers – such as Wanda and myself – were seated. She had her back to the railing. So I had a view of her set against a background of conspicuous consumption: executives waging power lunches; champagne corks popping; spruce men in leisure suits plying their mistresses with oysters . . . I recalled that this central area, the part that is now a restaurant, had once been a flower garden (according to Frank: Who Knows). I imagined the scene as a formal parterre: the businessmen were boxed trees or bushes; their silk ties were bursting into blossom. The women were elegant shrubs with neatly variegated foliage; or they were gorgeous sprawling flowers, at the very instant before they'd have to be deadheaded. The waiters were dishing up plates of soil-coloured food . . .

'Yes?' I said.

'. . . so that's why he married me' she concluded. She sipped my tea, then pulled a long face, the way people do when they taste X expecting it to be Y.

'I see. Yes. Er . . .'

'For my bread, mm?'

'What?'

'My bread.' By way of illustration she held up a Kaiser roll speckled with poppy seeds, which some previous diner had left on our table. 'My money. My inheritance. My fortune. My – '

'Yes, quite. One understands. But surely, that can't have been the only factor, I mean, an attractive young woman such as you surely were at the time, well . . .'

'No. He wasn't . . . interested in that. He only cared for his writing.'

'Well, actually . . . the point one was trying to . . . Your personality, surely. That must've been a . . . at the forefront of his . . .'

'No!'

'And, well, men marry for all sorts of peculiar motives. The desire, for instance, to have a mother for their children . . .'

171

'No, Emma. Not that. He didn't want any children. He wouldn't let me . . .' She was close to tears again. 'Everybody says you're so smart. Can't even you understand? I'm telling it like it was. I married him for one reason, one reason only, 'cause I luffed him. And he married me for his reason: he needed money. *My* money. My em-oh-en-ee-why. He needed money to write, to be a genius. And when we'd gotten married – we went to Nevada 'cause I was under the age – he took all my money, and soon he stopped pretending, and we split a year and a half later.'

'Gosh.'

She began weeping. I mopped her tears with a paper napkin. Some of her make-up came off on it, making brownish stains; her eyes looked older.

I said gently, 'And he seems such a nice man from his stories.' I thought it best to be forthright. 'So, Wanda, when did you find out he was deceiving you?'

'He never deceived me! Not really. I knew from the beginning, from before the beginning, he was only after one thing. Men always are! I didn't care!'

'You are alleging you married him because you loved him. Fair enough. But, by definition, one loves someone if and only if one admires that person. And how could you possibly admire a fortune-hunter?'

The napkin was quite soaked through, so I had to replace it with a Kleenex from my pocket. Fortunately I had a sufficient supply.

There were some striking lacunae in her account, which I wished to fill in. 'About Pertman. He claimed that it was he who provided Allgrobsch with financial support in the early years. Is it the case that he – '

'Mm. He was always soft on me, me and Elzee both . . . He was covering up for us.'

'I see. And one other matter. How can your ex-husband have taken *all* your money, as you stated. Surely, in the divorce settlement . . .'

'He needs my money. I don't. He's a genius. I always *knew* he's a genius. Geniuses are different than us. They've got different needs. And I was right, mm? When he won the Nobel, it was the second happiest day of my life!'

It's hard to remember that there are still women about who achieved maturity before the days of feminism. I said gently, 'Ah, the relations between men and women are often fraught with complexity. I could lend you a little paperback which – '

172

'I'm not men and women! I'm *me*. And he's *he*.'

And another thing: the sheer illogicality of the thought processes of most people. One forgets that many perfectly harmless and indeed pleasant individuals are in fact stupid. Or possibly . . . Wanda might have been reasonably intelligent once, but Love did this to her – or Luff did. I pictured Luff as a kind of Cupid afflicted with Down's Syndrome, dangling his quiver at a silly angle. Sometimes Luff bursts into tears and pummels people for no reason at all; sometimes he jabs them with his arrows. It could happen to anyone, perhaps; one might be quietly minding one's own business, behaving sensibly and thoughtfully – and suddenly one is pierced by Luff's arrowhead – and all one's rationality and intelligence go out of the window.

Indeed, if one sees it from that point of view, it was entirely Luff's fault – not Wanda's or Allgrobsch's . . . Well, no: that would be going *too* far. Yet it's hard to believe that a writer with the moral stature of Allgrobsch could be guilty of such inhumanity. One thinks of the moral clarity of his 'The Skater', for example, or that story of his about the duck. And his 'Bird's Eye Maple' simply bursts with compassion. He's so *good* in every sense . . . But now – given that one knows that in real life he was a cheat and a conman and a deceiver, well, the stories also seem cheats and cons and deceptions. What had seemed like purity turns out to be hypocrisy. What had seemed like strength turns out to be unfeelingness. His fiction is fairy gold!

And this is intolerable. How dare a trivial libel undermine the work of such a great writer! The flawed human being, Elzee Allgrobsch, was dying in St Kevin's – but the great writer, L.Z. Allgrobsch, must survive for posterity!

I calculated rapidly. 'So who knows about this?' I said.

'Nobody knows . . . Mm, everybody knows. I mean, Barbra and . . . plenty of guys at the club, they know the facts, but they don't know *why*.'

'So only you and I . . . and Pertman?'

She nodded.

She'd more or less run out of tears. I helped her to her feet.

I guided her out of the café and back to the foyer. We took the route by way of lots of deities – both Greek and Egyptian ones. They had the same expressions on their faces – bored or sneering or pious – as dons on High Table while grace is being said. I wondered if the gods would welcome Allgrobsch in their midst, permitting him to take his deserved place among the immortals.

173

I collected Wanda's black and my green coat from the cloakroom. I helped her dress herself, ready to brave the outdoors. I cleared my throat and said rather pompously, 'Tell nobody about your misfortune. And I too will tell nobody.'

She looked at me with disgust. 'I know you think I'm dumb,' she said. 'I *am* dumb. But I'm no fool.'

Nevertheless she hugged me tight and long, and kissed my cheek. She vanished into the great grey world outside – I saw the tip of her gloved hand, waving, perhaps for a taxi.

And just after she'd left I decided I'd misjudged her. Were she and I so different? We both were prepared – indeed, eager – to dedicate our lives to some great goal: Literature, in her case; in mine, Mathematics. I was fortunate in that I had the ability to be a mathematician myself; she could aspire to be a writer only by proxy. Her Luff wasn't a mentally retarded love-deity at all; he was just an old-fashioned muse with a headache. I wanted to explain this to her, and tell her how much I identified with her, and how deeply I sympathised (after due consideration) with her predicament – but it was too late now, and although I could and would tell her this on some subsequent occasion, it seemed it would always be too late.

I removed the red clip-on disc from my jumper and dropped it in a container for disposal of the same. It slid down a chute and ended up behind a vertical perspex screen: a multitude of such discs had accumulated there. They came in several colours, presumably a different one for each day, to stop visitors cheating. A pretty, gaudy, *pointilliste* effect. These discs reminded me of a kind of sweet of which I was fond in my childhood, known as a Smartie. Its name appealed. They came in a variety of hues: red, orange, yellow, green and brown – mingled in a cardboard tube. (The orange ones were my favourite.) Just the other month I bought a tube of Smarties for old time's sake. To my horror, they turned out to be all blue! But there weren't any *blue* ones. Why do people insist on tampering with the past?

Obituary for L.Z. Allgrobsch, New York Times, *17 February 1990.*

As much to the man on the street as to the lover of literature, the name of L. Z. Allgrobsch stands for all that is profound, questing, and yet ultimately resonant in the art of our times. I had the good fortune to be present throughout the many and varied stages of his much burnished career. His very first *juvenilium* – a sequence of lyric sonnets on the perhaps retrospectively significant yet scarcely original theme of rejuvenation in spring – was submitted to *Proton*, an émigré magazine which I had the honor of editing, in London in 1946. I returned the poems with a blank rejection slip. This did not dissuade him from submitting more, and yet more, verse, until, finally, I scribbled a note on the back of a slip suggesting that since his verse was so prosaic, and his lyric gift so limited, his talent might be better employed in prose. He did so. I published his consequent offering, his first work in print, a meditation on the subject of time, in the next issue of *Proton*. He went on to produce for us his marvellous prose poems, parodies, occasional journalism, and character sketches, throughout the 1950s, all still lamentably untranslated, as well as some crystalline short stories which, it is hoped, will be forthcoming in English translation with an introduction by myself, shortly.

His career as a writer of short fiction is, of course, well known. His first, scintillating collection, *The Skater and other stories*, which has subsequently received much favourable notice, received but little attention when it initially appeared, in our native language, in 1955. Much the same might be said of *The Barber's Song* (1958). But his first, faltering step into the English language, *The Vendor of Shooting Stars*, took the literary world by storm in 1960; and his reputation was only confirmed in subsequent volumes: *Somewhere, Rain* (1963), *The Snowman's*

Tale (1967), *The Twins* (1970), *In the Town of Sadness* (1975), *Bird's Eye Maple* (1979), *The Bubble Blowing Party* (1984), *For Want of a Bicycle* (1986), and finally, *Greater than Infinity* (1988). A further posthumous collection is believed to be in preparation.

His work – despite and in some sense because of its refusal to present solutions, and its unwillingness to offer easy identification with the victims of history – manifests a deep and moving compassion. Seldom indeed does it spill over into melodrama. His acceptance and yet not acquiescence in the face of tragedy, a rare virtue in our time, is positively Hellenic. I can speak from personal experience when I say that this burning *arete* was manifested in his quotidian activity as much as in his literary compositions. I well recall strolling with him along the Champs Elysées on a certain wet afternoon in the winter of 1958; he greeted an apparent stranger with the words, 'The man on the street corner is my friend.' On this occasion, the man in question was in fact an old and treasured friend of his (whose name escapes me) from pre-war days; but it is altogether characteristic of Allgrobsch that he should use such a locution to express universal human brotherhood.

In an era when the human values so treasured by him are passing away, and when such great changes – which he surely would have welcomed – are taking place in the land of his birth, we must pay our respects to a man of the past and the future, whose stern yet luminous humanity is an example to us all.

H. H. Gritz

32

Greater than Infinity

Just look at the mathematician. His cheeks are as smooth as a girl's. His forehead is unlined. His hair is too long. His hands tuck themselves into his pockets, and twitch. He wears thick checked fabrics, cut extravagantly in an alien mode. He says he has studied at Prague and Cambridge and Göttingen. He says he is on his way to visit his parents who live in a city not so far away whose name we all know. He stands in the middle of the town square – while carts rumble around him and women sidle past carrying baskets of red cabbages, mossy firewood, windfalls and cracked eggs from or to the market – asking if someone can put him up for the night.

But how can we accept him? Everybody else in the town has a definite placing: Levno the cobbler makes shoes; Dav the tailor makes suits; Fehma the part-time seamstress sews scraps of lace or velvet on to dresses to make them as good as new . . . but what does a mathematician make?

Finally Radka the inn-keeper does what inn-keepers must. He lists the attractions of the room over the stables (its warmth, its freedom from fleas, the comforting murmur of its perpetual creak) and demands cash in advance. The mathematician moves in.

All the boys and young men of the town observe him. We follow him on his afternoon strolls through the countryside – he swats wildflowers with his ebony stick and whistles at nesting birds – and trail him back to the inn before dusk. We are like wasps around a pot of treacle. The doorways and windows attract groups of us: individuals peek through knotholes. Radka does his best to drive us away (much stamping, shouting, cracking of the horsewhip) but we dive in the bushes, then sneak back. I can't weave through the undergrowth as fast as the others because I am asthmatic. Cautiously I crouch behind a bush and croak questions. 'What's the mathematician doing now?' 'He's drinking a glass of beer.' 'And what now?' 'He's about to munch a slice of veal pie.' 'And now?' 'He's

177

unbuttoning the thing he says is his Norfolk jacket.' 'Now?' 'He's relieving himself in the outhouse.' 'And . . . ?' 'He's climbing the rickety stairs outside the stable.' '. . . ?' 'I can't see: he's snuffed out the candle.'

The following morning – deserting our studies and our jobs – we keep track of him. We notice him promenading through the prominent streets of our town. He strides to and fro, inspecting façades from different angles. He taps with precise fingernails on plaster walls or the mortar between bricks. He marches backward to get a long perspective. He glances up at pilasters and archways, and nods to himself. He sees things we cannot see.

In the afternoon he goes for a walk by the river. He sighs several times. He spreads a handkerchief on the bank. He sits down. He stares into the gray flow. He uproots a fistful of grass and tosses it on the water. He does not seem surprised when we approach him. He half rises to greet us, then changes his mind, lowering himself again, smiling politely. We arrange ourselves on the bank in a semicircle around him. He taps the silver tip of his cane against his sharp shoes.

Somebody dares to ask him a question. Then another and another. Not that we don't believe he is a mathematician; not that we don't have faith in his grasp of abstract thought; not that we don't trust him . . . but we are living in troubled times, and we want to be sure – just as a lover might secretly read his beloved's diary.

'What is nine times seven?' 'Define nine. Define seven. Define the process of multiplication.'

'How many lines are in a square?' 'A square has an area whereas a line has none, so no finite number of lines can fill up a square.'

We nudge each other nervously. We dare each other to ask the question on all our minds. Finally one brave soul asks, 'Do you know everything?' 'I'm sorry,' he replies in his foreign intonation, 'but I don't undestand your idiom.' 'Do you know what will happen to us all?' He emits a curt, meaningless exclamation.

That evening the mathematician sits by the log fire in the inn, drinking, chatting argumentatively with Radka the inn-keeper and Portin the intellectual. We can only overhear scraps of the conversation – something to do with a possible reduction in the room rate, the cost of beer and veal pies, and epistemology. The firewood must be too green: there are loud hisses and crackles.

In due course the mathematician steps out into the yard. He calls into the darkness, 'I can't see you, but I know you're here. Listen. I cannot answer the question you asked me this afternoon – but I will solve a profounder problem. I will prove to you that something you think impossible – more than impossible! – you thinks it's absurd – is nevertheless true. In return I request a little favor: I happen to find myself short of . . . well, it could happen to anyone – so would you please . . . my . . . ah . . . pay what I owe at the inn?'

A long silence – then, swelling from the night: 'Yes!'

The next morning the mathematician is on the bench by the quay; a fountain pen is in his hand, and a bottle of black ink rests beside him. He is balancing a pad of paper, ruled horizontally in blue and vertically in red, across his lap. He scribbles on it fluently – some intricate array of symbols and numbers. He murmurs to himself: 'Infinity . . .' A windy, mysterious sound: it wafts out from his mouth and disappears over the river.

The regular passenger steamer is docked at the landing stage. It stops here once a day, bringing cousins and aunts and government officials. A few merchants disembark, swaying a little as they walk along the gangway to dry land. The sailors help unload planks, straw, cement; somebody lowers half a dozen crates of laying hens. The captain calls down, 'Anybody coming on, here?' The mathematician yells up, 'Wait for me!' The ship's steam whistle blows.

The mathematician talks very quickly – and all the while his pen is skittering over the pad, dashing off his thoughts; occasionally the pen – its nib is like the beak of a drinking duck – dips momentarily into the ink, spatters a dark droplet, and goes on writing. 'Infinity is defined as the number which is so big you will never reach it. For example, imagine saying: one, two, three, four . . . you may go on speaking for ever and you will never be silent.

'But now I will demonstrate there are several infinities, each of them lesser or greater than the others. This is ridiculous but provable! For suppose, for the sake of argument . . .'

∞

The mathematician has been discoursing on infinity. His speech has turned faster and faster, his argument has become more intricate, yet his assumptions are so elementary and his methodology so straightforward we all follow his line of reasoning. (The ship's whistle blows for the second time.) . . . And at last, resting his weight on his cane, he jumps to his feet, trots smartly along the gangway (which is hauled up after him), leans

179

against the railing, buttoning his Norfolk jacket with one hand while waving goodbye with the other (the last blast on the steam whistle), shouting the final deductions to complete his proof.

Suddenly a big man is elbowing past us, pushing towards the landing stage, bellowing, 'I'm not made of beds and veal pies! I'm not a millionaire! I'm not an American! Are you coming down or shall I come up and get you?!' It is Radka the inn-keeper. The mathematician smiles, scratches his smooth cheek, and points vaguely at the land.

The engine starts up with a deep loving sound. The ship gently and slowly slides away from the quay. The mathematician raises his hands in triumph and yells, 'Reductio ad absurdum! Quod erat demonstrandum!'

. . . and all the boys and young men of the town race towards the ship (all, that is, but one – for I have just tripped over a tree root, and lie on the earth, painfully out of breath). I see them jump by the score from the bank on to the deck, or leap forward and grab the aft railings: they close in on the mathematician (maybe because they love the proof so much they want to learn more – or maybe the proof seems empty and irrelevant: they want vengeance) as the ship angles into midstream, gathers speed, and steams away downriver.

© L.Z. Allgrobsch 1988

180

33

From the New York Times, *18 February 1990*

ERRATUM
We regret that an obituary for L.Z. Allgrobsch was published in yesterday's edition of the *Times*. It subsequently has come to our attention that Mr Allgrobsch is not yet dead. He remains in critical condition in St Kevin's Hospital, Brooklyn.

34

According to Frank (when I met him some days later during what shouldn't have been spring yet but was), that kind of mistake is always happening. Now that newspapers are computerised, it's so easy for a drunken sub-editor to fiddle with the keyboard, or a stray cat to wander across it, or a glitch in a program to cause a system crash – so a file gets recalled from memory, or erased, or printed back to front, ravaging the layout. A premature obituary is not the worst of it. He murmured the name of an illustrious London newspaper; once, back in 1989, its Fifty Years Ago Today column had been diverted to the front page: headlines screamed 'WORLD WAR DECLARED'. They'd had to pulp the entire issue.

I asked sternly, 'Is this anecdote actually true, Francis?'

He shrugged and smiled coquettishly. 'Well, Em, can you come up with a better explanation of the Allgrobsch cock-up?'

One would rather that subject were not mentioned, or indeed anything to do with the man. Of course one was determined not to reveal Allgrobsch's shameful treatment of his wife; in fact to steer clear of that whole topic, if necessary dragging red herrings *passim* – but deception happens not to be something one is talented at.

'Honesty is the best policy,' I said, quoting Mummy.

'Uh huh. An instance of a proverbial saying that's undergone a dialectical antitheticalisation. Originally, in the sixteenth century, in the era of Machiavelli, "policy" meant stratagem, so the meaning was: Telling the truth is usually a convenient ruse. But, in the context of the Victorian bourgois *mentalité*, it de-, and indeed re-, constructed itself to imply the, so to speak, valorisation of "truth".'

'Yes, well,' I teased. 'Things have moved on a little since you were young, back in the sixteenth century.'

He laughed heartily to show he wasn't the kind of person to take offence at jokes about himself, especially unfunny ones. He shifted his bottom to indicate that he wanted to change subjects.

'Y'know, Em. I've got this new theory about Whodunnit . . . It was H.H., for sure. See, H.H. funded Allgrobsch early on – that we know – and it must've been him who kept him in typewriter ribbons in the early sixties. And why? Well, maybe they had some kind of . . . relationship going on?'

'I really don't think – '

'I mean, you just have to look at H.H.'s ego-presentation in his obituary bit, transferencing like crazy! So he was afraid Allgrobsch would spill the beans, so – after he'd gotten himself appointed literary executor – he fed him a mysterious oriental poison and then let me write the biography because he reckoned I wouldn't discover the truth. But little did he know!'

Frank had narrated this so slowly and boringly that – until quite near the end, when he'd inserted a dramatic eyebrow wiggle – one hadn't realised it was supposed to be a shaggy-dog story.

'One tiny flaw in your theory,' I said. 'Allgrobsch wasn't murdered. He had a stroke.'

'Uh, yeah,' he said mock-childishly, 'if you're going to be so picky . . .'

'One worries about you, Francis, one really does. Your inability to distinguish reality from fantasy might be acceptable in a poet or a politician, but not in a supposedly serious academic.'

'Uh . . . We all need fantasy, I guess.'

'Frank, you're stealing my lines! The last time we had this discussion, *I* was the one who said the function of art was to provide fantasy, and *you* said it was a text to be analysed.'

'Ah, sure. See . . . it's not exactly "fantasy" I go for – it's meta-reality. And, uh, it's all around us . . .'

He held up his arms as if being crucified, to draw my attention to our surroundings. We were in a horribly trendy hang-out in the East Village much favoured by the likes of Frank, known as the Red Cabbage Café for some reason. Anyway, imagine: a basement room, largely painted black, with spotlights aimed randomly at clots of dust or somebody's knee, or the upturned wooden packing cases which serve as tables. A huge plaster red cabbage dangles from the midpoint of the ceiling; on the floorboards underneath it, a message is daubed in red Cyrillic script, stating (according to Frank's translation from the Russian): '*This is not a red cabbage.*' Fragments of nude tailor's

183

dummies and a purple stuffed mongoose jut from one wall – instant funk. Waiters and waitresses with self-parodic hairstyles, high-stepping grimly, pass round colossal crimson menus (the choice of foods is nothing if not eclectic: seven kinds of bortsch; red cabbage salad; pastrami on rye; frittered camembert with stir-fried kiwi fruit; cheesecakes . . .) printed in English but with all the R's back to front, to give a Slavic look. Disco muzak was rampaging from a jukebox in a corner.

'It's all rather, well . . . pretentious and vulgar,' I said. 'Don't you think?'

'I like it,' he said. 'It's my kind of place.'

Since it was teatime there was only a sprinkling of people: some of them were obviously supposed to be famous, since they were wearing sunglasses and/or floppy tugged-down hats; they were being stared at by the other category of customers: couples with nasal accents, pointing and going, 'Ooh, isn't he/she . . . ?' A specimen of this latter type – two teenage girls in dayglo outfits – had the privilege of being blown a kiss by Frank. They nudged each other, tittered, ogled him and their fingernails alternately.

He said profoundly, 'The ambience is streetwise.'

'Well, if you hadn't invited me here, I certainly would never have gone otherwise.'

He smirked, taking this as a compliment.

Frank had phoned me that morning, claiming that there was something frightfully important he had to discuss. He was as mumbly as he usually is over the phone (he uses inarticulacy as a tactic to show who's in charge); one couldn't get him to state the matter in clear English. Which is how come one had consented to meet him here – despite, as always, having plenty of maths to be getting on with. (A conference on scope theory was going to take place at the Institute in little more than six weeks, which provided a self-imposed deadline for completing my proof of the SPO.)

A bald waitress delivered Frank a frozen Mexican beer on a stick – the latest craze, she assured us. I received my daring order of a glass of kvass, a rather agreeable Russian drink tasting something like gone-off cherryade. (I'd acquired the taste during the SPO conference in Moscow the previous year.)

Several minutes later, when we were both rehydrated, Frank grunted a bit.

'Ah, Em. Can you do me a favour?'

'Er, yes, well . . . it would rather depend . . .'

'It's about Allgrobsch. It's why I asked you, y'know, here.'

He frisked and patted himself, taking incidental pleasure in the exercise; then sunk a hand into one of his suede jacket's ample pockets, slapping down on the table a hardback. It was a copy of Allgrobsch's latest collection: *Greater than Infinity and other stories.* He pushed it towards a spotlight's ellipse of illumination. The cover depicted a man on a boat on a river, but – when one looked more closely – this was composed of a repetition of the infinity symbol in various sizes and three colours. Jolly ingenious.

'Actually,' I said, 'I have the British edition sitting on my bookshelf in Cambridge; I've never got round to it, and the jacket isn't nearly as decorative.'

'It's the title story,' he said. 'I'd like you to read it.'

So I browsed through it, there and then.

'Hmm,' I said ten minutes later. 'It's not bad, really.'

'Can you, uh, explain it?'

'Oh. I thought *you* were the expert on that. Well, it seems quite straightforward. Basically, it's a variant on the Pied Piper legend; or it might be interpreted as about the dangers of tasting the Tree of Knowledge; or even Orpheus's Descent to the Underworld. A nexus of myths, really. That's Allgrobsch's style. Or' – I could hear myself imitating Frank's own show-off way of talking, but how else can one discuss literature? – 'to put it boldly, from a psychoanalytic perspective, just the way you like it, it's to do with the Death Wish, isn't it? There again, of course, taking a Marxian approach – '

'Are you trying to be funny, Emma?'

'Funny peculiar or funny ha-ha?'

'I don't need you to do me a mythemic breakdown! Let alone a naïve vulgar psychohistoricisation scavenged from Every Man His Own Marxist and You Too Can Have An Ego Like Mine trash thrown away by riffraff on the streets of Cambridge! I don't tell *you* how to do your equations! You lay off my lit. crit.!'

'Well, one *is* sorry. But you *did* ask me to – '

'Not the literature, Em! It's the *maths.* This is what I need to know. Has Allgrobsch got it right, or did he make it up?'

'Oh, *that* . . . One assumed everyone knew Cantor's Theory of Transfinite Numbers. How remiss of one . . . Yes, yes. If you'd like, I could sketch out the proof described in the story. It's so elementary even the layman can understand it. Here goes . . .

185

'Now: when we say that there are seventeen people in this room, we mean they can each be paired off with one of the integers one to seventeen. Counting is all about pairing off. Agreed?

'So, I'll prove that a list of all the whole numbers – 1, 2, 3, etc. – can*not* be paired off with a list of all the numbers that can be written as decimals: I mean, a list of all the numbers like 0.6598769268 . . . and so on for ever.'

I sketched the following diagram on the back of a napkin illustrated with a red cabbage:

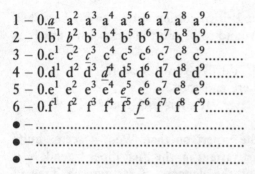

$1 - 0.\underline{a^1}\ a^2\ a^3\ a^4\ a^5\ a^6\ a^7\ a^8\ a^9$..........
$2 - 0.b^1\ \underline{b^2}\ b^3\ b^4\ b^5\ b^6\ b^7\ b^8\ b^9$..........
$3 - 0.c^1\ c^2\ \underline{c^3}\ c^4\ c^5\ c^6\ c^7\ c^8\ c^9$..........
$4 - 0.d^1\ d^2\ d^3\ \underline{d^4}\ d^5\ d^6\ d^7\ d^8\ d^9$..........
$5 - 0.e^1\ e^2\ e^3\ e^4\ \underline{e^5}\ e^6\ e^7\ e^8\ e^9$..........
$6 - 0.f^1\ f^2\ f^3\ f^4\ f^5\ \underline{f^6}\ f^7\ f^8\ f^9$..........
● – ....
● – ....
● – ....

'So, reading down the left-hand column, one has the list of all the whole numbers: 1, 2, 3, 4, 5, 6 – and all the other ones I haven't written in.

'And on the right-hand side, what I've put are supposed to be all the decimal numbers . . . Do you understand my algebraic notation? a^1 could be ^{6}, and a^2 could be ^{4}, and a^3 could be ^{7}, etcetera etcetera, so the number on the first line is 0.647 etcetera.

'So each row on the left spells out one decimal number. And all the rows are different.

'And let's make the list on the left so long – so *infinitely* long – that *all* the whole numbers are listed. And remember that for every whole number one decimal number is listed. Will the list on the right be long enough that all the decimal numbers are down there?

'Well, let's see if one can pair off all the whole numbers on the right with all the decimal numbers on the left. One can't! Because let's pretend – for the sake of argument – that one *has* paired them all off. Now look at all the underlined digits in the diagram. It's possible to construct a new decimal number, such that its first digit is different from a^1 and its second is different from b^2, and so on – hence this new number is different from all the other decimal

186

numbers, and so it isn't paired up with any whole number. *Reductio ad absurdum!*

'So in summary: the infinity which equals how many things there are in the right-hand list is smaller than the infinity which is needed to count all the decimal numbers. So there are two infinities, one of them bigger than the other. *Quod erat demonstrandum!*'

35

'There are more things in heaven and earth than are known of in your philosophy, Horatio.'

'What?' I said.

'Horatio,' said Frank. 'He's the guy that Hamlet is – '

'Well, yes. Of course one knew that. But why precisely are you reciting Shakespeare at this juncture?'

'Yeah. This is the moral of Greater Than Infinity, I guess: that there are things we don't know about which are very – '

I interrupted him, afraid to the verge of paranoia that he was hinting at the Allgrobsch–Wanda relationship. 'Before one can say Jack Robinson, you'll be letting rip with To be or not to be the quality of mercy is the winter of our discontent!'

The bald waitress arrived with Frank's order of blinis with genuine fake caviare, and for pudding: flambéed ice-cream on a steel platter. The latter was quite impressive: it looked like a ball of fire but apparently it had ice in its heart – hence it was doubly inedible. I was too jittery to eat anything, excusing myself with, 'One has to keep an eye on one's figure,' which was nonsense, really, since I'm naturally skinny, whereas Frank has a just perceptible tubbiness. The same thought seemed to be going through his head, since he was scanning my body in a rather disconcerting way.

Although I had covered no fewer than three further napkins in digits, algebraic symbols and diagrams, Frank still hadn't managed to grasp even the bare essentials of the Theory of Transfinite Numbers. It's simply a mystery how anyone of adequate intelligence can find mathematics difficult – perhaps all that comp. lit. stuff had eroded his brain. At no point in the conversation did he mention Wanda, or Allgrobsch-the-man (as opposed to Allgrobsch-the-writer) – which

188

struck me as suspicious: why was he being so cagey? I felt compelled to scratch the itch, to get the matter over with.

'How's your biography getting along, Frank?' I asked, casual-seemingly.

'Uh, fine. Fine . . . The image of a person trapped between life and death is deeply embedded in the American psyche, as evidenced by certain fictions of Poe. Allgrobsch will be seen in that light.'

'Well, that's certainly one way of looking at him.'

'Or compare the current flurry of media concern regarding the US hostages in Lebanon, as opposed to the lack of interest in the US marines who were killed there.'

'You mean, Americans are more interested in the living than the dead – unlike the clubbies, who are the other way round? I suppose you're right. Remember that funny public holiday they had on November the eleventh called Veterans' Day? Men with wheelchairs and sunglasses rolling all over the place. It's really on Armistice Day when people commemorate the fallen of the world wars – only here one is only interested in the survivors . . . Are you going to write about that theme in your book? A bit macabre, isn't it?'

'Uh, sure, Allgrobsch fits in the Gothic Horror tradition – Webster, Grimm, Kafka, King – but epistemology-wise rather than ontologically.'

'Oh.'

'See, I'm using my lack of knowledge about the guy as a thematic element. The death-within-life of knowledge itself. It constitutes a state of *agnosia* – knowledgelessness – in the biographer-biographee set–up; and this is echoed by the epistemic relationship of the consciousness-in-history to history *qua* history – and it's triply echoed by the deliberate foregrounding of the unknowable in the texture of his fictions.'

This sounded quite intriguing. Poppycock, to be sure, but *interesting* poppycock. I asked, 'You mean, for example, it's illustrated by the fact that Allgrobsch doesn't actually set out the proof in his Mathematician story? He just does the before and after, but not the during?'

'Sure. Its very non-existence emphasises its existence. Like Wittgenstein said: 'What we don't know shit about, thereof we can speak.'

'Francis. Did Wittgenstein *really* say that?'

He waved a hand airily. 'Naturally, I'm translating from the German . . .'

189

'And so . . .' I said cautiously. 'Any information you might gather about Allgrobsch's private life is in fact completely irrelevant as far as you're concerned?'

'Why?' He wiped a bead of roe off his chin, and sat back alertly. 'Do you know something?'

'Who? What? Ah, there are more philosophies, Horatio, than are dreamt of in your . . . er, you get the drift.'

He frowned.

I continued. 'So, then. May I take it you're proposing to put in your book a lot of stuff about yourself, and how you researched it? A sort of My Quest For Allgrobsch?'

'Uh . . . Kind of. But I'm trying to get away from the ego. And no linear thinking. My thing is to group the elements in units, each one centred on a, as it were, what you might call the locus/focus . . . focus/ locus . . .'

'Hocus pocus!' The words came out unintentionally and fast, almost in a sneeze.

Thanks to the tension, as much as anything, one had to dash to the smallest room.

I left Frank at the table, resting his chin on his hand, following me with a puzzled gaze.

The sanitary arrangements were not the cleanest, and the graffiti were jolly inferior. (One is used to a more intellectual genre of graffiti – for example the notorious third cubicle from the left at the Gents in the Department of Pure Mathematics in Cambridge, which contains an attempted proof of Fermat's Last Theorem scribbled in tiny handwriting around all four walls. There *is* a subtle flaw in Lemma XXXVI, just above the cistern – you can sneak a partial view through the window, and there's usually no one there before seven in the morning – nevertheless many visiting scholars have spent hours in there and come out none the wiser.)

I paused in the antechamber to examine one's image in the long looking glass. Actually I tried not so much to *look* at oneself as to catch sight of one's *doppelgänger* casually strolling past: to see how one would appear to others; an impossible task. Besides, my attention was distracted by the reflections of numerous couples and loners; this facility was more crowded than the café itself. One woman was painting a kiss mark on her friend's cheek, with lipstick. Another was adjusting her companion's coiffure with an electric drill and a soldering iron. A teenage transvestite by the hand-drier was sniffing a white powder.

A person in a leopard-fur-pattern leotard leant over to me, and talked out of the corner of her mouth. 'Mm, I got the hots for your lover. He's succulent.'

I felt called upon to defend Frank. 'Actually, I'll have you know he's not my lover. What's more, he has a doctorate in comparative literature from the University of Cambridge.'

However, as I returned to my table, I noticed Frank was not where I'd left him. I glanced around. He was leaning between the pair of juveniles I'd noticed earlier – the ones packaged in a fluorescent clinging material – exchanging telephone numbers. Then he peered down an excessive cleavage and remarked on it, 'Hey, you have a beautiful mind.'

Completely unabashed, Frank grinned at me, and sauntered across to our table. We sat down.

The flambéed ice-cream had melted into a white puddle.

'What's new?' he said, after a pause.

'Oh, nothing much.' I tried as hard as I could *not* to think about Wanda. 'Well, quite a lot actually: further developments on the Smart–Potts–Ostrovsky conjecture – we've arranged a conference in April – but I'm sure you wouldn't be interested.'

'Try me.'

I was silent.

'Oh, and Arnie was pestering me again this morning. Remember him? I described him to – '

'Ah, sure. I know. The nerd. What's his game?'

'He wanted me to explain the equivalence of the Schrödinger and Heisenberg representations of the quantum wavefunction. Does he think one has nothing better to do with one's time?'

'Yeah, he has a thing for you.'

'What?'

'Sure, Em. Plain as a pikestaff. He's got a crush.'

'Frank. Don't be . . . unpleasant. He's a plain little boy, and he said I reminded him of an idealised mother!'

'Yeah. That's always the first sign.'

'You surely don't suppose that . . . he and I . . . ?'

'Why not? He's closer to your age than I am.'

I forced a sarcastic, 'Ha!'

He looked down sullenly for a minute. Then he reached across the table and grabbed my right hand in his. He cradled my fingers in his palm. The pressure was quite strong. I could feel his skin getting sweaty.

'Well . . .' he said, in the way people do when they are about to say goodbye.

'Well, then . . .' I replied, likewise.

He lifted my hand to his mouth, and delicately kissed my fingertips in the manner I'd become accustomed to permitting him on parting. I was inwardly pleased with myself for not having mentioned anything on the Wanda topic. He licked my littlest finger. His rough chin scraped against the side of my hand. The rather attractive grey bits of his coiffure, just above the ears, gleamed. He proceeded to pass his tongue around my other fingers: a damp, ticklish, and not unpleasant process. Of course one would rather he hadn't − but his grip was firm; and one wouldn't want to make a fuss; and besides, fingers don't really count.

He murmured, 'You have a great body.'

'Oh? One was under the impression it was beautiful minds you preferred?'

'Ah, your razor-sharp intellect . . . Sure. But I can go for that virginal look.'

I tensed. (He was down to the knuckles by this point.) One is aware that that's what one is (and men can always tell, somehow) but one wouldn't wish it to be *blatant*.

'Did anybody ever tell you you have a delicious thumb?' he asked.

'It's not a topic that often crops up.'

'And you've got a real sensual pinkie.'

'Is that better than a fake sensual one?'

To be honest, I quite enjoyed Frank's absurd flattery. Of course, there were a dozen women in that very café with figures more voluptuous than mine, but still, it's sometimes nice to be white-lied to. The thing is: people are always praising one's intelligence − and quite right, too − so one's body tends to get rather overlooked. The compliments one does receive are so non-specific − wolfwhistle from a building worker, grab by a drunken professor − that they might reasonably be interpreted as an appreciation of the female form, but not of one's particular variant thereon.

I said teasingly, with regard to thumb-sucking, 'Surely you gave up that particular practice some thirty years ago?'

'Ah. You know what it's a sublimation of, right?'

'I'm not sure I want to know.'

He chewed my nails for a bit – the way I sometimes do when I'm nervous. Then his mouth drifted down: he nibbled my wrist. I passed the time by idly asking myself *why* being kissed there is not an outrageous liberty: arguably because one thinks of the hand as a peripheral and public part of the body (but why more so than one's mouth, say, or . . . ?); also one feels one could withdraw it at any time (but the same goes for anything else, given that Frank is not completely lacking in gentlemanly qualities). Actually I rather relished the sheer silliness of this activity. One felt childish and free . . . I thought of my youth with Otto Man and Shay Zlong . . .

Meanwhile the lighting had become dimmer: the spotlight formerly aimed on our table had shifted. The muzak was a slow wail. Nobody was seated near us – and in various obscure spots around the place, couples were canoodling.

Frank's spare hand moved round to caress my shoulder through two layers of cloth. Yes, well, but – one can't draw a line at shoulders.

He whispered, 'Y'know, Em. Sometimes when I'm with . . . another woman, I shut my eyes and I pretend it's you.'

I wrenched my right hand free. There were definite toothmarks on the wrist. I pushed back my chair and sprang up. 'That's the most disgusting thing one's ever heard in one's entire life!'

As I backed away, the spotlight shone directly in my eyes, as at an interrogation. I couldn't see him, or anything. I was transfixed.

His voice floated from the glare. 'What have I done? Tell me.'

'I'm not going to tell *you* anything! Because you're horrible, that's why! I don't tell secrets to horrible people!'

'Emma . . .' His voice seemed very distant.

'You're nasty! I don't like you any more! You're not my friend!'

'Emma . . .'

'You think you're such a clever clot! But I know something you don't know! And I'm not going to tell you . . . So there!'

'Emma, I don't understand . . .'

'The same to you with knobs on!'

Suddenly there was darkness. He must have been standing in front of me, blocking the beam from the spotlight. Then all I could see was the glowing corona of his backlit hair.

'You *will* tell me your secret, Emma.'

'Oh no I won't!'

'Your teensy weensy, itsy bitsy little secret?'

'No!'

'I'm your best friend, Emma. Remember?'

'Oh no you're not! You're my best enemy!'

'Uh huh. So . . . ?'

'I won't tell you anything!' I screamed.

'Sure you will. You'll tell me everything.'

. . . And of course, in the end, I did.

36

The Man Who Always Lied

The strangers come to our town. They ask the first person they meet, who as often as not happens to be Tidak, stationed at the crossroads, 'Does this road lead to the inn?' He replies, 'Yes,' though in fact it doesn't.

The strangers return to the crossroads. They ask Tidak again, 'Is that the inn over there?' pointing at the gate where Radka the inn-keeper stands waving. Tidak replies, 'No.'

The strangers pass once more by the crossroads. 'The road you told us not to take was the right one, and the one you told us to was wrong. Why were you lying to us?' He says, 'No, I wasn't.' They ask, 'Are you telling the truth now?' 'Yes, I am.' And – if they're wise – they add an extra question to determine what kind of a man Tidak is: 'Does two and two make four?' He answers, 'No, of course not.'

For Tidak, you see, is an incorrigible liar. He can't help it. He's not like the rest of us who lie only when it seems to our advantage, or to please the questioner, or when we think we'll get away with it. No, Tidak lies when it's convenient and he lies when it's inconvenient; he lies when lying is polite, and when it's impolite; he is absolutely incapable of telling the truth. So, sometimes, we envy him – for we are positioned high up on the saddle of Truth: we have to tug its reins hard to make it veer; and even then the snaffle often breaks and the beast gallops in the direction it prefers, or gives up, lies down, and won't go anywhere . . . but our envy is misplaced: Tidak's lying is nothing but a burden to him, a complexity, an awkwardness, a cause of isolation . . . Indeed, he is often attacked by frustrated strangers.

We point this out. We draw the moral. We urge him to give up his perfidious ways. But he rejects our advice. He claims that lying is at least as logical as telling the truth; in fact, under present conditions, it is more

195

logical, or rather, more comforting, which is (he claims) the same thing. Naturally his argument is a tissue of lies, but how can we convince him of this? He has lied so often that it seems he has forgotten what truth means.

Well, we have learnt to cope with Tidak's eccentricity. Simply: we ask him a question, listen to his answer, and insert a silent 'not'. For example: 'Tidak. Can you lend me some money? I'll pay you back next week.' 'No.' 'Why, thank you.' So you see that Tidak — for all his mendacity — is a generous and kind man. Indeed, it is his virtue rather than his vice which will eventually lead to his downfall.

Tidak is strictly an amateur liar. In the big cities (it is said) such as Moscow and Berlin and New York, there exist men who lie professionally and are said to make a decent income purely from untruth; they marry a wife on the strength of their lying profits and buy a house and a motorcar, and bring up their children on lies. But our town isn't large enough. A man may lie in a small way; he may dispense fibs and canards in the evenings or at the weekends, and so gain a little extra; but he must have another trade to get his daily bread.

Tidak is a bookseller by profession. It's a living, after all. In fact, he is the only bookseller in town. He has books sent to him from the city; they arrive on the Tuesday ferry. He piles them in his wheelbarrow and pushes them along the gangway; up the winding road; from house to house through the town. In the evenings he locates himself at the crossroads and waits for us to come home from work, craving a good read. Of course most of us are poor and can't afford to spend much on literature; still, the poorer you are, the more you need fantasy: an escape route. So he boycotts fact, and he won't even stock works about contemporary life, for that's too close to the bone; he only offers stories, translated from other languages, about Hollywood or cowboys or knights in shining armor. His bestsellers are science fiction: Jules Verne, for example, or H.G. Wells . . . We like to read about foreigners being miserable in impossible ways.

Sometimes the wholesalers in the city won't send any stock for months. They allege transport problems, or insist they haven't received payment for the last batch. Then Tidak has to use his ingenuity. He rents books out by the day. He writes new titles on old books, and lends them twice to the same customer. He gets hold of boring unsaleable volumes and describes them in an irresistible fashion. For example, he might have obtained Introduction To Geometry.

He stands on his barrow and hoists the book in the air. 'Welcome,' he cries, 'to the fair land of Geometry, an imaginary country located between

Algebra and Sums. Journey to its fair cities, Scalene and Equilateral, along the river Isosceles. Spy on the love between the noble knight Obtuse and his fair maiden Acute. Will their love be thwarted by Acute's father, King Tetrahedron? Or will they all be eaten by the fiendish monster from the planet Rhombus?' Of course we know he's lying – but fiction is supposed to be untrue, and there are no other new books in town, so we are desperate . . . In the end, half humorously, one of us pays the price.

The first sign that something is wrong appears on a pleasant spring afternoon. A bird is singing in the cornfields. Somebody passing by the book barrow remarks, 'That's a linnet.' Tidak nods. But it is a linnet.

An hour later, another person mentions to him, 'It'll be dark soon.' 'No, it won't,' he replies. But he is lying as usual – for look, the sun is setting right now; the big red disk is already cut through by the horizon.

The following morning he is asked if he slept well, and he claims he didn't, so he is telling the truth again, for it is obvious from his appearance – his unshaven chin, his bleary eyes, his hanging head – that he always sleeps badly.

The moral of all this is that Tidak has not converted to honesty. Rather, he now veers crazily between truth and its opposite. This might seem more upright than lying consistently, but indeed it is less coherent. Some take this for a sign he is on the road to recovery, while others allege he has sunk deeper into the morass. We don't know what to believe.

Soon we figure him out. It turns out that – unlike the rest of us, who sometimes mix truth and falsity in a single sentence – each of his replies is consistently true or consistently not. Hence it's not difficult to devise a strategy that will extract a grain of truth from the raw corn of his utterances. For example, Fehma the artistic has come up with the technique of paired questions. She might ask, 'Does two and two make four and can you lend me some oil?' If the reply is, 'Yes and yes,' or, 'No and no,' she borrows a little oil, 'No and yes,' or, 'Yes and no,' she doesn't. Whereas Portin the intellectual has devised a more elegant system: he poses a question in the conditional tense, such as, 'If I were to ask you if I have borrowed that Conan Doyle from you before, what would you reply?' Tidak, by sheer force of logic, is duty bound to reply in precisely the same manner as a truth-teller would – although in fact his answer may contain a hidden double-lie.

The next stage of Tidak's decline may be put down to an excess of generosity and humility. Books are in even shorter supply. A lesser man than he might have put the price way up; a more adventurous man would have switched to a different trade. But his response is to stand at the crossroads, as always, lauding the contents of his few suriving, much-read books. Now he has fallen into the habit of describing their contents in such elaborate detail – true or false – that his versions are superior to those in the actual texts. For example, he brandishes his copy of Wells's The Time Machine. 'In this book you will read how a brave explorer travels into the future and discovers a glorious utopia . . .' He expatiates on the delights of that fictional land, where life is easy and there is no need or temptation to lie . . . Those of us who are already familiar with the book know that in fact the hero ends up in a dreadful future, but why pay good money to read about that when Tidak's own stories are available for free? Portin interrupts with a sly question. 'If the hero were to venture into the future, what would he find?' But the rest of us hush him: we don't want to know.

And, in the last stage of his insanity, Tidak tells the truth about everything. Ask him about himself: he replies with utter frankness. Ask him what he thinks of our selfishness in listening to his stories but not paying him anything: he answers honestly; nobody is spared.

And that was the end of the tale entitled: 'The Man Who Always Lied'. But – as always – history continues after the story is over. Some weeks later the strangers returned to our town. They asked Tidak questions. He answered them all. He was never seen again – and the barrow filled with his merchandise was left at the crossroads. It was a fine spring day and the books burnt easily.

37

What should one do? Whom should one turn to? One had been a very foolish little Emmy in telling Frank all about Allgrobsch's mistreatment of his wife, and now one should make amends. But how? There again, surely even Frank wouldn't be so ungentlemanly as to publish those tawdry facts? Oh yes he would.

I needed sympathetic advice. After returning home from the Red Cabbage Café I'd had a long chat, in my bedroom in the dark, with Professor Absent – but he had the disadvantage of being imaginary, and so hadn't been able to offer a fresh perspective. The following day, during lunch-break at the Institute, I'd broached the matter with Fanny and Bridget. They, however, had got on their high horse, and insisted that all wickednesses should be trumpeted. Well, one agrees in principle of course – but not if it means devaluing the work of a great writer, and implicating oneself as a complete chump, to boot . . . To be sure, one did have a sole friend in New York who could be relied on to be sensitive and forgiving to one's own moral weaknesses, and subtly aware of the complications involved in exposing those in others – but that was Frank, and he was out of the question.

So (as Mummy always says) when one has eliminated all alternatives the one that remains must be right. I phoned Barbra.

Actually I rang up the club – and a deep voice said she wasn't there, and gave me her home number. Which I dialled.

'Er, hallo . . . is that you, Barbra? It's me . . . I mean, it's I . . . It's Emma.'

All I heard was scratchy telephonic noises; then some breathing; finally Barbra's voice going gruffly, 'Hh . . . Kind of busy just now . . . Lost a sock . . . And where's my black pantihose? . . . Ah, there you are, you wandering bra, you . . . Look, Emma, I'm occupied. Why don't we meet in the club some time, yes?'

'Well, you see, it's rather urgent . . . Not over the phone . . . Wonder if I might, well, come round to your place now?'

She was speaking with her mouth too close to the telephone. 'Emma, I am in the middle of one humungous pantihose cliffhanger. I put three in the laundry bag, and now there are only two. You tell me, Emma, does the bag eat them, or what?'

'Yes, but . . .'

'You have to count everything *before* you go to the launderette, and *after*. They steal things there, you know? I don't know how they do it. You sit there, all the time, watching the clothing going round and round, and you take it away and something is missing. Maybe they have a suction pipe sneaks in the rotating drum, or an octopus lives in the machine – *seee-oomf*! – you'll never see that blouse again!'

'Yes, but . . .'

'I'm just going to the launderette. You want to talk to me there, Emma, you can. Yes?'

She gave me rapid, detailed instructions. I descended into the subway. I set out bravely on the downtown train. I had a go at checking my route on my pocket-size colour-coded subway map, but it was far too complex to be worth bothering with. So I passed the time by reading an amusing *Am. Rev. Math.* offprint which had a definite error on lines 44–6.

An hour later I was in a nameless launderette sandwiched between a Dominican hair parlour and the He-Died-For-You Comfort Station, helping Barbra stuff her dirty clothing into a machine. She was clad in dungarees stamped 'STOLEN FROM ALCATRAZ'. She noticed me looking at them, and gave me a well-I've-got-nothing-else-to-wear shrug. Only a few other people were in the place – all female, mostly middle-aged, many staring at the vision of their rotating laundry. Signs posted *ad lib.* stated that the proprietors took no responsibility in case of overloading, flimsy fabrics, colour leakage, loss of personal property, armed robbery, rape, tidal waves, loose buttons, nuclear warfare etcetera.

'Not in *there*, Emma,' she said, clutching my wrist. 'Whites and colours get washed separately.'

'A sort of laundry apartheid,' I said.

She wasn't amused. 'I was *right there*,' she said, 'on the black section of a bus in Montgomery, Alabama, in sixty-four. You don't make cracks to me about racism.'

200

'I'm sorry. You seem in a . . . mood. Actually, I came to talk to you about – '

'I'm not in a "mood"; I'm in a mood.' She furrowed her brow.

'Yes, well. I wonder if you're aware of the circumstances surrounding Allgrobsch's marriage . . . ?'

While Barbra fed coins into slots, measured out soap powder and fabric softener, pushed buttons (selecting Hand Warm and Delicates) and closed the doors of two front-loading machines, I explained the situation to her.

Afterwards she said, in a rising then falling tone, 'I knew and I didn't know, from the beginning. See, the thing with Wanda, she's' – pressing her index finger against the side of her forehead, and twisting it clockwise and then anticlockwise through a hundred and eighty degrees – 'screwy, a little. Sure she married him for love, and he married her for money – but is this the whole story, I ask myself. She's okay looking, and she has her charm. A man could marry her for a whole bunch of reasons . . .'

'Gosh. Do you actually mean . . . I told Frank an untruth about Allgrobsch, and now he's going to put it in print, and it's all my fault!'

'Who knows?'

'You do agree with me, don't you, that – even if it's true – nobody should find out about it? Apart from Wanda and me and Frank and you, of course. And Fanny and Bridget and Pertman. Not the reading public.'

'But yes. It's wrong to print bad things about people. Even if they're true. Especially if they're true.'

'But . . . Oh yes, I do agree with you. But . . . The point I'm getting at is: it could absolutely knock him off his pedestal! It could simply ruin his reputation as – what did Gritz call him? – a moral luminosity!'

Barbra chortled and patted my hair. 'You know what they say: "Sticks and stones/ May break my bones/ But words can never hurt me." How can anything we say or do now damage Elzee's fictions? They already exist. They are outside him. They belong to the libraries, the bookstores, the readers, the translators, to literature! As for his stories themselves, *they* don't care who they got written by.'

'Oh b-b-b-but surely, it does matter. I mean, suppose one had a very fetching still-life on one's wall at home, over the mantelpiece, and then one discovered it had been painted by . . . Well, some very bad man. It would make *all* the difference, wouldn't it?'

'No. I'm a translator so I know. The work comes to me through the mail. Sometimes I get a proof copy, or maybe just some typescript, or a big printed hardback even – and this is *it*. Often I don't know the author from Adam: I don't *want* to know . . . Like, I met a translator at a conference, I'm not saying his name, he does French and Russian, and he is such a rotten . . . He is so bad, you can't think. But – he is a very good translator. Ay-plus! So who cares?'

'But that's different! Nobody cares about the moral status of a translator, any more than one does about that of the publisher or the bookseller, or the righteousness of the chap who chopped the tree they made the book paper from! Whereas the author is the fount of . . . Well, a truly great author is a figure to be looked up to, to be listened to, to be admired, to be loved!'

Barbra smiled. 'I guess Elzee will be pleased.'

I blushed. 'Er, one did get rather . . . carried away.' But I did mean it, all the same.

And all the while the clothes were revolving. A promiscuous muddle of socks and gloves, bras and some decidedly masculine looking undershorts (it occurred to me that one knew very little of Barbra's private life – and of course one wouldn't dream of asking, or even speculating about it really, though she *had* collected Mr Black's tea cup in a rather intimate way; and one had seen her exchange certain pleasantries with Mr Dozy; and she'd laughed at Mr Richman's improper joke . . .), plus lots of other incomprehensibly twisted garments. Things were swimming in there which one simply wouldn't put in a machine. (There was a little Chinese man in operation around the corner from my place in the Village; reasonable service, meticulous hand-wash, very civil.) A steady rumble-grunt.

I asked, 'Did you ever want to write your own stuff, instead of just doing translations?'

'Impossible.'

'Why?'

'Hah, you're so lucky, Emma. You have your own country and your own language. As for me, my mother tongue I don't speak well enough to write in it, and I write English fluently but it's not my mother tongue. I can't write my own poems or stories in any language.'

The clothing rotated in the machine. I thought of the Wheel of Fortune, bringing some up to glory and others down to whatever goes on down there. I looked through the broad window at the grey sky outside: rain might come, and sweep our world away – Barbra and I, and the black woman reading Genesis, and the housewife scratching a lottery ticket with a coin, and the bare bright fluorescent fixture, and the scraps of ancient yellowing magazines (*US News & World Report* and *Playboy* and *Plain Truth*), and the infant making googoo noises at her mother's laundry (just think: at that age one was learning algebra!) – round and round in a lukewarm flood. Well, that would solve a problem or two, anyway.

The machine whined and spun the clothing.

I helped Barbra transfer it to the drier. First we had to tug it into red and blue plastic baskets, then empty those (except for the items that Must Not Be Dried) into the maw of the bigger machine. The clothing felt soggy and very heavy, as if marinaded in molten lead; it clung to the hands; it was awkward to move.

An interesting experience, this clothes-washing affair – though one wouldn't care to do it too often. Of course one doesn't want to give the impression one had never cleansed garments before. Far from it. Naturally, in The New House we always had Mrs Thatcher from the village to do the rough work; and at Cambridge one tipped one's bedder, Mrs Golightly. But once, when she had laryngitis – and another time when she was visiting her son in Gildsey – one had done it all on one's own, and creditably too. 'If you ever get tired of that mathematics,' Mrs Golightly had said, 'there's a job waiting for you as a bedder.'

The drier made a noise like a distant air-raid siren. The cycle finished.

Barbra pushed the dehydrated clothes into a shopping trolley. 'I've got to go,' she said curtly. 'Have to lie down, think my thoughts.'

'What is it?' I asked, at last becoming sensitive to her feelings. 'Has something happened? Something bad?'

'No.'

'Well, then?'

'Not *bad* . . . I went to the hospital this morning. To St Kevin's. This is why I wasn't at work, why I was so . . . offhand when you called. I saw Elzee. He's still – you know – his face is grey and blue, and he's got colour-coded wires coming out of his head, and tubes in his belly, and . . . and you can imagine. Then I spoke to the senior physician, Dr Athanias. He says, he never saw anything like it. Elzee is getting better. Not much, a little. Not a little, maybe more. Maybe a whole lot more. He says there is no reason why Elzee shouldn't recover completely.'

'Gosh. But that changes everything! It could make all the difference. Don't you see? It's the best news in the history of the world!'

I hugged her hard.

38

Extract from H.H. Gritz, ed., The Function of Literature:
Twelve Writers Speak *(PEN, 1982)*

. . . *Every day I awake at seven, and write for five hours. Then I have a cup of coffee and a sweet roll. Then I write for two hours more. In the afternoon I nap. In the evening I examine what I have written that day, and throw away almost everything.*

As I become older, the task of writing becomes both more and less easy. Easier, in that there are some techniques I have at my fingertips; and I am confident that my position as a writer will be but little affected – either for good or bad – by what few stories I may still have in me. But harder in that history has moved on, and my warnings have had no effect. I have begun to think of myself as a figure from a past epoch. Sometimes, when I sit down at my desk in the morning, all words seem as light as feathers; they refuse to settle on the page. And at other times each syllable is as heavy as a millstone; I can scarcely set down ink on paper.

Ah, why do we old men write? When I was young, I wrote – as young men do – for vanity's sake. I wanted to impress my friends and enemies, and charm a certain young woman; and I wanted to be famous. I dreamed of dining at the same table as Eliot, Gide, Dos Passos . . . And now I am old and I have broken bread with most of the writers I so admired in my youth; I have been awarded the ultimate accolade of the Nobel Prize – its accompanying certificate and medal are lodged in a bank vault – all that remains for me to do, it seems, is to die and become a classic.

And yet I write . . .

I write because I am dissatisfied. With myself, certainly; but, above all, with the world. Writing is a sacrament or it is nothing. Sometimes, I think it is nothing.

The Cobbler's Tale

. . . *and, anyway, what does that all mean? Are we free to levitate? Are we free to pass through a fire and not get charred? Are we free to fly? Are we free to visit London or Tibet or the moon, or for that matter the capital city without an official pass, signed twice and stamped three times? Are we free to set out one morning, as is done in the fairy-tales, and stride as far as we can in a straightish line through the misty woods? No, no, no, of course not.*

But put it another way. Are we unfree? Can't we stroll round to our neighbor's? Can't we climb downstairs? Can't we awake at dawn, stumble out of bed, and put the right foot on the floor, and then the left, and take our first step? Because, granted that we can, voluntarily, do just one of these feats – that we can control our bodies in the slightest degree, make a little twitch then let it expand into a swing of the leg, a stumble-forward – then we are free to do all the others also, as near as makes no difference.

Strangers are always surprised to discover Levno has a small brown face with a big mustache, and hums as he works. 'But how did you expect him to look? How did you expect him to sound?' 'I don't know, really . . . Different, somehow.' He labors in a converted blacksmith's forge at the end of our town nearest the river. He is certainly no smith – though his hammer thuds, occasionally striking sparks; and he pants fit to fan a furnace. In fact his workshop has no fire, no heat at all – apart from his own sweaty energy. Sometimes the place is so cold as to be almost but not quite intolerable: the internal season is permanently on the boundary between spring and winter. He bangs nails (humming a low note) into cold strips of tanned cow hide . . . He stitches (a high note) leather on leather – manufacturing (the riddle solves itself in the stranger's head) shoes for everybody.

Cobblers tend to be revolutionary. Probably it comes from the business of repairing. *Give them a millionaire's used riding boot, and what do they observe? Some scuffs on the sole, dried mud in the storm-welt, a personalized smell; if the heel is worn down a fraction, well, it can be reheeled so that no one (the cobbler apart) will know the difference. Or give them a pauper's clog – the problems and the solutions are basically the same. So cobblers soon lose their illusions, and gain new ones.*

Yet Levno isn't politically active – *his cynicism and irony are confined to more personal matters.* 'You see young Dav the barber,' *he says, one afternoon, pointing,* 'That lad sitting on the fallen log. He's just decided he's tired, so he won't bother going to the house of Govya the beautiful, and standing beneath her window and sighing. And over there, near the river, can you spy Govya coming back from doing her laundry, happening to meet Vlob the tailor on his stroll? Both of them are exhausted. So they agree to rest, side by side, on the mossy bench a while . . .' *And Levno leaves the rest of the argument unsaid; he just hums a repetitive non-melody meaning:* It is the motions which govern the emotions. It is the feet which govern the motions. It is the shoes which govern the feet. It is the cobbler who governs the shoes. So . . .

Levno squats tailor-wise on the floor of the workshop, gazing through the open door. He has been cobbling for decades so he scarcely needs to think while he works. His mind is elsewhere. Since times are hard, there are no new shoes to be made, only old ones to be mended. He hums the remnants of a dance tune. Meanwhile his hands are performing their requisite tasks: they fit a shoe on to a last, hammer and nail, snip and glue, polish . . .

Enter a man: 'Are my boots ready yet, Levno?' *Or it might be a woman:* 'Can I collect my brogues, Levno, please?' *Levno pauses; glances up. No need for him to rise to reach his stock: all the completed shoes are lined up on low shelves behind him; he just has to swing a hand round, and grab. In fact he arranges his life so as to walk as little as possible – much as liquor-sellers try to avoid drinking, or many a tobacconist gives up the weed.*

He delivers the shoes to the customer. He accompanies this with a brief description of their special features. 'Here is a brass reinforcement on the tip to fit your boots for much hard usage.' 'Here is some padding on the instep: it will be soft for you.'

Then he twists his mustache and makes a little, unfunny joke. To the men he says, 'These are seven-league boots! You can leap from hill to hill in them!' *He whispers to the women,* 'Not only do these show off your elegant ankles to advantage, but they also make you as graceful and energetic as a ballerina. You will pirouette!'

At this point, the following fact must be admitted: Levno is not good at his job. In truth, he is bad at it. But since he is the only cobbler we have in our town he makes all our shoes nevertheless. We shout at him; we grumble about him to our friends and neighbors; we curse his name when we are on our own . . . But what can we do? We don't like him: probably he doesn't like us. We don't want to employ him: no doubt he'd rather be doing something else for a living . . . And his inane humming is driving us all crazy.

Imagine putting on a pair of Levno's shoes. For the first second they feel all right. Then a slow pressure builds up near the toes. A slight rubbing sensation at the side of one ankle. A throb under the instep. The toe-pinch intensifies. A new sharp pain on the ball of the foot, rapidly becoming more acute. A repeated jab at the big toe. An ache – both pointed and widespread – beneath the heel. A vice-like squeeze across the toe-knuckles. A searing pain on the sole. A complex, swirling constellation of agonies, attacking the foot from all sides, penetrating its subcutaneous musculature, burning within.

So what should we do? We could think about journeying to the cobbler in the next town. We could see if Vlob the tailor could turn his hand to a little shoe-making. We could buy ready-mades imported from a factory in Czechoslovakia. We could ask the strangers for advice . . . But life is difficult, so none of us has yet got round to accomplishing anything so imaginative. Instead we put on our old shoes (complaining all the while), and off we hobble to the market, or to work, or to play, or wander aimlessly up and down the hill and alongside the river. We are always planning to do something about our problem soon.

It is now several decades in the future, and I am thinking back over the affair of the terrible cobbler with nostalgia. I lean back on the rocking chair in my centrally heated apartment and – in so far as my arthritis permits – wriggle my bare toes. Were his shoes really so uncomfortable? Far from it! Remember the evenings, coming home . . . lolling in front of the fire . . . taking off our shoes. What a relief! The men leap up. They jump and cavort. They feel confident they could – should the fancy take them – bound seven leagues from mountain to mountain. The women raise a graceful leg. They swivel; they flex; they dance across the floor. There is no reason (it seems) why they shouldn't spring into mid-air, cross and uncross their legs in one amazing entrechat, *and never need come down.*

40

One of the pleasantest things about being a mathematician is that one can work anywhere. Granted, most mathematicians at any given moment are swivelling on swivel chairs in air-conditioned offices, or slumped across a library desk – but my first-year tutor at Cambridge always used to get his best inspiration in the bath (he claimed), and one knows a certain eminent Californian algebraist who conducts his research beside his Olympic-size swimming pool with an iced daiquiri always to hand. So, feeling rather melancholy in the aftermath of the discussion with Barbra, I decided, instead of returning to the Institute, to take the train down to the beach. The forecasters had predicted sub-zero temperatures: one wanted to wander in the open air while it was still tolerable. Besides, the coming week would terminate in something called the President's Day weekend (celebrating Washington and Lincoln's birthday: how terribly clever of them to have been born on the same day . . . almost), when all the tourist zones would be packed out. So I set out for Coney Island. I had vaguely heard of it as a place where people go to have 'fun', and one could do with some of that.

Exited from the subway station. A cool breeze. Ran downhill as far as the beach. There were no obvious signs of fun. Fun was closed down and packed up for the off-season, presumably . . . I strode along the boardwalk: a plank-floored raised way running parallel to the shoreline. The tide was out. The sand was a beigeish grey; the sea was a greyish grey. I zipped up my green-grey anorak, all the way to the chin, and pulled the hood into place. Suddenly and briefly the sun broke through the clouds – the whole beach was a tessellation of men smearing oil in their hairy chests; women turning on their fronts to brown their backs and avoid male leers; puzzled terriers with sticks in their mouths; leaping teenagers punching beachballs at each other; infants dropping ice-creams and crying. Simultaneously, in the same physical space, a fun fair was occurring: merry-go-rounds were doing their thing; dodgem cars were colliding; vehicles packed with screaming holidaymakers were sliding down the Big Dipper's slope, fluent and curvaceous as the long ∫ of the integration sign . . . Then another cloud pushed in front of the sun, and the vision vanished.

On reflection, the changeable weather matched one's mood, so one rather approved of it. I sensed the planks underneath my feet – their slight unevenness, their flexibility/rigidity, their 'give' – and felt jolly proud to be out here all on my own. I know that Mummy, although she never quite states this in so many words in her aerogrammes, is concerned about my being alone in this big bad city; she's heard the stories – who hasn't? But I'm not scared: crises afflict people in slums or Africa or broken homes; one is not the kind of person to whom bad things happen. A big wind blew at me – I blew straight back!

I made a deliberate effort to think about scope theory (a sensation of my mind altering, like pushing a heavy door on its oiled hinges): at will, diagrams illustrating the categorisation of scopes appeared; they turned, enlarged, contracted, altered, were labelled with symbols . . . Which is what makes one special: not that one is cleverer than normal people (though of course one is, too), but that one can focus one's thoughts on abstractions outside oneself. Presumably fiction writers, such as Allgrobsch, share the ability to escape from themselves – but only into another populated world; whereas the pure mathematican can contemplate what is true and important and nothing to do with humanity. One pities the great mass of normal people trapped inside themselves. Frank, for instance, doubtless has tremendously subtle and rich thoughts about Frank – but that must get fearfully boring, mustn't it? All young women, in particular, desire to get away from the mind–body stuff: that's why some of them go in for anorexia or masterful lovers or caring selflessly for an aged relative – if only one could tell them that the answer is pure mathematics!

I marched on into the wind. It held a high note – like one of those boy sopranos in the King's College chapel. I passed shut beefburger places; an exercising person; old men walking dogs; a pair of heavily bundled-up fellows seated at a table playing draughts. A pun, that: 'draught' and '*draught*'. I was on the verge of pointing this out to them when I realised that they wouldn't understand anyway, since in America the game is known as checkers. One felt cut off, unable to communicate, as when travelling in a foreign country whose language one doesn't speak.

And actually they *were* gossiping to each other in a foreign language – Russian, in fact. One's own Russian is strictly mathematical: limited to such phrases as the translations of: *absolutely convergent series*, or *summation with respect to the primed variable*, or *thus it can be shown* . . . If Gorbachev himself were to leap out from behind the hot-dog stall and shake my hand, I would be unable to so much as enquire about the health of his wife and children.

And (as I turned inland) all around me were shops with signs in mingled Cyrillic and Roman lettering. At first it seemed reminiscent of the Red Cabbage Café – one thought it was some superficial perestroika-induced trend – but then I heard housewives discussing the prices of potatoes in Russian; I smelled vodka. This was no vision: it was emigration.

A passer-by in a tweedy overcoat asked me something. In New York should one be addressed by a stranger on a street, it is the custom to walk rapidly past on the working assumption that an obscenity or a demand for cash has just been blurted; then one jerks one's head round and barks, 'Twenty till two,' or, 'It's the third block on your right.' I performed this routine automatically (one had become quite New York-ified!), saying (in Russian), '*I'm sorry, I don't understand. Do you speak English?*' (During the SPO conference in Moscow the previous year, I had had much practice in using these phrases.)

A quarter-second later, I realised that the stranger had in fact been addressing me in English all along; what's more (as came to my attention after another 0.5 seconds), the stranger wasn't a stranger, he was Ostrovsky. In a nice new coat and untrimmed balding hair, he was looking both smart and shabby: like the kind of semi-impoverished aristocrat who crops up in Chekhov and Turgenev, with whom one so sympathises.

'Hallo, Yuri,' I said. 'What are *you* doing here?'

Simultaneously he was saying words to the same effect. 'Hallo, Emma. What are *you* doing here?'

Then we went through the routine people always do in such cases, saying that our meeting like this was surprising, remarkable, extraordinary etcetera . . . Actually – as a result of my residence in a university town, and my attendance at various international conferences, and my extremely good memory – I know circa 10^4 people by sight; so few weeks pass when one does *not* bump into someone haphazardly. I discussed this with Ostrovsky. He claimed he knew twice as many people as I did, and *he* chanced on random acquaintances at least twice a week. For instance, once, buying a 'Good Luck In Your Exam' card in a tiny village in Peru, whom should he notice browsing through the adjacent rack but . . . Well, one can fill in the rest of the story for oneself. We spent an amusing ten minutes performing statistical calculations (with varying initial assumptions, boundary conditions and methodologies) as to the expected frequency of such encounters, and comparing the theoretical values with anecdotal evidence.

Then he felt it incumbent upon him to say how pretty I was looking and I made some remark about the weather.

I didn't hear the next bit of his conversation because a train was clanking along the overhead tracks. When he next became audible, he was reminiscing about Russia.

'Oh really,' I said. 'Does all this' – gesturing sweepingly – 'remind you of home?'

'No, not really. The folk here, they come from Odessa, I think. But I lived in Moscow.'

'Oh yes. People are always pining for Moscow, aren't they?' (One has a faded memory of *The Three Sisters*.)

He took photographs from his wallet. The first showed his flat in Moscow: a cramped place with ugly furniture, a red carpet, a broken guitar. No doubt it was full of memories for him. One made the appropriate comment.

The next was of a pretty, skinny, blonde woman – about my age at the time the picture had been taken. The sun had been shining on one side of her face, making her look especially three-dimensional. 'She's my wife,' he said.

'Oh. And . . . ?'

'She still lives in that apartment, I think. You understand, I am not like the other Russians, who waited for exit visas. I was impatient. I went to a differential geometry conference in Toronto, and . . .'

'Gosh. Can't you get her out legally? What with all that glasnost one keeps hearing about, surely one could – '

'Now she's somebody else's wife.'

I balanced the picture of the woman on my gloved hand. I thought of the figures in those old sepia photographs framed and mounted on the rear wall of the club. I examined it. Her eyes seemed shrouded, perhaps against the sun, mysterious, puzzled, scared . . . 'What's her name?'

He didn't answer.

Oh, it isn't fair, I wanted to say but didn't, *that you and the clubbies have got wonderful homelands you can get all weepy about, and you can moon over a photo of a woman who probably never loved you much in the first place, while all I've got to make me deliciously miserable is guilt about Frank and Wanda and – well, yes – nostalgia for a scrap of Olde England which never really belonged to my kind of person and certainly doesn't any more.*

Then we talked a bit about scope theory, rather aimlessly. I explained that I was within striking distance of proving the Smart–Potts–Ostrovsky conjecture.

'I think I must go now,' he said.

'Oh really. Must you?'

'I look forward to seeing you in a month, Emma, at the conference at your Institute . . . You know, you have a rival there?'

'A rival at *what*?'

'At proving the Ostrovsky–Smart–Potts conjecture, naturally.'

'Who?'

He put his hands on my upper arms, as if about to clasp me, but he didn't. He disappeared into a delicatessen and was last seen haggling at the smoked-fish counter – where it would have been rude to follow him.

I made my way back towards the sea, moving my legs in big curved steps: my special moody walk.

I crossed the boardwalk; jumped down on to the beach; shuffled across it kicking up sand – first the dry loose stuff, then the firmer damp kind – and stared out at the Atlantic Ocean. I waved at England.

Those little dark greenish waves, bunching and flopping, they resembled the cabbages in the Long Field on the north side of The New House. I let my eyes defocus, and I saw again that field – and Mummy crouching to root up a weed, and Daddy strolling between the rows, reading a preprint on hydrodynamics . . . Possibly this thought should have evoked heart-rending homesickness, but actually one felt jolly pleased to have come up with such an interesting and ingenious simile.

41

'Oh please, Frank, don't publish the truth about Allgrobsch's misdemeanour. Because that wouldn't be very nice. Would it?'

Which would be one approach.

Or instead:

'Wanda? *What* Wanda? Wanda *who*? How absurd, since there's absolutely no evidence that . . . Did someone suggest that Allgrobsch might have . . . ? Oh, surely not!'

Or, failing that:

'Now, look here, young man. If I say you won't print that poppycock then you won't! That's flat! *Or else!*'

But, on further consideration, one had another tactic at one's disposal which would probably be more effective.

I had to venture all the way uptown to see him, at his office in Nixon University. As I travelled northwards on the subway, I mentally rehearsed possible opening lines. The meeting place was of course his suggestion: he alleged he was too busy to visit a restaurant near my Institute for our fortnightly lunch together (not that we had any regular schedule; it just happened that we met every two weeks or so), so I prevailed on him to invite me instead to his buttery or hall (or whatever it's called there). No doubt he assumed he would be at an advantage on his home ground. Well, one was not cowed. Besides, it would be interesting to observe him in his natural habitat.

'I'll be with you in a moment,' said Frank's voice; his head poked out of an office door for an instant, swivelled around, and ducked back within.

So, then. One had to kick one's heels, in a long dull corridor on the fourteenth floor (actually the thirteenth: that number had been missed out in the counting – absurd superstition!) of a concrete teaching block, for Frank the professor to finish coping with importunate advisees. One cleared one's throat. One averted one's eyes and tried to think about something else. The place was cluttered with waiting students: surely one would not be mistaken for one of them!

The corridor was equipped with an iced-water machine (one pressed a lever with one's elbow, or a pedal with one's foot, and a little squirt appeared) and nothing else. No furniture; no amusements. Nary a pop video; not even a window. Several students, therefore, clustered around the iced-water machine: sipping from it, wetting their fingers in it, just playing with it. Others slouched on the floor with their back against the wall and chatted in pairs. Even by the general standard of undergraduates, this lot seemed none too bright. For example, two boys were engaged in an intricate conversation: the darker one described how he'd acquired a little plastic doll which, on squeezing a rubber bulb, would bare its buttocks – it was dangled inside the rear window of his car as a mascot; the paler one explained at some length how and why this was not amusing, and what he would do with it if it came into his possession. A girl was telling her friend about a boy she had dated: 'He came five minutes late. What does that *mean*?'

Various of them went in and out of Frank's door. They entered jaunty or laconic or scared; they exited dejected mostly, clutching essays scribbled over with red ink. Somebody murmured to a friend, 'C minus. He's a tough grader.'

Finally I managed to get in to see Frank. His room was small, had a big window and a filing cabinet, and was impressively book-lined. It smelled of the accumulated nervous sweat of many undergraduates, which made one feel jittery oneself.

Frank was seated behind his desk. He was looking unusually formal in suit and tie. He was wearing his horn-rimmeds: he performed one of the thoughtful-masterful gestures which can be done with them. He ostentatiously peered at me. He said in a dry British accent, 'Ah, it's Emma, isn't it?'

'You know perfectly well it's Emma,' I replied. 'And I'm not one of your students, so you can take that look off your face.'

'Take a seat,' he said, pointing at a low hard chair. I remained standing.

'And what have you come to see me about, Emma?' he asked, still in the professorial manner. Then he snapped out of it. He took off his spectacles. He loosened his red silk tie a little. 'I've been grading their mid-terms, Em. It's for Western Civ. one-oh-one: Plato to NATO. So

214

far, we're up to Machiavelli. A lousy class: no intellectual capability; most of them couldn't argue their way out of a paper bag.'

'Well, I suppose they can't help it. They haven't had the benefit of a decent education.'

'I'm a hard taskmaster,' he said, with a bully's grin, 'I don't mind admitting it. It's still only halfway through the semester. That's my tactics see; I'm a bastard at the beginning, to make them all work hard – or drop out of the class and give me less work – and then I let up near the end and give them good grades on the final exam. So they think I've got a heart of gold and I get a good course evaluation.'

'A *what?*'

'It's a kind of, y'know, report on how I'm doing, student-wise. The students fill in the forms, and the students' union compiles the results. It's important, on the tenure front.'

'That's like letting the monkeys assess the running of the zoo!'

Frank shrugged. 'Want to see mine from last semester?'

He slid a word-processed leaflet on quite glossy paper – *NU Course Evaluation. Fall Semester 1989* – across the desk. It was open on the page referring to himself. I read out loud: '. . . um um um . . . "with his British formality, um, imposes a high-level of intellectual rigor" . . . It's funny seeing it spelled that way, with no u; it always makes one think of *rigor mortis* . . . "and fair play, yet is accessible to students and is always willing to broaden their um, and relate the course material to issues in contemporary um . . . This course is strongly recommended . . ." I say, it makes you seem quite good.'

'I am good.'

It was followed by some meaningless statistics. Thirty-four per cent thought his class preparation was 'excellent', whereas 47 per cent assessed it as merely 'very good' and 11 per cent judged it a pitiful 'good'. Also students had to respond to a list of statements such as: 'I felt the course expanded my horizons' with 'yes' or 'I think so' or 'no'.

'How absurd!' I said. 'The first two responses are identical. By definition: if one replies yes to a proposition then one thinks so, and if one thinks so then one replies yes.'

'Em. I'm not personally responsible for the exact wording of this thing.'

'Yes, well. At least it must be some comfort to feel you have satisfied students.'

He put on a hurt expression, took off his spectacles, and rubbed the red mark at the top of his nose. 'I know what you're thinking, and it's not true. My rule is: no nooky with undergraduates – that's what graduate students are there for.'

'Nothing could have been further from my – '

He interrupted me by holding up a hand like a policeman. He clenched his fists and unclenched them again.

'I've been thinking,' he said, 'about the, uh, Wanda, y'know . . . You want a cup of coffee?'

'No.'

'And I feel, after taking all possible views into consideration, and . . . uh . . . my prime duty is to – or a cup of tea? – to the biography. Hence, as it were, I have to publish any relevant facts.'

'*What*? Are you seriously intending to put into general circulation some scandalous – '

He had a guilty expression on his face rather similar to the one he uses for purposes of seduction. He said weakly, 'I've got to be decisive at this point in the proceedings. A proper understanding of the biographico-literary nexus that goes under the y'know of L.Z. Allgrobsch necessitates analysing all the accessible data, specifically including – '

'But it's not *good*.'

'Uh huh.'

'No, you don't understand. One means, it's *bad*. You're chipping away at Allgrobsch's fundamental ethical – '

'I *am* ethical, too. I'm the ethicalest biographer in town. What you're suggesting – no, you can't interrupt, I want to make this clear at this moment in time – what you're saying is: tell a lie. Yeah, maybe it's only a small lie, a cover-up operation, a kind of mini-Watergate situation – but if you tell a little lie, then you tell a bigger one, and a bigger one, and suddenly *kerpow*! – a colossal Allgrobschgate!'

'But surely, common decency requires – '

'You think you're the only one with morals! You think just because your mummy taught you some old-fashioned sayings when you were a kid – "Love your neighbour as yourself" – "Discretion is the better part of valour" – "Undies worn twice are not very nice" – you think you're little Miss Goody-Goody! Well, let me tell you – '

'Now, let's not jump to conclusions . . .'

'Let me tell you, I've got morals too. Number one. You've got to be investigative about everything. That's my philosophy! If you know a scandal, it's your duty to go into it. If you don't like something, you

216

should challenge it. If you've got deep-seated motivations, you should act on them. Try to be upfront about everything, in your daily life too. This is why I'm a literary scholar. Yeah, I know you don't believe in literary, as it were, criticism. You're cynical. You're dubious. You've got a bad case of false consciousness. You think it's all just playing a game, just having your bandwagon and eating it, but I'm serious about lit. crit. I believe that if we analyse texts, and learn to see them in ways they don't see themselves – and not only texts but also "texts" in the inclusive sense, like oral records and history and any psychological materials – we can learn more about the world, and change it, and make it better!'

'That's a touch ambitious, isn't it?'

'And anything else – if you try to make it pretty, cosmeticise . . . You start telling a story that takes a real, flawed human being like Allgrobsch, and turns him into some kind of demi-god, then you're a fascist!'

'Oh. Do you think so?'

Frank didn't reply. As a consequence of his show of invective, he was rather red-faced and panting: this had the effect of making him look both beastly and passionate.

I said, 'Well, actually, one is feeling rather peckish, so perhaps we should . . .'

'*What?*' he said loudly, as if one had just made an indecent suggestion.

'. . . have lunch?'

'Uh . . . lunch, huh . . .' He found little items on his desk-top to fuss around with: an eraser; a stapler; a student essay with 'NO' scrawled across it in red; five paperclips linked in a chain; an executive toy consisting of suspended banging balls. 'I'm kinda busy . . . My research . . . My teaching commitments . . . So . . .'

'Oh. That's all right then. I've come all the way out here just to wait in your corridor and then have a nice twenty-minute chat with you and not get lunch.'

'Glad you see it that way,' he said crisply.

'Well, Francis. I was planning to mention this post-prandially, over the coffee, but . . . I thought you'd like to know.' I paused a little, relishing the suspense. 'About Allgrobsch's state of health . . .'

'Uh, sure. Got a . . .' He searched in a drawer and gave me some clipped papers: one of his interview transcripts. 'Here. I did a thing two weeks ago with a guy called Athanias, the physician in charge of

217

Allgrobsch. Gave me some ideas about why he got the stroke. Been meaning to show it to you, Em.'

'Francis. I've just heard from Barbra that Allgrobsch is getting better. He's on the road to complete recovery.'

Frank sank back in his chair. His horn-rimmeds slid down his nose; he banged them up into place. He dragged the phone towards him, gripping the receiver as if it were the handle of a shield.

I remained calm and composed.

Frank rose again. He shooed me from his office with great flurries of his arms. He slammed the door after me.

As I stood outside, with one's ear not far from the door, I heard him dialling; then calling, 'Hallo? Hallo? Is anyone there?'

42

'Hallo-o! Hallo, it's Emma Smart here! Hallo! Hallo? Oh, thank you.' The entryphone went *zdzdzdz*; I sprang up and pushed open the front door of the apartment building before the buzzing stopped.

Wanda's place, actually. It was in a surprisingly dignified part of the city, with decent-sized weathered houses and front lawns, reminiscent of surburban Cambridge. Well, one had to own up that one had leaked to Frank what she had told one in confidence: that was only proper. So I'd decided to come over and break the news. And I wanted to get it over and done with, so that I could settle down to my mathematics. To be sure, I was also curious to find out how normal New Yorkers live; the only homes I'd visited so far belonged to academics (Professor Absent's, of course; Ostrovsky's; Honthorst from the Institute) or to funny people like Bridget's mother or Fanny's boyfriend with the rottweiler, so they didn't really count. It had seemed simpler not to give her advance warning of my visit; on the other hand, while burrowing through my desk at home in search of a subway token, certain considerations had crossed my mind. Suppose she were out shopping: well then, one would wait. Or suppose she lived with a person: one could cope with that. And what to wear: one spent a good minute pondering the alternatives. Going just as one was might seem deliberately careless. There again, the semi-brogues and the flouncy Liberty skirt one keeps for best might show her up. So – since Wanda always wears black – it would be a thoughtful touch to copy her, wouldn't it? I slipped into my basic corduroy trousers and cashmere poloneck. I viewed my reflection in the full-length looking glass. Why yes: although my face is too cheerful really to fit the part, one did look quite sophisticated. I tried out a jolly downcast expression, doing it with the eyes and the mouth. One looked so miserable I had to giggle.

As it turned out, one needn't have worried. Wanda was at home, alone; dressed in black; and my outfit was perfectly in keeping with the ambience.

'H-h-h-h-hallo,' I said. 'I say, your apartment has a studenty feeling to it – and one means that in the positive sense: it's not the kind with books piled in old asparagus boxes and underwear draped over the radiator and a dismantled Yamaha on the bed – oh, no, it has an experimental air – not that of course one claims to be speaking as an expert: when I moved into my rooms at Cambridge Mummy lent me the old bedspread and the watercolours of Highland cattle . . .'

'Hi!' she said.

'Oh gosh, I'm gabbing away again, aren't I?'

'Sit down.'

I lowered myself. I looked around.

I made some conversation. 'I like the colour scheme in this room.'

'It's all black.'

'Yes, but *nice* black. Interesting, er, textural qualities of blackness on the wood shelving and the curtains, and the . . . all natural materials, too, and the black candles. Where did you get them?'

'They're on special in a discount store at Lexington and Twenty-third. They just leaped out and grabbed me.'

'Gosh, yes. I suppose they would, rather.'

'Now, Emma, tell me why you've come to see me.'

We were seated facing each other on neighbouring big beanbags on the floor of quite a large room. The curtains were drawn, so the only illumination was from the pair of tall candles fixed in ebony holders. Incense was burning somewhere, giving a pleasing aroma rather like that of the disinfectant Mummy puts in the sheep dip. Wanda was dressed much like I was, except that her feet were bare, and she'd ringed her eyes with eyeliner or whatever to make them bigger.

'Actually,' I replied, 'if I might just explain what one said to F-f-f – How are you?'

'My inner self is in a state of deep psychic depression, but I'm hiding behind a mask of sociability.' She said this in a dull, matter-of-fact way.

'Oh. How interesting.'

'How are *you*, Emma?'

'I'm very well, thank you . . . Er, have you thought of going out and meeting people? Join a social group, take up pottery classes, that kind of thing?'

'My ambition is to make my mind a blank.'

'Oh.'

'I have this strong feeling coming through, you want to tell me something . . . Mm?'

I admit I'm not very talented at consoling the unfortunate. In my first year at Cambridge I'd volunteered to assist an organisation known as the Samaritans for jollying up people who want to kill themselves. They always need new blood to sit in front of a telephone in the small hours. I went along to a special training course. It was frightfully good fun: we did a lot of role play in which I usually got to be the would-be suicide. I put on a Cockney accent and said, 'Elp! Elp! HI'm orribly hupset cos my usband it me! HI'll cut my ead hoff hand is!' And then somebody else would have to persuade me to drop the knife and have a nice cup of tea instead. But at the conclusion of the course one was informed – in the tactfullest possible way – that one just wasn't cut out for the job. My age, of course. Also I kept offering constructive suggestions whereas what you're supposed to do is just repeat what the person told you, but in a questioning tone, to encourage her/him to discuss the problem – on the principle, perhaps, that the kind of people who ring up the Samaritans spend most of their lives talking only to themselves, and any other mode of conversation would strike them as unnatural. I tried to use this approved technique on Wanda.

I said, 'You have this strong feeling coming through, that I want to tell you something?'

'Mm. You want to share it with me?'

'You are wondering if I want to share it with you?'

'Uh huh.'

'You are saying, uh huh?'

'Uh huh.'

We were like chess-players nearing a draw by repetition. I changed my tactic. 'Actually, Wanda, there *is* something I – '

'You told your friend Frank about what my ex did to me, and now he's going to tell the world.' Her tone was level – not to say flattened.

'My goodness! How did you know?'

'It's the reason I'm depressed.'

'Oh dear!'

'Subconsciously, I always knew this would happen, I guess. It's why I was open with you, because my inner being wanted to expose itself, to shuck off my guilt.'

'So you're not . . . angry with me?'

She shook her head. 'Hell, no. It's in your nature, and you can't go against that. You're the world's greatest gossip.'

'Oh. Is that so? One had never thought of oneself in that light.'

Then she hugged me (with remarkably good timing) which made one feel better about one's character.

That's the thing about normal people: they operate largely on instinct, like dogs and cats. No doubt they find this ability useful in the jobs they do – such as bus driver, prime minister, street sweeper and so on . . . I seem to spend a fair amount of my time puzzling out how their minds work; given that they're incapable of using consistent logic, they must have some other system for steering through their daily lives. Actually, if one examines each individual statement they come up with, it usually makes a rough sense; but they can't string them together to come up with a rational conclusion. They're like someone who can't swim but who can thrash about in the water, managing to stay afloat. They do get from A to B somehow. In the case of Frank – who straddles the clever/stupid borderline – the distinction is perhaps clearest: sometimes he'll come up with a remarkably spot-on *aperçu*; other times not. Even Wanda, who is always unintelligent, is nevertheless quite shrewd.

Anyway, now that the air had been cleared (metaphorically, that is; the actual stuff was thick with incense smoke), Wanda and I had a jolly chat about the clubbies. She knew the most frightfully interesting anecdotes about everybody (well, she would, wouldn't she); for example, the time Mr Richman had bought a bottle of hair-restorer that made him come out in a rash; or Mr Dozy's boast about his feat of valour in the Korean War, which turned out to be rather exaggerated; or what happened after Mr Brown won eighty-four dollars off Mr Black at poker . . . And she even mentioned a story or two about what Barbra had got up to with some of the regulars – well, one had noticed her patting Mr Richman on his bald spot, and returning H.H.'s pocket watch surreptitiously, so now that one put two and two together . . . Not entirely to my surprise, I found I was enjoying the companionship of Wanda. Her best friend couldn't accuse her of scintillating wit (but one has quite enough of that for two): on the other hand, her presence is comfy.

'By the way,' I asked, when the anecdotes had run their course, not really expecting a logical reply, 'I take it you receive alimony from Allgrobsch?'

'Alimony? I'm not divorced. He's my husband.'

'Really? I thought he was your ex.'

'Legally, we're still married. We have a joint bank account.'

'Oh. So you could take out all his money – all yours, that is – what you gave him?'

'I could . . . I sure won't. I want to help him.'

'Ah. Far be it from me to be excessively rational, but might I point out that, as a bestselling author, indeed a Nobel Prize winner, Allgrobsch doesn't need the money, whereas you do. Why not give up washing dishes and dispensing beer at the club, and become a lady of leisure?'

'You don't understand, Emma. I gave him everything I had, to help him. I can't stop now.'

'Yes, but . . .' I realised argument was pointless.

'I won't give up my sacrifice! And you can't make me!'

'And do you intend to persist in this conviction indefinitely?'

'When he dies . . .' She stopped talking and gulped. Quite possibly she was near to tears: it was hard to tell because the candlelight was so dim, just a shimmer across her face and long hair. She didn't look pretty, but beautiful. It wasn't difficult to see what attracted Allgrobsch to her – apart from her inheritance, of course.

By this stage I'd already taken my shoes and socks off, so as not to be standoffish. She extended her bare feet and rubbed her soles against mine.

I thought I'd give the Samaritan technique another try. 'You were saying, "When he dies" . . . ?' I was doing my best not to titter; her toes danced: one is awfully ticklish down there.

'Then I'll quit. I'll take what's mine – and I'll take off to – nowhere, San Francisco, Nirvana . . .'

'Which of the three for preference?'

'I know a friend, she wants to sublet her place in San Francisco. Want to come live with me there?'

'Supposing,' I said cautiously, 'just for the sake of argument, suppose Allgrobsch recovered again and was, well, alive and kicking, would you – and one is speaking merely theoretically, needless to say – would you still collect what's due to you, and go off to . . . the place you mentioned?'

'No way!'

'Oh?'

'You don't *know* what it *means*, to care for a man. If I do nothing in my life, I want to say: I sacrificed myself for a genius!'

'Well, we all have our differing ambitions . . .'

She muttered annoyingly, 'When you're my age you'll understand.'

The incense was ponging a bit. One of the black candles was about to topple over, but I caught it, and eased it upright again, which was as much as might reasonably have been expected of one.

43

Interview with Dr John Athanias (edited extract), New York,
16 February 1990

– Ye-e-es.

– We don't want to commit ourselves there.

– Hmm.

– He underwent what in a medical context we tend to call a stroke. Or, in the language you would probably be more familiar with, a cerebral embolism. With complications, of course. Ah, there are always complications . . .

– To retrace the, hmm, progression of the syndrome is never as easy as the layman . . . hmm. Substantially, what we have here is a blockage of the – and these off the cuff remarks are only speculations and should not be interpreted as binding or definitive statements in any way . . .

– Well, we're not in a position to make any comment on that.

– The ambulance took the patient to St Kevin's, arriving at . . . let me check our records . . . nineteen twenty-three hours. The treatment of the patient while under the care of the paramedical personnel was the finest possible under the circumstances. Though that statement was of course off the record and does not imply any guarantee on our part, and in no way are we representing or claiming to represent the official views of the hospital or any person other than . . .

– No comment.

– The patient underwent emergency surgery commencing at nineteen fifty-eight hours.

– No comment.

– You understand that, much as we want to assist you, Mr . . . hmm . . . 'Dr' . . . ah, Frank, there are . . . Well, complications may arise, yes, as there always are, of a medical, also a legal, and a medico-legal nature. As a professional person, we're sure you understand. We must all be circumspect.

– The prognosis, hmm. The patient's prospects for – as you would call it – 'getting better' . . . Ye-e-es. That would depend on the degree of brain damage, if any. We think it's safe to say . . . possibility of the patient regaining consciousness. In plain English, the chances are . . . Not to say he might not attain a complete recovery, of course. And our statement should not be interpreted as . . .

– Hmm, difficult to say . . . The original cause was probably some . . . possibly some action, some statement, some disturbance . . . We understand you were present when the stroke took place. Did you observe any unusual stress on the part of the subject, associated with, for instance . . . Did anyone make any demand or, hmm, surprising comment, or . . . ha, ha, leap out dressed in a gorilla suit, or otherwise cause, what you would call, shock?

– Hmm.

– Well, as you would say, time is money, and we really . . . Well, it's been good talking to you . . . In conclusion, we don't rule anything out. For example, we once had a patient with severe, ye-e-es, bullet through the brain – Mafia contract, in fact – occlusions of the . . . in a coma – we all thought he wouldn't last the night. But he did. He slowly regained normal encelographic status and functioning – marvellous thing, the brain – and finally he actually sat up and said, '*Mama*', and had a massive coronary thrombosis and died.

44

Adrift

This story is set during a period in our history when no ships steam along the river. Why this should be, we do not know. Maybe there is a blockage upstream, or a dispute, or some other imaginable problem. All we understand is: the regular ferry no longer docks at the landing stage bringing us our American cloth and our Czech watches, and our honorary aunts carrying spherical cakes wrapped in knotted kerchiefs; and fishing boats no longer sail past our town either; in short, the river is silent.

For a few days we pretend nothing has happened. Why should it perturb us anyway? Some of our supplies can be obtained via an overland route instead; and those that can't, can't. And if our friends and relatives are unable to pay us a visit – well, we will think kind thoughts of them, and they of us.

But then we start checking up on the river. The oldest are the first to do this: they mount to the viewing places where streets swerve to avoid plunging down the hillside, and stare at a unified vision of cloud, land and blank running water. The young follow next: they skip down to the riverbank; they point and giggle; they toss stones into the water to shatter its blandness and blaspheme against its calm. And finally those who are neither old nor young come to the river: they watch its languid flow with envy, then with satisfaction, and then with no thought at all.

But the river is not really silent. It is full of bubbles and green things. It is as it must have been in the days before man, we think. The word prehistoric *is on all our lips. As otter is sighted – a slick hairy wriggle – cavorting midstream and eating living fish.*

Since many of us have time on our hands, and since we are all gathered by the river anyway, the idea occurs to us to travel on the river by boat. Somebody discovers a small skiff half buried in a pea patch; the tendrils are creeping over the mossy wood. It is hauled to the landing stage. It is cleaned and patched and rehabilitated. Somebody else constructs a raft from some firewood and a ball of jute string. This design is soon copied. A canoe is found in the school. A dinghy has been lying for years under the butcher's slatted warehouse . . . And soon the river is adorned with many little rowing vessels, sweeping to and fro over the green water.

The river moves fast. There are two techniques to cope with this. Some of us prefer to zoom downstream on the flow, and then paddle hard upstream. Others do the reverse. Each group expresses its philosophy forcefully. The downstream-firsters claim they experience ease followed by worthy, rejuvenating exercise. They accuse their rivals: 'You are so exhausted by the time you come to float downstream you cannot possibly enjoy it. You are puritans, deniers of joy.' On the other hand the upstream-firsters claim they pay for their pleasures in advance, as one should, and then lie back and enjoy the free ride. As for their rivals, they say, 'How can you take pleasure in your sport when you know you will have to work hard afterward?' By the evening, when it is cool, both factions retreat to the land. All of us lie together on the bank, wet and quarrelsome, suspecting we should have adopted the alternative strategy, defending our own case with less and less conviction.

Then the old tell stories to the young. 'Have you heard of the city that was swamped by the waters? If you look down on clear days you can see the drowned roofs, and hear the bells chiming underneath.' Of course that could not happen to our town since this is a non-tidal river – so nobody bothers to gaze down through the ripples, or cup a hand over an ear, listening.

Which leads on to another story that the old are fond of telling: how there exists something called the sea, which is like our river, only much bigger. 'If you stand at the edge of it and look as far out as you can, you will not see the other side. If you are alone on a boat in the middle of it, you can look all around and, for all that you can tell, the whole of the world apart from yourself has vanished.' But the young are too wise to believe this story, although they know it is true.

§ IV

Fire and Ice

Then the princess kissed the toad.
Suddenly . . .

45

Gosh, one was proud of oneself. There I was, just inside the doors of the Institute, welcoming familiar and unfamiliar faces. Fanny and Bridget were seated behind a table, handing out 'HELLO I'M ——' badges, and packages of relevant information, and waving newcomers on towards the coffee urn and the bagel box. It was the long-awaited morning of Sunday the first of April: the day of the conference on the Smart–Potts–Ostrovsky conjecture, organised by Fanny and Bridget and oneself. And was April Fool's Day really an appropriate occasion to celebrate the hypothesis that most strategies will lead to a 'best' world? Why yes, one thinks so.

Everybody was here! Flixheim was in a corner, arguing with Habib and di Piero. Potts and Jed were smearing smoked-salmon-flavour creamcheese on each other's bagel and each other. Chang and Ostrovsky were over by the window, scribbling equations on sheets of scrap paper thoughtfully placed there in advance. (I'd scooped the stuff from the recycling bin: everything from fliers for the Free Mandela Disco to minutes of the Equal Opportunities Committee. Mathematicians prefer using second-hand paper: they feel freer to waste it.) Blogham-Smith was flossing his teeth with the string of a teabag. And there were plenty of strangers too: postdocs and graduate students, or visiting research associates, even one woman about my age. 'How *are* you?' I kept saying. 'How do you do? . . . Hallo! . . . I read your nifty little article in *Proc. Am. Math. Soc.* – simply splendid stuff . . .' My cheeks got quite exhausted from smiling. One felt rather like the Queen.

Most people were blinking as if they had just come out of the dark. And, in a sense, they had. I had, too. Naturally one had been labouring for weeks or months, perfecting the papers to be delivered here, the objections to be raised, the questions to be posed, the off-the-cuff brilliancies to be muttered during the lunch-break, so one had been going without much sociable chitchat; hence the dialogue was of that artificial sort in which every word seems subtly peculiar and echoes off the ceiling – in the style favoured by dropouts from a Trappist monastery. I pattered among the crowd, overhearing some conversations and participating briefly in others. Most dealt with the eternal academic grouses: underfunding, incompetent students, boring committees; they were expressed in terms of mathematical slang and sprinkled with in-jokes. 'My bank balance is asymptotically tending towards zero . . .' 'Not so much the Eternal Triangle, more the Eternal Infinitely Discontinuous Fractal . . .' 'I used to think he was square, but he bends a little; I guess he's a rhombus . . .'

'If you guys could just be finishing your bagels,' said Fanny or Bridget. Bridget or Fanny said, 'The proceedings will commence in the auditorium in one minute . . .'

We all filed in. The introductory piece was given competently by Ostrovsky: he summarised the history of the SPO – politely minimising his own role in just such a way as to make it clear he was politely minimising his own role. He complimented me three times. He ended with a quotation from Voltaire; then a little joke to which the punchline was, 'If this is the best of all possible worlds, then why is it so lousy?' Hearty laughter. Applause.

Ostrovsky welcomed me on stage. I took a deep breath, and outlined the agenda. 'If you turn to page twelve in your Additional Material folder, Ladies and Gentlemen, you will see . . .' etcetera. And a quick summary of ongoing activity in scope theory, to whet appetites. Of course I said something terribly flattering about Ostrovsky, by way of return.

Flixheim spoke on 'Three Paradoxes in Scope Theory'. Actually his speech was quite interesting – very abstract stuff – but I was concentrating on my own job: coordinating the question and answer period afterwards, always the trickiest business at conferences. Somebody is bound to feel aggrieved he wasn't called on to speak, and somebody (often the same somebody) won't shut up.

A coffee break.

Potts delivered his usual stuff on 'Applications of the Potts–Smart–Ostrovsky Conjecture', which one could doze through. Jed interrupted with the surprise announcement that Fermat's Last Theorem had just been proven: this was an unfunny April Fool; everyone shushed him.

Lunch.

And in the afternoon we broke up into small groups for seminar discussions. It was one of these, entitled (by Fanny and Bridget) 'SPO – What's Hot And What's Not', that I had chosen as the venue at which to reveal my proof of the SPO to an astounded world. Actually, the word had got around that I was proposing to do just this (well, one had mentioned it in passing to various concerned parties . . .) so this seminar had by far the largest attendance: fifty people were squeezed into a room big enough for fifteen; the latecomers had to sit on dragged-in folding chairs or the window ledge; the late-latecomers were standing. The air-conditioning whined so loudly it had to be turned off. The place became hotter and smellier.

Establishing priority is vital. It's no good discovering something which somebody else has already discovered. (Take the case of poor Johannsen at Houston: he very nearly got promoted to an associate professorship – then it turned out a fellow no one had ever heard of in Turin had come up with the same idea, so Johannsen didn't even get tenure. He was last heard of teaching Introductory Sums at a community college in Missouri.) But on the other hand it's not a good idea to announce one's discovery with blaring trumpets, a tickertape parade, and publication in *Am. Math. Rev.* – because there are always a few niggling little details to be worked out, and one doesn't want to print something faulty and then have egg on one's face. Which is why I was using this seminar for the purpose: it was public enough that there would be no doubt as to my priority, but not so public that if there were any error I couldn't retract it.

One cleared one's throat. The audience became calmer. An expectant hush. I switched on the projector (generating yet more heat) and slid the first transparency into place. As an overture, I sketched out the proof that the SPO is meaningful and valid for infinite simrel networks: actually this part had already been published and was uncontroversial. Then I launched *con brio* into the proof that the SPO is true for 'almost all' networks, using a rather sly technique known as 'downward induction' – which is tricky to explain . . .

. . . but the previous evening I'd had a go at telling Arnie about it because he'd been badgering me to.

'"Induction" has a special meaning in mathematics: it's the name of a strategy for finding a proof; it's best explained by giving an example. Here goes . . .'

For Arnie's benefit I wrote on a pad of yellow paper the following equation:

$$S_n = 1 + 2 + 3 + 4 + \ldots + \ldots n = n(n+1) \div 2$$

'In plain English, this states: consider the sum of all the whole numbers from one right the way up to some number called n; this sum is equal to n times the number next higher than n, divided by two. The theorem to be proven is: this equation is true never mind which whole number n is.

'Well, it's very easy to show it's true if n is any particular small number. For example, if $n = 1$ then the equation states . . .'

$$S_1 = 1 = 1(1+1) \div 2 \quad \text{(I wrote this on the pad.)}$$

'. . . which is true (check it for yourself); or if, for example, $n = 3$, then the equation states . . .'

$$S_3 = 1 + 2 + 3 = 3(3+1) \div 2 \quad \text{(I wrote that too.)}$$

'. . . which you can also check. But how can one prove that it's true for *all* values of n? Well, one will use the method of induction. First, one establishes a subproof: namely, that *if* the equation is true for a certain value of n, *then* it's also true for the next higher value of n. For example, one wants to prove that *if* the equation is correct about S_{100} *then* it's also correct about S_{101} . . . and so on . . .'

I began sketching out the subproof. But Arnie interrupted me. 'Sure, Emma. I can do the subproof in my head. It's easy algebra.'

'Fine,' I said. 'Now, what's been shown so far is that: if the equation is correct about S_1 then it's also correct about S_2, and if it's correct about S_2 then it's also correct about S_3, and if . . . etcetera etcetera. But it *is* correct about S_1' – pointing at the equation above – 'so it's also correct about S_2, and so also about S_3 . . . etcetera; so it's *always* correct; so the equation is proven. QED!

'Now that kind of proof – showing that if something is true in one special case then it's true in another, and using that to prove it's always true – is what we call induction.'

In fact an inductive proof is my favourite kind: I like the notion of building little local connections between the truth of different statements, and using them to establish something global. Well, all mathematicians have a preferred style of proof; for instance Ostrovsky is notorious for proving almost anything by *reductio ad absurdum* (i.e. supposing for the sake of argument the thing to be proven is *not* true and showing this assumption leads to absurdity): it appeals to his sense of humour.

Arnie nodded. 'So, you're proving the SPO by induction?'

'In a way, yes. Actually, one shows the SPO is true in the special case when the network is infinite, and then one shows it's also true for very big finite networks, and so on down to normal-size smallish networks . . . That's why the technique's called "downward" induction. Of course, extrapolating from infinite to finite things is subtle . . .'

A brief silence followed my presentation. Then questions flooded in. I was able to rebut a silly error made by Habib (he'd misread an insect on my transparency sign for a division sign!) and another more serious one from Chang; but as for a horde of other comments and queries (emanating, notably, from Blogham-Smith) I could only promise to consider these issues later. The point is: my proof was exceedingly complex, involving dividing all possible cases into a host (twenty-six, actually) of categories, and establishing the SPO in each separate case. Nevertheless one was confident that the proof was solid – and one got the impression that was the general consensus of the seminar, too – not because all the details were necessarily sound, but because it 'felt' right. One can tell.

Well, well. Of course one felt satisfied to have announced what was quite possibly the greatest triumph of one's career to date; yet on the other hand there is always a certain melancholy after any success; besides, although my proof was correct – a sturdy, workmanlike construction – it wasn't beautiful and neat; in short it wasn't what Daddy (in his naval slang) calls 'pusser'. And pusser-ness counts for a great deal in the world of mathematics. Often, when mathematicians are gathered, we pass the time by compiling lists of the Top Ten Proofs, selected on the basis of elegance, economy, surprise and originality: my proof of the SPO would never be on anyone's list.

It was intolerably hot and humid; one unbuttoned as far as decently possible.

A small dark woman stood up – the one I'd noticed earlier. I didn't know her personally, and of course one knows everyone in one's field, so I assumed she was a mere graduate student. She seemed quite comfortable in this tropical climate. She strode to the front of the room, picked up a blue boardmarker, and began writing equations on the whiteboard. At first one couldn't understand what she was up to. Her first equation was quite a well-known theorem in number theory concerning the distribution of prime numbers; it seemed to have nothing whatsoever to do with scope theory: one wondered playfully if perhaps she'd strayed into the wrong conference by mistake. Then – as she set down more equations – one began to understand: she was attempting to prove a theorem about the distribution of exceptions to the SPO in an exceedingly abstract way, borrowing analogous results from number theory. By the time her writing had filled the board, she'd succeeded in proving that theorem, and what's more, her result implied an indirect proof of the SPO itself!

She stated in a quiet, rather husky voice, 'I think this result agrees with Smart's.'

The 'NO SMOKING' sign loomed over the whiteboard – a representation of a burning tube cancelled with a red multiplication sign.

There was nothing more to be said! (Which, as always, implies that a lot was said: half the audience congratulated her, and the other half couldn't understand what on earth she was on about.)

In due course everybody left – all except for her and Ostrovsky and myself. He introduced us.

'Emma, meet Jane. Jane, Emma.' He turned to Jane. 'Emma needs no introduction, of course.' And then to me. 'Jane used to be a postdoc. in my department. She's really a number theorist, but I persuaded her to vacation in scope theory.' He gave a little smile to show he was making a witticism. 'I'll leave you ladies alone.'

He retreated through the door.

We were facing each other in the centre of the room. I was sweating; she wasn't. Only our 'HELLO I'M ——' labels were speaking to each other. She was standing with sleeves rolled up, arms akimbo, looking at me.

A silence took over. Which, as the more senior person present, it was my duty to break. 'Hallo, Jane,' I said. 'That was quite a decent piece of work you did.'

'Yes, it was.'

I added, 'In fact, it was really not bad.'

'Yes.'

In case she didn't understand the British convention of praise by

236

immoderate understatement, I forced myself to say, 'It was jolly good.'

She smiled. 'Yours, too.'

'No,' I said, 'that's not what I *mean*. Your proof is no truer than mine, but it's vastly more stylish. To use the rather vulgar American mathematician's slang, I "brute-forced" my proof, whereas you "magicked" yours.'

'Don't underrate yourself, Emma.' Her voice was low but clear. 'Some people don't like sealed-in clocks; they like the kind with the transparent back so you can check all the workings; Well, your proof is see-through, like that. There are many mathematicians who prefer it your way.'

'One is not "many mathematicians". One is *I*. And I happen to care about style and beauty and – yes – brilliance! *Your* proof is the one I want to have discovered. You've achieved what I'd wanted to, putting my own triumph in the shade!'

She moved her hand across her face and pushed her hair back. I noted that she was slightly shorter than oneself.

She said, in a precise, even tone that gave the impression she was choosing each word with care, 'We have another connection. Didn't Yuri tell you?'

'Yuri? Oh, Ostrovsky . . . Why, no . . .'

'I've moved to Berkeley now. The maths is hot there. Why don't you come and join us? I'm back in New York just for this conference. While I'm in California, you're subletting my apartment in the Village, right?'

'What? No. The apartment belongs to Professor Absent . . . er, a middle-aged fellow, a linguist, balding, wears bifocals . . .'

'No.'

'But . . .'

'The linguistic books are just stored there; they belong to my boyfriend. And I'm not middle-aged, or male, or balding, and I don't use glasses.'

The image of Professor Absent hovered over her. At first it was colossal: he was a twice life-size giant; then he shrank to her dimensions, and his genial wrinkled face was superimposed on her taut smooth one. And then he faded away.

'But this is absurd!' I said. 'It would be an incredible coincidence if – '

She interrupted me. 'Oh, it's not a coincidence. I think we make our

237

own luck, don't you agree? You got the apartment through the inter-university exchange computer in Illinois, right? I know a guy who works there. I asked him to put you in my place. I hope you like it . . . We women mathematicians have got to help each other, surely?'

It seemed so unfair. At that moment, staring into her calm, strong, dark eyes, I hated her more than anyone in the world. And at the same time I admired her terribly.

I said, 'One is a genius.'

She didn't disagree.

'Oh, and one question more,' I whispered. 'How old are you?'

'I'm twenty. Twenty-one next June. Why do you ask?'

'Oh . . . nothing.'

46

The Boy From Nowhere

*Radka the inn-keeper is trying to buy a jar of beetroot and sell a carved
balustrade veneered in tulipwood; Dav the barber wants to barter his flute
for an egg; Vlob the tailor is offering an overcoat for a leg of lamb; Gam
the pious has fish – he needs a loaf; Dama the respectable is seeking a
turnip in return for a used wedding ring; Portin the intellectual is offering
to exchange the complete works of Spinoza (in red calf binding, slightly
foxed) for just about anything . . . In these difficult times everybody in our
town gathers in the marketplace, muttering and arranging deals, in quest of
the necessities of daily life. What will we sacrifice if need be? Everything,
almost – even those items of intense personal value that remind us where we
came from and who we are: heirloom candlesticks, family portraits in gilt
frames; a treasured glass puppy (souvenir from a Venetian honeymoon); a
grand piano with a scarred lid.*

*And we are so harried, so involved in our intricate business, that we fail
to notice the entrance of the nameless boy.*

*Well, presumably he entered the town somehow. He must have crawled
in, up from the river or down from the hill; or maybe somebody deposited
him here . . . Surely there must have been an amazing entrance scene
(which all of us overlooked – but we can imagine it in retrospect) when the
little naked creature, making inhuman mewing noises and padding quietly
on four hands and feet, first arrived behind the pyramid of tawdry
cabbages; and it cried.*

*Not 'it': he. He cried . . . He cries, and – Govya the beautiful pats his
little shaggy head; Gam the pious pulls a funny face to amuse him; Fehma
the artistic rocks him; Levno the cobbler plays a counting game with the
infant's toes . . . Eventually he becomes silent; he curls up on his side and
sleeps.*

*He belongs to nobody, so we all look after him. We move him from house
to house – whoever has a spare blanket and a little place near the embers*

239

can take care of him for a while. We don't have enough to eat ourselves, but surely we couldn't deprive the poor innocent boy. He is beautiful; he is sweet-natured; he is very little trouble; he never complains; he is easy to hug.

One problem, though. He can't talk. A child his age should be able to speak simple sentences; a few score words, at least. But he only whimpers and growls. 'Ah well,' we say, 'no doubt he will learn in time.'

And some other awkwardnesses. He prefers raw food – meat, for preference – tearing it apart with his nails and teeth. He persists in not standing upright. He marks the boundaries of his living space with his urine. We shake our head and say, 'Boys will be boys.'

And one especially worrisome matter. He has no name. Evidently it's pointless asking the boy himself. No individual in our town has enough authority to assign him an identity. The idea of making a collective decision occurs to us – but surely that would be absurd: it is as if we were all to gather in the marketplace one morning, point to a cloud passing overhead, and declare, 'We hereby name it such and such!'

So we try to find him a nickname. Nicknames are common in our town, anyway: we all have several. They come and go. The process of their evolution is mysterious. It's not as if a nickname is invented by any individual or group. It's not the case that somebody wakes up one morning and suddenly everybody is greeting him in a new way. Rather, they appear slowly and they disappear slowly . . . So what shall this new boy's nickname be?

Various suggestions pass into temporary use and then oblivion. It seems a good idea at one time to name him Dirtyfeet – since he has; but then his feet are washed, and that nickname becomes pointless. Or he is known as the Stranger – but soon he isn't. Or he passes under the title of the Crawler – but in time he sits more or less straight. Or the Mute – then he learns a little of our language. In the end we give up: we realize that names slip from him like water off a duck's back. We just refer to him in the third person as 'him', with a special emphasis, or 'that boy'.

He grows up a little. He reaches the age when he is no longer automatically cute. Of course we all still look after him. We let him sit in the market behind the vegetable stalls. We give him scraps of cabbage leaf or broken parsnip. Still, he is beginning to seem suspiciously like a beggar. He is becoming more embarrassing to explain to visitors. We realise we have forgotten why we adopted him originally.

Portin the intellectual tries to make sense of the phenomenon. He tells

240

the rest of us the tale of Romulus and Remus, raised by a she-wolf, who founded Rome. But this sounds like a parody, a sick joke: he is obviously never going to found anything.

All the same, we love him.

The enemy comes. Some of us flee. Some of us are taken away. The rest of us are allotted identity cards with bad photographs. Except for that boy. Since he has no name he has no official status. He can't be arrested or given rations. He is forbidden to live or die.

I don't remember how this story ends. Forgive me, but after all I was only a boy myself at the time, about his age. From the fact of my non-memory, I can deduce only that his end cannot have been very dramatic. Maybe he vanished quite early. Or maybe he never disappeared: he could have stayed on, nameless and untouchable, throughout everything. He might still be living in the town now, decades later. It's terrifying to think how much happens in detail which is only recalled in general. Think of fog, for example. I know there must have been some foggy days in our town back then. Fog, surely, is a well-understood meteorological condition and the town didn't have some special environmental anti-fog feature . . . Besides, I do recall the existence of fog in an objective way (much as one might if reading in a textbook of physical geography about its occurrence in China or Patagonia). But I have no actual, sensory memory of the stuff. I don't recollect thick gray mists sweeping up from the river and settling along the winding road and the marketplace. I can't see in my mind's eye fog obscuring the heaps of small onions and the bartered pearl earrings, and all our faces, our smiles and our tears . . . Yet I know this must have happened.

47

My entire apartment was filled with steam. It was emanating from the
bathroom door and being sucked in by the grille of the air-conditioner.
It was condensing on the sitting room ceiling, and blurring the titles of
the books on the shelves. For I had turned the shower on at full heat
and full force, and – as always in America – that was hot and forceful
indeed. I needed cleansing. I had come home from the conference
grimed and sticky. Naturally one does not object to a delicate film of
one's own perspiration – but I seemed to be coated with other people's
sweat as well: an alien, smoky gunk. My very clothes smelled as if
borrowed from somebody else. Just as I'd turned the shower on, I'd
suddenly been struck with the fear that I'd forgotten to lock my front
door. I'd rushed out and checked it: no, all was secure. And now I
returned into the heart of the steamworld: nothing was visible in the
bathroom except for a white thickness, and the ceiling lamp glowing
dimly through it. A mighty roar like Niagara. I stripped off. I draped
my clothes over the chair. My hands groped for the temperature
control; I adjusted it. I stepped forward, exposing my skin to the
obliterating onrush. I made liberal use of a rather nice lemon-'n'-honey
head-'n'-body-shampoo; its aroma was reminiscent of the hot drink
Mummy used to make for me when I had a nasty cold. I scraped and
tickled myself with the big loofah. Afterwards I set about wiping
myself down with a shaggy towel as big as Otto Man . . . The steam
thinned, and became no more than a mist; it couldn't clear away
though because something was amiss with the washer on the hot tap,
and boiling water dribbled . . . Well, one was comforted a little . . . But
how could one ever get over that frightful shock of the alternative proof
of the SPO? Besides, one's period was definitely coming soon . . .
Everything was really *too* bad.

Actually one gets on quite well with one's body. It *is* reasonably trim and efficient. To be sure, one's tummy gurgles a bit after meals (that's the worst one could say about it), and one's monthlies are a bother (one did feel rather itchy), but simply nothing compared to the stories one hears . . . Of course Frank would insist one shouldn't think of one's body in this way at all; in fact he had made that very point on several occasions. 'The mind–body dichotomy is rooted in a historically located bourgeois conception of the Self,' he declared. 'The distinction exists only in the context of patriarchal power-relations. As a liberated woman in your case, and a post-feminist person in mine, let us throw off the shackles of worn-out dogma.' To which I retort, 'That's all very well in theory, Francis. But one happens to be in the business of using one's topnotch mind rather than one's perfectly ordinary body. I dare say if one were a sumo wrestler or a professional contortionist one would take a different attitude.'

One felt hot; perhaps one was coming down with something. I walked through the apartment in search of some clothes. Meanwhile I tried to chat with Professor Absent. I needed his sage advice . . . but now he was truly absent. His treasured collection of works on linguistics had reduced to no more than Jane's stored volumes. His helpful notes on public transport and plumbers were signs of Jane's helpfulness. His abandoned jigsaw piece was just Jane's. His roll of translucent Saran Wrap on the kitchen shelf had turned into Jane's Saran Wrap. His *Tassajara Bread Book* with a curlicue of dough stuck on his favourite recipe for molasses-and-walnut loaf was Jane's too. The Scrabble game on top of the bedroom cupboard was set up with words he might never have known: they had been composed by Jane and Jane's adversary (I considered dismantling these words, muddling them down into their component letters; but such revenge would be pitiful indeed.) He had never gazed into the full-length looking glass on the door of the bedroom wardrobe, as I was doing. I didn't see his benign reflection – only that of my own naked body, which (perhaps the glass was dusty or my eyes were full of water) seemed smaller than usual, and darker; more like Jane's.

I slipped my cassette of Debussy's *Pelléas et Mélisande* into, er, Jane's stereo. Which was located in what I used to call the sitting room but had come to think of (under American influence) as the living-room. Strange name: as if all the other rooms were for dying in. *P. & M.* is my favourite opera. The heroine, Mélisande, is a beautiful maiden who does nothing at all and is perfect, while all the men rush about trying to do things and get into trouble. The music soothed me just a little.

I was seized with a desire to brush my teeth. I wanted to clean every crevice and cranny, to remove every last trace of the (actually not bad) supper with Jane and Ostrovsky at the Italian restaurant which one had been duty bound to attend after the conference. So I roamed back to the bathroom. I set about scrubbing the deepest recesses of my gums – the molars, the wisdom teeth – by means of repeated longitudinal strokes, in the manner recommended by Mummy.

I switched on the overhead infra-red lamp. The name is a misnomer really, since by no means all its radiation was in the invisible infra-red end of the spectrum: it emitted a bright red glow, making the bathroom glint like a furnace and converting the steam into pseudo-smoke. It also had the handy side-effect of evaporating condensation on the mirror. At first impression, this lamp had seemed completely useless, but one had always felt it had to have *some* use; at least let it dry one's hair a little. According to Frank (who knows every shady mode of cheating ever devised) the sole function of the lamp is to raise my rent: New York City law requires that the rent can go up faster than inflation only if some 'improvement' is made to the property, so landlords have a vested interest in adding such facilities as remote-control venetian blinds, electronic mosquito traps, or indeed infra-red lamps.

While I was thinking about all this, and meanwhile polishing my incisors, the entryphone buzzer sounded. I ran, still clutching my toothbrush, to speak into it.

A voice said, '*It's me.*'

'Oh, it's you, Frank. Talk of the devil!'

'*Can I come up? Please, Emma. It's urgent.*'

'Oh, gosh. It's not very convenient, actually . . .'

'*Please . . .*'

'Hang on a minute . . .'

I slipped into my spacious dressing-gown in navy blue towelling material (Daddy had given it to me for my 21st). I undid the complex system of latches and locks and let Frank into the apartment.

'In fact I'm glad you've come,' I said hurriedly. 'Something rather peculiar happened at the conference, and you'll do to talk to about it.'

He looked at me with a very queer expression. I thought at first perhaps my dressing-gown had flapped open . . . but no. Then I realised I was frothing at the mouth.

'I'm not rabid,' I said. 'It's only Colgate freshmint.' I swallowed some of it and licked my lips. I looked down at my bare wet feet on the

'WELCOME' mat. 'Now, what happened was this . . .' But one was reluctant to tell him everything – possibly one was afraid he might take Jane's side rather than one's own; after all, she was younger and more intelligent – and youth and intelligence are qualities which evidently appeal to him.

My toothbrush was in my hand. 'Here, what shall I do with it?'

I looked up.

His expression was one of desperate sadness. He took my toothbrush and threw it over his shoulder like a Russian finishing with his vodka glass; it ended up in the bathroom. 'I've got to speak to you, Emma.' He mumbled something about 'misery . . . pain . . . loss . . . the end'.

'What happened?' I asked. 'Has somebody . . . Did somebody . . . Who . . . passed away?'

'Allgrobsch!'

'Oh no! But only the other day one gathered he was doing quite well, in fact a complete recovery was on the cards . . . Yet now . . . "In the midst of life we are in . . ." Well, well, well.'

Frank was going in for another spot of mumbling. I tried to guide him into the living room but his legs kept staggering bathroomward so I let him go in there anyway. I sat him down on the lone chair for want of anywhere better; his bottom was squashing my dirty clothes.

'Now you just keep calm and tell me what the problem is,' I said in my maximally maternal manner. I squatted on the floor beside him. This wasn't a comfortable posture, so I levered myself on to the edge of the chair, next to him. I patted his hand.

But he was not altogether coherent. As far as one could gather from his utterances, the main drift seemed to be that he'd been tremendously fond of Allgrobsch, but hadn't realised it until now, when it was too late. He said something to the effect that he yearned to find out every last detail of Allgrobsch's life, and that the passion of the biographer for the biographee is the *ne plus ultra* of human desire. I asked him why. And he replied with further emphasis on the craving of the biographer to merge with the subject; he distinctly mentioned something called, 'the *princesse lointaine* phenomenon'.

And he wept.

So of course one pressed his head against one's breasts (through a layer or two of thick dressing-gown material) and stroked the wodge of grizzled hair above his ear. One pushed closer against him so one could sit more easily on the chair. He hooped his arms around the small of one's back. Pelléas and Mélisande, that doomed couple, were singing of their undying love. The looking glass reflected, amidst the red glare and the red steam, two figures in an inferno.

His conversation became even harder to catch. He definitely cited Shakespeare or somebody. 'Stay me with flagons and comfort me with apples for I am sick of love . . .' One presumed he meant this request figuratively. (Besides, all one had in the kitchen was half a bottle of dry sherry and a tangerine.) Then – as his mouth tilted up and down, rubbing against my collarbone – he murmured some more quotes.

'Excuse me,' I said, trying to push his head back to where it belonged. 'I didn't quite catch that. *What* is like a tower of marble in the valley of Jezreel? And could you kindly explain the *exact* relevance of two comely fauns basking in the wilderness of Kadesh?'

One had never realised before just how heavy a man's head is: it was quite an effort to shift it at all, though I had one hand levering on the side of his neck and the other just inside his shirt, tugging at his shoulder. Eventually his head slid down diagonally; I felt the roughness of his chin scraping against the skin beneath the left dressing-gown lapel. I had to yank quite hard on the nape hairs to make him retreat.

'By the way,' I asked. '*How* did you hear the sad news about poor old Allgrobsch? I mean, only the other week Barbra was bruiting that he was getting better. And now . . . Well, it's a "Dead, dead, and never called me biographer" kettle of fish. Isn't it?'

Frank lifted his head and looked into my eyes. There was a puzzled expression on his face – which turned into a crafty one.

He said, quite clearly and slowly, 'You're saying . . . I'm saying Allgrobsch is dead, and you want to know how I found out about it?'

'Yes . . .'

'Ah.'

He paused with his jaw hanging open. (One does wish his mind and speech moved more swiftly.) He continued, 'Now, the big, as it were, question you want to ask me . . . Am I going to publish the whole truth about him, including the scandalous – '

'Ye-e-es,' I interrupted, somewhat up in the air as to what direction the conversation was supposed to be going in. 'No doubt that remains an issue.'

'Uh . . . and just supposing . . . and I'm not saying anything, y'know, it's . . . Just, if I said to you, I'll cover up the scandal, to make you happy . . . I mean, what do you think?'

'What do I think about *what*?'

246

'. . . Make you *happy*, huh? In return for not printing the whole truth about him . . .'

'Francis! Are you seriously suggesting that – '

He nodded.

'What? One does the whole . . . the complete . . . everything?'

His right hand squeezed one's bottom.

'Oh golly gosh. That's practically blackmail . . . What can one do?'

Well, needless to say, his suggestion was wicked, not to say improper. And one was disgusted. Obviously his own conscience should be quite enough to prompt him not to publish disgraceful facts about Allgrobsch without any need of a bribe from oneself. One might argue that, under the circumstances, given that his conscience was notoriously feeble, one might be justified in supplying the requisite bribe . . . But surely one should consider one's own interests also. Should one submit to a man's foul lust simply in order to protect the reputation of a well-known author who was elderly and sinful and wouldn't even know what one had done for his sake and a foreigner to boot? Unthinkable! Yet one recollected what Wanda had said about the attractions of self-sacrifice: the notion of surrendering what one most treasures in order to assist a man, a genius . . . and the fact that one achieved no tangible benefit as a result – far from being a counter-argument – would in fact add to the appeal. Which reminded me of the graffito I'd perused over the basins in the Ladies at the Red Cabbage Café: '*She offered her honor/He honored her offer/And all the night long/He was honor and offer.*' The spelling of 'honor' with no u made it look Latin – one of the old Roman virtues! Isn't it wonderful to think that each woman possesses this private virtue, this delicious secret, hers to guard or offer up, just as she wishes? One thrilled at the very concept of Honor: one tingled from top to toe . . .

. . . And while one had been weighing the pros and cons, the issue had more or less been decided, for it was evident that one's dressing-gown belt had been unknotted and Frank was shirtless. In the looking glass I spied a scarlet light and an artificial, operatic mist, and a man and a woman in the middle distance, clinging to each other, with their mouths open just like Pelléas and Mélisande singing a love duet on the stage of La Scala, only of course they wouldn't be taking each other's clothes off there and then . . .

Which recalls a previous attempt on my honour. It was at Cambridge, between Lent and Trinity terms in 1987. Frank and I were both staying up at our respective colleges during Easter Vacation in order to get on with work. One rather balmy afternoon, I was leaning from my bedroom window to admire the sunset across the Backs. The river and the meadows were dyed a pretty rose tint. Clouds were arranged dramatically in the sky . . . When who should come barging into my rooms and all the way through to tap me on the back and squeeze my shoulders and say, 'Hiya, Emma!'

'How do you do?' I responded coldly.

'Cute, huh?'

'What?'

'The twilight. It's good.'

'You're saying the twilight is good?' I'd been taking the Samaritan training course, and this kind of response popped out automatically.

I explained this to Frank, and he promptly informed me that, according to the Byzantine historian Procopius, writing a few centuries after the New Testament, almost the entire Samaritan people was massacred by the early Christians on grounds of heresy, which is why one doesn't come across many Samaritans wandering around Cambridge these days. I accused him of deliberately reading the nasty bits in history books. And he just smiled.

He didn't beat about the bush. He took from his jacket pocket the *Cambridge Book of Metaphysical Verse*. A convenient little volume; I noticed it was much thumbed and dog-eared at various poems he had no doubt found efficacious in the past.

He sat down on my bed, and put his shoes up right on the Liberty print bedspread with the peacock pattern Mummy had given me!

'Take those off at once!' I said. (And wished I had phrased my request differently as soon as the words had left my mouth.)

'Uh . . . sure.'

Soon he was lounging barefoot on the bed, with his head propped on one fist – a romantic pose. The twilight softened his features, making him look younger and more innocent than he was. His head was backdropped against the framed watercolour of Highland cattle and the big drypoint engraving (after Constable) of The New House, and, on the mantelpiece, the crystal vase crammed with iris and daffodils. His feet were decidedly hairy. He might have been a faun in some Arcadia . . .

He was reciting. 'And this is by Marvell. It's called "To His Coy Mistress". "Had we but world enough and time – "'

'I really don't think – ' I interrupted.

He didn't seem put out. He flipped further on in the anthology. 'And this one's by Donne. "I wonder by my troth what thou and I *did* till we loved . . ."'

Etcetera. He then whispered, in what was presumably supposed to be a seductive tone, another poem by Donne: this one about a flea; it wasn't nice.

'Really, Francis. This isn't fair at all. After all, *I* don't recite equations at *you* to make you change your mind. So why should *you* practise your literature on *me*?' (I can hear the childish whine in which I made my complaint.)

But of course he wasn't listening. He was gabbling another verse. All I could hear of it was a yelp of, '*O! my America!*' (surely he must have dog-eared the wrong page?), because his hands were squirming all over one.

I thrust him away from me. He rolled across the bed and ended up on the Persian rug on the far side. For a moment he simply looked baffled. (Had no one ever resisted him before?) Then he got angry and up, and hurled the vase on the floor. It didn't break and the flowers were undamaged, but the carpet got quite soggy . . .

The carpet was soggy, of course, with condensed steam. The very notion of carpeting a bathroom is peculiarly impractical; nevertheless common, they say, among the middle classes. The atmosphere was warm and humid. We were naked. (Well, I was; he was still wearing his striped socks.) Not that one looked so very nude; what with the mistiness and the illumination, our bodies looked more like romantic abstractions than the real thing. Finally he had the decency to remove his socks. Then he displayed that thing they're always going on about in the AIDS commercials (one had always wanted to see one from close-up) and took it out of its package.

'Em,' he said. 'There's something I got to say to you, before we . . .'

I sat up straight with my back against the tub, and crossed my hands on my lap. 'Yes?' I said. One wondered if he might have a social disease. One wouldn't put it past him.

'I cheated. I told you a white lie.'

'Oh really. Which one?'

'Y'know, you were saying I was saying Allgrobsch was dead. And I was saying I was sad because y'know . . . Uh, it's true and it's not true.'

'What?'

'You see, what I meant is, as it were, Allgrobsch is getting better – '

'You . . . you fibber!'

'Uh, I told you the truth, in the first place, but you refused to listen . . . Like I said, Allgrobsch is getting better, and maybe – probably – he'll survive; so I went and phoned my publisher, and my publisher redlighted the biography because of libel. I mean, if he dies, then I'm okay. A dead man can't sue for libel. But if he doesn't . . . I'm shipwrecked!'

As he explained this, I realised I'd known – or should have known – what he'd meant all along. One hadn't been blackmailed at all, really; and one wasn't self-sacrificing either. Which was jolly demeaning.

The red light glared luridly like the ones that are hung in certain disreputable districts in foreign cities.

'So much for one's honour!' I cried.

'My biography is dead! My poor, poor biography!'

I set the crystal vase in its place on the mantelpiece again. I picked up each poor, fallen flower – the irises and the daffodils with their contrasting hues, their delicate, infolded centres – and hugged them against my chest.

'One doesn't do things like that,' I said.

Frank stroked his own left elbow, on which he'd landed. He looked hurt in the broader rather than the more limited sense. He folded his arms, copying me. He stepped quite close. I backed against the window. He bowed from the waist in a rather Japanese style; his head hovered a little below my chin. He bit off the head of a daffodil. He chewed it thoroughly. I could see little yellow bits protruding from the corners of his mouth. Then he opened his mouth wide – shut it again – opened it – and spat the contents on my nice clean blouse.

'You've simply ruined one's best white one!' I said. 'You're no gentleman! You're not even English! You think you're so attractive, but one doesn't care for your sort. So there!'

He forced a laugh. 'Who's this "one" you keep talking about? Who is she?' He switched to a falsetto. '*One* is a brilliant mathematician! *One* is a child prodigy! *One* is a posh lady! *One* is ooh so innocent!' He returned to his normal voice. 'You think you're the only "one" in the world, don't you? Well, you're not. There are two people in this room, so stop hiding behind your maths and your girlishness and grow' – *swear word* – 'up!'

I wanted to shout some bad language back at him; however, such expressions don't come naturally to one's lips. 'Oh, you think you're so charming and so forceful, do you? Well, if that's your style, you can practise it somewhere else! *One* doesn't care for it. You're nothing but a . . . a pain in the bottom!'.

He took a step closer towards one.

One pushed him hard on the chest – and the flowers fluttered once more on to the damp carpet. One yelled, 'Get out! Get out of one's room and one's college and one's country and one's life!'

And now the red light had changed meaning again. It meant STOP.

'Oh dear,' I said. 'What a pity you told me that. Otherwise I would have surrendered one's honour. But now . . . well, one would seem such a fool.'

'I don't want to lie to you, Emma. I like you too much.'

'Ye-e-es.'

'Couldn't we . . . anyhow . . . I mean, it's kinda silly to take our clothes off and do nothing?'

'Ah, Frank. One rather liked the image of you as a wicked seducer – some villain from a Victorian melodrama, twirling the tip of his waxed moustache. And now you turn out just to be sleazy . . . just dear old sleazy-Frank.'

He slid on his bottom towards me across the carpet and put his arm around my shoulder. Although he's handsome, one doesn't want to actually look at his bits – so I reached up and switched off the light.

We talked in the dark. We confided our worries. I told him about Jane, and one's own fear of not being a genius. 'I mean, I used to assume one was the most brilliant person in the world – and this makes for a kind of neatness; there is oneself up the top, and everybody else arranged down below. But if one is just a normal person . . . well, then, *why*? It's all so random! So untidy! Where does one fit in?'

'Here,' he said – and pressed my body against his.

'But the same goes for one's honour,' I said. 'One had always imagined one would offer it to the perfect man, one's husband presumably, Mr Right . . . Granted that's an absurdly old-fashioned notion – but what is there to replace it? I mean, I wouldn't mind if one were seduced by the best man in the world or the worst man in the world, but to be coupled with a random in-between fellow – why, that would be intolerable!'

Then Frank told me a little about his life. About how he'd been brought up by wealthy cosmopolitan parents and step-parents, who were always quarrelling and bribing him with expensive gifts, and

251

flying him round the world. How he'd seen the body of world literature as something of eternal value, something steady and important he could contribute to. How he'd realised he lacked the temperament and imagination to be a creative writer himself, but he had the skills to be a critic. How he'd put all his best efforts into his career, and how his interview for tenure had taken place yesterday, and if he were successful he'd have a job for life in the centre of the literary universe – New York – and if not, well, he'd been offered a position in a two-year college in Vermont . . . ('Oh no!' I said. I hated to imagine him trapped in a small college town in nowhere, making passes at provincial professors' wives) . . . and the success or failure of the Allgrobsch biography could well make all the difference.

Then we talked for a while about the snakes and ladders on the academic gameboard. In one's own case, one could never sink so low as Frank could; one could always become a fixture in Cambridge (one already had tenure there); or one might be able to stay on in New York (Fanny and Bridget had promised to do their best to secure one a permanent position at the Institute); or . . . doubtless most universities would be happy to have one. But one wanted to be at the *best* place. And where was that?

'Let's do it now,' said Frank.

'Oh. All right.'

'I want to see you,' he said.

He switched on the infra-red again.

He kneeled. He stretched me out on my back on the carpet. Something was scratching my bottom; it was the toothbrush; I wriggled away from it. The radiation warmed my whole front, as if one were sunbathing. Then he lay down beside me. His body was an ember.

Suddenly there was a loud triple knock on the front door. Its echo reverberated. A voice called, 'Emma! Are you in there? Emma!'

DAMN.

48

I dragged on my dressing-gown again, urged Frank to stay put in the bathroom, and scampered to the front door. Who could it be? Perhaps Raoul the janitor come to mend my leaky washer? I peered through the spyhole at the figure outside; his open palm, raised for the purpose of slapping on the door, was magnified by the fisheye lens; the hand looked like a flapping pink parasol, or one of those titchy amoebas viewed through a microscope.

'No you *can't* come in, Arnie,' I said. 'I'm busy.'

'Aw, please, Emma. It's important!' His voice through the door was muffled but still loud, like a politician heard on radio.

'If you want to ask any more questions about Special Relativity, you'll just have to wait until some more convenient moment. There's a time and a place for everything, you know.'

'No, Emma, it's not about relativistic electrodynamics . . . It's . . . It's . . . let me in . . .'

I went *humph* quite violently to relieve my feelings. Then I undid the locks.

He stood in the doorway, scratching his spotty chin.

'Well, come in if you're coming in, Arnie. One hasn't got all night.'

He shuffled into the alcove where coats and scarves are hung up. His shaggy dirty-blond hair merged with my mohair shawl. He knocked over an umbrella, and set it up again.

He gulped. Then he said rapidly, 'See, Emma. It's about my friend. This is why I've got to see you. My friend . . . my friend's in bad trouble . . .'

'Oh dear,' I said. One would rather he didn't force the role of mother substitute upon one, but what can one do? I took him by the elbow and sat him down on the living-room sofa.

'So you got your "friend" into trouble, did you, Arnie? Er, how many months?'

'What?'

'How many months has she been in . . . a certain condition?'

'What? No, you don't understand . . . My friend, he's in love!'

'Ah, yes. That is a kind of trouble, indeed.'

'He's in love with a girl – a woman, really . . . He can't get her out of his mind.' He whispered, as if reciting a magic spell. '*She's an older woman.*'

'Oh?'

'And what my friend wants to know is . . . What's the thing my friend must do?'

'Er . . . Perhaps you could tell me a little more about this "older woman". Is she agreeable? Is she beautiful? Is she fond of your "friend"?'

'Oh, she's the cutest, beautifullest creature in the galaxy! And she's a *genius*. You know that? She's got a fantastic brain! She's so clever she can . . . Just look at the mind on that woman! . . . But I don't know, my friend doesn't know, if she loves him. What do you think?'

His mouth gaped. He stared up at one with a look of dumb appeal.

I sat down beside him and tried to be tactful. 'My advice to your friend is: that he should proceed with extreme caution . . .'

Arnie echoed my words, as if pondering the pronouncement of an oracle: '*Proceed with extreme caution.*'

'In fact, it's rather implausible, isn't it, on an *a priori* basis, that this – as you have described her – extremely intelligent and attractive older woman would be drawn to your friend? She doubtless has quite enough problems of her own to deal with.'

His face crumpled. He looked devastated. 'So you're saying, Emma, I . . . my friend hasn't got a hope in hell?'

I paused. On the one hand the last thing one wanted was to encourage Arnie; on the other, just possibly, he really *did* have a friend who was enamoured of an older woman, and one wouldn't wish to pre-empt what might become a beautiful relationship. Besides, he seemed so miserable.

'In my considered opinion,' I said slowly, 'er . . . Would you like a chocolate chip biscuit?'

'What?'

'Or a glass of milk? I could fetch you the carton from the refrigerator?'

He shook his head dolefully.

'Oh, Arnie,' I said gently, 'you are an awful nuisance.'

He smiled wanly. Just for an instant, I suspected him of doing a Frank: deliberately exaggerating his dejectedness in order to appeal to one's maternal instinct. But no, a boy of his age and immaturity surely couldn't be so Machiavellian, could he?

'You see, Arnie, I have my own concerns too. Or rather . . . My "friend" has a problem. My friend – she's a woman, about one's own age, appearance, intelligence and so forth – she has a relationship with a man. A rather puzzling, infuriating fellow. On the one hand he is undeniably sophisticated, handsome, experienced, but there again he sometimes behaves in the most immature, not to say babyish manner imaginable!' (I was speaking loudly to ensure Frank could overhear: it would do him good to listen to my point of view for a change.) 'What should my friend do? Sometimes she wants to hug him, and at other times she wants to throw things at him!'

Arnie made a brief, deep, grinding noise resembling an engine starting up, presumably to indicate that the machinery of his intellect was coming into operation.

Then he said, 'I guess your friend is crazy.'

'Well, possibly . . .'

'But you know what I think? I think my friend and your friend should get together, huh? I mean, they have the same problem . . .'

He rested his hand on one's knee.

'Ah, I don't think you quite understand, Arnie!' I gabbled, wriggling away. 'My friend has nothing whatsoever in common with your friend. In fact the two definitely can't stand each other, they're horribly incompatible, and unless you let go of my dressing-gown cord and stop sliding your hand up my leg *this instant* I'm going to scream!'

One second later, Arnie was lying on the floor, cringing, rubbing a bruise just under his left eye – and a large, slightly damp, entirely naked man was standing over him.

'Gosh,' I said. 'I hope you haven't hurt the poor boy.'

Frank snorted triumphantly. He waved a loofah like a battle club. He slapped his palms together, metaphorically wiping off the dust. He looked considerably more nude in the living-room than he had in the bathroom. His skin was quite hairy, and there were disconcerting pale patches in various places.

I gave Arnie a helping hand. He tottered to his feet.

'Are you all right, Arnie?' I asked.

255

'He'll live,' said Frank.

Arnie grunted.

'Oh, and by the way, Arnie,' I said, 'meet Frank. Frank, this is Arnie.'

I smiled politely and waited for the two men to, reluctantly, shake hands. Mummy always says one should settle quarrels immediately, and one should never let anyone leave in a bad mood. 'Now, if you'll both just settle down on the sofa, I'll bring in a nice pot of Earl Grey . . . or would you rather have cocoa?'

'Hot chocolate,' Frank translated automatically.

'Or I believe I might have some dry sherry in the kitchen – I'll just have a peek.'

So a minute later the three of us were settled on the sofa, enjoying a light repast of tea, oatmeal cookies, some Bath Oliver biscuits with slices of cheddar, and a schooner of amontillado for Frank. One was surprisingly hungry. It was all rather like *Déjeuner sur L'herbe*, except of course that the genders were reversed, and anyway Frank had partially made himself decent with the aid of a back issue of *American Mathematical Review* and a tasselled satin cushion.

Nobody spoke for a while. Then I felt it was one's duty to clear up some possible misunderstandings.

'Oh I do hope no one got hold of the wrong end of the . . .' I said.

The men didn't reply.

'That is, Frank, all Arnie was doing was kindly telling me about the problems of his friend . . .'

'*Sure,*' Frank said.

'And might I just explain, Arnie, that Frank and I weren't actually . . . I mean, there's a perfectly innocent explanation for . . .' I said, gesturing vaguely at Frank's tassels.

'*Sure,*' said Arnie.

'Well, I'm glad *that's* cleared up. One wouldn't want the evening to end in a complete brouhaha, like some French farce.'

Arnie held up a cookie like Sherlock Holmes peering through a magnifying glass. He looked at Frank. 'What's *his* problem?'

Frank seemed to interpret that simple question as a challenge; he clenched his fists.

'Now, really,' I said. 'It's all quite straightforward. You see, Frank is rather tense because he went before the tenure committee at his university yesterday. I'm sure he won't mind you knowing about it . . . do you, Frank?'

Arnie grunted. 'This is *it*?'

'Naturally,' I added, 'Frank has other things on his mind, too. For example' – turning to Frank – 'and after all it's no secret you're writing Allgrobsch's biography, is it?' – turning to Arnie – 'Well, the publisher has put a stop to the project, saying that Frank might be libelling Allgrobsch . . .'

Arnie spoke across me to Frank, 'Uh, why don't you ask All . . . Awg . . . that guy . . . if *he* thinks you're libelling him?'

Which struck everyone as a jolly good idea. An obvious one, indeed – so obvious that it hadn't occurred to one before.

One set about putting the plan into operation. Frank retreated to the bathroom to put on his clothes. (A flash of red light and a puff of steam as the bathroom door opened and shut.) Arnie ate all the remaining food, including a cube of cheese that had been left on Frank's plate. And I telephoned Barbra with a view to finding out the visiting hours at St Kevin's.

Of course, the upshot is that Frank and I never consummated our passion that night. One might call it bad luck – Arnie galumphing in like that – if one believed in luck. Well, well. To be sure, the frustration of one's plans was annoying – but not as annoying as all that. After all, one doesn't do it for the sake of physical pleasure – everyone knows it's jolly painful the first time (one has heard some dreadful stories: *vide* Linda/Lirda) but out of a desire for knowledge. Curiosity, that's the reason. One simply wants to unveil the mystery. Which is what growing up is all about . . .

And as for the bare facts – well of course one has known them since one was 12 (Mummy explained them quite lucidly) and actually one had grasped the gist at a much younger age . . .

Which leaves the physiological experience. And, ah, one has often imagined it. It happens in one's dreams, in the middle of sleep – or just before, or just after. Like *this* . . .

One is naked. One reaches out and touches one. One smiles. One laughs. One nudges one. One's mouth floats towards one's mouth. One kisses. One is kissed. One murmurs a little private noise which no one in the whole world could ever understand except one. One clings to one. One presses against one. One is drawn towards one – unresisting, irresistibly. One feels a silken tingling as one glides all over one. Waves of delicious otherness sweep from end to end inside one. One gasps. One gasps. One and one unite.

49

The Vendor of Shooting Stars

Dav the barber knows a splendid one about a drunkard and the moon, while Radka the inn-keeper chimes in with a scurrilous story concerning a famous actress; Gam the pious pretends he is a rabbit; Vlob the tailor expatiates on a cryptic pun; Zemla the yellow-haired illustrates some topical satire with the aid of a red cabbage and a forked stick; Levno the cobbler recites rhyming doggerel; Govya the beautiful sticks her tongue out and rolls her eyes; Portin the intellectual invents a shaggy-dog story concerning twenty-three men who set out to climb a mountain; Dob the big-eared performs a cartwheel . . . And yet Blog the vendor of shooting stars does not laugh.

Not that what he sells is literally 'shooting stars' – that is just the name we use in our town for sweet-smelling fallen apples, wrecked pears, beige plums, injured quinces, bird-pecked cherries, crazed peaches . . . any fruit that has tumbled from its bough before its time and rests, damaged but not worthless, cushioned on undergrowth. Across the orchard floor, his eyes jerking from side to side, shuffles a short man – Blog – whose round ruddy head resembles some kind of windfall. He is searching for windfalls. He sights one: he moves toward it in big limping strides and, with one practiced swing of his right hand, half scoops, half throws it over his shoulder. It lands in his bonnet-shaped basket. He sidles off in quest of the next fallen fruit, dragging the basket by a rope as if it were a recalcitrant dog. When he has collected enough, he will haul his load to market. He will stack his wares in the shape of a pyramid. He will perch on top of a barrel beside them. He will chant, 'Shooting stars! Buy my best shooting stars!'

This is one way Blog makes a living. But there is another . . . It is the custom in our country to invite a crude, coarse jokester to every party. At any wedding or festival you will notice him, leaping about or cowering under the table, standing on his head or posing uncomfortably in some high place. He pokes fun at the hosts for supposed miserliness and covetousness;

258

he constructs elaborate scatological puns based on their names. He devises personalized smutty insults aimed at each guest. He kicks up his legs in a drunken can-can. He makes rude noises with his lips. He winks slyly at the ladies. You will wonder by what right he was included in the guest list – until you realize. The fool is the life and soul of the party. The fool drives away the demons of priggishness, solemnity, hypocrisy. The fool makes the rest of us feel wise. The fool makes us laugh.

Yet Blog cannot laugh . . .

What kind of man becomes a fool in the first place, anyway? Sure, ugliness is an advantage (and Blog is certainly ugly); so is poor coordination; a wandering mind; a croaky singing voice (Blog has all these qualities) . . . but above all it is lonesomeness that fits a man for this career. Blog's wife is dead. All his children are gone or dead. He lives in a shack near the forest with a gray cat and a bottle of plum spirit for company. Nobody tells him how to behave. No woman hangs on his arm whining, 'Oh, Blog, be decent.' No child yaps, 'Oh, Daddy, don't.' Of course everybody in our town is miserable nowadays, what with the latest troubles (though somehow we still find things to laugh at) . . . But Blog has been unhappy for so long he might be expected to notice little difference . . .

Yet he never laughs . . .

But why should he laugh at his own jokes? Should a wineseller drink his own stock? Should a king address himself as My Majesty? This was what we argued at first. Indeed we claimed to detect a wry, savory humor in his lugubriousness. We praised the authenticity of his deadpan delivery. We put down his melancholia to fatigue or professionalism.

But now his misery has become irritating – even contagious. We go to the market to buy an egg or a book, a cabbage or a roll of insulating tape . . . then, drawn by the visual appeal of stacked red, yellow, brown, green rotundities, and the aroma of sweet rot, we pause beside Blog's pyramids of shooting stars, pondering which windfall is the most delicious, mulling over our options. At last we make our choice. We seize – carefully – one fruit quite near the base (the pyramid does not collapse) and place it in our basket, on top of all our other provisions, for safekeeping. Blog is roosting on his usual barrel. We reach up to him; give him a coin. Suddenly we become aware of his sore eyelids, his slant stare like a kicked dog's, his twisted grimace . . . He cracks a joke . . . And our whole day is spoiled.

So we decide to make Blog laugh . . .

I say 'we'. I say 'decide'. In truth there is no collective decision: it just comes about somehow that each of us – should we happen to be passing through the market and observe the hunched figure in the sackcloth cape and the broad-brimmed, topless, dun hat (its crown vanished long ago) who is squatting up there on his barrel – tilt our head back and bark some jollification. Of course we all try to amuse Blog in the manner in which we ourselves would like to be amused – as if he were no more than a mirrored version of ourselves. Levno and Dob have a go at obscene horseplay. The stylish crowd – Vlob, Dav, Govya, Zemla (the men in thick knotted neckties, the women in flowing dresses) – gather around the barrel to drink glasses of tea and narrate knowing anecdotes about moderately famous public figures. Gam the pious chortles sweetly, silently. Even visitors from other towns come to the market (news of the challenge has spread) and try to please Blog with their exotic gags. (Still he doesn't laugh . . .) Portin the intellectual suggests an innovative approach based on a Freudian analysis: he claims that laughter is no more than a euphemism for sexual release; so we persuade Dama the respectable to do her best (she demands, and receives, in view of Blog's ugliness and scent, twice the standard payment); she reports afterwards that he sighed, groaned, even smiled once, but never laughed. Some stranger thinks that black irony will do the trick. The stranger's voice roars, 'Blog! Your house has just burnt down! Your plum spirit has evaporated. Your gray cat has roasted!' A one-hour pause. 'Blog! I was lying.'

Yet Blog never laughs . . .

Did Blog ever laugh? I have questioned as many survivors as I could find. I have pleaded with them to scour their memories, to seek out any vague recollection of Blog having submitted to laughter, having let out so much as a weak giggle . . . It appears not. Nevertheless I do not think our quest was ignoble. It is true that we never did find a joke that could amuse him, but I believe that somewhere, hidden in a dark place, that joke exists.

50

Let's go in search of Allgrobsch! Barbra (I'd rung her at the club) had announced that the visiting hours at St Kevin's were specially extended that very evening (whether to accommodate Sunday night idlers or April Fool pranksters): the opportunity seemed too good to miss. Frank and I had piled into a taxi to speed us there, and Arnie had insisted on tagging along as well. One was driven through Manhattan streets crammed with bouncy people and glittery things – then across a bridge over dark water – and down into a quiet suburban part of Brooklyn: a park; a lone old woman walking her dog; tall houses recessed from the road; a triangle of whiteness where two walls met: remnant of the last snowdrift of the winter of 1989–90! Already the period I had spent in New York was beginning to seem historical, as if one were recollecting it from some vantage point years in the future.

Mercury lamps glared. A black-on-white sign conceded: 'ST KEVIN'S HOSPITAL'. The taxi bumped and swerved past iron railings; then glided between stretches of pale concrete, planar and vast as a Siberian tundra . . . We got out.

The automatic gates slid open.

Now we had passed into the hospital's capacious atrium: one was in another continent and another season. A sense of space and hidden light. Here it was already spring – summer, almost. Smiles of greeting flashed in the warm dry air; one heard murmurs of '*Welcome*'. An ornamental fountain plashed. Greenery tumbled down from the mezzanine level. In one corner, gaudy pictures daubed by patients in the paediatrics and psychiatry units – orange stick-figures with green heads; a blue tree; a purple sun – were blooming behind glass. The whole floor was covered in bean-green linoleum, resembling a meadow as viewed by a short-sighted person.

Where, in this arcadian setting, could Allgrobsch be secreted?

The focal point of the atrium was the gift emporium by the entrance. At my insistence we dropped in: one must always bring a little something when visiting the poorly – as Mummy does when she pays a call on Mrs Hodgson or Mrs Spratly in the village. Indeed this shop more closely resembled the one in the village than any in the Village; its ambience was scatty but friendly. The rather dotty assistant tried to interest Frank in an 'I GOT BETTER AT ST KEVIN'S' keyring and Arnie in a 'MY MOMMY WENT INTO THE MATERNITY UNIT AND ALL I GOT WAS THIS LOUSY T-SHIRT' T-shirt. One examined the rack of Get Well cards, but none seemed altogether suitable or seasonal; they tended to feature drunken green bunny rabbits with thermometers in their mouths, cleverly melding St Patrick's Day and Easter themes . . . Oh well, one can't go wrong with flowers. I selected a pretty and ingenious speckled orchid; Arnie loaded himself with a bunch of blowsy daffodils; Frank economised on two two-for-the-price-of-one green plastic carnations. (Trust Frank to pick what doesn't exist in nature!) On the way out I glanced at the racked newspapers: the *Wall Street Journal* headlined the depreciation of sterling: one tried not to take it personally. *USA Today* was open on a lurid diagram in red, green, blue – not some bodily organ in cross-section, but a false-colour weather map of the United States – chill in the north-east, warmth in the south-west.

Where was Allgrobsch? The assistant waved us on.

We climbed an upwardly and then downwardly sloping ramp . . . Imagine hauling oneself through a narrow crevice in the side of a mountain and passing into an inner system of potholes and mineshafts. We had left the bright lights and the airiness behind; now we were in the mazy interior of the hospital, as intricate and functional and mysterious as the human body itself. Everything gleamed dully. Everywhere echoed. The wheels of distant trolleys squealed. The air-conditioning system made a noise like a gently sleeping giant. The few figures that drifted by were locked in their own thoughts and didn't look up. An otherworld.

Multitudinous doors presented themselves. Each had a notice on it declaring what lay behind; it was like walking through one of those Look-and-Say books used by children learning to read, where the cat tagged with a C-A-T label sits on a mat imprinted with M-A-T. Some signs suggested the possibilities of life and renewal: 'OB/GYN', for instance, or 'COFFEE'. Others hinted darkly: '**ONCOLOGY**' was stencilled in big, heavy letters. And yet others were enigmas: what was the significance of 'NEUROLOGY'; what was the hidden meaning of 'CHECKROOM'? We were following the arrows towards 'INTENSIVE CARE'. We yomped for what seemed like miles. Every time we reached a fork in the corridor, or a stairway, or a liftshaft, another sign would appear to direct us; it was as if one were being guided by a guardian angel.

Frank took a portable telephone from his hip pocket. He tried to contact his own university switchboard. Not surprisingly, at this hour, nobody was there.

We strode past 'PHLEBOTOMY'. Arnie explained this was the blood department.

Frank, irritated, put on his professorial British accent. 'Yes. We *do* know.'

Arnie: 'My friend, he went to the hospital to – '

Frank, interrupting: 'We've heard *quite* enough of your friend for one night, thank you.'

'My friend – see, he's having a medical check-up for his insurance – nothing wrong with him, it's only for his insurance, see. He goes in the hospital, and he meets a guy in a, like, white coat and everything, he's like a doctor, a physician, you know. So he says to the . . . Uh, and I forgot to say, my friend's only having his blood tested, right, he's in good shape, nothing wrong with his . . . he's *okay*. So he – that's my friend – he says to the guy, the guy in the white coat . . . Uh, and I forgot to say my friend has a speech problem, he swallows the beginnings of words, like he wants to say New York he says Ew Ork . . . Anyhow, my friend says to this other guy, he tells him he's come for his phlebotomy – and before he can do anything the other guy sticks a needle in his vein and straps him down in the operations theatre, and cuts out the front lobe of his brain!' Arnie burst into raucous laughter. He stared around wildly. 'You get it? Get it?'

Frank cleared his throat in exaggerated embarrassment.

Arnie said, 'Phlebotomy! Lobotomy!'

One tried to keep the peace. 'Yes, a pun can be quite droll, arguably, in its own, rather special way.'

'April Fool!' Arnie shouted. 'It's only a story!'

'Oh, that's all right then,' said Frank. 'You had me worried for a moment.'

Arnie grinned, not noticing or ignoring the sarcasm; or nervously.

And meanwhile one had conducted a bypass operation all the way around 'CARDIOLOGY', sidled past 'MEN'S ROOM' and had arrived at

'INTENSIVE CARE'. A large sign insisted: 'FAMILY MEMBERS *ONLY* PERMITTED TO VISIT'. Which was frightfully annoying, because (1) one would have to white-lie; and (2) it was grammatically incorrect; or rather, the stated meaning (i.e. that family members were permitted – as opposed to being obliged – to visit) differed from the intended one. We had a quick whispered conference.

A tall nurse on duty was seated just inside the door. Her hands were fidgeting as if tying knots in an imaginary string.

'Excuse me,' I said. 'One is the patient's daughter.'

She looked me up and down very hard.

One got goosepimples.

'Leave your flowers out here,' she commanded, pointing at a table already loaded with numerous bouquets in varying degrees of freshness and wiltedness. A jumble of climates and seasons. With a world-weary air, like Sherlock Holmes on a cocaine binge, she commented glumly, 'I've known cases where a single grain of pollen can be fatal.'

'Oh, yes?' I said.

'You and him have got the same European look,' she told me. 'Sunday evenings are always the busiest. We're expecting a full house tonight. Your sisters are here already.'

'My *who*?' I asked.

But she had already turned to Frank and Arnie, who were introducing themselves as Allgrobsch's son-in-law and grandson respectively.

Before being let in, one had to put on a smock, a lower-face mask, a cap, overtrousers, slippers, gloves – all in white mercerised cotton – lest a speck of dirt pollute the ward. One dressed with care. One felt very pure: a vestal virgin on the point of entering the temple . . .

And soon we had penetrated the holy of holies. The walls, ceiling and floor were as white as our costumes. We were in a kind of temporary winter. (I thought of the peculiar weather pattern in New York this year: from snow to sun to snow to – perhaps now at last – real spring.) The three of us were burlier than in our external existence, and slower moving; we might have been a family of polar bears padding across an ice floe. Some silvery tubing glinted. Liquids gurgled within pipes. Insulated wires led from X to Y. A powerful air-conditioning unit sucked air out, cleansed it, and blew it back in; the breeze was soft but utterly steady, like an arctic wind . . .

No (on reflection) it was more like cosmic rays beating across the vast interstices of the galaxy. This place was isolated, not belonging on any planet. Indeed it was furnished more like a space station than an earthly building, not least in that the contents were bolted indifferently to walls, floor and ceiling – there seemed no especial reason why the whole entity shouldn't be rotated upside down.

We turned a corner. The room resembled a laboratory rather than a conventional hospital ward. More and more complex machinery abounded. A gas pipe was slinking along the floor like a dachshund. A valve-connector had as many openings as the heart. A fuzzy wavepattern heaved across an oscilloscope screen. It was impossible to gauge distances here since there was no natural scale: one couldn't tell if this volume were spacious or cramped. (Where was Allgrobsch?) I had the impression more people were present than had come with us; it was hard to be sure because of our identical, enveloping costumes, and because anybody with an averted face merged into the background . . . Two erect figures appeared in what seemed to be the distance. They were dressed in the standard ward clothing. Suddenly it became evident they were only a few feet away.

'Hi, Emma!' said Bridget or Fanny. Fanny or Bridget said, 'Hey, Emma, it's good to see you.'

'What on earth are you doing here?' I asked.

'Your neighbour, Mona – she told us you were at the hospital. She was very helpful.' 'And I always wanted to meet L.Z. Allgrobsch. He's our favourite.'

A pump gulped.

'Do we break it to her gently?' 'We're trying to tell you you can have a permanent position at the Institute, starting next Fall.'

'I don't know what to say,' I said, meaning it literally. I didn't know whether to be pleased or embarrassed.

'We fixed it for you, Emma. Aren't we clever?' 'Oh, say you'll accept it, Emma! We came all the way here specially to ask you. Say yes!'

Before one could respond, one had been tapped on the shoulder by a handful of wriggling fingers. The nurse passed on a memorandum slip stating that one had to ring a certain number urgently. Oddly, the number was my own.

I borrowed Frank's portable telephone. Meanwhile he was chatting with Fanny and Bridget. He leaned towards them and they leaned away, like grouped figures in some baroque statuary.

'Hallo?' I said cautiously into the telephone.

A familiar voice answered: '*Hallo. You have reached the answering machine of Dr Smart. Please leave your name, your number and –* ' One had the illusion one was conversing with another version of oneself belonging to a parallel universe in which one had made the decision not to bother visiting St Kevin's. Who knows how one's life might have been different in that case? (Who knows how one's life might have been different if one had taken the other path any time the road forked? Suppose one had gone to Oxford rather than Cambridge? Suppose one had refused on principle to speak to Frank the first time we had met? Suppose one had decided against coming to New York? Suppose one had chosen not to visit the club originally?) How all one's decisions pen one in! A brief but suffocating feeling of claustrophobia washed over me. I desperately wanted to ask other-Emma what on earth she was up to. What would she reply? Then another voice cut in: *'Hello. It's Jane. Listen . . . I'm still in New York. I'm catching a cab to the red-eye to California in five minutes, so I can't speak long. I came by my apartment but you're not here, so . . . Well, Emma, do you know why I'm phoning you?'*

'N-n-no,' I said. Had one mistreated her apartment in some way? Was she complaining about excessive condensation in the bathroom? Or cockraoches in the kitchen? Or scuffmarks on the sofa?

'I just spoke to my chair . . .'

'There's some interference on the line,' I said carefully. (When one had studied Latin, there had been a jolly translation exercise in the textbook concerning the correct way to address a table, but . . .) The world was out of joint.

Her voice increased in volume. *'I spoke to my department chair, and he said he can definitely fix you with a tenured associate professorship starting in the Fall. Salary and conditions negotiable. He wants a decision by next Monday. What do you say, Emma?'*

'J-j-j-jane. Er, it's very kind of you to arrange this on my behalf, but one really had no definite plans to . . . And actually, honestly, one is flabbergasted. I mean, firstly by your kind offer – which I suppose one ought to think over – after all, it would be an alternative to returning to Cambridge – and . . . You see, just one minute ago I was offered an opportunity to stay on here at the Institute. What an amazing coincidence!'

Jane laughed. *'There are no big coincidences in life, Emma, only small ones. Don't you believe it! Haven't you heard of the inter-university agreement? The professor-hunting season starts in April, to limit competition. They're not allowed to offer anyone a job before. So today's the day when department chairs phone their first choices.'*

'I see. How silly of one not to realise.'

'*Well, Emma. I'm sure a first-rate theorist like you has many options. I put your name forward to the committee, you know. It's your decision. Where do you want to be next Thanksgiving: in the ice of New York or the sunshine of California?*'

'Well, quite,' I said. 'I'll call you back on Monday. Thank you.'

We said our goodbyes, and she rang off.

Now I understood why Frank was carting his portable telephone around with him: evidently he was hoping for a call from Nixon University (or elsewhere) offering him a tenured position.

(Where was Allgrobsch?)

Somebody was hailing me. And then a different somebody hailed me. Because of the matching costumes, each speaker seemed to be the same person with a changed voice, like an impressionist, or a medium at a seance possessed in turn by a range of spirits. And I wasn't even sure if I were being addressed or merely overhearing an echo.

At last I managed to identify one person, both by accent and appearance.

'You look rather oriental in that get-up,' I remarked, 'as if you were wearing a yashmak. Quite a contrast to your usual colourful attire.'

'You look kinda weird yourself.'

'Oh, one didn't mean it like that . . .'

'Sure.' Barbra's speech trailed off.

All I could see that was recognisably *her* was her furrowed forehead and deep-set eyes. Then I couldn't even see that – for she was glancing at a disturbance behind her.

The nurse was appealing to the doctor. 'This lady says she's the patient's wife. They can't all be his family!'

The doctor shrugged.

'She is too,' said Barbra. 'I'm Elzee's sister, and I guarantee her.'

'Hallo, er, Mom,' I said to Wanda.

Wanda addressed me in a hushed tone for some reason, as if one were in church or a library. 'Barbra told me to come. She said seeing your husband come back to life is an important aspect of married life. But I think it's . . . mm . . . spooky.'

I thought it the better part of valour not to comment on Wanda's appearance. Being dressed in white instead of her usual black made her complexion seem darker and more rugged, not to say older. What's more, the visible fractions of her own clothing were peculiarly bright: fluorescent orange socks and royal blue velveteen cuffs.

'You're looking at my gear, Emma. I can see.'

'Oh, not especially, actually . . .'

'It's fun and real tacky, mm? I like it.'

'You do?'

'Oh *yeah*. You know, I really appreciate what you said to me. It changed my whole perspective on the ego situation. I realised I just wasn't *thinking* about my es-ee-ell-eff, and it's time I stand up and say: I am proud to be a person.'

She talked more and more vociferously. '. . . and now I know I was hung up on my own feelings of frustration and aggression and, mm, bereavement. But why should I sacrifice my own being for anybody?'

'Well, it's not necessarily harmful to – '

'I'm going to follow your advice, Emma, and stop caring about my ex!'

'Did one advise that?'

'Like you said, Emma, I have to change my life, so I'm going to go west, and if you want you can come too, to esseff!'

'To do *what*?'

'SF.'

'Science fiction?'

'California.'

'Ah, yes. One has heard of it.'

She yelled, 'I don't care if he's a genius! I don't care if he comes to life again and says he wants me! I'm the new me and I'm not the old me!'

One looked the other way as if the source of this outburst had no possible connection with one.

'Incidentally,' I said to the nearest non-Wanda to hand, 'where is Allgrobsch?'

But this person wasn't listening to me but to the nurse. He was busy assuring her – in a prissy voice instantly identifiable as H.H.'s – 'Aha. In fact I have the privilege to be the elder brother of the great author.'

The place was crowded and yet not crowded. It was as if strange warps and pockets of hyperspace abounded – for no one, or almost no one, was within permanent view or earshot. Presumably this was in part a consequence of the stacks of irregular-shaped apparatus (it was easy for someone to be screened behind an oxygen cylinder or a computer monitor), and in part due to camouflage (the rear view of anyone beside a wall was invisible); speech was masked by the rumblings of piped gases and liquids, and the whinings of machinery.

For all that, it was certain that a horde of visitors was somehow secreted within this ward. Allgrobsch – who in reality had no living relations apart from Wanda – had acquired an honorary brother and sister, three daughters, a son-in-law and a grandson. All of us belonged to one imaginary, extended family . . .

One could only catch glimpses of H.H. and Frank, and one couldn't really overhear their conversation. Evidently they were arguing about something. H.H. was wagging his finger. Frank was looking guilty (but then he usually does).

Afterwards Frank wandered across in my direction. He was shaking his head. He was muttering, 'I mean, it's not like I did something *bad*.'

'Anything the matter?' I enquired.

He cornered me in a narrow space between a wall and a waist-high horizontal surface.

'Ah . . . uh . . . It's the obituary.'

'You mean the premature one for Allgrobsch? What *was* your part in that affair, actually?'

'Look, all I did was phone a guy I know at the *Times* and tell him – I didn't even *tell* him, I just *hinted* – and now H.H. is blowing his top – '

'I understand. But why did you do such a thing?'

'The way I see it, the only real good publicity is dead publicity! I'm doing Allgrobsch a favour. I'm helping build up media interest. If he recovers – and I'm not saying he will and I'm not saying he won't – he'll bless me from the bottom of his bended knees because I increased his sales. So what's H.H. got to be upset about?'

'Well, that's certainly a point of view . . . One does sympathise with you: there's something touchingly naïve about your self-righteousness. Your misdemeanours are venial. After all, it's not as if you actually killed the man.'

'*Exactly*,' said Frank. 'You've hit the nail on the tip of my tongue.'

'Oh?'

'Ah, somebody might argue that, so to speak, actual death will be the best for his enduring fame, and it ensures he doesn't ban my biog. – and his last collection – did you ever read it? – *Greater than Infinity and other stories* – well, it wasn't up to his earlier standard, so in fact he should be *grateful* if somebody did him in, a kind of euthanasia, really, but who's going to do a wicked thing like that?'

'I'm sorry. I don't think one quite caught the gist of that argument.'

'Ah, it's nothing, Em.'

'Right-o. Glad to hear it.'

Frank grunted. 'Like you were saying to me the other week, how Allgrobsch the writer is more important than Allgrobsch the man . . . ?'

'Yes. I do believe one made that remark in a certain context.'

'Well, my biography too is valuable, and so I should be prepared to defend it even if it means – '

'Your potential biography most certainly won't become an undying classic. Surely you will grant that. Not to say that it may not be a splendid work of literary criticism, in its way . . . Hence it would be illegitimate to further your writing at the expense of Allgrobsch's.'

'Uh, sure, but . . . Well, you're proving my point! His writings are really what matter about the guy. As a person, he doesn't in fact, as it were, exist – like you implied – '

'I implied *what*?'

'Anyhow, I wouldn't do a cheating thing like kill him . . . not actually kill him . . .'

'One trusts not,' I said sternly.

Then I noticed his eyes were aglint.

'Really, Francis, your joke was not in the best of taste. Frightfully improper . . . Where is Allgrobsch, anyway?'

Frank gripped one's arm rather too tightly. 'I don't see what you've got to be prim and British about. It's all your fault in the first place, Em – and I'll prove it!'

Frank beckoned in a grand gesture, like a wizard summoning a genie.'

'Athanias,' said a deep voice. 'Dr John Athanias.'

'Oh yes. Rather,' I replied. I couldn't tell from which body this voice was coming. 'You're the top doctor here aren't you? I'm Smart. Emma Smart. That is . . . Emma Smart-Allgrobsch, actually. The patient's daughter.'

'Oh? Frank was saying you're a British mathematician.'

'Well, yes. That would be an alternative point of view . . .'

I asked the voice how Allgrobsch was, and was informed that I couldn't be given a definite commitment on that point. I enquired if the patient could speak; the reply was maybe. I explained that one had come here to communicate with him; no answer . . .

Frank entered the conversation. 'Doctor,' he said. 'Will you just tell my . . . my . . . the patient's daughter here what you told me? About the cause of the stroke?'

'Hmm,' said Athanias. 'Well, of course, without wishing to make any definite statement in any way, we feel, from a medical angle, that the embolism was instigated by a sharp rise in blood pressure in the cerebral capillaries, concomitant with . . . well, frankly a number of possible factors . . .'

'Such as . . .' I prompted.

'Such as sexual excitement, extreme anger, laughter. Those are the textbook categories.'

One cast one's mind back to September; the club; the eminent writer L.Z. Allgrobsch seated all alone at a table, crumbling a bread roll with his left hand whilst spooning some red soup into his mouth with his right; then standing up; then falling down . . .

Frank said, 'I guess we can rule out the first possibility.'

I nodded.

'And anger . . .' said Frank. 'Well, I don't remember he was in that state . . .'

'Barbra said he'd complained about the lukewarm bortsch,' I suggested desperately.

Frank shook his head. 'So this leaves the third possibility. Now, tell me, Emma, what do you remember? Who said something which might make a distinguished elderly writer burst into laughter?'

'I don't know *what* you're talking about, Francis!'

'Maybe you've forgotten . . .'

'All one might have said was a perfectly innocent comment. Nothing remotely humorous. One merely suggested that doubtless everyone in the club was a passionate admirer of Allgrobsch . . .'

Which made Frank's eyes wizen with laughter, and even Athanias panted with suppressed humour.

'I don't see what's so funny about that!' I objected.

Frank guffawed audibly.

The doctor became visible momentarily – he was shorter and darker than I'd imagined. Then he vanished into the unstable whiteness from where he'd come.

'I don't like you, Frank!' I said. 'You're not my friend any more!'

He chuckled loudly. 'It's not funny!' he gasped. 'It's not funny at all! It's the unfunniest, sickest, blackest joke!' And he swayed and rocked, while his lips wriggled behind the face-mask like lovers under the sheets.

Everybody in the world was here. Everybody was nosing forward from their camouflaged niches, and turning to stare at one. Barbra and Wanda, Fanny and Bridget, Frank and Arnie, the doctor and the nurse and H.H., oneself and Jane's voice, also. Well, not quite everybody. One almost expected Ostrovsky and Sydenham-Blom to show up; perhaps Sunny Jim too, waving his arms, or Mona with her pile of papers; and why not Edmund as well, in his apricot-coloured robe, and Daddy, clutching an offprint on hydrodynamics, and Mummy holding up her secateurs the way saints on altarpieces always grip the emblematic instrument which tortured them?

And of course Allgrobsch wasn't to be seen . . . Yet now his physical presence seemed virtually irrelevant.

'Where is he?' I asked. 'Where's Allgrobsch?'

I sidestepped towards the horizontal surface covered with a mass of catheters, wires, pipes, cloths; thick plastic tubing and a circuit board were suspended from wall-brackets; assorted machinery was making its characteristic inhuman or humanoid noises. As one gazed at the surface one became aware that, tucked below the life-saving apparatus and masked by its penumbras, a draped human body was present. ('Hey! Watch out!' cried someone. 'You're about to bump into the feet!') It was sprawled longitudinally: an elegant integration sign. Languorously its chest rose and fell: some life was trapped there. Its head nestled in the deepest shadow . . . And now that one looked at its face, one could recognise the features one had last seen seven months ago during supper in the club, but they were tinted violet; and the mouth was fixed in an awful smile.

'Hallo,' I said to the face. For the benefit of the nurse I added in an undertone, 'Hallo, Father,' as if one were about to confess to a priest.

I asked the doctor, 'Can he speak yet?'

'We wouldn't like to state the . . . hmm, definitely. Possibly he can understand everything we say. The long-term prognosis – though we certainly can't be certain – is positive. At this moment in time, he may or may not be able to communicate.'

Frank pushed past me. He leaned as far forward as he could over the body, and spoke directly to the mouth. 'Listen, Mr Allgrobsch. Are you or are you not prepared to support the publication of a biography of yourself authored by me? Yes or no?'

The jaw seemed to stir a little, but no sound came out.

Foreheads and eyes clustered around the body; they wobbled slightly. The body itself was almost perfectly still.

Arnie suggested, 'Maybe he can move his eyelids? I saw a movie where the hero had a car crash and – '

'Good thinking,' said Frank, in the tone used by Batman for

addressing Robin. He moved his head closer to Allgrobsch's nearer ear. 'When I say go, please blink. One blink means yes and two blinks means no. Ready – steady – GO!'

But Allgrobsch didn't blink.

Barbra suggested, 'Maybe he's forgotten the question. Why don't you repeat it?'

Which Frank did. Still no response.

'What if he can only move one eyelid?' said Fanny or Bridget. Bridget or Fanny said, 'Wink, not blink.'

Which was tried. But no winks were forthcoming.

H.H. had a go. He spoke softly as if addressing a child. 'Hello-o. It's your old friend H.H, remember me? Now, this young man here wants to know whether or not you forbid his biography. Well . . . ?'

No response.

Finally Wanda said, 'Elzee . . . please . . .'

With remarkable sluggishness, so slow their motion was indetectable, the right eye closed. It opened. It closed again.

'Hah,' said H.H. 'Two winks means no.'

Frank said, 'Hey, he made one wink twice.'

'Anyhow,' said Arnie. 'It was one and one half winks. I was counting.'

'Besides which,' I pointed out, 'it's unclear if the reply was to the positive or negative version of the question.'

So one tried again to get Allgrobsch to commit himself, using varying stratagems, for all of half an hour. There was no clear signal. He was almost as unreachable as the dead.

Finally the doctor said, 'It's best not to tire him any more. Now, official visiting hours end in ten minutes. So . . .' He added as an afterthought, 'And remember he can hear what you're saying maybe, so take care not to give him SAL.'

Arnie asked what that meant.

Wanda mouthed, 'Ess-ay-el.'

The nurse replied, 'Sex, Anger, Laughter.' She ticked them off on her fingers. 'The three big no-no's for stroke patients. It's why there's such a high fatality rate in New York City.'

While the nurse was telling Arnie about the stresses of New York life, Frank was whispering something to me.

'It's like the story of Herostratus,' he said.

'Who? Never heard of him.'

'Sure. That's the point. Herostratus was a forgettable dude in the

273

Ancient Hellenic World. Joe Nobody. But he wanted to be famous. So what he did was he burned down a – or he killed a – y'know, I can't remember, but it doesn't matter. He destroyed something important, okay? The punchline is: the reason he did it was for the publicity. So the Greek court, they decided his name should be blotted out from the records, and nobody will ever hear of him again. But . . .'

'Gosh. What a sad tale.'

Frank cocked his head. 'I've got a neat idea for a whodunnit. A literary biographer murders his subject in reality as well as, as it were, metaphorically, so as to become more famous than his subject . . . ?'

'Francis, one assumes that was intended as a joke – '

'Uh, sure. A "joke" . . .'

'And one in extremely bad taste, to boot.'

Frank nodded piously.

I swivelled. I marched away.

I collided with the opposite wall. I marched back.

I was stopped by Arnie.

'It's your Frank!' he said. 'He's sticking shit in the stiff's ear!'

'It's all right,' I replied. 'He's simply badgering Allgrobsch with his questions again.'

'No, but *listen*,' said Arnie.

Due to the various mechanical noises and echoing chatter, one couldn't hear what Frank was saying exactly. One caught just occasional words. He was informing Allgrobsch about somebody one had never heard of called Mrs Goldskin and somebody else called Mrs Rosenthal. Then he appeared to have switched subjects, and to be describing a train journey he had once taken. There were various other people in his compartment, including a Scotsman; another fellow traveller was Irish, and a third was English. With surprising rapidity, he launched into a new topic. He was asking Allgrobsch some question concerning the fixture of lightbulbs, specifically in regard to the number of personnel required for this purpose. And once more the subject altered: he was declaring that pure mathematicians do something or another (one didn't catch what) only in theory, whereas fiction writers do the same thing in imagination, and critics can't do it at all. And at last, as I realised what Frank was up to . . .

(His portable telephone bleeped. He hopped back, cradled it against his neck, much as violinists do with their instrument, and jabbered into it.)

. . . a wave of sheer emotion surged through me: it was so powerful I

274

couldn't tell if it were pleasure or pain. Now I'd caught Frank out in something worse than sleaziness: he was actually doing evil. Which meant all the fantasies one had constructed around him went up in smoke. So I was free of him! I was liberated! I was grown up! One was so happy one wanted to hug Frank or anybody.

I skipped as close to Allgrobsch as possible. 'Allgrobsch. Elzee. You mustn't listen to what Frank is telling you. He's trying to narrate comic anecdotes because he wants to make you laugh – and we all know what that means. A biographer trying to murder a biographee: isn't that a kind of parricide? And it's not funny, either. He's serious about it' – somewhere in the distance Frank was grunting, '*Wrong number*' – 'I said, the thing's *not* funny, so you mustn't smile . . . You mustn't see the comic side of it because there isn't one . . . It's *just not a j-j-j-j-joke . . .*'

But Allgrobsch's mouth was hooked in a terrible upcurving rictus. His eyelids jerked open exposing bright, bobbing eyeballs. His lips separated. His whole sheeted body rocked and shook gently, and made a strange cracking noise like an ice-cube in hot water. His throat rattled. And innumerable croaking black toads of laughter leapt up from between his teeth and tongue, and vanished in the dry air.

I looked around. My companions had disappeared beyond or behind the complex instrumentation, or perhaps they had simply turned round and camouflaged themselves – for one could make out nothing more than shifting shapes in the whiteness. One thinks of the opening passage of Allgrobsch's early story 'The Skater', which is set:

. . . on a certain day in spring. Although this day looks much like yesterday, or the day before that, or the day before that . . . somehow we know it is different. Maybe the sun is a fraction stronger or the breeze is a little more vigorous. We youngsters run along the road winding downhill from our town, singing a nonsense chant as we go.

We reach the river. It is – still – a smooth and perfect expanse of ice. The noon sun has turned it into a bar of pure light. A skinny duck waddles from bank to bank.

Suddenly, a noise like thunder! Now the ice is covered with a network of fissures, branching and multiplying before our eyes. Within a few seconds there are too many cracks to count. And, in the course of the afternoon, while we stand on dry land, waiting and watching, the ice divides into floes and slivers and panes – which will, quite soon, drift away downriver.

Epilogue

Gosh how *young* one was when one was young. A number of years have passed since one was involved in the Allgrobsch affair, and one feels jolly superior to that Emma Smart one used to be – though one envies her naïvety just a little. One's hair has grown long again. Lots of new politics has washed over Central Europe, but one still keeps a bit of the Wall for old time's sake. Naturally, after the sabbatical at the Institute, one didn't return to stuffy old Cambridge. Nor was there any point in staying on in New York; the best mathematicians no longer favour the East Coast. No doubt about it: one made the correct decision in accepting the Berkeley professorship. Jane and I have collaborated on several papers, but on the whole we work in separate fields. After all, she's a genius and one is not. Scope theory is rather dated anyway; besides, one has reached the age when most pure mathematicians think of veering into applied. One has some rather original ideas on chaos theory, actually.

And what happened to everyone else? Allgrobsch had a grand funeral; H.H. delivered a splendiferous eulogy. It turned out Allgrobsch had written the story of his life just a few months before his death. The upshot was that no publisher would take on Frank's biography. Of course Frank didn't get tenure at Nixon. When last heard of he had some temporary research fellowship in Paris . . . He'll survive.

The autobiography was a whopping bestseller (it contains scandals about everybody, yet Allgrobsch somehow converted them into Literature; the critics all agree it was his swansong). Lucky Wanda inherited the proceeds and is doing her best to spend it. Pertman died soon after Allgrobsch and she got his estate too. She appears on chat shows to tell the world what he was 'really' like; evidently she's in her element there.

And yes, one does share a frightfully stylish Victorian house with her and three other women. It's in the Haight district of San Francisco, just a block from Golden Gate Park. One goes jogging there every morning. During the finer afternoons one lounges on the sun deck, with a stack of scrap paper, a pen and a copy of *Am. Math. Rev.*, occasionally pausing to rub a smidgeon of patchouli scented sun oil on to one's gently darkening skin. In the evenings we sip kiwi daiquiris on the deck, as we gaze out towards the Bay. No, it's not paradise – we have the most thrilling quarrels about whose turn it is to clean the wok – but it's as near idyllic as any grown-up has a right to expect.

Well, well. One had always supposed one's life would be structured like a fairy-tale: one meets a prince, marries him, and lives happily ever after. Actually one hasn't reached a happy ending but a happy beginning:

Once upon a time, long long ago, in a land far far away, there lived a beautiful, wise, contented virgin . . .

$$\infty$$

A NOTE ON THE AUTHOR

Jonathan Treitel was born in London in 1959. He has worked as a physicist and lived in San Francisco and Tokyo. He is an acclaimed poet and short-story writer. *Emma Smart* is his second novel, following *The Red Cabbage Café*. A collection of his stories is to appear in 1992.